Also by Tom Reppert

The Far Journey

The Captured Girl

Assassin 13

THE LIGHT AT MIDNIGHT

THE LIGHT AT
MIDNIGHT

Tom Reppert

Helen's Sons Publishing

ISBN: 978-0-578-78391-8

CONTENTS

PART ONE: NASHOK

CHAPTER ONE

An unusually cold winter hung on in Nashok like a wolf with its teeth deep in a deer's leg. Even in March, temperatures still plunged below zero. The Neman River that cut our town in half was frozen, and snow covered the countryside. Those early months of 1941 were uneasy ones. Herr Hitler's angry speeches railing against Jews could be heard almost daily, blaring from radios in neighborhood homes, and many people, including Papa, worried about the Germans on the Polish border ninety kilometers away, but I took no notice of it.

On that first Sunday in March, bundling in our warmest clothes, my friends in the Young Guardians and I joined townspeople on the ice and skated down the river, racing past the trees on the banks, ducking under the small bridge. Tall for a fourteen-year-old girl, I felt clumsy in my stork-like body and spent much of my time fearful boys would gawk at me. But on this day, I imagined myself as clever as Sonja Henie, leaping into the air with a spin—that was till I fell. Some people skating by laughed. Sharply waving off Peretz Frischer's concern, I gathered myself up and chased after the Guardians.

Then, glancing back at him, I grinned. "Catch me."

He laughed and gave pursuit, but I reached our friends first.

Peretz was sixteen and thought of me as a little sister. In my secret dreaming of castles and fantasy worlds, I thought of him as my prince. And Nashok as our fairy kingdom. Here, I had my family, friends, school, the Young Guardians, and Peretz. Our kingdom of Jews had been on the Neman River for eight hundred years, a town of stone buildings, wooden houses, and synagogues. These days, more than four thousand of us tried to live in harmony with several hundred Poles and Lithuanians who numbered among our neighbors. Some of them liked us; many did not. It wasn't all beautiful sunsets and good neighbors in the kingdom.

But I loved Nashok anyway. I loved the winters, but summers were a special time. With the windows open to fight the heat, you could hear music throughout the day and much of the night. Someone was always playing a violin, and we had two pianos in town. I loved to hear the klezmer band play. Late at night, I would sneak up to the cupola on our roof and listen to them performing at a wedding somewhere in town. Even if they were on the far side of Nashok, I could hear the faint melodies drifting on the air. I imagined myself hand in hand with Peretz dancing at our wedding.

Summer meant the best market days. On Wednesdays, I ran down to the square early to watch the gypsies arrive in their covered wagons and prepare their stalls and performance areas. By eight o'clock, farmers from the region and merchants from Belorussia had set up their wagon stalls with produce and a variety of goods. The town shopkeepers moved their wares outside while Jews and Christians crowded into the square to bargain noisily. Often, I saw two merchants arguing over a single customer, each pulling on his jacket. With horses, pigs, chickens, and a few cows, you had to watch where you stepped.

As long as the gypsies were in town, parents kept their children close and clutched their purses to their bodies. Everyone knew gypsies kidnapped children and, being master thieves, stole whatever they could. Yet, we all found ourselves spellbound by their talents. Amazingly, they swallowed fire, walked across the rope strung from the row shops to the firehouse, sang such beautiful songs that people wept, and told fortunes with mystery and wonder.

This world changed for us in 1939 when the Russians came the first time. They were replaced by the Lithuanians for a bit, then they came back again just seven months ago on market day when their tanks and truckloads of soldiers rolled into Nashok. They drove down Vilna Street into the square. It was late afternoon, and already many merchants and farmers had left for home. The rest dispersed quickly, none quicker than the gypsies. I ran home to tell Mama.

She was kneading bread dough in the kitchen alongside Janina, our Christian housekeeper, and only shrugged. "Did you get the kerosene?"

"But, Mama, the Russians are back."

"If the electricity goes out, Rivka, how are we to light the lamps without kerosene?" Sighing, she stopped kneading the dough and looked at me. "Before these Russians, we had the Lithuanians. Before them we had the communists the first time, then before them we had the Poles, and before them the Germans from the war. Always somebody wants to tell us what to do. What do you think I can do about it?" She wiped her brow with a flour-dusted hand, leaving a white slash, and began working the dough again. "Rivka, we must live our own lives. When our new masters are gone, we will still be here."

Yet, Mama sent Janina back for the kerosene, not me.

An hour later, as I was ironing one of Papa's shirts, the door flew open and my older sister Hanna rushed in, her long, black hair tumbling out when she pulled her black beret off.

"Mama, the Russians are back," she announced.

"She knows," I said.

Hanna frowned at me, then said to Mama, "Well, I should go tell Papa."

Our mother was taking bread from the oven. She set the pan on the counter, glancing at Hanna. "I'm sure he already knows. He has his patients. Don't bother him."

"I'm supposed to help at the clinic anyway."

Mama shrugged as if Hanna could make her own choices. My sister rushed out the front door as fast as she'd come in.

Chagrined, I frowned because while I did the ironing, my sister ran off to the clinic to help Papa. But then, to be fair, she wanted to be a doctor and I didn't.

After that, the Russian takeover moved swiftly. They appointed several local Jewish communists to a Revolutionary Council to govern Nashok and placed Malka Henske, one of our own neighbors, in charge. Having grown up with her, Papa knew her well. A real communist, her first order of business was to seize the great Polish estates in the region and parcel them out to Polish and Lithuanian peasants. Papa's five hectares of land outside town where our family had kept cows and apple trees for untold generations fell into Malka's hands.

I wondered what Mama thought about the Russians now.

On that first Sunday in March when Peretz walked me home after skating, I sat in the living room with my family. Papa, Mama, and Baba, our grandmother, talked about Malka's latest outrage, especially Baba, who hated her and the Russians, while Hanna and I worked on our studies. She had a biology book in her lap while I read one of my German books, *The Nutcracker and the Mouse King*. I loved this story about a young girl's Christmas gift, the Nutcracker, coming alive and fighting evil in the form of a seven-headed Mouse King. When the Nutcracker defeats the Mouse King, he takes the girl away to a magical kingdom made up of dolls.

Pulling my sleeve, Hanna interrupted me and leaned in close. She whispered something she'd heard that day about a farmer who'd received land from Malka but was not so grateful. Drunk in a Nashok bar, he shouted for all to hear, "That bitch Jew has no right to take Polish land."

I giggled at the swear word.

Upset we were not paying attention to her tales of outrage, Baba asked, "What's so funny, girls?"

I shrugged. But when Papa asked, I told him about the man, dropping the word *bitch*.

He'd heard the story too. "Leopold Sadoski. I don't think he is a happy man."

I asked Papa why a man just given land by Malka Henske would say that about her. "I've never seen her at temple once," I added.

"Doesn't matter, Tsigele. You know the answer as well as I do." He still called me *Little Goat*, even though I was hardly little anymore. He was trying to read the local paper, now an underground publication. He shrugged as if to say *isn't it obvious?* "They hate us."

Then he went back to his newspaper.

His answer frustrated me. Of course they hated us, but why? For a Jew, even in Nashok, this hatred was our life as much as rain and snow. Each time I witnessed it, each time it was directed at me and I saw faces contorted with fury, I could not understand from what dark abyss such a thing arose. Only that it did.

One man in particular frightened me, Radek Karnowski. The Karnowski brothers Radek and Lucek owned a grocery shop in the market square and belonged to the Polish Endecja party, an anti-Semitic gang calling for Poland to be free of Jews.

At one time, the brothers had pictures of Jesus and Mary in their store window with a sign that said, **No Jews in this store.** Now, they had pictures of Stalin and Lenin. The sign forbidding Jews stayed.

Radek was the worst of the two. He was a broad man with a long, dark beard that made him appear like Rabbi Herskowitz. A heavy drinker and brawler, he frequented Nashok bars with ten or twelve of his mates, then came out looking for Jews. They carried cudgels and knives and sent many men to Papa's clinic.

On market day the next Wednesday, I encountered him while he and his bully boys were on a rampage. Winters didn't stop people from bartering and selling. Bitterly cold, women vendors hung braziers inside their dresses to warm themselves. After school, my best friend Mila Frischer and I, bundled in our wool caps and thick coats, hurried hand in hand to the square, making straight for Luba

Hadash's pastry shop. She baked the most delicious lemon cakes and for us would throw in warm tea, then let us sit in her kitchen to eat them.

Mila was what people called cute. Her dark hair was slightly lighter than her cousin Peretz's, whose shaggy, black locks gleamed in any light. She and I had been talking about lemon cakes for the last hour. I had a few coins I'd saved from my work translating German, Russian, and English documents into Yiddish and Hebrew, mostly for one of the Rabbis or even Papa. I was good with languages. Actually, I was very good.

This afternoon, the sun floated above without heat. The square was crowded with farmers and merchants. The air smelled fetid from all the pig piss and the horse and cow droppings, all the slop. But not as bad as summers since it froze immediately.

Under the communist, market days were much smaller affairs. The Belarusian merchants no longer attended because the Russians had closed the border, and most shop owners feared being labeled bourgeoisie and shipped off to Siberia if they appeared to be doing too well. So instead, they sold their goods on the black market.

And the gypsies no longer came.

Now, Malka Henske had her minions hammer posters onto the telephone and electric wire poles and passed out leaflets praising the merits of communism. Some of her lieutenants stood on boxes and made speeches everyone was too cold to listen to. Not exactly as riveting as gypsies eating fire. These days, people came in the hundreds, not the thousands. But they had to eat so they came.

As we turned the corner to Luba's shop, Mila and I pulled up short. Passing a bottle of vodka back and forth between them, Radek and ten of his mates blocked the door. At first, refusing to be turned away, men and women just pushed past them into the store. Drunk, slurring his words, he spit and cursed at them, "Dirty Jews, there is no place for you in Poland."

He seemed to forget that, at the moment, we were part of the Soviet Union.

8

For a few seconds, Mila and I watched from fifteen meters away. I noticed Avigdor Koppel, a young man who worked at the furriers, start up the path to the shop with two of his friends. His father repaired bicycles out of his house on Starka Street and exchanged repair work with Papa for getting his arthritis treated. Radek and several of his buddies stepped in front of Avigdor. I knew this would be trouble. The yelling got louder and the shoving more violent.

Mila said softly, "Maybe we should go to Mr. Gelman's. He has nice bagels."

Fear getting the better of me, I said, "Maybe we should."

We turned to go when Radek yelled, "You." He and another man strode straight for me, ignoring Mila. I would have run, but fear locked my legs in place.

He stopped a foot away, a menacing presence in work clothes and heavy boots. Spittle dripped down his beard. His eyes burned with madness and hatred, and I could not fathom why. My heart wracked my chest with its furious pounding. Even though Radek had been a patient of Papa's for years for something about chronic tendonitis in his feet, my father never charged him a single coin, yet here he was threatening me.

The other man who hung a step back I didn't know. He was thin with a pockmarked face, grinning like this was a puppet show.

Radek shouted at me as if I were on the other side of the square, "You're that Jew doctor's daughter, aren't you? The noble Dr. Resnik. Living in that big house like a king. Treats the rest of us like shit. Thinks he's better than anyone else."

His yellow teeth looked like fangs. His foul breath shot out in white gusts. Frozen in panic, I couldn't answer.

"Jew brat, you and your bastard father don't belong in Poland. Take all your dirty Jew family and get the hell out!" He shook his fist at me. "I should knock your teeth in."

His screaming eyes told me he would do it. That I was a girl smaller than him didn't matter a grain of wheat. I stood my ground though, but from absolute terror. I couldn't move. Yet, from somewhere within, anger welled up. It formed in my chest and grew massive. I was not any less frightened, but I felt the same exploding rage that came to me at rare moments. A bit insolently, I said, "If my father leaves, who will treat your flat feet?"

The pockmarked man sniggered. Radek's eyes flashed with fanatical rage. He drew back his fist and would have hit me. That was when Avigdor punched him in the face. A small man, he did little damage except to enrage Radek even more. The Endecja leader turned on him savagely and began pummeling him. Several of his cronies joined in. A wild brawl erupted when Avigdor's friends came to his rescue and several men from the market flew into the fight.

Mila grabbed my hand and we ran.

"That was the bravest thing I've ever seen," Mila said as we raced from the square. "You are amazing."

I wasn't amazing; I wasn't brave. I was a coward. What bothered me was that Mila believed I'd stood up to the monster. It seemed Avigdor thought the same thing. Afterward, he told people that Dr. Resnik's daughter Rivka was as brave as Yosef Trumpeldor himself. But when I told everyone I'd actually been too scared to move, they thought me just modest. In fact, I was shaken for days after the incident. The look in Radek's eyes plagued my dreams and made the night frightening. I'd seen madness and hatred in his eyes before to be sure, but there had been something else this time, something I could only describe as dark and evil.

At the same time, another thing began to fascinate me even more. That anger that arose out of me. I could not control it any more than I could control my fear. It took shape, something ferocious, a companion that was on my side. It had visited me once before when I was ten. At that age, the woods were forbidden to me because they could be dangerous, but I wandered their paths, not straying too far from home.

One day I ran into Stannis Karnowski, Radek's oldest boy. A wolf cub had been caught in one of his traps, and he was poking it with a sharp stick. The cub was two, maybe three months old and snarling at Stannis. The moment I saw this, the rage surged through me, fearless and monstrous. Screaming at him, I picked up sticks and rocks and began throwing them. Miraculously, he backed away, not afraid of me, but at a loss as to how to deal with this screaming, wild girl. The wolf cub bit me in the forearm when I released it.

As it dashed off into the brush, my rage disappeared, and I looked at Stannis with dread. When he saw this, he chased me, and I scrambled up a tree. He was too heavy to climb, but still I had to wait till dark before he left. Later, I snuck back in the house and cleaned up just before supper. I should have told Papa about the bite, but I was too afraid of his and Mama's punishment, so I hid it and feared for the next two months I was getting rabies. Ashamed of being such a mad girl, I never told anyone about it.

Now, the rage had come back.

In those days in March of 1941, many people came over to our house in the evening to visit Mama and Papa, the main topic of conversation always the communist, and I listened, pretending to be reading. It seemed throughout Malka's rule, the Revolutionary Council had many things to do to bring about their communist paradise. Fiercely anti-Zionist, they banned all Zionist organizations including the Young Guardians and Betar Trumpeldors calling them reactionary. I knew the word but didn't know how it fit me. I belonged only with my friends and Peretz. Besides, how reactionary can planting a few potatoes be?

Malka wasn't finished. She closed down the Hebrew school I attended and prohibited speaking Hebrew anywhere in the shtetl since it was the language of Zionism. The school became Yiddish only. Next day, Malka's own son, Liebke, and four of his mates began attending.

Mr. Kopelman, our grade teacher, ignored the decree and continued teaching in Hebrew. Someone reported him. The following day, Russians came to school and arrested him. By the afternoon, he and his family were on a train to Siberia. I wouldn't miss Mr. Kopelman. He had been brusque with the girls in class, thinking them unequal to grasping the full lessons of history, but even so, it was a hard thing to do to him and his family.

We all know Liebke Henske did it. Now, all day long in class, he spouted his mother's communist propaganda in Yiddish, and no one dared stop him.

I adjusted to the town's overlords, as did my family and friends. As Mama said, we lived our lives. We spoke Hebrew whenever we could; the Young Guardians and Trumpeldors held meetings in secret, always speaking Hebrew. Hanna, a Trumpeldor, and I attended our different youth groups, even though we knew we also could be shipped off to Siberia. This made me feel really brave.

One afternoon, she and I argued about my belonging to the Young Guardians. She had recently celebrated her seventeenth birthday, and that made her think she now possessed all the wisdom in the known universe and could lord it over me. She wanted me to quit the Young Guardians and join her Betar Trumpeldors.

"Sisters should stick together, Rivka," she said. "Especially now that the Bolsheviks have made us outlaws."

I shook my head. "I don't like your uniforms. They're like military uniforms."

Waving her hand dismissively, she gave a scoffing snort.

It was a lame answer, but I didn't like how the Trumpeldors marched around in their uniforms like toy soldiers, singing boisterously as if they were the best at everything. They did this in the woods, of course, far from town since both youth clubs had been outlawed.

Hanna already bossed me around at home enough. I didn't want her to boss me around at my youth club as well. What did it matter? Both were Zionist groups and did the same things, farm, farm, farm, hike, hike, hike, ski the forest in winters, study berries and edible roots in summer, and spoke only Hebrew, all in preparation to make Aliyah to Eretz Israel. Which we would never do. Not now anyway. So why change clubs?

When Hanna and I argued today, she needled me about going only because Peretz Frischer was one of the leaders. "You have no chance with him, Rivka. He's sixteen; you're fourteen. He doesn't even notice you."

I thought of a thousand brilliant things to say but not till later. Instead, I ran outside and fed the chickens by throwing the corn and wheat seed at them. Oh, how I hated my sister.

She was right, of course. I was in love with Peretz and had been all my life. Tall and handsome like an American movie star, he was closer to being an adult than a child, at least he thought he was.

Last week, I told him how I felt, and he patted my cheek. "That's nice." Like I was six. A sewing needle in my eye would not have hurt worse. For that moment, I wanted to kick him.

Yet, walking to school this morning, he told me to make sure I came to the Young Guardians tonight. He had something important to tell me, but I would need to keep it secret.

With a coquettish smile I'd been practicing in front of the mirror, I teased, "Important, is it? How important?"

He didn't notice my smile at all. "The most vital of all things."

"And you can't tell me now?"

He shook his head. "No."

"Well, if it's that important, I'll be there, just like I always am."

When we arrived at school, he went off to his upper grade class, and I to my own, dreaming about what it could be. Was it possible he felt he same about me? Could that be it? I was dying to find out.

CHAPTER TWO

Later that evening, the Young Guardians met at the Schanzer home. I sat squeezed into the big, cushiony chair with Shoshana Erlich, listening to the evening's debate about what grain to plant in the spring, oats, wheat, or potatoes, though I didn't think potatoes were actually a grain. It couldn't possibly matter. We were not farmers. We just played at it.

All the Young Guardians wore a white bow pinned to their shirts to signify that they spoke outlawed Hebrew. A fire crackled in the fireplace. Nearby on the dining room table was a birthday cake with candles, though it was no one's birthday. This in case the police raided the house to break up this desperate band of subversives.

"Are you going to try out for the new play?" Shoshana asked me. "Please do."

"Sure. Maybe, I'll get the lead this time."

"Maybe you will."

I knew I wouldn't. Shoshana had real talent. She was always chosen for the lead in the plays put on at the Firehouse, at least when it called for a teenager, and this new one did. Though I liked to be part of it all, I was never chosen for the lead, maybe because I was not a particularly good actress. Shoshana was a prodigy, people said. Some day she will go to Vilna to be in the Yiddish theater or even to Warsaw if the Germans ever allowed it.

In the center of the living room, the eight boys and three of the seven girls of YG vociferously defended their positions on which grain to plant in the spring, especially Yankl Glazman, who demanded it be wheat as if the future of the Jews depended upon it. I glanced at Peretz, watched how his unruly hair refused to stay in place no matter how many times he ran his hand through it, watched how his beautiful grin would quell any argument instantly. A couple times, he glanced my way, showered me with that grin, and I'd perk up. He then gave a slight nod as if to say, *soon, soon, he will tell me the great secret.*

Shoshana sighed, exasperated. "This is the same old argument every meeting."

"Leah will settle it tonight," I said. "It will be potatoes."

Leah Adler was the leader of the Seven, our social club. We girls who belonged to the Young Guardians had grown up together, attended the same classes at school, and did so much together that people sometimes called us the Seven. So that's what we called ourselves.

Tonight, Leah had jumped right in among the boys to argue her position for planting potatoes. She always knew what to do. By the strength of her personality and her decisiveness, everyone followed her, even the boys. I knew tonight they would choose to plant potatoes, much to Yankl Glazman's chagrin. Me, I was no leader. I seldom put myself forward, not making suggestions. I knew no one would follow me.

Looking at my other girlfriends, I realized something shocking. Among the seven of us, I was not the best at anything. And that made me the least of them. A pretender, the one that didn't belong.

Mila was the most likeable, Leah the leader, Shoshana the most talented actress. Then there was Esther Gershowitz, the prettiest. Nordic blonde hair and blue eyes. Why Nordic was always the standard for beauty I didn't know, but Esther had it. She would turn heads with any color hair, but that blonde look killed the men. She had been the first one of us Seven to get breasts as big as cabbage heads. Mine came in the size of grapes. When I confided in Mila about my concerns, she told me not to worry, they'd grow, and I would fill out.

Maybe, but now no boys turned their heads when I walked by unless it was to call me *the Stork*. I hated the nickname.

In cross-country skiing, Genesha Blum always won, by far the best athlete among us. I was a good skier but had no chance of winning any of the races. My only goal was to beat my sister Hanna whenever we skied against the Trumpeldors, which I never could.

I realized I was not even the smartest of the group. My languages were good, but Sarah Shlanski was a wizard at math and achieved top scores in everything. She did most math problems in her head and finished before the rest of us had slogged halfway through. She was another prodigy.

Together we were the Seven, and desperately I hoped they would never find me out, find out how poorly I measured up to them.

Finally, the Young Guardians' meeting ended with potatoes being agreed upon as I knew it would. I hurried to the closet to put on my coat and wool cap, then tapped my foot impatiently for Peretz to walk me home. As we left the Schanzer's house, his warm eyes told me he actually did love me. That we would someday be married. That had to be it.

Outside, a gray sky lay suspended above by a thread as twilight hung on as it always did in Nashok. Our boots crunching on the packed snow, I walked close to Peretz, bumping into him occasionally. He was silent, so I began counting his steps aloud.

"What are you doing?" he asked.

"Counting how many steps you take before you speak."

"But you're not speaking."

"I am. I'm counting."

He chuckled and shook his head.

To stay off the streets, we took a path behind the neighborhood houses and in among the shadows of trees. I didn't fear the Russian soldiers, but it was good to be prudent. The Russians didn't patrol much, remaining in their warm quarters most of the time. A battalion or regiment of them, I didn't know which, lived in an encampment fifteen kilometers from Nashok. Generally, when they did wander out into the streets, they were friendly enough. I'd even spoken to a few, though my Russian was only rudimentary, not nearly as good as my German and English.

The main rule Papa had was to stay away from the Russian soldier who was well into his bottle of Vodka. Those could be dangerous to females of all ages. He didn't detail what the danger was, but we all knew. Mila and I even talked about it when we were alone.

Peretz's expression deepened like the world's troubles fell on his shoulders. "Have you heard from your brother?"

I beamed. Though it had only been a couple months, I missed Ben Zion. "He's coming home for the Shabbat."

"How long will he be staying?"

"Just the weekend. He has to return to Vilna Monday. He has classes he can't miss."

In his first year at the University of Vilna, Ben Zion studied medicine in preparation for the day he joined Papa in his practice.

"I will come see him Saturday then," Peretz said.

"He'll like that."

He took my arm to guide me over an icy patch as if I couldn't manage it myself, but his touch on my arm felt good, even through the thick, winter coat.

"What did you think of the meeting?" Peretz asked.

Moving my head side to side and thrusting my fists in the air, I mimicked Yankl Glazman in a fierce voice, "It must be wheat. We must plant wheat this spring. Wheat, I tell you. What is more important than bread?"

He laughed. "He's probably right though. We probably should plant wheat in the spring."

"What does it matter? Oats, wheat, potatoes? We're not feeding the masses. We're only practicing to be farmers when we all go to Palestine, which we will never do."

He grinned as if I'd just stumbled onto the answer to a great puzzle. Understanding hit me instantly. I grabbed his arm. "My God, you're going to Palestine. That's your secret."

He shook his head. "No, not Palestine. To America."

Of course. His father and uncle had been in America for years, sending money back regularly. I tried to be excited for him, proud of myself for that. "When? When are you going?"

He held up his hands. "Wait. It's not official yet, so you can't say anything. Papa and Uncle Moishe—he's Morris now—have just become American citizens and put in the paperwork for us to join them. Aunt Miriam and all my cousins too. The American embassy will notify us for our interviews. Till then you can tell no one, not even Hanna."

"Why would I tell Hanna?" I said too petulantly.

He shrugged. "Just don't tell anyone. Not even Ben Zion."

"I won't." I hesitated a moment then asked, "Why did you tell me?"

Clutching my elbow, he stopped me. "Because you're my closest friend, Rivka. We've been friends forever. Who else would I tell?"

That felt good. Me, his closest friend. If not romantic love, at least he saw me as someone special in his life. Maybe, it could grow into something more. Then, it hit me like the Vilna bus. He would be leaving forever. I would never see him again. And Mila, too, my best friend. She was his cousin. Their leaving stabbed two big holes in my heart, but I could see how excited he was, and Mila talked about nothing but America and Hollywood stars, dragging me to the firehouse to watch the latest movies from America when the town got them.

As we walked on, his face became serious again. "You should talk to your father about leaving Nashok too," he said. "Go anywhere. Far away."

"Why? The Russians aren't too bad, but Mama says we will survive them. Where would we go anyway?"

"Don't be silly, Rivka. They're not good," he said, sharply.

That hurt, and I looked away into the nearby forest, which had grown dark.

"But I wasn't thinking about the Russians. I was thinking about the Germans," he said.

"The Germans?"

"Yes. They're only a hundred kilometers away in Poland." Worry creased his face. "We had a man from Warsaw staying with us named Jacob Spielman. I've never heard of him, but he's a famous writer. He's trying to reach Palestine.

"He'll never make it."

"He will," Peretz insisted. "While he was with us, he told us terrible things about what the Germans are doing to Jews."

I felt a chill race up my spine. "What things?"

Peretz hesitated for several seconds, glancing at me twice before deciding to go on. "He was hiding with gentiles in Warsaw, but it became too dangerous. He says the Nazis are killing all the Polish leaders, the writers and university professors. And Jews. One Jewish family was betrayed and taken by the Gestapo along with their Polish hosts. All were executed, Rivka. Most of his former colleagues, Jew and gentile, at the university are in labor camps or dead. Near the apartment he was hiding, there was a mass killing at a small clinic like your father's. Spielman left Warsaw that day."

He waited for my response. I had none. Shocked, I just looked at him dumbly. I never knew what to believe. With Nashok on the direct train route between Warsaw and Vilna, thousands of refugees from the German occupied territories had come through town since 1939. They told horrifying stories of Jews transported to the Warsaw ghetto or to labor camps, and worse, mass killings by the Germans. Most people dismissed these tales as wild exaggerations.

"I don't want to scare you, Rivka," he said, "but you should know. It won't be safe for you if they come."

"I'm not scared," I said with fear boiling in me. "Baba says those are all false rumors. She says the Germans are much better than the Russians. They were in Nashok during the first German War.

All of them sweet boys, she says. She has stories about them she tells us all the time."

His face crumpled into a closed-eyed grimace. He balled his fist and thrust them behind his head in frustration. "Such nonsense. Your grandmother is wrong. Just tell your father what I said. Please, Rivka. When we go, I will worry about you."

I didn't know what to think. Believe Peretz and a man I've never even met or believe my grandmother and parents. My parents were worried but not overly so. They went about their day to day lives as always, and so should I. I thought of the hideous face of rage I'd seen on Radek Karnowski, but then he had not killed anybody, even though he'd probably like to.

I was dealing with too many terrible emotions far from what I expected ten minutes ago. The horror of a killing horde just over the horizon, and the very real prospect of losing the two people outside of my family I love best in the world.

As we approached the back door of my house, I felt his last words were as good as I would ever get from him. Then someday soon, I would never see him again.

CHAPTER THREE

I n the Department of Human Heredity and Eugenics, twenty-four-
year-old Max Bauer stood in a conference room at the Kaiser
Wilhelm University, defending his PHD dissertation on the superiority of the Aryan race. Down a long, polished table, he faced three
professors in black robes who sat like medieval prelates judging his
worthiness for holy orders. He barely hid his contempt for them,
certain his worthiness to discuss this topic far exceeded theirs to
judge him.

In a nearby glass cabinet, he caught his own reflection appearing
like a Nazi poster of the tall, muscular Aryan with his blond hair
that gleamed almost metallic in the lights. His gray, double-breasted
suit had been tailored to show off his lean body and erect, military
posture learned in the Hitler Youth. On the other hand, his blue
eyes, enlarged behind the lenses of his wire rim glasses, gave him
the presence of an intellect.

As he spoke, he held his hands out, illustrating the size of a
skeletal head. "Among numerous other factual examples, the math-
ematically derived Skull Index shows with scientific precision the
most desirable races are the Nordic and Westphalian. We see the
Aryan type today in Germany and Scandinavia, and also in the art
of ancient Greece and Rome, Renaissance sculptures such as David,
and German heroes such as Otto von Bismarck and Frederick the
Great."

"And in yourself, I might add," Professor Heissmeyer said with an ingratiating smile. He tapped a pen nervously on the tabletop.

Bauer gave a slight nod of acknowledgement. Heissmeyer was a sycophant and would vote to pass him. Bauer had no personal power over the man, but it would take a bold and foolish professor to fail a dissertation on the genetics of race when they knew it was so fervently promoted by the Nazi party and the Führer himself.

"Tell us about the bottom of the racial scale," Dr. Adler said, the oldest of the three.

Bauer had prepared for the question. "The least desirable are the Slavs, Romani, and Jews, but the Jews are the true Untermenschen, the true subhuman. Again, physical measurements prove the point. The Jew skull is narrow, four centimeters less than the Nordic by comparison. Jew features are distinctly angular and measurably darker. Their bodies decidedly shorter." He warmed to his topic. "According to recent studies in Galicia, Jews were shorter than the Poles and Ukrainians by a significant margin. Half were below the average height."

"Does it not follow, therefore, that half were above the average?" Dr. Hoenig asked.

This took Bauer up short. He had not expected anyone to challenge him, not even Hoenig. A proponent of eugenics, the professor nevertheless did not believe in the inferiority of any race, though he did not speak of such things anymore. The students believed he was an anti-Nazi.

"There is no data to suggest that, Herr Professor," Bauer replied.

Dr. Heissmeyer folded his hands in front of him, indicating the exam might be finally coming to an end. "If you pass, what are your post-dissertation research plans, Herr Bauer?"

He stood straighter and said with pride, "After graduation, I plan to join the SS."

They couldn't hide their surprise. Hoenig nodded derisively. "Of course you will."

That was three years ago in Berlin. Bauer had passed the exam by a single vote, two to one. Next day, he informed on Hoenig to the Gestapo, then travelled down to Bad Tölz in Bavaria and reported to Waffen SS officers training school. Like all Waffen SS officers, when he graduated, his blood type was tattooed on the underside of his left arm in Gothic lettering. It was a badge of honor and the proudest moment of his life. Now, he was an SS Hauptsturmführer, serving in Warsaw, while Dr. Hoenig, if still alive, resided in the Dachau concentration camp.

"We are nearly there, Herr Hauptmann," Oberleutnant Keppler said, breaking his reverie.

It was after midnight, and he rode in a black SS sedan with an army truck following. They sped down a cobbled street and screeched to a halt in front of the Church of the Holy Trinity. Soldiers leapt from the back of the truck and surrounded the small chapel. Bauer and four other SS men in gray uniforms exited their cars and strode up the steps, six soldiers carrying rifles close behind.

Bauer tried the brass handle, but the oak door didn't budge. He nodded to one of the soldiers who pounded his rifle butt against it. The soldier did it two more times before they heard the bolt inside being thrown back. A stocky, middle-aged priest in a faded cassock swung the door open.

Inside, with only a few lighted candles along the stone walls, gloom filled the nave. Two younger priests stood back near the stone pillars watching. Bauer gave the priest a look of astonishment. "Father Mazurek, you bolt your door at night? What about all those poor, troubled souls seeking sanctuary?"

"Different times, Herr Hauptmann. Can I help you with something?"

Bauer pushed past him and strode toward the sanctuary at the front. Father Mazurek hurried after him. Abruptly, the German pivoted around on him. "Jews are hiding here, Father."

Father Mazurek shook his head. "Herr Hauptmann, I am hiding no one."

Bauer scolded him in a mocking tone, "Lying, Father? Isn't that a mortal sin?"

As the priest began to answer, Bauer waved him to silence. "No harm will come to them. We are only transporting them to the ghetto. All Jews must live there. No exceptions." He smiled winningly. "It is their new homeland, their Eretz Israel."

The priest stepped around Bauer and held up his hand blocking the way. "We do have a few sick and poor who have nowhere else to turn. They are our parishioners. I do not want you disturbing them at this late hour."

Bauer gave a nod of understanding, holding out his hand for one of the soldiers' rifle. After studying the end of the stock, he lifted it up to the priest. "Can you read what is written there, Father?"

When Father Mazurek leaned in to search the bottom of the stock, Bauer smashed it violently into his face. The priest's nose burst, spraying blood over his cassock, and he collapsed to the floor. The two priests watching screamed. One of them ran forward holding his hands in the air. "No more, no more. This is a house of God."

Bauer tossed the rifle back to the soldier, drew his Walther pistol, and aimed it at the young priest's head. "Hiding Jews is punishable by death. We know they are here. Someone betrayed you, Father. Unless you tell me now where they are, I will execute every person we find in this church, and you will be the first. You have three seconds to choose, and I will not count aloud."

In the silence, dripping water could be heard coming from somewhere. At two drops, the priest shouted, "In the basement. In the basement."

Bauer lowered his pistol. "Show me."

Twelve Jews were found in a hidden room below the sanctuary and prodded out to the transport truck by the soldiers. The church was emptied of people, the priests, including Father Mazurek, six nuns, and several Poles that had been staying at the dormitory, all hauled out to the trucks, except two famous Polish writers who were kept back. Bauer and his four Einsatzkommandos, his SS Death Squad, took them into the courtyard at the back of the church.

The Polish intelligentsia had been marked for death the moment the first German soldier stepped onto Polish soil. Eliminating a country's heart in this way gutted their ability to resist. Bauer and his fellow Einsatzgruppen rounded up countless thousands of the influential, wealthy landowners, clergymen, government officials, university professors, army officers, and writers, Jews and Poles alike. They executed them in mass graves or sent them to concentration camps to die. He had become especially efficient at dispatching the enemies of the Reich, as his many medals show. This was his pride, each medal his due.

The old man who walked stooped over with a cane seemed not particularly frightened. More resigned to his fate than anything. He had been identified as Leopold Zahorska, who had written on Polish history for five decades and stood at the pinnacle of academic writers. The woman was Maria Pytel, whose fame was of a different kind. Not yet thirty, her novels of Polish life and her famed beauty had made her a glittering star in the literary firmament. She had been in hiding since the day Poland fell to German forces.

In the darkness, the two writers stood against the church wall facing the SS men. Bauer stepped up to the woman. "You are Maria Pytel, are you not?"

Her voice quaked. "Yes, Herr Hauptmann."

He smiled with warmth. "I have read one of your books, *The Light at Midnight*. It was translated into German. Quite wonderful, fraulein."

"Thank you, Herr Hauptmann."

He studied her for several seconds, then said, "It would be a crime that a beautiful woman with such a brilliant mind should be killed." He backed up and gestured toward the gate. "Leave. Go on. Walk out of this courtyard. You're free to go. Don't look back. But leave Poland."

She glanced at Zahorska, who nodded. "Go, my dear. Don't sacrifice yourself just to die here with an old man. Take Herr Hauptmann's generous offer."

She looked again at Bauer then stepped past him, walking hurriedly toward the back gate. Before she had gone six feet, Bauer drew his pistol and shot her in the back of the head.

Next, he turned and fired a bullet into Zahorska's forehead.

Snorting a laugh, Oberleutnant Keppler said, "Nothing more gullible than Polish writers."

Afterward, Bauer ordered all the valuables within removed and the church boarded up. The Jews were then transported to the ghetto and processed into a few city blocks, already housing nearly four hundred thousand people, while the Poles, including the Catholic priests and nuns, sent to concentration camps.

Exhausted, Bauer returned to his quarters at the SS garrison on the outskirts of the city and went quickly to bed. Satisfied he'd done his best, he slept well and awoke at noon.

CHAPTER FOUR

D arkness gathered outside and in our house. With the lighting of the candles and saying the blessings over the wine and challah bread, my family began the Shabbat meal without guests, an unusual occurrence. Usually Papa would bring one or two home from the clinic, or Mama would invite our uncles and aunts and their families.

Scrubbed, we wore our finest clothes; the table had been set to perfection by Hanna and me under the strict supervision of Grandmother, whom we affectionately called Baba, though she's not always that affectionate. We set out the ivory-bone china with gold trim, the silver pitchers of wine, the kiddush cup, and the fine silverware.

Like everyone else in Nashok, we tilled a garden, kept chickens, and even raised a few cows. Because of the scarcity of food these days, we had to be careful with our chickens, using them for either eggs or barter. With Russians restrictions, market stalls and shops were nearly empty.

The Revolutionary Council had taken most of the cows in town, including ours, and confiscated food supplies like coffee, tea, cocoa, most of the sugar, and now butter too. So, for this Shabbat, Mama cooked a nearly meatless chicken for later, an ancient hen that had probably been old in Baba's time. Old chickens didn't retire. They made it into the soup or onto the plate. We also had noodles and kugel but without raisins, which cost a fortune on the black market.

Over the gefilte fish, Hanna held forth on her intention to attend Vilna University in the fall as planned.

Of course, as always, this shocked our grandmother. Baba wore a large, blue jacket better to conceal her bulk, tugging at the lapels as if an attorney about to address a jury. "You can't possibly," she said. "No good Jewish daughter needs such schooling. She only needs to marry a good Jewish boy and read her tkhines."

"Yiddish prayers written by men for women, Baba," Hanna said.

"Of course by men. Who else? And besides, the Russians will have you on your way to Siberia as soon as you arrive."

Hanna waved her hand, dismissing the concern. "Still, I will go, Baba. Just say a few Karl Marx quotes, and they'll leave me alone."

Papa squirmed in his chair. She turned to him. "Papa, you promised me."

Grandmother snorted. "That was when you were ten. You can't hold him to that promise now. Not now with the Russians back in charge. Shipping off professors and students like cattle. You could be one of them, then what are we to do?"

Upset, Hanna said, "Ben Zion is a student at Vilna. Why should I not be?"

Mama placed her fork carefully beside her plate, and everyone fell silent. "Hanna, I have one child I must constantly worry about. I cannot suffer through worrying about two. You must stay here where it's safe."

"Papa?" Hanna pleaded.

"Your mother is right," Papa said. "But this is what we can do. We will register you, and if the situation settles, and your mother agrees, you may go. But if it remains this bad, you will not. Is that understood? I may even bring Ben Zion back."

Hanna grinned, taking that as a victory. "Yes, Papa."

After that, our dinner talk was unrestrained even though the train from Vilna with Ben Zion aboard was long overdue, and we'd heard nothing about why. How could everyone else be so offhand about it, as if it were nothing? I imagined a massive wreck and my brother bleeding in some field. Or more likely, the Bolsheviks boarded the train as they often did and dragged him off. Ben Zion would more likely spit in the commissars' faces than pretend support for them. He was worse than Hanna in that regard.

Papa appeared unconcerned, conversing with the same enthusiasm he always did, seemingly insistent on the conversation proceeding as vibrantly as always. Which was why my fear doubled. After a sip of the chicken soup, he calmly asked about the new play Hanna and I were rehearsing at the firehouse. My sister had a substantial role, while I played a rabbit in a furry costume, barely on stage one minute. Hanna described the entire play as if she were the only one in it.

I glanced over at the dark wood clock on the mantel. Nine fifteen. No Ben Zion. I looked at Mama, who met my gaze. For just a moment, I saw fear in her eyes, but it was instantly gone. There was no one stronger than my mother. Not Papa. Not the great Malka, who ran all of our lives, not any of the Russians. She was the sun around which the entire family orbited. Without her, we would all fly apart like rogue planets and disintegrate. If she could be strong about Ben Zion, so could I.

"I met your new 8th grade teacher, Mr. Fischbein, at the bathhouse today," Papa said, his thick eyebrows coming together in a scowl as he fixed his attention on me. "He said you are a fine student, but there have been times he has caught you daydreaming. This cannot be true, I told him. My daughter Rivka, the scholar, she would never get lost in a girlish reverie."

Unable to meet his eyes, I dropped my head and didn't reply. When Malka and her council shut down the Hebrew school, the curriculum changed, became more Russian. Science, communist history instead of Polish, math, and so on, but in Yiddish. The Torah was still taught in secret.

Papa reached over and turned my head to face him, but I still didn't meet his eyes. Truth was I studied as hard as I did, earned the reputation as a scholar, only to please him. Most days I'd rather be out skiing or in the summer running the forest paths.

Grandmother shook her head in disgust. "The world is coming to an end. In my day, girls did not study the Torah."

"Yes, Baba," I said, making my voice contrite.

A sudden pounding at the door made me jump. It could be Malka and her communist strong men come to take our home. We had expected her to run us out someday just like she had with all the best homes in Nashok.

"Who would interrupt us on the Shabbat?" Baba said uneasily.

"Go to the door, Papa," Mama said. "It might be news of the train."

As he rose, the door opened, and a handsome, curly haired young man strode in, grinning at us. Hanna and I screamed in delight. It was Ben Zion.

With a gasp, Mama jumped up and rushed into his arms while the rest of us gathered around asking questions all at once. Her fear catching up with her, Mama began to swoon and flopped down on the arm of a chair. Papa got water and a cloth from the kitchen and dabbed her face over and over. Reviving, she shoved his hand away. "This man has gone crazy. He's trying to drown me." She stood up. "Ben, come to dinner."

The next morning, an old man passed us on the street as Papa, Ben Zion, and I were walking to the town square. He gave a deferential nod. "Good morning, Dr. Resnik and young Ben Zion. Another cold day. Will this winter ever end?"

I hung back, trying not to be noticed. With the sun glinting off the ice and packed snow, I squinted at him from behind Papa's shoulder.

"Good morning, Mr. Edelson," Papa and Ben replied together. Papa added, "Surely it must end soon."

"If you say so, Doc."

When we passed people, they always went out of their way to greet Papa with respect. Me, I didn't think Mr. Edelson even noticed.

As on most Saturday mornings, Papa and I strolled down to the central market, mostly so we could be alone together, and he could talk to me. It was the time in the week I most treasured, even though it seemed I needed a lot of talking to.

This morning, Ben Zion walked with us, excited to expand on the tales of his first year at university he'd begun last night. Beaming, I marched between them, my hands in the crook of their elbows.

"I am walking with the two handsomest men in all Nashok," I said, then added, "No, all Europe."

"Only Europe?" Ben Zion said.

"Well, surely there must be a few men in Hollywood who outshine you, but not many."

My brother laughed and ruffled my wool cap. "You are such a comedian."

"Stop that." I pulled the cap back down over my ears.

Since he had long planned to be a doctor, Ben Zion worked in Papa's clinic when he was home. For some reason, Hanna wanted to be a doctor, too, and got angry whenever anyone suggested she be a nurse instead. She too worked at the clinic. I hated the sight of blood, which made doctoring not my best path to follow. Since I was not very good at anything, I didn't know what I should do with my life. Maybe being like Mama wasn't such a bad thing.

A few minutes later, several of Ben Zion's friends caught up with us and dragged him away. He waved as they ran off to do whatever boys of his age do together. Pretend to be men most likely.

"Papa, do you still want me to become a doctor like Ben and Hanna?" I asked.

He laughed. "I never wanted you to become a doctor, Rivka. You are not suited to it. This, I know." He grinned. "Remember when

33

you brought my lunch to the clinic that time and saw Isaac Blum bleeding from a bad cut?"

Irritated he would recall that, I said, "I fainted. So what, Papa? I was little."

"Yes, you were. But I don't think you would like the constant routine of healing people."

How would he know what I would like? I didn't know myself. "If not a doctor, then what will I become?"

He shrugged. "I don't know. Something bold I think."

I was aghast. "Bold? Me? Hanna is the bold one. Not me."

Rubbing his chin, a playful grin on his face, he said, "You're my paradox, Rivka. Bold and shy. But you are the dangerous one, not Hanna. Not Ben Zion. You."

What was he talking about? That's crazy.

"Three years ago, when I sent you to Kovna to spend the fall with your aunt," Papa said, pressing his gloved hands together, searching for his next words. "When I sent you to Kovna with Rebecca, you went to a Polish school for a semester."

I had gotten into fights daily with girls and even a few boys. I was not the only Jew attending the Polish school, and it seemed we all suffered the same daily taunts. But I'd said nothing about that to Aunt Rebecca, despite coming home with the occasional torn blouse or bruise. I would not quit because of it.

"Your aunt told me your teacher said something terrible about Jews in class, and you took your books and walked out. You spent the rest of the semester in the library."

The teacher had said something about Jews, goats, and our papas. The school marked me present each day and allowed me to remain in the library. I never knew why they did that. They only required me to take my exams at the end of the semester. I did and passed them all.

I shrugged. I did not grasp Papa's point. I thought he'd be angry at what I'd done so never told him. But he wasn't angry.

34

"That's what I mean about dangerous." He shook his head and waved his hand as if dismissing any possible contrary argument. "The point is, Rivka, if you hang back because you are, indeed, shy, that's fine. But if it's because you believe you do not measure up to Hanna or Ben Zion or some other standard, then that is foolish. You do. So take risks, but with care. When you see the road you want, take it."

I thought I had an inkling of what he meant, but just then a car with the single red star screeched to a stop in front of us, blocking our way. A man got out of the passenger side and opened the back door, motioning us in with an unforgiving nod.

Riding in the back seat of the car speeding into the center of town, my panic eased. Moments before, when the car stopped, I had almost run off but could not abandon Papa. The man had handed him his medical bag, surely picked up at home from Mama. Obviously, an emergency somewhere. Not worried at all, Papa chatted with him as if an old friend. So, I decided I could relax. I would not be shipped off to Siberia today, at least.

We were taken to Revolutionary Council headquarters at the hotel in the market square. The sturdiest and tallest building in Nashok at four stories, it had been the first confiscated when the Russians arrived. We were led to Malka Henske's office and greeted by her male secretary, a young man in his twenties behind an immense, worn desk. The white cuffs of his shirt stuck out from his suit jacket, which was much too small for him. He waved us to a bench and picked up the phone on his desk.

"Dr. Resnik is here," he said.

Papa and I waited in silence. I heard the muffled click-click of typewriters somewhere down the hall. Except for the secretary, we were the only two in the reception area. Across the room on a long table were stacks of confiscated goods. My mouth dropped open slightly since it held so many food items I had not seen for months: raisins, spices, tins of coffee, tea, cocoa, and so many other things.

Most people could not afford these things on the black market and some items like cocoa only a Rothchild could afford.

The office door opened, and Malka Henske stepped out. Barely into her forties, she was a sturdy woman with a square face framed by brown ringlets. She was too stern to be attractive, but when she smiled at Papa, I saw that she could be if she wanted.

Papa approached her. "Working on the Shabbat, Comrade Henske?" he said in a mock scolding tone. "Whatever will your parents say?"

"I don't recognize Shabbos, Abraham. Speak only Yiddish. No Hebrew. You know this," Malka said. Her tone had no playfulness in it. "Thank you for coming."

"I had no choice."

"I knew you would not abandon an old friend." She saw me on the bench. "Good morning to you, Rivka."

"Good morning, Mrs. Henske."

"Comrade Henske," Malka corrected, but without her usual sternness.

"Good morning, Comrade Henske."

A trim, wool jacket with lace at the collar didn't quite conceal her heavy body. She was clearly pregnant. Turning to Papa, she said, "Come in. We must discuss something."

When the door shut behind them, I leaned back against the brick wall and stared longingly at the food items on the table.

"Don't you want to take off your coat, little girl?" the secretary asked. He was a Jew from some other place, not Nashok.

"No. And I'm not a little girl."

He shrugged, smirking.

Now, getting hotter, I wanted to take off my coat but couldn't without appearing foolish.

A couple minutes later, the secretary stood up, grabbed a stack of papers off his desk, and hurried down the hall. I heard a door open, the sound of typewriters louder, and then the door shut. For a full minute, I stared at the food. All this stuff had to come from not just Nashok but the entire region. Struck by an impulse so powerful, I sprung up, strode across to the table, and snatched the tin of cocoa, sliding it into my pocket. I quickly returned to the bench.

Fear flooded my stomach. What had I done? Stolen something for the first time in my life. Guilt ate at me. I needed to put it back—that was clear—but sat frozen to the bench. The secretary could return, or worse, Papa and Malka come out of the office just at that moment. He would be humiliated and so ashamed of me that I would break apart. Malka could gladly send me to Siberia then.

Words bounced like cannons inside my head. *Put it back. Put it back.* But I couldn't move. I kept watching the door to Malka's office. Finally, I stood, hesitated, took a single step forward, then another toward the table. So slowly was I moving that I felt exposed. I did not want to get too far from the bench so I could dive back in case they came out. Finally, I pulled the tin of cocoa from my pocket and reached it toward the table. Just then the door opened, and Papa stepped out.

He was glancing back at Malka, saying something I couldn't hear. She said, "Thank you, Dr. Resnik. I can have my car drop you back at your house."

Just as the secretary returned, I made it to the bench. He didn't look at me or the table.

Papa shut his bag with a snap. "No, I think Rivka and I will finish our walk. I'll come back in two weeks to check how things our progressing, but I see no reason to worry."

As we left the hotel, he said, "Are you all right, Rivka? You seem pale." He touched a hand to my forehead.

"I'm fine, Papa. I'm perfectly fine," I said, gripping the tin of cocoa still in my pocket.

CHAPTER FIVE

On Sunday, the Young Guardians and Mr. Schanzer hiked up into the hills surrounding Nashok, singing songs as we went. We all wore green pants and gray shirts, our simple uniform. The terrible winter had finally broken about a month ago, and spring rushed in like a flash flood. The smell of spruce and pine hung in the air. Wildflowers were pushing up through the meadows, and the trees had grown greener. The day was chilly and overcast, threatening rain, so hoisting our rucksacks, we were hurrying through the forests toward home. I walked alongside Peretz, a lock of his dark hair pushing out from his wool cap, making him look roguish.

"Have you heard anything about America?" I asked him.

He glanced around for anyone close enough to hear, then said, "We received a letter from Papa two days ago. Our application to emigrate to America has been approved in Washington. So now all we have to do is wait till this approval reaches the embassy in Vilna. When they notify us, Mama and Aunt Miriam will pick up our visas and get our tickets."

I squeezed his forearm "That's wonderful, Peretz. I really am happy for you."

"Are you? You look sad."

"Of course I'm sad," I said, frowning. "I'm losing Mila and you. My best friend and the boy I want to marry. Now, that won't happen."

39

Irksomely, he sighed as if at fifteen he was infinitely wise. "Oh, Rivka, there are years and years to come for all of us. Who knows what will happen? Perhaps you will come to America, then we will see. But when you grow up, you will be a great beauty and want nothing to do with me."

I did not like the *growing up* comment but did like the *great beauty* one. Hoisting my ruck a little higher on my shoulders, I shook my head. "No, I will never come to America. Papa will not leave Nashok. He says he is too important to the people here. And I don't want to go. Except for you and Mila, all the people I love are here."

He said nothing to that, but I did see sorrow on his face.

When the Young Guardians returned to Nashok, the boys went off with Mr. Schanzer to do whatever boys did while the Seven gathered at Mila's house for a surprise, hot cocoa for everyone. Aunt Miriam had found sugar and milk and using my cocoa had the hot chocolate ready when we got back. Everyone screamed with delight.

We sat in the living room. Mila's younger brothers and sisters were at neighbors' houses, so they were not underfoot. Each of us wore the white bow indicating we only spoke the outlawed Hebrew. As we always did, we talked about our hopes and dreams, or the math problems we had trouble with—all but Sarah, who never did—and the boys we were interested in. I kept my heartache at Peretz leaving to myself.

"Where did you get the cocoa, Mila," Leah asked. "I thought no one had chocolate."

Mila pressed a finger to her lips. "It wasn't me. Rivka came up with it."

Sipping from her cup, Leah turned to me. "Where did you get it?"

I had to be honest with these girls. "I stole it."

Their jaws dropped. "What!" A couple girls gasped.

"Who from?" Shoshana asked.

"The Council. Malka called for my father, and I was with him. They had boxes and boxes of confiscated stuff on tables."

Esther's pretty face twisted in a grimace. "You committed a mortal sin."

Everyone fell silent. That was the heart of it. They were uneasy. All of them had been raised in Jewish families who believed in and practiced the tenets of the religion. I did too. Stealing, even from the wretched Malka Henske, was breaking a sacred commandment.

Finally, Mila said, "Nonsense. It was an act of rebellion. Rivka is fighting back against our communist oppressors."

Genesha and Shoshanna laughed. I looked gratefully at Mila, and she smiled back.

Leah raised her cup. "And we, by drinking this cocoa, are committing an act of resistance. We are partisan fighters." She took a sip and sighed with a heavenly expression.

Genesha said, "Malka must be searching everywhere for the culprit. She will hang someone for this vile act of treason."

"I hope not," I said.

Shoshana raised her hand motioning for silence. "How did you steal it?"

I shrugged as if it were nothing. "They left me alone in the reception area. The tin of cocoa was there. Suddenly, that cocoa leapt off the table and landed in my pocket."

They chuckled. Esther said, "Now she's adding lying to her crimes." This time she said it lightheartedly.

Mila wagged a finger at me. "Young woman, your father will be very upset with you."

"No, he won't," I said, "because he will never know."

Leah said, "He won't know from us."

They all nodded agreement.

With our bellies warmed from hot cocoa and exhausted from the long hike, it was time to go home. We hugged each other and left. Walking the path back behind the houses, it came to me that no longer was I not the best at something among my friends. Because now I was. Something that would shock Grandmother into a stroke. I was the best thief. I laughed aloud.

CHAPTER SIX

BERLIN, JUNE 15, 1941

The screech of the train's iron wheels entering Berlin's Anhalter Bahnhof brought Bauer out of his nap. As always, he was instantly awake. Sliding his reading glasses into a pocket of his field gray uniform, he stood up, adjusted his cap, and grabbed his traveling pack off the rack.

Moments later, he stepped onto the platform and peered over the crowd, searching for his wife Klara and boy Hanzi but didn't see them. He slung his pack over his shoulder and headed for the exit, pushing his way through the hundreds of soldiers heading for their troop train.

Off to war, Operation Barbarossa, though that was still a closely kept secret. When Bauer first arrived in Berlin three months ago, Barbarossa was postponed so the Wehrmacht could first destroy the upstart Yugoslavs and then help the worthless Italians conquer Greece. Back then, he had only remained in Berlin for a week and a half, enough time for the powerful leader of the SD Reinhard Heydrich to pin medals on his chest and preside over his promotion to sturmbannführer for Joseph Goebbels's newsreel cameras.

In that ceremony, his wife and son stood off to the side along with his parents, who had come from Nuremberg to witness it. Meeting

Heydrich after the ceremony, his parents bobbed their heads with comical, embarrassing deference. Heydrich limply shook hands with them and Bauer's wife, patted Hanzi on his blond head, then ignored them, and pulled his new sturmbannführer aside. "Now you are a major. That means more responsibility, Bauer, the fun is over for you. The Wehrmacht have their part to play in Barbarossa; we have ours. You are assigned to Pretzsch where all preparations for our work is being made. I'm driving down today. You can accompany me."

Bauer snapped his boots together. "Yes, Gruppenführer. It would be my honor."

When he arrived at Pretzsch, several thousand men from the ranks of the SS, police, and security services had already reported to the police academy for training. For the next two and a half months, he worked with Oberführer Oscar Muller, his old commander from Poland, on their plans. They were to be attached to Army Group North, which would pour across the border into the Baltic states, destroy Russian forces, and take control of the ports. Commanding an Einsatzkommando unit, Bauer's mission was to cleanse an enormous swathe of land between the border and the city of Vilna.

Now back, a week before Operation Barbarossa's probable attack on Sunday June 22, he scanned the crowd for his wife and boy.

He heard her call. "Max! Max!"

He broke into a wide grin when he saw Klara waving and pushing her way through the crowd toward him. She tugged his little boy Hanzi in his Hitler Youth uniform by the hand. At four, he was too young for the group, but he loved his father in a uniform and so always wore one himself. Setting his pack down just in time to catch Klara in his arms, he kissed her, hugged her, and kissed her again. A few people around them applauded, and one soldier boldly called out, "I hope a Fraulein as pretty as this greets me when I return, Major."

"My beautiful Klara," Bauer said to her, eating her alive with his eyes. He felt a surge of desire. In a devilish voice, he whispered, "The girl with the perfect body."

She threw back her head and laughed. Turning to his son, Bauer lifted him in the air. The boy giggled. "My, my, you're becoming a big man."

He set him back on the platform. "Practicing your football?"

"Yes, Vati."

Bauer ruffled the boy's hair, lifted his pack onto his back, and with his arm around his wife and taking his boy's hand, he made his way out of the station.

At just past 10:00 AM next day, Klara drove her husband to Hitler's massive new Reich's Chancellery. After kissing her cheek, Bauer stepped out and hurried up the steps into the building.

Inside, he stood for a moment like a schoolboy at his first trip to a Nazi rally in awe of the magnificent structure. It must be the grandest palace in Germany. Polished floors, high ceilings, leather bound furniture, and the line of SS guards standing in their uniforms with their polished black boots. The great hall churned with coordinated chaos, soldiers and civilians rushing about as if the world would soon end or begin. His chest swelled with pride. All this was for Operation Barbarossa, and he had his own important part in it.

"Bauer," someone called in a booming voice that echoed in the reception hall. He saw Oberführer Muller striding toward him like a miniature **Göring**, his puffy face twisted in a smile. Not everyone was the ideal Aryan, Bauer thought. They exchanged salutes.

"Good morning, sir," Bauer said.

Muller rubbed his hands together excitedly. "Well, here we are. This is the real beginning of the war. Make no mistake, Bauer, Poland was a field exercise. First time hearing the Führer speak in person?"

Muller had the bad habit of spraying spittle when he spoke, and Bauer eased a half a step back. "No, sir, I heard him in Nuremburg with a hundred thousand people. It was quite a thing, but this is different."

"Yes, different."

A young lieutenant approached them and clicked his heels. "Will you follow me, sirs?"

He escorted the two SS officers down the hall to a large reception chamber where at least eighty men in uniforms and civilian suits sat in rows facing a podium. On the stage, a magnificent, gold eagle perched atop a black swastika while giant, red and black flags draped from the wall. Each man had the same special mission to accomplish, and today, Hitler planned to detail that mission in exactitude so no one would misunderstand the task at hand.

Bauer and Muller scooted in and found seats toward the back. Up on the dais, several of the Führer's top men sat in chairs waiting for his appearance. Himmler was cleaning his glasses while listening to Heydrich make some point or other. Next to Heydrich, Goebbels's good leg bounced nervously. He checked his wristwatch and then looked out over the audience. Bormann sat like a statue, his facial expression never changing.

The only one not sitting was fat **Hermann Göring**, who strode back and forth on the dais in his pristinely white uniform, one he created for himself. His chest was bedecked in medals, most of which he had actually earned in the last war, but to Bauer, he looked more like a maître d than a Reich's Marshal.

At exactly 10:30, Hitler marched into the room, and **Göring** darted into his seat. Everyone shot to their feet and snapped their arms out in salute. The Führer casually returned it and gestured for them to sit. He spoke in a barely audible voice, so everyone strained to hear. "In the course of my life, I have been a prophet. During my struggle for power, the Jewish race laughed when I said I would one day become leader of the German state, and that I would then settle the Jewish problem. For some time now, however, they have been laughing out the other side of their faces. In a few days, we will implement the final solution to the Jewish problem. Let them laugh then."

The men snorted and guffawed. As Hitler's voice steadily rose, he held his fists in front of his face in rising fury, veins popping in his neck. "This is a war of extermination. The Jewish-Bolshevik intelligentsia, the oppressor of the past, must be liquidated. It is right, moral, and necessary for the survival of the German people."

He harangued against Jews and Bolsheviks for the next half hour, rambling in his declarations, but that didn't matter to Bauer. He saw the certainty in the Führer's beliefs, the great passion igniting in his eyes, the power of his voice to convey meaning. The words struck deep into Bauer's soul and fired him with determination.

Leaning forward, Hitler gripped the sides of the podium. "This is not a matter for military courts. You will not be bothered with such things. The officers under your command must know what is expected of them, and the soldiers must be ready to carry out their orders to the utmost ruthless measure. There is no room for mercy, for such mercy will not be extended to you. When Operation Barbarossa begins, you will follow close behind our army and remove the enemies of the Reich from all captured territory."

Abruptly, Hitler fell silent for several seconds. To Bauer, the silence had physical substance as the Führer held them all in his grip.

"I call on you to perform your sacred duty," he said and pointed a shaking finger at them. "The extermination of all the Jews in Europe."

He stepped back from the podium and extended his right arm. "Sieg."

Every man leapt to his feet again, Bauer among them, and roared back, "Heil."

Hitler repeated, "Sieg."

"Heil."

"Sieg."

"Heil."

"Sieg"

"Heil."

Abruptly, the Führer turned and strode from the room.

CHAPTER SEVEN

The day broke overcast and remained so throughout. June 19, 1941, the terrible date carved itself into my memory for this was the day Peretz was going to America. The Neman River swelled from the recent rains and threatened to come over its banks, a reflection of how I felt. Rain and gloom.

At 9:00 AM, my entire family and I walked to the Frischer house on Zigmond Street to say goodbye. With his mother Mina, a stout woman we all loved, and his siblings, he was scheduled to leave on the train to Warsaw at noon. Switching trains, they would travel down through Germany and Austria into Italy where they were scheduled to catch a ship out of Naples bound for America. Going through Germany right now would not be the route I'd choose, but it was the only route they had.

When we arrived, a number of people had already gathered. When someone emigrated to Palestine or America, it was a big event, almost as big as a wedding. Peretz was talking to several people, so I wandered into a small library where he and his siblings studied. Alone, I sank into a soft chair and stared at the shelves on the one wall that had books.

After a few minutes, he found me. "Rivka, there you are. Hiding from me?"

I stood up and stuck my hands in my dress pockets. "No, it's hot in there. Just trying to cool off. I was about to go back in."

He gave a snort. "I don't even know half these people. So, have you changed your mind?"

"About what?"

"About coming to America."

My temper flashed. "No, I'm fourteen. I can't just hop on a train and tell the conductor I'm going to America."

Peretz shrugged. "Not now. In a few years maybe."

"I'd never leave my family, and they won't leave Nashok. Papa's the doctor, and Mama will never go without Baba."

"My grandmother was the same," he said. "If she were still alive, we wouldn't be going to America."

I sighed. "I guess I'll have to marry Yankl Glazman."

He laughed, shaking his head, tossing a lock of hair over his brow. "I like Yankl."

"So do I."

We stood there awkwardly silent for the first time in our lives. After another moment, I turned and walked away.

Back in the crowded living room, I made my way across to my girlfriends, the Seven, beside an empty glass cabinet, which once held knickknacks of all kinds that had been in the Frischer family for centuries. Mila hugged me. We both had things today that saddened us. Her small sister, Aneta, had caught the measles, and their own journey to America postponed till the girl got well and Aunt Miriam could get new visas. Everyone hoped for a month from now. At least I had her for a while longer.

"I think I would have chosen Palestine," Genesha said. "I'd live in a kibbutz, then farm and keep cows."

"Ambitious," Esther said sarcastically.

"It's not like Peretz has a choice," Sarah said. "His father's in America."

"I'm not going to either one," Leah said. "I'm going to Moscow first chance I get to join the Bolshoi." Her voice had a catch in it. She was apparently nervous about sharing this secret with us. It seemed a joke. Leah had no athletic or dancing ability. But she was serious.

"The Bolshoi?" I said.

"Yes."

Esther said, "It's a little late for that, isn't it? You're already fifteen and can't dance."

Undeterred, Leah shrugged, "I can learn."

Mila said, "You will go the Bolshoi and take over. Run the place and invite all of us to watch the performances." We all chuckled, nodding. That would be more like Leah. Mila added, "Maybe you'll even take over for Stalin someday."

Leah shrugged. I could see she would not give up on the idea.

"I'm trying to get my parents to go to America," Shoshana said. "Peretz' father told him there's wonderful Yiddish theaters in New York. That's where I want to go. Isn't it amazing they would speak Yiddish there just like us?"

Esther shook her head. "Not at all. There're a lot of Jews in New York, my Papa says. Many from right here in Nashok like Peretz's and Mila's fathers."

Mila nodded. "This is true." She turned to Sarah. "What about you. Where are you bound?"

She was already fifteen like Leah and Mila. I would not be for another five months. "I'm staying here," she said firmly. "This is my home. I have no plans or desires to leave."

That was the biggest surprise for all of us. Sarah, the math genius, should be studying at some big university in Germany or England, not tilling the soil and taking photos like her mother. No one said anything.

Leah turned to me. "What about you, Rivka? Are you going to be running off to America after Peretz and Mila?"

I shook my head. "No, I'm staying here like Sarah."

Leah threw up her hands. "My God, our two best scholars, the two best in the shtetl, are not going to even go to Vilna for university."

I smiled mischievously. "Maybe I'll take trips to Vilna or Warsaw or Berlin. After all, I'm clearly the best thief among this band of cutthroats and I may have to go from time to time to where the thieving is better."

They laughed.

When it got hot and stuffy, the Seven went out onto the lawn where the town's best photographer Erna Shlanski, Sarah's mother, took our picture. We all had on our best dresses, and we sat on the grass, smiling at the camera, full of ourselves. We knew if anyone could conquer the world, at least our own private worlds, we could. When Mrs. Shlanski snapped the camera, I felt a great sense of pride and even wonderment. She was capturing us for our future generations to see. We had just achieved a bit of immortality with the photo.

A little later, we returned inside where dreading Peretz leaving, I avoided him the rest of the morning. Back inside, I kept watching the clock, as if by doing that I could stop time. I couldn't. Time just ran over me. At 11:30, about sixty of us trooped down to the train station with the Frischers for final goodbyes. A small town station made of worn brick, it had four tracks because it was on the route between Vilna and Warsaw.

Among the crowd, all the Young Guardians stood on the station platform as the train to Warsaw eased in with squeals of metal on metal and bursts of steam. While I stood off to the side, they hugged Peretz and wept. People filed before Aunt Mina and the rest of her children, saying goodbye.

All their baggage had been loaded, and the conductor was announcing the train's departure.

"That's enough," Papa said. "They must go. They must board."

All but Peretz climbed aboard. He was still saying his farewells to friends. He glanced at me and came over. "Don't you want to say goodbye to me, Rivka?"

He reached his hand out to me, and I took it in mine. My hand trembled, and I knew I was blushing furiously. He said softly so only I could hear, "No one could have a better or truer friend than you, Rivka."

"Go in good health, Peretz," I said, a quaver in my voice. I kissed his cheek.

He climbed onto the train, turned once and waved, then disappeared into the car. Moments later, it pulled out of the station.

When the train was lost to sight beyond a row of buildings, I sprinted from the platform and ran home without slowing. I burst into the house, took the stairs two at a time, and climbed the ladder into the cupola. I looked out over the town, saw the roof of the train station in the distance, the spires of the synagogue, the Hebrew school, all Nashok. I swung my eyes up into the hills, searching to the southwest and found the opening in the woods where the tracks rise out of the valley and curve around a knoll.

I stared for several seconds, a minute, and no train appeared. I feared I'd missed it, then it chugged up the incline, Peretz's train, headed for America. I watched it till it was gone and when it was, it felt like my body had drained of blood. Tears rolled down my cheeks.

A yell came from below. "Hey, what are you doing?"

I looked down. Standing on the street, shielding her eyes against the sun, Hanna was watching me.

"If I jump," I said. "I think I could fly, and if I could fly, I could catch up with him."

"Well, don't do that."

She came inside, and moments later I heard her footsteps on the stairs, then on the ladder up to the cupola. Oh, wonderful, I thought as she stepped up beside me. My sister Hanna was now going to tease me unmercifully for being such a childish person. Instead, she took me in her arms and held me. I sighed in them, and for the first time today cried.

"We've all been in love," she said gently. "You know you're in love because it hurts so much."

"Who were you in love with?" I asked between sobs.

"You know that boy Ben Zion brought home for shabbat last year? The one he goes to university with?"

I stepped back still holding to her. "You mean him?"

She nodded. "Don't you know? That's the real reason I want to study medicine at good old Vilna."

Wiping my eyes, I laughed through tears, then sat down on the floorboards and rested against the wall. Hanna sat beside me and put her arm around me. I leaned against her.

"Like I said," she remarked, "we sisters have to stick together."

As the train to Warsaw neared the Polish border, Peretz sat facing his mother and two sisters. He was trying to reconcile the sadness he felt at leaving his friends with the sense of adventure ahead. He was going to America. There was no future in Nashok for him. But he would miss them all, the Young Guardians, all his school friends, and Rivka, such an unusual girl.

He saw her in his imaginings hovering in front of him, a pretty, dark-eyed girl looking at him with mockery and affection, what she thought was love. At fourteen, she was too young for the kind of love she spoke of. He loved her, too, but more as a sister, though she did have alluringly slim legs.

Crossing the border into Poland, the train slowed to a stop at a small station. Peretz's heart jammed up into his throat when four border guards entered the car and began checking passports. The gray uniforms of the front two gave them the appearance of police.

Peretz looked at his mother, who remained calm, nodding at him to do the same, but he couldn't. He took his passport from his pocket and gripped it tightly, bending it. Religion was stamped on all passports, and theirs had a red J for Jude. His mother reached across and rested her hand on his, and he relaxed. Shouldn't frighten his younger brothers and sisters. Down at the far end, the two men in front were briskly conducting business, taking only seconds to scan the passports as if they were looking for something in particular.

As the men worked their way toward Peretz and his family, he attempted to feign an air of indifference he didn't feel and stared out the window at the small station, a red brick building with several people waiting on the platform to board.

Out of the corner of his eye, he saw one more row of seats and then they would be at them. "Your passport," one said, reaching out toward Mina. She handed hers to him. He flipped it open, then held it for the other man to see. "Mina Frischer, Juden."

In halting German, Mina said calmly, "We have visas for America. My husband is…"

He held up his hand to silence her, then looked through the passport. Finally, he returned it. "Congratulations, Frau Frischer, your visas have won you the lottery."

About a half hour later, when the train clamored out of the station, Peretz began to relax. Next stop Warsaw, then down through Germany and Austria. But immediately outside of town when the countryside opened up, he saw something that froze his heart. Along a cobbled road, a long line of tanks rumbled toward the border. The tanks seemed endless. In the farmer's field about a half kilometer beyond, a vast array of tents and soldiers and army vehicles seemed caught up in organized chaos, everyone moving with some unidentified purpose.

There were thousands of men. Thousands of vehicles.

"Mama," he said. She was tying his youngest sister Elena's shoe. When his mother looked up, he nodded out the window. Her mouth dropped open, and alarm came to her eyes.

The rest of the day and into the night, their train had to stop for long stretches of time to allow what were clearly troop trains moving in the opposite direction. They did not make Warsaw till after midnight and stayed in the station till morning when they climbed aboard the Berlin train.

In Berlin, they quickly changed trains and made it down through Austria and into Italy. It was a long, exhausting journey. Peretz was surprised that all the border checks threatened them not at all. To Peretz, the American visas cast a magic spell that covered them with a cloud of invisibility. They made Naples around 3:00 in the afternoon of the third day, stayed one night in a portside hotel using most of their funds, and sailed out the next day onboard the MS Vulcania bound for America. It was June 22nd.

CHAPTER EIGHT

A pale sliver of light coursed across the eastern horizon as Max Bauer, commander of Einsatzkommando 4d, checked his watch for the third time in the last hour. 2:55 AM. Barbarossa, B-hour imminent. Along with several of his men, he stood on a ridge overlooking the small stream a kilometer away that marked the border. The land was vast with fields, swamps, meadows, and great swathes of dense forests.

Lifting his binoculars, he scanned Russian territory, spotting nothing but shadows, not a spark of light, no movement. On this side of the border, however, he did see activity, a lot of it. Under the cover of darkness, the 20th Motorized Infantry was advancing toward the small stream. Their mission was to push up through the Vilnius axis, destroying the enemy in its path, and he and his unit would follow.

The excitement of the moment had spread through his men. In ten minutes, the greatest invasion in the history of the world will be unleashed on the unsuspecting Russians. Like Muller, though, he didn't know whether the German army would achieve complete surprise or not. The Wehrmacht will annihilate the enemy anyway.

Lowering the binoculars, he took out two cigarettes and offered one to Oberleutnant Keppler. Reassigned from Bauer's old detachment in Poland, Keppler had just reported earlier that evening after taking a detour to Berlin for the birth of his first child. Bauer understood and said nothing about it. He valued Keppler for the work ahead. Covering his match, Bauer lit both cigarettes, and they smoked, cupping their hands to block any light.

"Thank you, sir," Keppler said, taking a drag and exhaling through his nose. "It won't be long now. I wish I could be with them."

Bauer wasn't sure whom he meant by *them*, his wife and new baby or the soldiers attacking tonight.

"So do I," Bauer said. For him, he meant Klara and Hanzi, not the soldiers. "How is Helga and the baby?"

Keppler grinned instantly. "Both are fine, sir. Thank you for asking. I got a message a couple hours ago from the doctor. What was his name? I'm always forgetting his name. You can imagine how difficult it was to get a message through today. Anyway, both are doing fine." Stretching the bounds of the physically possible, his grin widened. "It's a boy."

"Congratulations, Franz. What's his name?"

"Eric, after my father." Keppler took another drag on his cigarette, then frowned. "Sir, I feel I must ask about procedure. You see, I know what our mission is but not exactly how to do it. Nothing like this has ever been done before, at least not on this scale. Sorry, sir, if I'm out of line."

Bauer plucked a piece of tobacco off his tongue. "These difficulties have been discussed. You weren't here." He let that sink in. "You'll be fully briefed when the opportunity presents itself."

Keppler nodded quickly, deferentially. "Of course, sir."

Exhaling smoke into the night air, Bauer fell silent for a full minute. A frog's croak came from the nearby marshes. Distantly, an engine started. From several meters away, he heard the hushed voices of three of his soldiers. Then he said to Keppler, "To some, the difficulties of our 'special tasks' are insurmountable. People call our mission 'special tasks,' dancing around calling it what it was, but we will not. It's cleansing the continent of Jews. We must not fail, Keppler. The Führer is depending on us to do our job."

"Yes, sir. I understand."

"The fact is there is no manual to follow. No outline of how to do it. We will be creating the manual as we go. There are nearly 300,000 Jews in Lithuania, so the way I see it, to accomplish our goal of making Lithuania free of these Jews is a matter of organization. Most problems in any field of work can be solved with good organization."

"Yes, sir."

Bauer flicked ash off his cigarette. "When I was a boy, my father took over a failing produce business. We bought produce from farmers and distributed it to grocers. We had seven workers who did a little bit of everything. My father sacked some, hired some, and trained all employees to do one thing and do it well. We prospered. Organization, Keppler. That's how we will get this thing done."

"Yes, sir. It seems like common sense, doesn't it?"

"Each of our operations must be exhaustively planned. A reconnaissance of the city, district, or town. Depending on the number of Jews, a place for the pits must be found, and the pits dug. When the time comes to carry out the action, the Jews will be assembled in one holding area, if possible, and then transported to the pit. We will be busy." He glanced at Keppler. "I hope you will have a chance to see your wife and child at some point during all this. I certainly intend to see mine. Are you planning on a large family, Keppler?"

The oberleutnant grinned. "We are. Helga wants four. I want six."

"Then it will be five." Bauer tossed his cigarette into the grass. "Of course, we don't have the manpower to deal with the Jewish problem on our own. We'll need to work with Lithuanian partisans. Most of them hate Jews more than us."

"Yes, and Poles, I should think. Oh, Dr. Rosner. That's his name. My wife's doctor."

At that moment, the world exploded with fury. Thousands of artillery guns unleashed frantic shellfire onto Russian territory. The thunderous roar shook the earth around Bauer. Flashes like distant lightening could be seen up and down the line for kilometers. The bombardment pounded the enemy for several minutes before the infantry and a nearby Panzer battalion thrust across the border and swept the stunned Russian soldiers before them.

CHAPTER NINE

Four days after Peretz left for America, the Germans came, rumbling into Nashok with a great roar of clanking and grinding. It was 5:00 AM, and I thought the world was ending. Mila, who was spending the night, bolted upright in our shared bed. "What is that?"

The sun already blazed through my open window. Throwing back the sheet, I leapt up and ran to it. Below, tanks rolled along our street with their deafening clamor.

"Come on," I said to Mila, grabbing her hand and pulling her out of bed.

We ran for the hallway and scrambled up the ladder into the cupola where we saw something breathtaking and terrible. Everywhere, a great army swarmed through Nashok. They were rolling through my neighborhood and seemingly every other street in town, bucket-seat motorcycles and open-air cars, then tanks and cannons on flatbed trucks and soldiers, soldiers, soldiers.

Above all of it flew an armada of planes.

"My God," I breathed.

"My God," Mila echoed me.

One of the marching soldiers below spotted us and waved. Hesitantly, we waved back. Then, a monstrous roar rumbled inside my chest, and I turned to see a plane flying straight at me. I ducked. In an instant, it shot by just overhead.

From the hall, Mama shouted up at us, "Hey, you two, what are you doing up there? Come down right now before the Germans shoot you."

The entire family gathered downstairs, Mama and Papa, Ben Zion back for the summer, Hanna, Baba, and Mila, too.

"Close the windows and shutters. Quick," Mama ordered.

We did and hid behind our locked doors all morning, as if that would stop a German tank. Being the town's doctor, Papa had a phone and sent word to Aunt Miriam that Mila was safe and would be staying for a while. I wondered then if this invasion would prevent her from going to America. Her family still had visas. I hated to lose my best friend, so I admitted to a little selfishness. If she went, I would be happy for her; if she stayed, I'd be happy for me.

While Mama and Baba began preparing breakfast, Mila and I tried to help but, too frightened by the roar outside to do anything useful, mostly got in the way.

"What do they want?" I asked.

It must have been a stupid question because Hanna, standing at the kitchen window watching several soldiers tramping through our garden, looked back at me and rolled her eyes.

Grandmother gave a sharp cackle. "They want the Russians. They want Stalin. This is Armageddon between them, and rest assured, the Russians are running."

I knew that to be true. The Germans had ten times, a hundred times, more men and war things than the Russians.

"I'm not sure which is worse, the communists or the Germans," Mama said, trying to hide her worry as she set kugel bread on plates.

"Don't be foolish," Baba retorted. "The Germans are here to liberate us from the communists. They were here in the last war. They are good boys. It's a cultured country, not like those crude Bolsheviks." At the stove frying eggs, she glanced at Mama. "You remember. You were a young girl then, and they treated you like a princess."

Mama said, "Their fathers did. Not these Germans, Mother."

Grandmother shook her head. "They are the same. It will be better now. You'll see."

Hanna said, "The refugees from Poland say the Germans are killing people. They're putting the Jews into ghettos where they starve to death."

Grandmother flicked her hand as if swatting away a fly. "They say, they say. They say. Just crazy talk. Rumors. Scare stories. Nothing more."

Just then, we heard distant thunder, and she gave an amused snort. "There, you see. That's the Russian base. The Germans are blowing it up."

Soon, we ate a light breakfast, eggs and kugels, then gathered in the living room, trying to stay busy, sewing, reading, talking in hushed tones. Mila and I huddled together in one armchair as I read aloud from Grimm's Fairy Tales, translating the German to Yiddish as I went. Papa preferred I read Goethe, but Goethe is so dreary. No one liked him. Inside our cloistered home, a growing sense of dread settled in me, minute by minute. Mila, too. She clutched my arm so tightly I could barely turn the page. I kept glancing at the door as if soldiers would crash through any second.

"What will happen to us now?" Mila whispered.

I didn't know what to answer, but Papa heard and interrupted Ben Zion who was saying something about going out. Papa turned to us and said, "We go on as before. We live day to day."

I loved Papa, but I was not reassured. Russia was Malka, the devils you know. These were the Germans, who had overrun Poland and if Hanna and Peretz were right, killed people only because they were Jews.

At around 10:00 AM, when the sound of the rolling tanks and marching soldiers finally ended, Papa and Ben Zion went out to discover what was going on. Through the cracked of the window, I watched them dash across the street and through Mr. Rabinowitz's yard.

Later, when we were back in the kitchen preparing a light soup for the noon meal, neither had come back.

"Have the Germans killed them?" I asked in a faint voice, a little child again.

"Don't be ridiculous, Rivka," Hanna snapped. "Why would the Germans kill Papa and Ben Zion?"

Baba shook her head. "Of course, they didn't kill them, child. They're fine."

How do you know, I wanted to shout at both of them, but didn't.

Soon though, Papa and Ben Zion returned, saying what was already obvious. The town of Nashok had new masters. Hundreds of Poles and Lithuanians had turned out to welcome them, cheering and presenting bouquets of flowers, the Karnowski brothers and their families foremost among them. They'd already placed several pictures of Adolf Hitler in their storefront window, and each of the brothers wore the faded, brown uniform of the Endecja party.

As Papa and Ben Zion talked, I could see both were shaken. Papa's hands trembled, and as a doctor who conducted many surgeries, his hands never trembled. And Ben Zion was hectic, moving like a windup toy that had its spring tightened to bursting. They were hiding something. Mama picked it up too. Her face clouded with worry. All this had the effect of scaring me.

Reddening from excitement, Ben Zion spoke so rapidly I found it difficult to follow him. "Baba was right. The Russians ran. They didn't even fire one rifle, took off in their trucks. Malka and the Council too. All the Bolsheviks gone."

Grandmother nodded sagely. "Of course. Now, things will get better."

"Malka?" Hanna said at the same time. "She's nine months pregnant. She looks like a cow. She can't travel."

Mama frowned at her. "Someday you too will look like a cow, as you say. Then what about your big talk then, Hanna?"

Only slightly chagrined, Hanna threw up her hands as if to say, *it's the truth.*

With a great effort, Papa calmed his trembling. "We have a curfew," he said. "Just Jews. Nine PM. No Jew outside. I think the Germans will be very severe with anyone who breaks their rules."

As if I would be going out. I could sneak out but then that would take more courage than I have. The Germans shoot people who break their rules, no matter what Baba might say.

By late afternoon, Papa felt it was safe enough to escort Mila home. I wanted to go with them, but he wouldn't allow it. I hugged Mila and told her I would come and see her when I could.

Later that afternoon, I overheard Ben Zion telling Hanna what had unnerved him and Papa so much. It was such a momentous thing that, I think, he could not remain silent about it any longer and had to tell someone. Of course, it would be Hanna. They were closer in age and like souls, fierce, bold, and unafraid, almost as if they were twins. When he and Papa reached the square this morning, several hundred Poles had gathered to greet the Germans, applauding and cheering.

Off toward the firehouse, a smaller group, maybe fifty of so, had congregated. With pistols, knives, or cudgels in their hands, they were focused on something entirely separate from the arriving Germans, so Ben Zion and Papa made their way toward them. Surrounded by the crowd, Radek Karnowski swaggered about in his uniform, hurling insults at seven men on their hands and knees, all Orthodox Jews with long beards including Rabbi Herskowitz. They had buckets of soapy water, and they were scrubbing the cobblestones. Karnowski kicked the rabbi. The other men watching thought this hilarious.

Papa and Ben Zion pushed their way in among them, and Papa faced Radek, demanding that he stop.

Radek grinned. "Get down and help him, doctor. There are enough brushes."

"Stop this," Papa said.

Radek placed his boot on the back of the Rabbi's neck and pressed it to the cobblestone. "Help him or I will snap his neck.

This is the way it is now, Doctor Big Shot. Down. Both of you, or I will break his neck."

Ben Zion saw all the other men grinning as if this were a comedy show at the Firehouse. They hoped Papa would refuse. Papa nodded to Ben Zion, and both knelt on the cobblestones, grabbed brushes, and began cleaning. A roar went up from the other Poles watching, and a few slapped Radek on the back.

"Was ist das? Aus dem veg." A German officer pushed his way through the mob. "What is this?" He was a gray-haired man in a Wehrmacht colonel's uniform. He seemed upset.

Radek drew a finger across his neck. "Yids kaput."

The colonel's jaw clinched. To Papa, Ben Zion, and the other Jews, he said, "Get up. Go."

Quickly, Papa and Ben Zion helped the Rabbi up and all of them hurried from the square.

The rest of that day and well into the night, we spent tiptoeing around in our own home as if making noise would draw the attention of the Germans. Exhausted by the tension of the day, I went to bed early but then couldn't sleep.

It was stiflingly hot. Long after dark, I sat at my open window trying to catch a cooling breeze. There was no moon, but a brilliant sky. Sounds of a drunken revel came from the market square. I was sure it was the Karnowski brothers and their friends, surely hundreds of them, celebrating the new order of things.

Just past eleven, a car, its headlights off, coasted down our street and stopped a little beyond our house. Moments later, Papa hurried out our door, carrying his medical bag and climbed into the back. Headlights still off, it drove away.

I was scared to death. Where was he going? I was sure the Germans would shoot him. I waited by the window, clutching my hands in front of my stomach as if I could keep the fear in by doing that.

Time moved at such a slow pace that I was sure several hours had passed by the time the car dropped Papa off. I could see my clock in the starlight and made out it was just after midnight. Little more than an hour had passed. I slipped downstairs and listened at the closed door just outside Papa's office. He was arguing with Mama in hushed tones, so I could not tell what they were saying, but I heard the anger in their voices. Mostly Mama. Papa was more defensive. I heard the words *treatment* and *dangerous,* then the name *Malka.*

Suddenly, I realized they'd been silent for several seconds and then heard the knob turning. I only had time to dart into the hallway shadows as light spilled from the door and Mama stepped out. With a disapproving frown, she glanced back inside, then shut the door. Standing there for several seconds, she adjusted the hem of her sleeves. I could barely breathe for fear of making the slightest noise and Mama catching me spying on them.

Her voice was low. "You can go to bed, Rivka. Your father is safe."

As I started past, she stopped me, held my face in her hands for several seconds, then kissed my forehead. "Go to bed."

CHAPTER TEN

The next day, the main German army resumed its advance on Vilna, leaving a large detachment of soldiers behind. The officers seized the best Jewish homes close to the market square for their use, allowing the former owners to remain as servants. In the afternoon, Hanna came back from buying food on the black market, carrying a handful of leaflets the military had distributed.

I grabbed one and read, *The German army has come to liberate the Polish and Lithuanian people from the scourge of the Jews of Moses with his seven heavens, from the Jew-communists who are the friends of Roosevelt and Churchill and Stalin. For too long, they have oppressed Christians by using unfair business tactics, hoarding wealth, and leaving scraps behind for everyone else. But soon, all the Jews will be gone.*

My spine went cold as ice flows. All the Jews gone! What did that mean? I looked to Papa and could see worry on his face, but he said nothing. Hanna held one of the leaflets out to Grandmother. "See, Baba? What do you think of your Germans now?"

Baba waved it away. "Of course, that's what they say. They have to say that just like the Poles did and the Lithuanians did. Blame the Jews and say you're going to do something about it. Everyone is satisfied, then life goes on."

However, apprehension over the occupation eased, at least among the older people, by some of the soldiers themselves who seemed friendly enough. Ben Zion told us he spoke to one, asking him straight out how long he'd be in Nashok. The German, a young private, took no offense, but instead, seemed happy to talk with someone who spoke his language. He'd been wandering through the square, looking at the shops. Now, he stopped and shrugged. "Not long, my friend. It will be a short war." He grinned. "Here today, Moscow tomorrow."

In that first week, when no one broke into our house, my own fear lessened somewhat. I had to wonder who was right, Hanna and Peretz, who said the Germans were murderers, or Baba and her friends, who evoked the friendly Germans from the old war. While most Jews ventured out now, forced by necessity to work and find food, I did not. Mama allowed me in the backyard only, so I could tend our garden and chicken coop, like a prisoner. Rapunzel in the tower, but my prince was on his way to America. Being my age, many of my friends were kept home as well, all princesses to be protected.

When I went out into the backyard to do chores, though, I slipped off into the forest, my dark kingdom, and ran like a deer over paths of soft green sprigs and brown pine needles, free and wild, till I collapsed, out of breath. Then climbed my favorite tree, a giant oak standing thick and magnificent in a ray of sunlight and surrounded by skinny pine and fat spruce. Up on a high limb, I heard the far-off rattle of a train clattering toward Vilna or Warsaw. Up here, the air was clear and sweet. This was the world I escaped to. No Germans here. No one could catch me in my woods.

In this way, I met my own German soldier.

I was coming out of the forests into our backyard, carrying a small basket of mushrooms, daydreaming as usual, my eyes cast down as I composed my next letter to Peretz. He'd been gone eight days, surely not even in America yet, and I'd written twelve letters to him. These last few had been mostly about the Germans.

"Hallo," someone called. Startled, I froze and looked up

"Guten tag, fraulein," A man stood in my path, decked out in lederhosen and a backpack, smiling roguishly at me. He was blond and blue eyed, handsome to be sure, with a purplish scar on his right cheekbone. "Sprichst du Deutsch?"

I did, but didn't know whether I should tell him, or even speak to him. But he blocked my way, and I'd have to go around the chicken coop to get past him. What did it matter?

"Ja, I speak a little."

He gave me that smile again. "You speak it very well."

"You can tell that from so few words?" I said skeptically.

"Now I have more. I'm Max Bauer. What's your name, fraulein?"

"Rivka."

He held onto the strap of his backpack with one hand and a walking stick with the other. He nodded as if my name met with his approval. "Rivka, that's a pretty name. It means Rebecca, does it not? How old are you, Rivka?"

"Fourteen, but I'll be fifteen in October." I winced when I said that. As if desperate to show this man I was older.

"I'm from Bavaria, Rivka, the Black Forest. So far from home. Have you heard of it? The forests are beautiful like these." He gestured behind me. "I thought I would explore yours today. Do I have your permission? I bet you know them well. I bet you wander the paths all the time."

"I'm not going to wander them with you," I said sharply.

By his expression, my words stung. "I mean you no harm, fraulein. Truly."

"Leave her alone," Hanna shouted from the back porch. She dashed past him and grabbed my hand. He backed out of the way to let us pass. Without looking, we strode rapidly to the door. I glanced back, not sure whether I should smile. He seemed more like one of Grandmother's Germans.

"Meine schönen Mädchen," he called after us. "You are Jewish, ja?"

With my auburn hair, it wasn't obvious that I was, but Hanna had brilliant, long black hair and looked like an ancient Israelite that had just stepped from the Bible. We spoke in unison, "We are." Hanna more defiant than me added, "Are you going to shoot us now?"

His face was a dramatist's mask of sadness. "No. I'm sorry for you. Very bad times ahead for the Jews." He spun around and headed into our woods.

Startled, I asked Hanna, "What did he mean by that?"

"I don't know. Why ask me? Just talk," she said uneasily.

The next week, life in Nashok changed. The Gestapo arrived, five men in fedora hats and business suits who took up residence in the hotel, Malka's old headquarters. Everyone had heard of the Gestapo, and everyone feared them. They were the monsters that inhabited a child's nightmares. They got right to work, appointing an entirely new police force, mostly local Poles led by two Polish volksdeutschen from Kovna.

The man they selected to be their police sergeant was Radek Karnowski.

Before dawn on Saturday, the new police sergeant and two of his Gestapo masters banged on our door, rousting us out of bed. Papa answered, and Radek ordered the entire family into the street immediately. When Papa asked why, one of the Gestapo men drew a pistol and shouted, "Schnell!"

Shoved outside, we saw all our neighbors had formed into a single procession of sixty or seventy people, all of us in our nightclothes. Confused and terrified, I clung to Mama as we fell in with the column while a detachment of soldiers herded us along toward the market square. Radek and his policemen strode up and down the line, screaming at us and prodding us on with the barrel of their rifles. Papa walked just in front of us, straight and tall, and behind us, Hanna and Ben Zion flanked Baba.

"They are going to kill us," a man nearby said. "They are going to kill us." It was Samuel Glazman, Yankl's father.

I trembled at that. It didn't make sense. Why would they do that? After all, we weren't criminals. We'd done nothing wrong.

"Don't be ridiculous," Baba shouted at him.

"Shut up, Mr. Glazman," Mama snapped, her face locked him in a fierce glare. "You'll scare the children." Then under her breath, said, "Old fool."

"What do they want with us, Mama?" I asked.

"I don't know, Tsigele. It will be all right."

That didn't reassure me. If she didn't know what was happening, how did she know it would be all right? She draped her arm around me, and I held her hand with both of mine.

When we reached the square, there were already more than five hundred people there, the Judenrat out front, and Papa joined them, having been chosen for it by lottery. I saw both Mila and Leah, saw the fear in their eyes, and wanted to say something comforting, but I didn't have the will to climb out of my own despair.

I tugged at Mama's sleeve. "What's happening, Mama?"

"I don't know, Tsigele. It will be all right," she repeated.

"Mama…"

She pulled me closer, and I fell silent. A half hour passed, then finally a squad of twelve soldiers led a group of people also in night-clothes out of the hotel and down to the firehouse, all with their hands bound behind them. Some of them were children, which seemed odd, shocking even. What could they have done wrong? Stolen an apple? Why bind their hands? Though I desperately wanted people to see me and treat me as an adult, I felt like a child again. I truly did not know what was about to happen and looked on with as much curiosity as anxiety.

My heart quickened when I realized who the people were, Malka Henske and her family. Except for Malka, they were all crying, her husband Jacob, son Liebke, and two daughters Sarah and Miriam. Struggling to walk, Malka held her massive, pregnant belly as if the baby would fall out if she let go. Her face contorted in pain. Blood trickled down her bare leg. Helpless, the Judenrat watched. Beside them, the five Gestapo men watched. Radek and his police, spread out in front of the crowd, watched.

An officer with a drawn pistol ordered the Henske family to stop in front of the firehouse wall, and then he took up a position by the squad. I recognized him. It was Max Bauer. His uniform displayed the SS lightning bolts on his collar. I didn't know German ranks, but his seemed significant.

At that moment, I finally realized what he was about to do, and that's when my innocence died.

The action then went by in pieces, like a film with a broken projector lurching the frames forward. At Bauer's command, the squad turned as one to face the Henskes. He shouted another order, and they lifted their rifles in unison. He screeched one more rasping command. The volley jolted me as if the discharge of rifles had blown away the family's skin and tissue and left only their bones. I turned away.

CHAPTER ELEVEN

In the days following the execution, I was afraid all the time. I didn't leave the house, not even to venture into my woods. Mama allowed me my despair and only had me do chores inside. Because Papa was so respected, people came to our house to talk about the situation. Many dismissed the execution as any reason for alarm. After all, Malka was a communist and chair of the Revolutionary Council, and the Germans were at war with the communists.

"Of course, they would execute her. It is war," my grandmother insisted.

But then why Liebke, I wondered. He was a little *shvants*, but he didn't deserve to die for it. And the girls. Why them? Still everyone hoped this belief was right, that the occupation would not be so harsh.

Somehow, a bribe I think, Radek told us Major Bauer had been sent here specifically to capture Malka. Someone had betrayed her, informing the Germans she had remained in the area. Dark rumors hinted that wherever Bauer went, death went with him. After the execution, he left Nashok with his squad, and I was relieved to see him go.

Hope for a not so punitive occupation proved to be a fictional dream. Throughout the days and weeks ahead, the Nazis unleashed a storm of humiliation, torture, and deprivation on us, mostly on the men like my father, and along with the other Jews in town, I was forced to watch. Each time the Gestapo devised a new way to torment, they herded the women and children out to the spot to bear witness to the new humiliation.

In the square under Gestapo supervision, the police hacked off the beards of more than a hundred Orthodox men as the Polish crowd cheered and laughed, and the soldiers snapped memorabilia pictures. Any refusal to play along with this grotesque game was met with a barrage of rifle butts and kicks till the victim lay bloodied and unmoving.

That Saturday during the Shabbat service, Radek and his policemen pushed in among us and ransacked the synagogue, stealing everything of value, gold crowns on the Torah handles, the candelabras, the inlay of silver on the pillars, and some gold and silver coin. The police finished by stamping on the Torah itself, and Radek drove over it in his motorcycle till nothing remained but bits of torn parchment. Satisfaction on their faces glowed as if they'd participated in a religious ceremony.

Then, on a vivid, blue sky Sunday in late July when Hanna was off searching for kerosene to keep out lanterns lit—we had no electricity most of the time—Mama, Baba, and I were rousted out of the house and marched with hundreds of others to the market square. Over a thousand women and children had been gathered by the time we got there.

What I saw drove a spike into my heart. On their knees, several men, all from the Judenrat, were scrubbing the cobblestones, a favorite Gestapo torment. Papa was one of them. I gasped in anguish. The three of us, Mama, Baba, and me, held each other in a hug as the crowd started chanting, "Juden kaput. Juden kaput. Juden kaput."

Always at the center of these things, Radek kicked Papa in the ribs and then again and a third time till he rolled down in agony. I screamed and Mama took me in her arms.

When Papa got home, Mama bandaged his black and blue ribs. He moved around like an eighty-year-old man for the next couple of weeks after that. Unable to stop thinking about it, I wept for days.

From these incidents, it became clear how helpless we were, how no laws or even a sense of moral decency protected Jews, if they ever did.

Just the opposite was true. Anti-Jewish laws came at us like periodic blasts from a cannon. In August, the police posted new racial laws prohibiting any social or working contact with non-Jews, even those who were our friends, though few would claim such bonds now. In tears, Janina told us she must quit her job with us and left after hugging everyone. She'd been our housekeeper since before I was born and was almost as much a mother to me as my own.

They kept posting new ones.

From this date, all Jewish trade unions, social gatherings of three or more, and Zionist organizations are illegal.

The Young Guardians and Trumpeldors outlawed again. Such fear of teenagers.

Jews are banned from non-Jewish shops.

I thought of how Radek had finally gotten his wish to keep Jews out of his store by law.

Jews are forbidden to leave Nashok without a travel permit by penalty of death.

No travel permits were issued.

As the summer wore on, food became scarce, and I lost weight, looking like one of the storks that built nests atop so many of Nashok homes. More and more the Gestapo demanded supplies including valuables, even fur coats. Everyone had a fur coat, including me. You needed one in a Nashok winter. Now no one had one. When one woman complained at the confiscation of her beautiful coat, Radek chuckled. "You will not need it."

At the end of August, all Jewish schools were banned, and we were already prohibited from attending Polish schools. Who would want to go to a Polish school anyway and be forced to fight your way from class to class? Still, Mama insisted on my education and set up a system for lessons to be taught in a few homes. In this way, I saw the Seven again and the boys of our old school like Yankl Glazman. Though nobody tried to resurrect the Young Guardians or the Trumpeldors, at least not now, we still wore the white bows on our shirts.

Yellow Jewish stars must be worn on white armbands. Failing to do so will be punishable by death.

Not following any of these laws was punishable by death. I could not believe they would shoot us for forgetting to put on an armband but remembered all too vividly Malka and Liebke and the rest of her family lying in their blood. Shivering at the image, I knew they would shoot me.

Now, every morning at dawn, his new armband on, Ben Zion and all Jewish men between sixteen and sixty reported to the market square for work details somewhere outside town. Since Papa was a doctor, he was given an exemption. But then the Nazi's closed down all Jewish businesses, including Papa's clinic. They still allowed him to treat Jewish patients at home, but his clinic near the Neman Bridge was to be taken over by a doctor from Vilna.

The summer was brutally hot, more so than usual, spiked by violent storms nearly every day. Most of our streets were paved with cobblestones, but a few dirt lanes turned into mud thoroughfares. On the night of the announcement shutting Papa's clinic, a storm had raged up until midnight, blowing a tree into a street two blocks down, but then the gale abruptly ended, leaving the night chilled. Somewhere around 2:00 AM, Papa, Ben Zion, and Hanna snuck out of the house and slipped along the backyards, avoiding those houses that had dogs.

I knew where they were going. Incensed at being left behind, I grabbed my empty rucksack and ran through alleys and across darkened streets, reaching the clinic before them. A car sat down the street, one of the black Gestapo sedans, and I saw two men in the front seat. I went around to the back, climbed a tree, and leapt onto the roof of the clinic. From there, I slid through a second-floor window into a room where patients sometimes stayed.

Downstairs in the surgery room, I opened a back window and waited, thinking of how Rivka Resnik, the great thief, had expanded her repertoire to include burglar. Soon, I saw Papa, Ben Zion, and Hanna sneaking along the riverbank, each carrying rucks and rushing across the ground toward the building. They were going to go around front. I hissed, "Halt!"

Maybe they thought I was a German for they froze comically in stride. "Come in this way," I said. "The Gestapo are out front."

"Rivka, damn it," Hanna snarled in a low voice.

"Rivka, what are you doing here?" Papa whispered.

Ben Zion chuckled softly.

"Come in this way," I said.

They climbed through the window.

We filled the rucksacks with as many drugs, medical utensils, and equipment we could. Papa cut us off, saying there had to be something left behind. We snuck back the way that they had come, intending to hide most of our take in the forest. Since I knew the woods best, Papa asked me where we could conceal our cache best. In the darkness, I led them straight to an old, hollowed out tree a half kilometer from home, its trunk covered with thick brush. Wrapping the supplies in oilcloth, we stuffed them in the hallow, taking home only what Papa would need for the next few days.

As we walked back home, I whispered to him, "Papa, can I tell you something?"

"Of course, Tsigele."

"You know, since what happened to Malka and the Henskes, I am always afraid."

He put his arm around me as we walked. "I know. We all are, and I'm sorry. I wish I could make it all go away."

"But tonight was different. I wasn't afraid. Well, not a lot. I was afraid, especially when I saw the Gestapo, but it was different. I don't know. I don't know what I'm saying."

"Well, whatever it is, you were brilliant tonight. Just don't tell your mother you came out with us. She worries about Hanna and Ben Zion. She can no longer protect them like when they were children.

It would be too hard on her right now if she could no longer protect you. If she had to worry about you, too."

"All right, Papa," I said, not sure how anyone could protect me.

By mid-September, grim rumors of Nazi killings filtered into Nashok. According to the occasional refugee, Jews in towns and cities from Kiev to the Baltic Sea were being slaughtered, entire populations wiped out. And now, German murder squads had killed all Jews in the towns around us, and the circle was closing in on Nashok. The name of Major Max Bauer, the German SS officer who shot Malka Henske and her family, was mentioned three or four times in connection with this slaughter.

Frustratingly to Esther Gershowitz's father, Joseph, most people still could not believe any of this to be true. It seemed too fantastical to them. At a meeting in Rabbi Herskowitz's house, Old Mr. Koppel scoffed at the rumors, "The Germans just slaughtering people. Let's not be absurd. No, they want our money and our property, but that is it. All this is just scare talk."

Mr. Gershowitz railed at this for being criminally thickheaded, and the rabbi had to calm the meeting down. Esther told us about this at our makeshift school, which still met but only twice a week now. She said her father was certain of the rumors and was looking for ways to save their family.

I must admit, like all the Seven except Esther and Leah, I didn't know what to think. I was a fourteen-year-old girl whose mother kept me inside the house most of the time. The stories did seem too incredible to be believed, but they persisted. At my bedroom desk, I wrote all this to Peretz in letter after letter, everything that was happening in Nashok. Pootzi, my little stuffed bear, sat at the back of the desk like a bear Buddha, watching me. When I finished this letter, I picked up Pootzi and kissed him. Then I folded the letter, placed it in an envelope, and stuck it in the drawer. I stopped mailing them, certain that Mr. Palak, the Polish postmaster the Germans put in place, was not posting them and probably reading them.

After dark on October 1st, two weeks before my fifteenth birthday, we heard a soft knock on our backdoor. It was Rabbi Herskowitz. Soon, several other men arrived, including all the Judenrat. They squeezed into our living room. With the occupation getting worse by the day and the rumors of killings nearby, the rabbi had called another meeting. On dining room chairs, Ben Zion and Hanna joined them, as did Mama and Baba, both knitting sweaters for winter, sure to give their opinion freely. I sat on the stairs just off the living room but with a good angle to see everything that went on.

The Rabbi began by stating he now believed the end of our community was near. He recited everything that had been happening over the last few months and said he had one new piece of information. "I sent Stefan Wajda to Solkenik to investigate these rumors of killing," he said. "You know him. He is a good man, a good Christian, and a friend."

Silence followed, everyone waiting for his report.

"Well, rabbi, don't keep us in suspense," Mr. Gershowitz chided. "What did he say?"

"He said the shtetl of Solkenik is no more. Bodies lie in the fields. Only Christians are left. And Sturmbannführer Max Bauer is there."

Gershowitz turned on Mr. Koppel. "There you have it. You can no longer deny the truth. The Germans plan to kill us all."

For several seconds, no one spoke, then Koppel waved his hand dismissively. "That Wajda, he can tell a tale, especially when he's into his cups. How much vodka did you give him, Rabbi, for him to go?"

"None," Rabbi Herskowitz said emphatically, then sighed. "I will admit he was well drunk when he returned. But I believe him. Why should I not? He has no reason to lie. It's time you think about saving your families. I urge all of you to leave Nashok. You must flee."

Leave Nashok? I gasped audibly, but no one heard me. Papa, who had been silent throughout, bowed his head as if he'd lost a patient in an operation, and Mama turned to Ben Zion and Hanna, her expression one of deep concern. Then, she searched for me in the darkness of the stairs, knowing I was there. I almost said *I'm all right, Mama,* but remained silent. Her gaze fell on Papa, and they exchanged a silent communication, no doubt, developed over years of marriage. But what that was, I could not grasp.

Mr. Schneider, the Judenrat chairman, stood up as if to make a speech. "Flee, Rabbi? How can we? Hundreds of soldiers patrol Nashok these days. And the Germans have patrols in the fields and forests. It would be hard for a family to slip away even in the dark. And if we did, where would we go? The Nazis are everywhere. We all have friends among the Christian community here and elsewhere. But under Nazi threat, can we trust them? I have given some of them my valuables to hold for me. Then, I realized this is quite an incentive to turn me in to the Gestapo, is it not?"

Koppel pulled Schneider back into his chair. "Enough, Isaac. Rabbi, your heart is always with us, and I thank you, but rest assured, the Germans will become more civilized when the war is won, which surely will be soon. Besides, they wouldn't hurt women or children, and the men should be safe enough if they do what they're told."

In frustration, Gershowitz literally pulled at the hair on the side of his head. "Have you gone mad? Have you forgotten Malka and her children, gunned down by Bauer?"

Koppel threw up his hands in dismay. "Joseph, think for once. They were communist. The Germans are at war with communists. Not we Jews."

The rabbi gave a sigh. "Dr. Resnik, you have said little tonight. What do you think?"

Everyone respected Papa and waited for him to speak. Turning in his armchair, he fixed his eyes on them all. "I think we are looking into our graves."

When everyone remained silent, I thought that must have settled it. We would be leaving. But it didn't settle anything.

After several seconds, Baba set her knitting down and said, "You people may go leave here, but I am an old woman. I was born in Nashok, and I plan to die in Nashok, not in a strange city being chased by German dogs or dying of starvation in the forests. I will not leave."

That changed everything, at least for our family. We would now stay, for Mama would never leave without Baba, her own mother, and Papa would not part from Mama.

The Rabbi looked to Hanna, then to Ben Zion. "You are the youngest here. You have the most ahead of you. You could survive on the road."

They exchanged glances. If they decided to leave, would they take me with them? And would I go? Would I leave Mama and Papa? I didn't know the answer.

Ben Zion said, "Wherever our family is, that's where we will be."

Hanna nodded.

Baba said with finality, "This too shall pass."

When the meeting ended and the rabbi left, I didn't think I'd ever see a more dispirited man. Moments later, Baba passed beneath me on her way to her bedroom. Hanna went out through the kitchen to smoke a cigarette on the back porch while Ben Zion, exhausted from his long days on the German labor detail, climbed the stairs for bed.

Passing me, he ruffled my hair. "Time for bed, Rivka."

"In a minute," I said, resting my head on my knees and wrapping my arms around them. I watched Mama and Papa. She crossed over to him and sat in his lap. Papa kissed her on the lips, and they hugged. She rested her head on his shoulder.

I heard their hushed voices. "I'm sorry. I'm so sorry," she said. "I cannot go without Mama. She could not survive on her own. Who would look out for her?"

Papa looked down at her. "What about our children? What about Rivka?"

"I know, but will it be any safer on the road? Can we trust people who might turn us into the Gestapo for our boots?"

"We know many good Christians like Janina."

"What? All six of us living in Janina's house and for how long? Years? Her house is not half the size of ours."

I almost shouted from the stairs that we could live in the forest. All of us. I knew it well enough from the Young Guardians and all the time I spent in it, but then realized this idea would be seen as foolish and childish. Live in the woods. Baba? No, not possible. When my parents rose and started to walk from the living room hand in hand, I scurried upstairs to my room. I knew Papa would not give up. He'd work on Mama relentlessly so in the end we might, indeed, flee Nashok.

The day after this meeting, Major Bauer and his SS squad returned to Nashok.

CHAPTER TWELVE

Though the sun was bright, the woods that covered the hills seemed dark and endless, reminding Bauer again of the Black Forest where he grew up. He sat in the back seat of his sedan with Oberleutnant Kepler, the rest of his Einsatzkommando unit in the following three cars. The ninety-mile drive down from Vilnius this morning had been harrowing with the convoy speeding through endless stretches of destroyed vehicles, overturned carts and dead horses decomposing and stinking on the side of the road.

Beside him, Keppler was once more studying the orders Bauer had issued for this next Action. To maintain efficiency, all steps must be followed exactly, and he was not sure if the Oberleutnant was capable of doing so anymore.

Keppler set the papers aside and said sourly, "Today, it's another provincial town. They all become one, Herr Sturmbannführer. It's like living the same week over and over again." His eyes lost focus. "They all scream the same way." He shook his head. "What's the name of this town?" He snatched up the papers again and began flipping through them, searching as if the war depended on him finding the name.

"Nashok," Bauer said. "You remember it. We were there a few months back."

Setting the papers back on the seat next to him, Keppler nodded. "Of course, the Malka Henske situation."

"Yes, the female Stalin. A pleasant, little town."

The car slowed for a checkpoint. A guard waved the vehicles off to the side and came over. Bauer rolled down the window.

"A convoy coming through, Herr Sturmbannführer," the man said.

When he returned to his post, Keppler fidgeted in his pocket for his cigarettes, pulled out a pack and found it empty. "Damn. A soldier should never be without a cigarette."

As usual, he was jittery before an Action. Jittery clerk with a pencil. That's all he was, and that was why Bauer accompanied him more often than his other squad leaders. Some men could not handle the pressure of the immense task the Führer demanded of them. More and more of late, the oberleutnant hesitated, and when he hesitated, control could be lost. If that happened, the task would explode in his face, getting shit all over Bauer's own boots. His boss, Reinhard Heydrich, would not be happy. He'd have to make sure the oberleutnant stayed calm during this operation. Afterward, reassess and replace if necessary.

He held out his pack of his Eckstein cigarettes, and Keppler took one. "Thank you, sir."

Lighting both, Bauer inhaled the smoke. "It's quite ironic, don't you think, Keppler, that the cigarette ration of the German army is a Jewish brand?"

Keppler chuckled dutifully. Just then, a long column of supply and troop trucks rolled by on their two-day journey to Leningrad where Army Group North had laid siege.

"Part of me wishes I was with them," Bauer said.

Whenever he saw the Wehrmacht, he said that, but he didn't wish it at all, especially now. With the Russian winter looming, he suspected a frozen hell worse than the Arctic would descend upon them. After nearly twenty minutes, the last of the convoy passed by, and the guard waved them through the checkpoint. A few minutes later, they drove onto Vilna Street, the main cobbled thoroughfare of Nashok. Hundreds of men in faded uniforms, peasant garb, some even barefoot, were marching through town, bellowing unintelligible songs, and firing rifles and pistols into the air. Few other people were out on the street, not even non-Jews.

They were Bauer's men, his Lithuanian *shooters*. To keep them happy and doing their job, he provided them a steady supply of bread, cheese, sausages, cigarettes and, most importantly, schnapps and vodka. As the four cars sped by with their Nazi flags on the fenders, several waved to them. Ahead, Bauer spotted a synagogue back from the street, its rounded towers and red mansard roof etched against the cloudless sky. Two bearded Jews hurried along the walkway toward it, desperate to get off the street with all the shooters about.

As the car crossed the bridge over the Neman River into the market square, Bauer announced, "Welcome to Nashok."

Keppler swallowed as if he had a lump of coal in his throat.

On the morning of October 3, I was skipping rope with Mila and Genesha. Mama had allowed me to go to Mila's house only a few doors down as long as I stayed either inside or in the back yard. But when Aunt Miriam went to speak with a neighbor, Mila and I hurried across town to Genesha's house. For the next hour, the three of us jumped rope in the backyard.

When any of us were together, we used to talk about boys, schoolwork, and things we planned to do with the Seven. Now, we talked about what our families did to get food, how long the Germans would be here, what we did all day since we were not allowed out anymore.

As Mila and I swung the rope, Genesha jumped in and danced like she was from the Bolshoi. What an athlete she was, so agile and quick. That's when her father stepped out onto the back porch. "You girls must go home," Mr. Blum said to Mila and me. "The Nazis have ordered us to the square. All Jews. Hurry now. I'm sorry I can't see you home. Be careful."

We looked at Genesha and she sighed, fear in her eyes.

"What now?" Mila said.

"Let's go," I said and broke into a run around to the front street with Mila just behind. We stopped instantly. Five Lithuanian riflemen were striding down the walk toward us as if they owned it. Two women raced away from them and ducked into houses. We waited till they passed and dashed across the street.

In a couple minutes, we made the woods and hurried through them to the backyards along our row of houses. We reached Mila's house first and stopped, out of breath. Between gasps, Mila said, "Are we in trouble?"

I knew what she meant, not with our parents, but all of us with the Germans. "I don't know."

"I'm afraid, Rivka," Mila said.

"I am too. I better go." We hugged in affection and desperation.

When I got home, Mama was angry. "Where were you? You should have stayed at Mila's."

"The Germans have ordered us to the square," I said.

"We know," Ben Zion said. "Papa just told us."

We were all there, Papa, Mama, Ben Zion, Hanna, and Baba.

"It's that Major Bauer," Hanna said. "He ordered this. What do we do, Papa?"

He wiped his hands on his suitcoat as if they were damp and he couldn't get them dry. "What can we do? We must obey."

At that moment, gunshots rang out from somewhere in town. Hanna and Ben Zion rushed to the windows. I followed Papa upstairs where we climbed up to the cupola. Everywhere we looked, we saw the Lithuanians, several hundred of them, occasionally firing off their rifles and pistols. They manned every street in view, and German soldiers and trucks surrounded the town. I glanced at Papa, who gave a heavy sigh, one that tore me apart. It's our fathers who are our ultimate protectors. Our fathers who can do anything. I always thought mine could. But what could he do about this? From the look of helplessness and despair on his face, I realized he could not do anything.

I slid my arms around him and hugged him. "I love you, Papa. I'm the luckiest girl in the world to have you and Mama."

His eyes welled with tears. After nearly a minute, he said, "We better go down."

Just before eleven, thousands filled the streets and began making their way to the square, but we remained in our house. This roundup seemed different. With all the stories of mass killings, there seemed to be a finality about it. If we tried to sneak away, we'd be shot. That had already happened to a family on the north side of town. All of them killed.

Terror began bleeding into my stomach.

Just then, raucous shouting came from outside, and I rushed to the windows with all my family as fifty or so Lithuanians entered our street and began breaking into houses. In moments, they were throwing things out into yards, then hounding anyone there outside. Our door crashed open, and four men rushed in our house. I screamed, and Mama ran to my side.

They pushed and shoved us out into the street where many of our neighbors had already begun moving toward the square. When Ben Zion asked one of the Lithuanians what was happening, the man struck him in the jaw with his rifle butt, knocking my brother onto his hands and knees, blood trickling from his mouth. Stifling a scream, I feared the man would shoot him. Quickly, Papa and Hanna lifted him to his feet, and we stumbled with hundreds of others toward the center of town.

When we reached the market square, a barrier of solid wooden fences, barrels, and ropes held in more than four thousand people, the entire Jewish population of Nashok and more from nearby villages, all milling about, all scared. The wails of women and the crying of children resounded like cries from hell. Around the barrier, hundreds of Lithuanians and Polish police stood guard along with German soldiers. A couple soldiers met us at the entrance and demanded we fill their buckets with our valuables, including rings, bracelets, and brooches. Anything shiny was ripped off our clothing.

Some of the Poles held shovels including Radek Karnowski, who called out to Papa, "Dr. Resnik!"

We all turned to look, and he grinned at us, patting his shovel. I did not know what he meant by that, but his look sent chills through me. The well of terror grew.

Working our way through the mass of people, we found space for the six of us near the firehouse wall where Malka and her family had been shot. We sat on the cobblestones, Baba on an empty wooden crate. Immediately, the soldiers separated the men from the women and children. One of the Germans ordered Papa and Ben Zion to join the other men.

Gesturing with his rifle, he screamed, "Schnell!"

When they were moved across the square, I felt a sense of momentary relief because, if I stood on Baba's crate, I could still see them. Yankl Glazman, who was only a year older than me, tried to stay with his mother, but he was a tall boy, and the Germans forced him to go with his father. For some reason, he glanced over at me, held my gaze for several seconds, and then fell into line.

"It will be all right. They only want our money. You'll see," Baba said.

A small army of Lithuanians patrolled up and down the square between us and the men, preventing any contact, as if that would pose some kind of threat, but mostly, they were looking for valuables. As it turned out, Mr. Gershowitz, Esther's father, had been hiding Deutschmarks, a large wad of them. This was a treasure for the two grinning Lithuanians who made the discovery. But Mr. Gershowitz didn't hand it over. Instead, he turned his back and tore the bills rapidly into shreds, tossing them in the air.

The two men beat him to the ground with their rifle butts, hitting him again and again, long after his body stilled. I could hear Esther's screams from somewhere deep in the crowd. A German officer identified as a Leutnant Keppler drew his pistol and shot poor Mr. Gershowitz twice. The crowd fell silent, replaced by a murmur of despair. At least, I thought it was despair because that's what I felt. No one tended his body, just left it there. Squeezing next to Baba, I buried my head on my knees.

All day, the sun burned down on us like the dead of summer. Hours passed, some quickly, some slowly. Most of the time, I felt like a trapped animal, and I thought that's how Mama and Hanna must have felt. We had little food and no water. Quickly, I became thirsty but said nothing because there was nothing to do about it.

Mama told me not to wander about, which I had no inclination to do anyway. No one did. I saw a couple of my girlfriends from the Seven, but with all the guards around, it would be too dangerous for us to gather. Anyway, I'm sure we all were mired in our own desperate misery. I saw Mila not too far off. Our eyes met, and she gave a tiny wave. I waved back. My heart cracked when I saw her. Mila, who should be in America with her father, with Peretz. Now, she was here. In this square.

By common consent, an area was left open down at the end of the firehouse for people to relieve themselves. As long as I could, I held my water, not wanting to go in public or with guards watching, but then by twilight, it became too unbearable, and I asked Hanna to accompany me. Hurrying to the edge of the building, we squatted, our modesty protected by our dresses, and did our business.

When it got dark, the heat of the day vanished. With the temperature dropping, Baba, Mama, Hanna, and I huddled together. Brushing her gray hair back, Baba said, "It will be better in the morning. I'm sure of this." Her confidence in German humanity was both steadfast and pitiable.

"How?" Hanna demanded.

Baba shook her head and did not answer.

A bright, three-quarter moon settled onto the night. Exhausted from the tension, I quickly fell asleep in Mama's arms, but kept being awakened by madhouse screams and occasional gunshots. Not far off, with great cries and groans, one woman gave birth. I heard the baby wailing. A baby born into this? In my religious teachings, there was no hell comparable to the Christian Hell. If that one existed, this was it.

Sometime around midnight, Mama sent Hanna to search for a way for her and me to escape, but whenever she approached the barrier, a guard would spot her and proposition her. Each time, she retreated back into the crowd, and by morning, returned to us, shaken and despondent.

With the sunrise, the day warmed, but nothing else had changed. Still no food or water. Thirst dried my throat. The stench from the privy area now drifted over us like a poisonous cloud. During morning prayers, Radek rode his motorcycle into the crowd, cursing and shouting like a madman, but a madman who was thoroughly enjoying himself. Finally, with the help of the Lithuanians, he got people listening to him, and he read out another German decree from Major Bauer. The men would immediately proceed to the forest outside town to build a ghetto. When it was completed, the women, children, and elderly would move in while the men would be transported for work to labor camps.

They were formed into three large groups of three hundred each and marched from the square. My father and brother were in the last group. From across the way, Ben Zion took in each of us, a thin smile on his boyish face. Papa shouted something. I thought he said, "We'll come to you tonight when we can."

As they moved off with the other men, I watched them till they passed from sight beyond the buildings. I did not think I would ever see them again.

CHAPTER THIRTEEN

An hour after the men filed through the barrier, the distant sound of machine gun and rifle fire reached us, and chaos erupted. We knew now they were slaughtering the men. Slaughtering my father and brother. Mama stood up and screamed. Other women throughout the square did the same. We became a boiling pot ready to explode. Panicky, the SS officer named Keppler and a few of the Lithuanian guards fired into the crowd, and the screaming became worse. Hanna, Baba, and I flattened onto the cobblestones, but Mama continued standing with the rest of the wives, shouting and screaming.

The firing ceased. Just then, an open-air military car entered the square followed by a flatbed truck carrying sloshing barrels of water. In the car, Major Bauer stood up and used a bullhorn to address us. "Look. Look. I've brought you water. What is all this fuss?" He spoke passable Yiddish. "The men are working and may finish the ghetto by tomorrow, at least enough for you to move in. Be patient."

I did not believe him, though he was so smooth and convincing, the women calmed, even Mama. By the hopelessness in her eyes, I saw she didn't believe him either, but what was there for her to do? Someone called out, "We heard shooting."

Bauer waved that away as if it was barely worthy of comment. "The soldiers taking target practice, nothing more, and some shooting

93

birds. This training must continue all day, I'm afraid. Nothing to worry about. Stay calm, and all will be well soon."

Mama called to him, "Your murderers have wounded some of us. What about them?"

"Be patient. We will get to them when we can. Doctors are on their way from Vilnius. You must take care of them for now."

As he spoke to Mama, his eyes hesitated on me a fraction of a second but no more. He'd recognized me, I was sure, and I wondered if he felt any sympathy. In a normal world, a person would, but his cold eyes told me in this nightmarish one, he did not.

I began to know I was going to die.

Not until twilight did the gunfire stop. A few minutes later, the Lithuanian shooters roared back into town on their motorcycles and parked at the empty end of the square where the men had been earlier, not too far from us. Mama stood as they stepped off their vehicles. I could see they were drunk. A few of them were local men, men we knew, men Papa had treated in his clinic. One of these dropped his rifle clattering onto the cobblestones, pulled out a bottle of something, and took a long drink. Stumbling about, he dribbled half of it over his chin and onto his clothes.

Taking several steps toward him, Mama shouted, "Why, Petros? How could you do it?"

Angrily, he glanced around, searching for the person who'd spoken and saw my mother. Blinking several times, he stared at her, trying to focus, then in answer patted the bottle.

That second night in the square I cried in Mama's arms and sometimes Hanna's. My sister was so strong; I was so weak. Those hours passed with me having little awareness of things around me, my mind transported itself to a place and a time with both Papa and Ben Zion. Whether they lived in my dreams or my waking mind, I didn't know, but they were there and real. They spoke, they laughed, they lived.

A gunshot wrenched me out of my web of dreams. The German soldiers were ordering us to stand. It was just past dawn, and the air had a drenched, wet feel to it, the sky overcast. With so many children, there were more than three thousand of us, three times as many as the men, so they organized our departure differently. Selecting three hundred or so at random, the Germans and the shooters moved the women and children from the square using wagons provided by local Poles. We were not among the first group taken out. Not long after the first women and children left, we heard the echo of gunfire. I recoiled at each volley.

There was no more pretense. Bauer didn't rush in with water. Heavily guarded, we just waited for our turn. Throughout the day, a cold drizzle fell as one group after the other was marched from town. Slowly, the square emptied. Mila was gone. Genesha was gone. Leah. One by one, I saw all my friends of the Seven but Esther taken away.

Any hesitation was met with an onslaught of rifle butts and truncheons. Once, someone refused to go and was beaten to death on the spot. Die here or somewhere out there. What did it matter? But who wanted to give up that last breath? None of us did. I felt I was about to wet myself, but when I went to the open area, I could not pee.

Amid the dwindling prisoners, Mama, Hanna, Baba, and I huddled together, waiting. Mama kept staring at me and Hanna as if she had failed us. That crushed me. "Mama, it's not your fault," I said, trying to keep the tremble out of my voice. "It's not Papa's. Not Baba's. It's no one's fault but…"

"…but the damn Germans," Hanna swore, interrupting me, "and their friends like Radek. That's whose fault it is. God, how they hate us."

In the early evening, the rain stopped, but in our clothes, we shivered from cold and dread, one feeding the other. That's when the Germans moved the last of the women and children, maybe a hundred of us, out of the square. The well of terror inside me exploded like a grenade, sending panic flooding through my body. My legs faltered, and I had trouble following along with Mama, whose arm never left my shoulders. Many of the women, including Baba, began to chant the Viddui, the final confession before death.

As our procession marched away from town, crows flying above escorted us. Their cawing blended with the crying of babies and children, creating a madhouse symphony. It took us nearly half an hour to reach our destination, upward past woods to an open farmer's field where a long pit held thousands of naked, blood-soaked bodies.

It was then the wailing began.

My mind fractured into a thousand pieces. From then on, I could only grasp things in the most basic level of awareness. Two women ran, a mother and daughter. Radek shot them down. Not far away, the German officer Keppler was rubbing furiously at his uniform trying to remove blood that had spattered on him. Beyond him, my eyes focused on the meadow that led to the forests. In the middle, pushing up through the grass, was a single Iris flower that had already turned a brilliant yellow.

When we reached the trench, Bauer ordered Radek and his police to line us up, crowding us back to the edge. Just behind us were the bodies, so many bodies. The coppery smell of blood filled the air. Already, the Germans had machine guns set up, one in front of Mama and me. The shooters spread out on line facing us from ten meters. In the trees nearby, the crows sat in a neat row quietly watching us. My body trembled. Silently, in my head, I screamed, *why, what have I done?*

For just a moment, my mind escaped. I left that place. I saw Peretz at our wedding. I saw Mama and Papa escorting me down the aisle, me circling him, him breaking the glass and everyone shouting, "Mosel Tov." I saw Peretz and me in a house with a cupola. I saw...

An uproar broke the spell. To the left, Radek and three of his policemen were dragging a young girl my age from her mother. It was Esther. Pretty Esther. Dragging her toward the woods. She screamed; her mother screamed and ran to her. Esther kicked and scratched and flailed her arms. Finally, rage exploded from the men. They struck them again and again with rifle butts and truncheons till both were dead, then tossed their bodies into the pit. A great wail erupted from me and rippled through all the women. I noticed Bauer standing a few feet away rewinding his pocket watch, indifferent.

Near him, Kepler held up his hands as if surrendering and stepped toward us, his face ashen. "Please. You don't understand. We're trying to save children pain. We are not monsters."

Like a gunshot, Bauer snapped, "Oberleutnant." A sharp wave of his hand sent the officer retreating back into line.

Slipping his watch back into his pocket, Bauer ordered us to undress. "Take off everything. Anyone who fails to do so will have their clothes ripped off by the Lithuanians, and what they do then, I will not stop."

This last humiliation was like a hammer striking my spine. What did it matter, clothed or unclothed when you die, but it did. When we stripped bare, I lost control of my body. Urine swept down my leg onto the grass. Bauer spotted me and strode toward me, blood spatter on his uniform. But it was not me he came up to but Hanna, who had not taken off her dress.

"Remove the clothes," he demanded. "Schnell." Then, he noticed me and the puddle at my feet. He smiled. "Rivka. Yes, that's your name. I remember you. Such a pity we never wandered in your woods together."

I did not have the power to speak.

"It will all be over soon," he said kindly, just a man doing an unpleasant but necessary job, and that's what he said next, "This is my duty, you understand. I take no pleasure in it." His voice sincere, his regret appealing, almost real. He reached out to chuck my chin.

Tears in her eyes, Hanna took a half-step toward him and shouted, "Schweinhund!" No worse insult could be made to a German. Hanna. My wonderful Hanna.

Eyes flashing with fury, Bauer drew his pistol and shot my sister. Her head snapped back, and she tumbled into the pit. I screamed and screamed. Spinning about, he strode back to the machine gun.

Mama turned to me, placed her hands on my cheeks. I stopped screaming. She said, "Live, Rivka. Live for all of us."

With that, she thrust me into the pit, then swung around just as the machine guns and rifles let loose. I saw the bullets blow through my mother, and she tumbled down on me. Her blood drained onto my body. The deafening gunfire went on and on as bodies fell all around me, then silence. I heard the moaning. People were still alive.

Peeking out past Mama's shoulder, I saw Bauer, Kepler, Radek and a couple others fire pistols into the pit, into bodies, finishing them off. So close was I to Bauer, I thought he saw me, and I ducked my head in behind Mama. I lay unmoving, praying he didn't see me. She had protected me all my life and she protected me now. Bauer moved on. Soon the pistol shots ceased. No one was moaning now.

With so much pressure on my chest, I struggled to breathe. Suddenly, I started crying, my chest heaving. I could not stop. Terrified they could hear me, I gritted my teeth and focused on the sleeve of Hanna's dress next to me, blue flowers on a yellow background, studying each one. She loved that dress. After that, I don't know how much time passed. Eventually, my crying eased, and I became aware of the horrendous stench of excrement, the dead having voided themselves.

Darkness fell. People were speaking only in Polish now, no German or Lithuanian, so peeking out again, I could make out shadowy figures shoveling dirt onto the mass grave, and I almost panicked. I did not wat to be buried alive. But somehow, I remained quiet. The Germans had gone, as had the shooters; these men would too. Within a few more minutes, they covered all the bodies including me with a thin layer of earth.

Someone called out, "Why should we be here while they celebrate and get drunk. We finish in the morning."

Throwing down their shovels, they all cheered and trooped off. Someone shouted back at the pit, "See you in the morning, Sardines."

Moments later, I heard the roar of motorcycles, and then they were gone. Sardines. Laying amid the bodies, packed like a sardine, I shook uncontrollably.

"Live, Rivka. Live for all of us," Mama said to me. She was dead, but she still talked to me.

Live, live, live.

Wriggling from under her, I punched up through the dirt, and covered in dried blood and filth, crawled up onto the grass. I coughed, then stifled the next, not knowing if anyone was still about. No moon. It was full dark. I threw on a dress from the piles of clothing and stumbled barefoot from that place.

CHAPTER FOURTEEN

R adek drank from the bottle of vodka and surveyed his town. Here in the market square, which hours before held so many Jews, several bonfires roared, sending sparks high into the night air while men and women danced around them, the men shooting their rifles skyward. To him, it was a celebration as festive as Christmas and New Year's, though he had forbidden his wife and daughters to participate despite their pleading, not with all the drunken men around. The diggers who had been covering the gravesite came down from the fields, too dark to finish their work, and half the town's Poles had come out to join the festivity.

Many, however, remained in their homes, and he suspected some even regretted the necessary action against the Jews. Those Poles had been friends with them. If they loved the Jews so much, Radek was thinking as he walked toward the old firehouse, why didn't they go join them now? He chuckled at that.

The firehouse was where movies had been shown and plays put on. In the dim light from a single bulb, he rummaged through the costume room, found a fake, white beard that hung to his chest when he put it on, and a long, black coat like what a rabbi would wear, also a black silk hat. Now, he looked like Rabbi Herskowitz.

Tottering for a second, he regained his balance and headed back outside. When several men saw him approaching, they froze for a moment, then one of his own policemen, pock-face Corporal

Glickenhaus, recognized him and burst out laughing, slapping his knees. "Bless me, Rabbi, for I have sinned," he called.

"Bless you, my son," Radek said, waving his hand. "Say four Hail Marys."

When they all realized who it was, they cheered. He danced and chanted gibberish in a high-pitched voice. They thought it hysterical.

Disoriented, I walked the shadows through town, through one Jewish neighborhood after another, all dark. No lights in the windows. Silent. Empty. Nothing moved. Nothing lived. I swiped both hands at my neck, and they came away bloody. Always bloody. So much blood. I rubbed again and again, each time wiping my hands on my dress. So much blood. Drying and sticky. I couldn't get it off me.

My throat aching with thirst, I thought to go into one of the houses for water, but I kept going. I knew where to go, and I needed to get there. Near the square, light blossomed into the night, and the raucous sound of a celebration carried over the rooftops. I skirted the area and crossed into the Christian section of town.

Lights were on in homes here. I went around to the back of Janina's small house and knocked softly on the door. I knocked again and finally someone came.

Janina looked at me with alarm. "Oh, God, Rivka." Glancing about quickly, she pulled me inside and drew me into a hug. I wept. In her arms, sorrow began to devour me.

This was my second mother. As much as my own mama and Baba, she raised me. I wanted to cry but couldn't.

"We need to get you cleaned up," Janina said.

Taking me by the arm, she pulled me through the kitchen into the dining room where her husband Herman, their two grown sons, and their wives and children were having supper. Mouths open in horror, they stared at me standing barefoot, covered in filth and dried blood, wearing a dress too big for me.

I froze. They were eating off our gold-rimmed china plates. Other things of my family's were everywhere, the silverware, the tablecloth, and just beyond in the living room our mantle clock over the fireplace. One of the children even held onto my stuffed bear Pootzi.

I looked at Janina. She could not meet my gaze, dropping her head as her eyes grew wet with tears.

"We thought it would be better we have these things than someone else," she muttered. "I thought you would want that."

Her husband stood. "I am sorry for you, Rivka, but we can't help you. I have my own family to worry about. The Jews are gone. Go, Rivka."

Red-faced, the men saw me in fear. Janina had her face buried in her hands. There was nothing here for me. I would not be safe. I knew then there would be no safe place for me anywhere. As I left, I said nothing to the woman who had helped raise me.

Outside, I ran from Janina's house, ran toward the dark neighborhoods. In packs, men wandered the streets, some looting homes. I kept running, crossing streets so fast they either didn't see me or were not sure what they saw.

I went home and found chaos inside. Wall pictures and tables lay scattered on the floor with Papa's books. The heavy couch had been moved into the center and the chairs turned over. I stepped over the debris and climbed the stairs to my bedroom where everything seemed intact, except for a few of my things taken like Pootzi.

I went to the bed and collapsed on it. Within seconds, I was asleep. Within seconds, the horror filled my head. Images bombarded my dreams, one more hellish than the other.

Radek thought it was time to go. In the eastern sky a hint of pink edged the hilltops. In the square, the bonfires had burned down to embers, and only fifty or so men remained of the raucous celebrations that had gone all night. The rest had drifted off, many to find beds to sleep on in empty Jewish houses.

Of his police, only Corporal Glickenhaus and the Kroll brothers stayed, intent on finishing the last of the vodka. Glickenhaus handed him the nearly empty bottle.

"You peasant, you left me only a dribble," Radek said and finished it, gave a satisfied sigh. "That was a hell of a night. Only men of strong will and vigor stood with us." He shook his fist as the other men nodded. "Now, I think it time to get some sleep, don't you?"

"Oh, no, please," Glickenhaus pleaded. "I go home now. My wife will be waiting up for me. She will screech at me like a hen."

Radek laughed. "You fool, you can sleep anywhere. Pick a nice Jewish home. Go there. I am going to find a bed in the best house in Nashok. The one with the cupola."

"Dr. Resnik," Janus Kroll guessed. He was the older of the Kroll brothers.

"Yes, the late Dr. Resnik. I plan to move my family in tomorrow. You three can come with me. There are many big bedrooms, and we can eat the good doctor's food when we get up."

They agreed, and the four men staggered drunkenly from the square, leaning on each other for support.

"Rivka, wake up. You're sleeping away the morning. Wake up now." It was my mother's voice getting me up for school. "Wear your print dress. It looks so nice on you."

My eyes opened, but I couldn't see her. Maybe she'd called from downstairs. Not wanting to be late, I glanced at the clock for the time. It was gone. I sat up. Pootzi was gone. A monstrous, black shadow hovered just beyond my consciousness. I knew it was there but didn't want to face it. School. I must get ready for school. I threw off the odd dress I was wearing, far too large for me. I think it was Baba's. How did I end up wearing Baba's dress?

I hurried into the bathroom and ran hot water into the tub, then climbed in and let it run over me, soaping myself like I always do, washing the dirt and grime from my hair and body. As the water rose and steam rose from it, I sank in its warm comfort. When it neared the tub's rim, I turned off the spigot. Despite the dark menace perched on my shoulder, drowsiness settled into my head like cotton. I was nearly back to sleep when I heard the front door burst open, then footsteps on the stairs. Male voices slurring, shouting. One of them was Radek Karnowski.

Radek led the way as the four men headed upstairs onto the second floor landing. "Find a bedroom and sleep all day," he said. "You have my permission to miss roll call."

"I have to piss," Glickenhaus said.

"Do it in the corner," Janus Kroll said.

"Yeah, in the corner," his brother echoed. "Who cares?"

"I do," Radek snapped. "This is my new home. You do not piss on the floor in my new home. Use the bathroom, but I am first."

He went to the bathroom door and stared in surprise. The other three men joined him.

"What is it?" Janus asked.

"The tub is full of water," Glickenhaus said.

"So?"

Radek walked in and felt the water. It was dirty and warm. "Someone was here."

For several seconds, they stared in silence at each other, then Glickenhaus said in jest, "Maybe it was the ghost of Dr. Resnik."

Radek frowned at him, then sloshed the water. "Who cares? They're gone now. If they think they can take this house from me, they're mistaken. I am the police."

He staggered to the toilet and relieved himself. The others followed in turn, then each picked out a bedroom and fell asleep immediately, except for Radek, who went back downstairs, still concerned about someone being here and comfortable enough to take a bath. But he was too exhausted and too drunk to think clearly. He sat on the couch for a moment, then lay down, and in seconds was asleep.

I had squeezed my body into the towel cupboard. After fifteen minutes when I heard snoring coming from the bedrooms, I silently slipped out, wrapped a towel around myself, and crept into my room. On my bed, a man lay snoring. A bitter stench filled the air, and I saw the vomit on my bed and the floor. Outside, morning twilight had begun, but the house was still cast in darkness.

Remembering where the creaks were in the wood floor, I moved slowly and quietly to the closet and slid out my rucksack. Painstakingly slow, I dressed in ski trousers, boots and a long-sleeve shirt, then packed clothes for winter. It was coming, and it would be cold, and as Mama said, I must survive. Every time the man on the bed moved or sputtered in his snoring, I froze, then continued readying myself to flee the only place I'd ever known.

Finished, I lifted the rucksack onto my back, slipped out and down the stairs. At the foot, I unscrewed the knob of the banister, lifted out a cloth pouch, and pulled the draw string. Inside was a wad of deutschmarks and two pieces of Mama's jewelry we had hid from the Germans. One was a solid gold necklace that had been in the family for generations, destined to be passed on to Hanna. The idea of that lurched in my heart.

The other had been in our family even longer, how long no one could guess. It was a gold pendant encasing a bronze coin with the worn image of an ancient queen or goddess, her gaze turned slightly to the right, her hair falling in decorative curls. It had been intended for me.

Mama had loved these pieces, insisting the image on the coin was Shelamzion Alexandra, an old queen of Judea. She longed for the day she could pass them on to her daughters. Next year for Hanna, a few more years after for me. Breathing hard, I felt the sob growing in my chest. Clutching the old coin pendant, I squeezed my eyes shut so I wouldn't cry, though inside my heart had already drained of tears. I needed to be stronger. I could not fail Mama. Regaining control, I put the bracelet and pendant back in the pouch and slid that into a pocket of the ruck.

Coming from the couch, Radek's loud snores filled the house. I went over and stared down at him. He had herded us to the pit. He had made sure no one could run off. He'd killed Esther. His snoring was ragged. Drool slid from his mouth and snot from his nose. Then his eyes opened, and he stared right at me.

In the darkness, I did not move, but I stood right above him. He could not fail to see me. Moments of terror passed, then his eyes shut again and in seconds the snoring went on. Quietly, I hurried out through the back door and headed toward my woods. At the storage shack, I stopped abruptly and stared at the cans set against the wall, two of them. Kerosene. It took me only an instant to run through the scenario in my head. I felt no fear. No anger even. Just an irresistible hatred. Dropping my rucksack, I picked up the two cans and hurried back into the house.

With one, I went upstairs and soaked the floors then used the rest on the stairs, making sure to keep it off me. The smell was over-whelming, and I was sure it would wake them up. With the second can, I drenched the floor around the couch, then the rest of the downstairs. Both cans were now empty. In the kitchen, I found a kerosene lamp and lit it with matches from a drawer by the sink.

At that moment, Radek awoke. He sat up and sniffed. Standing, he took two steps toward the kitchen. When I held the lamp up so he could see my face, his eyes went wide. He shook his head, blinking rapidly, then stared at me. "Rivka!"

I threw the lamp at him. It hit the floor at his feet and exploded in flames. In seconds, he was a torch. His wild screams lasted several seconds then died.

The flames rapidly spread, and I darted out the back door. Without stopping, I snatched up my rucksack and sprinted into the forest. When I looked back, my home was already engulfed in flames. No one could have escaped. As I raced deeper into the woods, I realized something had broken inside me. I was no longer the same girl and would never be that girl again. I felt no pity. No remorse. Any sorrow left I drove deep into my soul and closed it off. Inside me now was a core where only emotions hard and cold as winter ice could live.

CHAPTER FIFTEEN

A cold rain fell as I ran through the woods, pressed by a desperate need to get far away from Nashok, not slowing down for kilometers, running and running. My legs burned. I gasped for breath but kept on. Every few strides, I looked back over my shoulder, sure the Germans were in close pursuit. Gray skies cast gloom over everything. The trees dripped with black moss. Shadows ate into the path ahead. For an instant, I felt like I was trapped inside a ghastly Grimm's Fairy Tale. No, I was trapped in something far worse.

My destination was a ski hut seventeen kilometers from town that the Young Guardians had used numerous times in cross-country ski outings. There, like a wounded animal, I could come to ground and heal, though I knew I would never heal. My wounds would lay open and fester for as long as I lived.

By midafternoon I reached the hut. Inside, a potbelly stove stood in the corner with wood stacked beside it. At seeing it, I breathed a sigh of relief, but I was too frightened to risk starting a fire. Shivering, I sat on the cot and checked my pack. I had enough food for four or five days if used sparingly, and I could find enough berries, roots, and mushrooms to live off for a while. I could construct snares to catch rabbits or other creatures. This would keep me alive till I found some sort of purchase on life. At least that's what I thought.

But in the next few weeks, I came to realize how wrong I was. I could not keep myself fed. For a while, I did find berries, roots, and other edibles, but it wasn't nearly enough, and I lost weight. As for catching rabbits, in little more than a month, my snares entrapped exactly one. I had no problem killing, skinning, and cooking it, but the meat lasted only a couple of days. I grew thinner and weaker. Nightmares plagued my sleep. They seemed so genuine that I awoke screaming. They hung on into the first waking moments, taking me several minutes to grasp I was no longer in the pit.

In this way, October swept by, me not even noticing my fifteenth birthday had come and gone. The first snows came with November, nearly a foot, but enough for me to experience a rush of fear. The berries were gone, and the roots covered up. Having nothing to hunt with, I would starve to death alone in the woods.

Scores of small villages and farms dotted the vast forest south of Nashok like oases in a green desert, now covered white. In this area, the farmers were Polish with a few Lithuanians. They knew the only people wandering the countryside and asking for help were Jews who had escaped the slaughter in hundreds of villages and towns. They feared German reprisals for helping us, but that was too kind. To me, they just hated us. Hadn't they proven that?

Hoisting my pack onto my back, I plowed through the snow and in the days ahead tried to survive by stealing food like eggs and the occasional chicken and slept in barns. But it wasn't nearly enough. To survive, I needed to ask for food. The first two farmers turned me away with threats and curses. One shouted, "Jew, go back in the grave where you belong."

Starving, near the end of my strength, I approached a small farmhouse outside the village of Pajkoi just as the sun was falling behind the far off trees. A middle-aged man with a stubble of beard answered the door. There was fear in his eyes when he saw me. "What do you want, girl?"

I must have appeared ragged, grime on my hollow cheeks, my coat drooping on my shoulders. In a strained voice, I asked, "Can I have something to eat?"

Frowning, he glanced back into the house, then at me again. He sighed. "Come in."

I stayed with them three months. In that time, Henryk Tabak, his wife Perla, and their twenty-year-old son Rudy saved my life and treated me with kindness I had not expected. They took care of me. They fed me. I worked. Mornings before dawn, I fed the chickens, gathered eggs, milked cows, chopped wood and filled the wood box, and continued working till long after sunset, only taking a break to eat lunch, and then I did it reluctantly. Some days almost dreading it. I dreaded stopping and getting caught in my own dark thoughts. Keep moving, keep busy, keep my thoughts only on the task of the moment.

In the cold mornings, I made it a point to get up even before Perla and get the fire started. In early December, when I was stoking the kindling and adding logs, Hanna came to me in a remembrance of long ago and I allowed it in. While climbing a tree one summer when I was nine, I fell and broke my arm. Papa set it and put it in a cast, then that evening, in pain, I lay in bed alone feeling sorry for myself. Still twilight, everyone was outside visiting neighbors or friends, having fun. So I was surprised when Hanna showed up in my room with two cups of hot chocolate. Three years older, she normally wanted nothing more than to be rid of me and be with her friends.

But this evening, we talked and laughed and retold stories of my earliest days tagging along behind her and her trying to shoo me away. Hanna's long black hair tossed about when she laughed. She was so beautiful, not like me, so plain. Even when we finished the hot chocolate, she stayed till I became drowsy and fell asleep. Then, weeks later when my arm healed, Hanna took me into the forest to find the tree I fell from.

"Let's go up," she said, and we both climbed the tree, something she had never done before or to my knowledge again. I had already gone back to climbing trees in my woods, feeling no particular fear about it, but didn't tell her that. As I stoked the fire in the Tabak's house, this vision played out so vividly I thought I could speak to her and she'd respond.

Then, I shrieked and jumped back. The vision turned red, Hanna lying beside me in the pit, her flowered dress drenched in blood, Mama's and Baba's bodies pressing down on us. In this new, hellish apparition, Hanna turned her head to me, her eyes glassy and vacant, a gaping hole in her forehead. "Please help me, Rivka," she whispered.

The vison wobbled but held. In desperation, I stuck my hand in the fire, felt the instant sting of flame, and jerked it out. Hanna was gone. Then, my hand not badly hurt, I got up and pressed on with my morning's work, pressed on with the day, because there was nothing else I could do except start screaming and never stop.

This was my life. Nightmares invading my days, constant dread the Germans would come, and a bitter hatred of them scalding my soul.

And what now? I didn't know what I was going to do. As much as Perla wanted me to stay, I couldn't stay with the Tabaks long. With the Germans and their collaborators everywhere, that was too dangerous. Should I move from place to place, just attempting to survive the war? Mama had cried out for me to stay alive, and surely I must. But that was not enough. The Germans were masters at slaughtering. I saw it. I was a part of it. They took my family, everything from me I loved and ended the world I knew.

And I alone am still here.

A flare of guilt hit me but nothing more because Mama desperately wanted me to survive, and because of her, I did. In my heart, I knew there was something more she wanted me to do, something more they all wanted me to do.

What happened next set me on a path toward that.

On days working inside with Perla, I would glance out the front window from time to time, out to the snow-packed road where horse-drawn wagons occasionally passed but no troop trucks or cars. Only Germans and their collaborators had cars these days. If I saw them turning up toward the farm, I wanted time to race into the woods. One day in early February as I stood at the window, Perla came up beside me. When she smiled, her crinkled eyes carried pain. The Germans had killed one of her sons and taken the other to a labor camp.

When she put an arm around my shoulders in a motherly gesture, I stiffened and she removed it. I could not bear to be touched nor could I handle the closeness she wanted.

"You're safe here, Rivka," she said gently. "The Germans won't come. We are not important."

I nodded, knowing how foolish that was.

Then, I froze. Two black sedans with small swastika flags on the fenders and a troop truck sped into view on the road. I held my breath as they came to the turnoff to the farm. About to run, I took a step back, but then they passed by and disappeared beyond the edge of the forests.

Perla put her hands to her face. "I hope it's not Pajkoi. I hope they're not stopping there."

At seeing the Germans, my hatred ignited in a white-hot burst. "Monsters! Killing and killing." Then, a guttural moan escaped from my chest.

Immediately, Perla took me in her arms and held me. My body shook from sorrow and fear, but also an overwhelming rage. I saw Radek stumbling about engulfed in flames and felt nothing but a sense of satisfaction. That in itself troubled me, for shouldn't I feel remorse? I didn't. This was not what Mama and Papa taught me. It wasn't what the rabbis taught me. I felt only the slightest twinge of twisted guilt for not feeling anything about it. What was wrong with me? I should feel something for killing him, but nothing inside me could produce normal human emotions anymore.

That night, the Tabak's daughter Adela walked from the nearby village of Pajkoi. "The Germans are close," she said entering without greeting, shaking snow off her coat. "They burned down Sanok. They passed through here and burned the entire village for supporting the partisans. They killed the men and took the women and children away in trucks."

Her face was flushed with cold or fear, or both, as she stepped to the fireplace to warm her hands. With the Germans being so near, I subdued an urge to grab my pack and run right now.

"The partisans came to Sanok months ago, back in October and demanded food," Adela said as Perla brought her a mug of tea, "and the villagers had no choice but to give it to them." She glanced at me, accusation in her eyes. "The Germans may be coming to Pajkoi next."

She meant I was a threat to her parents. They would be executed if the Germans found they were hiding a Jew, and surely some in the village knew. But for me, it was the word *partisan* that riveted my attention. Until this moment, I had not been aware that this was what had been propelling me forward all this time. I wanted to do something, and this was it. I needed to find and join the partisans.

I asked Adela where they were.

She shrugged a shoulder. "I've heard they operate out of the forests around Drosknik."

Rudy waved his hand dismissively. "*Operate* is a bit generous. They probably have less than fifty people, and they don't do much. Hardly more than steal towels at the spa the Germans use. All they do is anger them like a mosquito."

Drosknik was a famous spa town sixty kilometers south that I had visited several times with my family. Now, it was infested with Nazis. I knew then I could not survive unless I killed them. Maybe, I could never kill enough, but it was what I must do. I stood up and announced, I'm going to join the partisans. I'm going to fight the Germans."

Rudy smiled, but Henryk laughed. "Don't be crazy. You're fifteen and a girl. They won't take you. They might even kill you if they learn you're a Jew. Some partisans do you know." He shook his head dismissively.

I knew what they were all thinking. What a silly girl. Playing at war. But things were different. It wasn't like I had announced to Papa a couple years ago that I was leaving home to join the army. If you were Jewish, you were always at war. I did not want to die without fighting back. It was like coming across a wolf in a clearing and your choice was to kill or die.

I thanked Henryk and Perla for helping me, but I could not risk their lives anymore. "I'll leave tonight," I said.

Perla shook her head. "No, Rivka, you must not leave."

More calmly, Rudy held his hands up as if to slow my race for the door. "No, Rivka, wait till morning. It's snowing and not even the Germans would come out on a night like this."

Not wanting to face the storm now, I thought it worth the risk and agreed to stay.

The next morning, I woke before dawn and dressed in wool stockings, my flannel ski pants, a sweater over my long-sleeved shirt, and heavy wool socks. The storm had abated, leaving about half a foot of new snow and a cloudless sky above with waning stars.

After a quick breakfast, Rudy pulled me aside. "I know you want to join the partisans, but you won't find them in the winter. They're in caves and bunkers till spring. The Dainava Forest is a thousand square kilometers, Rivka. You won't find them. I can't say I think it's a good idea, but since you'll try anyway, wait till the snow thaws. They'll have to come out then looking for food. Find a place to shelter till spring. There's a convent of nuns near the village of Posner. They might take you in."

I wondered how he knew all this but didn't ask. "Thank you, Rudy," I said.

A few minutes later when we all stepped out back, I was surprised at the tears in Perla's eyes. She had cleaned and ironed my clothes, folding them into the pack, putting in bread and cheese. Now, in the cold, the tears froze on her cheeks. My emotions had flattened months ago, but a spark of genuine warmth filled my chest, and I hugged her.

Henryk brought out a pair of cross-country skis, poles, and a pair of tiny goggles. "These belonged to my son Roman. The Germans killed him. I know he would want you to have them."

After strapping my boots into the skis, I thanked the Tabaks again, pulled my wool cap down over my ears, and started out, turning once at the edge of the forest and waving. By noon, the temperature plunged, and I skied into a blizzard. My fingers inside the mittens were going numb. Trying to burrow deeper into my scarf, I continually wiped my goggles clear. I needed to find shelter quickly and pushed hard for Posner and the convent like my friend, the great athlete Genesha of the Seven, would have, praying the nuns would take me in. They would have to, wouldn't they?

CHAPTER SIXTEEN

In late afternoon, with the air still heavy with furious snow, I began thinking about a place to build a shelter in the woods and take my chances when an open field appeared before me, and soon a road. Within moments, the single tower of the convent loomed out of the storm.

A fierce nun in a black habit answered my knock and gave me a severe appraisal. "Yes?"

Yes? My anger flared. I stood outside in a blizzard, and she asked *yes?* "I was told you could take me in." When her face didn't change to one of kindness as I hoped, I added, "My father was a doctor. I know a little medicine. I'm good with the sick."

What a lie, but she didn't know that. The morality I had lived all my life was peeling away like the layers of an onion. Don't lie, don't steal, don't kill. I'd broken them all.

"We're full up," she said, staring hard at me as if trying to decide if I carried the plague. "But I won't turn you away."

She stepped back from the door. Quickly, I took off my skis and carried them in. A desperate fugitive, that's how I entered the Sisters of the Precious Blood convent. The nun was forty years old or so, square-shouldered and tall with a strong face and prominent chin, someone who looked more like a harsh forest spirit, the Leshii, than a follower of Christ. She directed me to put my skis and coat in a mudroom then come with her. "Tell me your name?"

"Rivka Resnik."

"I'm Mother Johanna, the mother superior. Follow the rules of our order, and you can stay."

The convent was gloomy and cold, lit by candles and oil lamps and warmed by the occasional brazier.

Mother Johanna led me to the chapel where she knelt, crossed herself, then folded her hands in prayer. "Kneel with me and pray," she directed. When I didn't, she glanced up.

"I'm Jewish," I said, ready to argue. Though not following the Shabbat in months, I wasn't looking to convert.

She sighed. "I know you're Jewish. I have fourteen Jews already hiding here. When the Germans come looking for runaway Jews, and they will, we can't hide all of you. While you're here, you will wear a habit and learn our ways well enough to fool the Gestapo. Even the men we have must do this on occasion. Learn as if your life depends on it, because it does." She pointed to the floor beside her. "Now kneel and cross yourself."

I did.

Later, I was fitted out in a habit and given a bed in a small monastic cell with a young nun named Sister Agneta. I asked her if she were a real nun or a pretend one like me.

"Oh, I'm real. I'm a novitiate, and that's what you are," she said with a dimpled smile. "A nun in training. That's why we wear the white veil not the black one. That's for the true nuns, the ones who have taken their permanent vows."

"Veils? Oh, you mean hoods?"

"No. Veils. We're not bandits," she insisted, nodding several times, then put a hand on my forearm. "Some advice, Sister Teresa. Don't ask that question of anyone else. If they are Jews, I mean. You'll scare them half to death, and it's best you don't know."

Right then I became Sister Teresa. Learn quickly was my commandment. Something bothered me about the mother superior, so I just asked. "I don't think Mother Johanna likes Jews, so why is she helping us?"

Her eyebrows lifted in dismay. "I think because it's what Christ would do. She's a saintly woman." She leaned toward me and whispered as if someone might overhear. "Sister Teresa, you should know something about her. Three of our nuns protested hiding Jews and threatened to take the matter to the civil authorities, meaning the Germans. Mother Johanna told them she would expel them from the order and excommunicate them. They backed down."

That surprised me. "Were you one of those who wanted to report us?"

Sister Agneta shook her head furiously. "Oh, no. I would never do that. It's not Christian."

"So, you don't think we killed Christ?"

She smiled at me. "I know *you* didn't."

I smiled back. Just then, a bell rang somewhere in the building, calling us to supper. At least twenty people wearing habits filed out of their tiny cells and headed for the refectory—I was learning the proper names of things already. The nuns sat at a long, wooden table with Mother Johanna at the head. Hidden within their hoods, only a few faces were visible to me. Everyone ate in silence, which was fine with me. I had nothing to say to them.

Set before us was meager fare, but I was the beggar here. A good, hard bread and bowls of some kind of mush mixed with vegetables. I nudged Sister Agneta with my elbow. "What is this we're eating?"

A loud thwacking rang through the room. Mother Johanna was pounding her spoon on the table, staring at me, eyes filled with outrage. I got the message: silence.

That night someone screaming woke the entire convent. It turned out to be me. Another nightmare. This one had been especially vivid, me back in the great pit of bodies with my family being covered by layers and layers of earth. Major Bauer, gleaming in his uniform and perfect blond hair under the cap, stood above me with his shovel covering my face with dirt. When I awoke, Sister Agneta was holding me. A few seconds later, several other young women in night shifts came to the door, a couple with lit candles. One asked if everything was all right, and Agneta nodded. "Bad dream."

Wriggling out of her arms, I sat up just as Mother Johanna appeared. Before she could say anything, I gave a sharp shoulder shrug. "Sorry."

"Go back to sleep, all of you," she said. She scowled at me before leaving. I guessed she couldn't get that expression off her face.

The next day, thinking I actually knew something about medicine, Mother Johanna assigned me to work in the infirmary with the convent's long-time nurse, Sister Irmengard, a slender, small woman of about sixty with olive skin like my own. She was considered a saint by the other sisters. Certainly not Papa's clinic, it had five beds along one wall and another five across the room. The glass medicine cabinet had a few rolls of gauze, corked bottles of rubbing alcohol, and what looked like tincture of iodine in a brown bottle. Stacked in one corner were several sets of crutches. Maybe a lot of people broke their legs around here. And next to them was an old wheelchair. It wasn't exactly a well-stocked clinic.

We had one patient, and she was permanent, Sister Humilitas, the oldest nun in the convent at nearly ninety. The old nun had trouble moving about and at times could be absent-minded.

"She sleeps here where we can take care of her," Sister Irmengard said, then sat me down. "The mother superior said your father is a doctor, yes?"

"He *was* a doctor."

She nodded, understanding. "Then you must know about medicine. That will be helpful."

I gave a shrug. She would soon learn how little of Papa's knowledge and skill rubbed off on me, but I saw no need to tell her that.

"This infirmary is not like clinics you are familiar with. You will find it is very, very different. Now that the two doctors in the area have been taken away by the Gestapo, we not only treat the sisters but the local people as well. We do not work miracles here. God does that. We work medicine, and that includes old remedies I've learned over the years."

She sounded like a gypsy healer living in a cave. It didn't matter. I wouldn't be here that long. A few weeks at the most. I thought about the medicine Papa, Hanna, and I stashed in the forest near Nashok, at least thirty kilometers away now, but the idea of going anywhere near the town to retrieve it sent shivers through me. She waited for a response, so I nodded.

"Good." Sister Irmengard slapped her knees, stood up, and handed me a mop. "After you do the floor, clean the surfaces with a solution one part alcohol and one part water."

So, between calls to prayer, I spent my first day in the infirmary cleaning floors, tables, chairs, door handles, and walls. A healer I wasn't, but I could do hard work.

In the next weeks, I did learn home remedies that surprisingly worked. Most often, our patients from the convent and the nearby village came in with colds and chilblains. For the one, Sister Irmengard prescribed drinking lots of liquids, something I knew, and for the second, soaking hands and feet in a small bath of oats and cooking oil, something I didn't know.

Twice, parents brought children from the village with broken arms which the sister set and cast as well as my father could have. Of course, with no anesthesia, there was a lot of screaming. Before, that would have sent me running from my father's clinic in destress, but no longer. I'd seen too much that was far worse. Now, in the infirmary, I stood fast and held the children down.

For me, I could have been tilling a garden. The only emotion that plagued me every day was fear, every hour of it. I never felt safe. The Germans were everywhere, and this being a convent saved us from nothing. The nuns felt their God would protect them. I intended to protect myself.

Quickly, I fell in with the ways of the convent, all the bells, the constant call to prayers, all the learning. Though I could not know how to be a nun in depth, I tried to pick up bits of information that when used correctly might convince the Gestapo I was a novitiate.

The mother superior would quiz me whenever our paths crossed. *What is the Nicene Creed?* I stumbled through a reasonable answer. *What is the Eucharist?* I answered that one like I'd been raised Catholic. *Who is your patron saint?* Having researched this in the convent's meager library, I'd found one that I liked.

"Saint Olga," I said, pleased with myself. She was the bloody patron saint of revenge.

Mother Johanna's permanent scowl deepened. "Choose another saint."

After a trip into the village to treat a bedridden pregnant woman, Sister Irmengard reported she'd heard that German units just burned a village fifteen kilometers away for harboring Polish and Russian soldiers. They were steadily removing the Lithuanian and Polish people from the countryside.

Already desperate to leave, I now dressed in my winter clothes each morning and skied into the forest looking for a ready passage, but even in late March, there was still too much snow, nearly three feet. You could not travel on foot in three feet of snow. The partisans were still burrowed into bunkers somewhere in a vast forest.

One night, unable to sleep, I made my way to the small sisters' chapel near the storerooms. The room was dark and cold, the candles unlit except for two that flanked the cross where Christ hung impaled. As I slid into a pew toward the front, I was startled by two men sitting across the aisle in their night clothes.

I knew about them from Sister Irmengard. The Kanski brothers Isaac and Jacob, talkative old lawyers from Kovna. Draped in blankets, their bare legs stuck out of their sleeping gowns at the knees. Like a doddering professor, Isaac's wire rimmed glasses had slid to the tip of his nose. On his head, a tuft of gray hair stood up like a waterspout. He had a reputation for being a pleasant, thoughtful man. His brother Jacob didn't. He wore a permanent sour expression that fit most of his speech. A complainer, nothing was good enough.

Glancing at me, they both nodded. Isaac said, "Sister, I hope we are not disturbing your prayers."

"No," I said. Still in my habit, they thought me a real nun.

In hushed tones, they went back to arguing about something. I tried to ignore them but something one of them said shot a bolt through me and riveted my attention. A name. They had said a name.

I asked, "You know Max Bauer?"

Isaac flinched, and neither brother answered.

"I'm from Nashok," I said and that was enough explanation.

"Of course we know him," Isaac said. "He is the known man, the face of the Nazi killing machine, the SS officer that directed the phony pogroms in Kovna that killed so many of us." His face took on a haunted look, and his mind went somewhere else for the moment.

I waited, certain he wanted to say more. He rubbed his forehead. "Bauer opened the prisons and let murderers and rapist out into the streets, gave them crowbars and hammers, and told them to kill Jews. A so-called 'spontaneous' pogrom. In Kovna's main square, they ran down and beat scores of people to death. Blood soaked the cobblestones, and there was Bauer standing with his Germans, watching. He might have been waiting for a bus."

Jacob shook his fist as if the German stood before him. "He took pride in it. The man strutted around in that hideous uniform of his as if he were a great military hero. He wore an Iron cross, and for what? Killing helpless, innocent people. What a hero. I was there. I barely escaped."

Isaac said quietly, "The Germans. They are killing the entire Jewish race."

Jacob folded his arms across his chest, his jaw thrust out. "And they are hunting us still. This is what is important. They will not rest till we are all dead. They will come here to this very convent, mark my words, and soon. We will leave for Vilna soon. We have friends there who will hide us. If we stay here, we will all be finished."

We did not speak anymore. Enough had been said. I knew he was right. I leaned back in the pew and gazed over at the statue of Christ, flanked by the candles, searching Him for any answers to the madness. I found none. But studying the figure impaled there, I was caught by the way the light flickered over it, giving Christ an almost living air as if He were writhing on the cross.

Two weeks later, the Germans came.

CHAPTER SEVENTEEN

It was an odd thing for Mother Johanna to do, at least I thought so. After breakfast, she led us all outside to build a snowman, or more precisely a snow nun, of all things, before it all melted. The men were dressed in habits like the rest of us so seen from a distance nothing would seem amiss. Sister Irmengard and I put Sister Humilitas into the wheelchair and pushed her outside and down the front walk which was always swept clear. Immediately, she struggled out of the chair and, like she was twenty again, began to pack snow.

The sun burned from a cloudless sky. For the last week, temperatures had risen and the snow was melting. In a few days, the forests would be passable on foot, and I'd leave. Building their snow nun, the sisters laughed like little girls. Finally, when the thing stood fat and bulging, Mother Johanna draped a black cloth over its head to serve as a wimple and hung a chain with a wood cross around its neck.

"Our newest novitiate," she announced, and everyone applauded, even me.

Not watching, staring down the road, Sister Agneta gasped, "Look."

Something in her voice made us all turn and follow her gaze. A half-kilometer away, two cars with swastika flags and an army truck rushed toward us. A tremor of fear swept through us as palpable and hot as a firestorm. My heart pounded. I damped down the urge to sprint for the woods. I would not get far in a nun's habit anyway.

Mother Johanna said evenly, "Walk calmly to the chapel. Men to your hiding place. Families the same. The rest of us, we will await our guests."

Trying to control my swelling panic, I helped Sister Irmengard assist Sister Humilitas into the chair. As we entered the convent, I glanced back. The convoy had closed to within a quarter of a kilometer.

"Now would be a good time for you to practice your praying, Sister Teresa," the old nun said with a rasping laugh.

I patted her shoulder. "You do it for me, Sister Humilitas."

Back in the infirmary, the old woman remained in the wheelchair. I actually looked around for a weapon and spotted a scalpel but thought how ridiculous. Me, Rivka Resnik taking on the Wehrmacht with a scalpel. I snatched it up anyway and slid it into my pocket.

With certainty, it came to me that none of this was going to work. Mother Johanna's great plan of hiding all of us would not fool the Nazis. No one who gave half a glance at the pretend nuns would be fooled. The trap door in the chapel that hid the men and families was so obvious it might as well have a sign that said, JEWS BELOW. I should have run. Sister Irmengard and I pulled up chairs beside Sister Humilitas's wheelchair and sat waiting for the Germans.

Less than a minute later, the hollow clack of the iron knocker reverberated through the convent. In my mind, I could see Mother Johanna opening the door, see the Nazis rush inside. I heard the marching of boots and the cries of shouted orders. Fear shivered through me. I kept repeating under my breath, "I will not be buried alive again. I will not be buried alive again." Sister Irmengard clasped one of my hands and Sister Humilitas the other. I took a deep breath and exhaled.

The great commotion was coming this way.

126

Seconds later, Mother Johanna rushed in with two SS officers. In turn, they were followed by two more soldiers, rifles slung over their shoulders, carrying a third officer. They laid the man down on the nearest bed, one placing his cap on the nightstand. He was pale and sweat glistened on his face. He couldn't be much more than twenty.

Immediately, Sister Irmengard went to the man's bedside, and I followed her, picking up the cap and putting it on the nightstand. The lead officer was stocky with a short neck and heavy shoulders, reminding me of a stout chest of drawers, this one in a smart, gray SS uniform, his thick legs stuffed into knee-length boots. He spoke passable Polish. "I am Sturmbannführer—Major—Dietrich. You are Sister Irmengard?"

Without looking up, Sister Irmengard replied, "I am, Major, and right now I'm trying to discover what ails your man."

He scowled at the other officer and spoke in German, "I should have sent him back to Drosknik." He turned to Sister Irmengard, speaking Polish again. "We had to pull the car over twice for him to vomit before we got him here. This man is Untersturmführer—Lieutenant—Schwarz. What is wrong with him? Is it the Spanish flu?" he asked with fear in his eyes.

Before I was born, this pestilence killed millions across the globe. No country was spared. No city or village. Some form or other of it had returned though with not as deadly a result. Mentioning its name still caused people's faces to drain of color. Not answering him right away, Sister Irmengard put a hand on the sick man's forehead and checked his red eyes.

"Open your mouth," she said.

Understanding her intent, he dropped his jaw wide for her.

I looked in, spotting a bit of redness. I'd seen Papa do all this, but I didn't know what any of it meant. Obviously, he was sick, but I couldn't say of what. How was I to know?

Sister Irmengard stood up. "Too early to tell what's wrong for a certainty, Major. If he has the Spanish flu, we'll know by this afternoon."

I didn't know what he had, but I knew it wasn't that. She was letting the German think his man just might have the deadly virus.

Mother Johanna said, "Leave him with us, Major. We will take care of him."

The officer's nod was barely perceptible. "We have an action to conduct north of here. We'll return for him afterward."

An 'action.' I dreaded what that could be.

When the mother superior led them out, Sister Irmengard and I took off the lieutenant's boots and clothes and gave him some water. In his underwear, he crawled under the covers, looking at me as if I were the healer. "Danke, you are my angel of mercy."

As Sister Irmengard directed, I put cold towels on his forehead hoping he would fall asleep and stay that way forever.

Moments later, Mother Johanna returned and called us into a far corner. She appeared sick herself, her face drained of color. "They're gone. Is he badly sick? He doesn't have the Spanish flu, does he?"

Sister Irmengard glanced at the lieutenant holding the cloth to his own forehead and whispered, "No. A little food poisoning, I think. Painful, but he should be fine in a couple of days."

"How are you going to treat him?"

Sister Irmengard shrugged. "Not much to do. He's going to be voiding himself from both ends most of the day. We'll just try to get him to the toilet in time." She said to me, "Get some buckets ready in case we can't."

Not something I looked forward to. I asked in a low voice, "Isn't lying a mortal sin with you people?"

I thought Mother Johanna would answer, but her attention remained on the lieutenant across the room. Sister Irmengard said, "So, if the Germans ask if we are hiding Jews, we should tell the truth? God is no fool, Sister Teresa."

Unexpectedly, Mother Johanna's face crumpled. Looking like she would cry, she pressed her hands against her cheekbones in anguish. This fracture in her toughness unnerved me nearly as much as the Germans' arrival.

"I think they came to transport us all to camps," she said, her voice strained. "God forgive me for saying so, but thank the Lord for the man getting sick. Maybe they will spare us now for treating their man. They've sent so many priests and nuns to those camps."

If that was the cause for Sister Irmengard's little game, I didn't think it would work. No good Nazi would pass up a chance to murder innocent people for any reason.

Finally, Mother Johanna hissed like a blown steam valve and regained her composure. Her breakdown had lasted less than a minute. Her old self again, she said to me, "You want to join the partisans. You should prepare to leave while you can."

At first, I was surprised she knew, but then she would know everything that went on in her convent. I glanced toward the lieutenant. "I'll stay till he's gone, if that's all right."

We heard a gasping sound and looked over at Sister Humilitas, thinking her suddenly ill as well, but instead, her face had broken into a wide, toothless grin, and she was laughing.

During the day, when Lieutenant Schwarz had to gush out one end or the other, I slung his arm over my shoulder and led him quickly to the toilet across the hall. Sister Irmengard and I fed him broth and kept him drinking water. Lying in bed, he appeared like a harmless boy, his brown hair tousled, his puppy eyes watching me, as if I personally were saving his life. Despite his youth, I needed no reminder. This was an SS officer. But it wouldn't have mattered if he'd been a common German soldier. I wanted them all dead. Still, my stupid smile never left my face all day.

"Am I going to die?" he asked once.

"No, Sister Irmengard will not allow it." I spoke German with him.

"I'm Warner Schwarz, by the way. Tell me your name, please."

"Sister Teresa. Open your mouth."

When he did, I spooned in a runny concoction of cooking oil, red wine, and flour that Sister Irmengard had prepared. It had no medicinal value, but it was harmless. He took it dutifully. Who would have thought nuns could be so deceitful? He told me he was twenty-one, newly graduated from the SS officers' candidate school. If he survived the war, he intended to study education, get married to a beautiful young girl like me, and make a large family.

When he finally went to sleep, I asked Sister Irmengard if I could go outside for a bit. Being with him all day had left me desperate for fresh air. I walked outside into the twilight. The sky was clear and gray; no stars had appeared yet. An easy breeze came from the east, dry and not cold. Large swaths of green and brown earth had punched up through the melting snow. Spring had arrived in force. The snow nun seemed to be standing guard near the walkway, but already shrunken.

I breathed in the sharp air and began to plan my escape. Not tonight, but early tomorrow morning. Then what? How do I find the partisans? You can't go up to people and ask, "Excuse me, sir. Are you with the partisans?" They don't wear signs. Of course, if they're in the forest, who else would they be? But that forest covered an area so vast that several cities could fit into it. I had to admit I had no idea how to do this.

At that moment, I recoiled. German sedans with their swastika flags and five canvas covered military trucks roared up the road toward the convent. Certainly, Major Dietrich returning for his officer and maybe for us.

I hurried back and told Mother Johanna that the Germans were returning.

"Go to the infirmary," she said calmly and went to the front door to await them.

In the infirmary, we awaited Major Dietrich, hoping the trucks weren't for us. Lieutenant Schwarz had pulled on his boots and was buttoning his tunic when the major strode in with Mother Johanna. He eyed his man and nodded.

He said to Sister Irmengard, "I see you haven't let him die."

"Of course not. I would not do that even if it were you, Major."

I turned rapidly to see how he would respond. He actually smiled. "So, not the Spanish flu then."

"Not the Spanish flu. Just don't eat so many raw sausages."

Dietrich turned to Schwarz. "How are you, Lieutenant?"

The young officer snapped to attention. "Fine, sir."

Major Dietrich gave a bow to Sister Irmengard. "Your reputation is deserved, sister. You have my thanks."

I could smell smoke on the major's uniform. He'd burned a village today, and in the back of those trucks were likely those who'd survived the fire, now on their way to labor camps. For a few seconds, I couldn't keep the white-hot hatred from my eyes. Was it Pajkoi? Perla, Henryk, and Rudy either in the trucks or dead. Or maybe the Germans had not gone the three kilometers out of town to their farm. Maybe. But no. No one was that lucky in this war.

I had to find out. When the mother superior escorted the Germans outside, I came with her. The lieutenant gave me a look filled with longing, and the major nodded his thanks to Mother Johanna again, then they climbed into the first car. Seconds later, the convoy sped away.

Mother Johanna and I stood outside till long after the vehicles had disappeared through the village of Posner, unable to quell the sadness squeezing our hearts. It had been Pajkoi. As the convoy had pulled away, we saw into the trucks where people huddled together on benches or on the truck bed. German soldiers sat at the open flaps guarding them. Mother Johanna gasped and clutched her throat. I tried to spot the Tabaks but couldn't. Then the last truck went by, and there I saw Adela, the Tabak's daughter. She rose up from the truck bed and stood for two or three seconds, looking directly at me before a German soldier yanked her back down.

That night, I left the convent.

PART TWO:
CHILDREN
AT WAR

CHAPTER EIGHTEEN

As usual on a warm, Sunday afternoon, women, children, and the elderly crowded into the Tiergarten. The men were off to war. A gentle, cooling breeze shifted through the trees as Max Bauer, his wife Klara, and their five year old son Hanzi strolled the park with Bauer's good friend Karl Schneider and his wife Frida. Neither man wore his uniform. The two wives walked ahead while Hanzi ran out in front kicking a soccer ball.

The two men first met at the Bad Tölz SS Military Academy where Schneider, an obergruppenführer—general, was an instructor in Civil and Financial Administration. His class was excruciatingly boring, and Bauer was the only one who paid attention. With the colonel also a friend of Bauer's uncle, that connection was enough to make a friendship. Since then Schneider had helped his protegee at several important points in his career. Now, the general worked for Reichsführer Himmler, monitoring the administration of concentration camps, the one who brought Bauer back from Russia in late January, most likely saving his life.

Last year in Russia had been a brutal, frozen hell. In early October, the cold settled in, and neither the army nor the einsatzgruppen units remaining were prepared for it. They had all thought Russia would have fallen by then. In January, temperatures dropped to -40 below, and men going to sleep at night froze to death by morning. Though the Wehrmacht laid siege to Leningrad, it was almost as if they were the ones besieged, for they could not retreat. The Führer wouldn't allow it.

With the earth frozen and covered in several feet of snow, Bauer could not dig pits for captured Russian prisoners and Jews. He had cursed and asked himself why he was even here. Nearly a million men had been killed, wounded, or gone missing. Lines of supply had reached their limit. The Wehrmacht could go no farther. Even so, Bauer still had faith in Adolph Hitler, but not the generals. They had let the Führer down. Then, in mid-January, for some reason, he was awarded the Eastern Front Medal, which men called the Order of the Frozen Flesh.

That was when Schneider worked his miracle and gotten him called back to Berlin. He was more grateful than he dared tell anyone. Saying Operation Barbarossa was doomed would not be tolerated, even by an SS officer.

When they walked the Tiergarten that Sunday in September, except for the absence of young men, you couldn't tell a war was on. Everyone seemed cheered by the beautiful day. There were shortages and some rationing, but the war was being won. That's what Minister Goebbels told them daily on the radio and in the papers. And eventually, it surely would be.

Hanzi ranged far ahead with the ball, and when his mother called for him, he raced back, one of his dribbles shooting passed the women. Bauer caught the ball with his foot and smoothly stroked it back to his son.

"Control, Hanzi," he shouted. "The good players control the ball."

The two men talked for a time about his current assignment in Oranienburg, twenty-five miles north of Berlin, then Bauer mentioned that Klara was pregnant. "It doesn't show yet, but the doctor is sure."

136

Schneider grinned, patting Bauer's shoulder. "Congratulations, Max. At this rate, Klara will receive the Gold Mother's Cross in a few years."

Bauer laughed. "Not likely, sir."

The Nazi Party awarded a gold medallion to women who gave birth to eight children, a silver one for six children and bronze for four. Like the Olympics, he thought, but in this case for filling up the Reich with good, Aryan children.

"Don't let her hear you say that," Bauer added. "When we got married, she had said we would have the eight. Then after going through a difficult labor with Hanzi, she said maybe six. We waited for the next baby, and now, I think after this one, we'll be lucky to reach four." Hesitating a moment, he added, "We took on one of the Lidice children."

Schneider raised his eyes in surprise, then they hardened. In a harsh whisper, he said, "They should have wiped out the whole damn country, not just that village."

"Yes, sir. He was a great leader. He will be long remembered."

More than two months ago, Reich Security Chief Reinhard Heydrich had been assassinated in Prague, devastating the SS for a time. In reprisal, Hitler ordered the nearby village of Lidice flattened. Quickly, the SS drove the nine miles out from Prague to the village, executed all the males, carted off the women and children to camps for later disposal, then burned the town. Some of the young children with Aryan features were spared and adopted into SS families. Bauer had taken a little, blond girl of five who seldom spoke, but then she did not understand German yet. Still, she was a sullen girl, and he wondered if he'd made a mistake. They'd left her at home today with the nanny.

Ahead, they saw the iron gate entrance to the zoo, their destination. "You know, Max," Schneider said in a lighter tone. "I'm a native Berliner, and I've never been to the zoo once."

"Terrible, sir. I don't know how you can live with yourself."

Schneider chuckled.

The next morning, Bauer sat with his two children at the break-fast table of his home in the Charlottenburg section of the city, next to the Tiergarten. He wore his uniform with his Eastern Front Medal and the Death's Head insignia on his right collar. When he had come into the dining room, the Czech girl, whom they now called Hannelore, recoiled at his uniform. It irritated him then and still did. He'd tried to bring her into his family, and one would have thought she'd be grateful.

Taking off her apron, Klara came in from the kitchen and joined them at the table, proud of the meal she'd prepared. Good German bread, cheese, wurst, a boiled egg for each of them, and coffee. Bauer's position in the SS allowed her to obtain food other Germans could not get without standing in long lines. As they ate, she described to him her coming day, first shopping, then visiting Frida Schneider, and later a meeting of NSF, the party's women's organization. He listened dutifully, nodding at all the right times.

Fifteen minutes later when the driver arrived, Bauer kissed his wife's cheek, ruffled Hanzi's hair, and leaned down to hug the Czech girl. She shrank back, looking away. Annoyed, he stared at her quivering lip, and for the first time wondered if she were Jewish. That country had Jews, and surely Lidice had them.

As the car set out on Oranienburger Strasse, Bauer sat in the back reviewing financial papers from his briefcase. Under his su-pervision, several Jewish artisans produced counterfeit American and British currency, worth millions in dollars and pounds. The program was created by Heydrich to undermine the enemy's econo-mies and fund intelligence operations. Also, hundreds of Russian prisoners arrived daily. It was surprising how much it cost to dispose of them. Too bad he couldn't have his Jews counterfeit a few marks.

It took nearly forty minutes to reach his destination, Sachsenhausen Concentration camp where Bauer served as the assistant commandant. Such a position of prestige should lead to another promotion soon. They passed under the entrance with the sign Arbeit Macht Frei. Those words were appearing at other camps now, some as mockery, for few if any ever got their freedom except by death, but most SS Death's Head officers like himself saw it as an almost mystical way in which hard work could lead to spiritual freedom. It was a humane way of dealing with Jews and other Untermenschen.

CHAPTER NINETEEN

With only a few weeks to graduation, Peretz Frischer, known to his friends as "Pete," sat in high school American History just after lunch period. In front of the class, Mr. Edelstein rambled on about Manifest Destiny, America expanding its nation from sea to shining sea. However, Peretz's entire focus was on Geraldine Rosen's legs. She sat in the row to his right, one seat up, and her skirt had ridden up to her knees. To him, she was the prettiest girl in class. With her plaid skirt, she wore a "sloppy Joe" sweater. All the girls wore them like Lana Turner, the actress, the original "sweater girl." In fact, Geraldine looked a little bit like Lana Turner with her long, golden hair. He desperately wanted to ask her to the prom next week but had not yet found the courage.

Abruptly, he sat back in his chair when she crossed her legs and he saw a glimpse of pink thigh. His mouth went dry. He swore to himself he would ask her right after class. *He swore.*

"Mr. Frischer, did I say something that alarming for such a reaction?" Mr. Edelstein quipped. He thought he was funny.

"No, sir," Peretz said, then amended that. "Well, surely interesting though, sir."

A few people chuckled, catching the hint of sarcasm. Peretz was no longer hesitant to speak in front of people. A neighbor and newspaperman named Stanley Greenberg spent an hour each day after work reading to him and his siblings from his New York Herald Tribune. After two years, his accent was nearly gone. And his command of the language was good enough for him to attend Brooklyn College next year, intent on medical school after that. His father would only accept medical or law school instead of going into the clothing business with him and Uncle Morris. Both his brothers were eager to follow that path.

When the bell rang, jolting him back to awareness of his purpose, a flood of panic rushed through him. But he swore he would ask her. Now or never. Gaging his exit from the classroom to match hers, he spoke with a croak, "Geraldine, er, Geraldine."

She turned to face him, looking surprised. "Pete? Hi." She smiled.

He walked down the hall with her toward her next class, which he knew was Home Economics. "I wanted to…speak with you." His shoulders slumped. The accent he'd worked so hard to get rid of was flooding back. He took a deep breath. *Say it. Say it, you coward.* "I was wondering if you would go to the prom with me. I'm sure you already have a date, but…"

She gave an easy laugh. "Why, Pete, I never thought you'd even speak to me, let alone ask me out, and to the prom. I don't have a date, and yes, I will go with you."

His heart surged. "Really? That's great. I should have asked earlier, but, well, it's called cowardice. If I ever tried to join the army, they'd tell me to go home. We only want boys with enough courage to ask out the prettiest girl in school."

Instead of reacting to the compliment, an alarmed expression took over her face. She grabbed his arm. "Please don't tell me you plan to join the army too. So many of the boys are so eager to run down to the recruiting offices right after graduation."

He smiled, pleased by her concern. "No, I'm attending BC."

"Good. So am I. I heard you're going into pre-med?" She was about to add something else when her eyes lifted to something behind him. "Who in the world are they?"

Peretz glanced back. His father and Uncle Morris were walking toward him, their faces fierce images of worry.

"What is it, Papa? Is anyone hurt?" he asked.

"Everyone is fine. We've come to pick you up. An old friend of yours just arrived from Nashok. He'll be at the community center in half an hour. He can tell us about your aunt and cousins, and if any of the terrible rumors are true." His father nodded to Geraldine. "I'm sorry, miss. I must take him away from you for a bit."

With his family all right, Peretz apprehension eased, but he felt a little embarrassed by his father automatically connecting him and Geraldine as a couple. He didn't mind, but she might.

"I understand, Mr. Frischer," she said and placed a hand on Peretz's arm, then turned and went into the classroom.

He asked his father, "An old friend. Who?"

"Yankl Glassman."

Peretz sat in the back of the family's 1940 Plymouth Road King, his father driving and Uncle Morris in the front passenger seat. They were mirror images of each other, though his father was two years older. Slim, swarthy, square solid faces, they both wore expensive, pin striped suits. It wouldn't do for the proprietors of the successful Frischer Brothers men's clothing store to wear ordinary brown suits.

Throughout the drive across Bensonhurst, Uncle Morris talked nonstop about his family still in Nashok, Aunt Miriam and the kids, including Mila. It was if his rapid talking would not allow space for any harmful possibilities to intrude.

"I'm sure they're fine," he said for the third time. "Miriam, she's a good woman. She will see the children are cared for, and Mila, my Mila, she's a smart one. She'll charm the Germans. All this talk about the German iron fist is just that, talk. They will make it through. We Jews always do."

The community center was a wide, brick building where mostly Eastern European Jews gathered. As Peretz, his father, and uncle hurried up the stairs, a sense of foreboding settled onto Peretz. He told himself the people of France were surviving, even resisting. Why not Eastern Europe? Why not his cousins and his friends? Guilt plundered his thoughts as if it took a scimitar to them. He had been safe for the last two years, and those he loved in Nashok had faced unspeakable trials. They had to be all right. They just had to be. If Yankl was unharmed; surely, they would be too.

They made their way into a small auditorium where some fifty people, both men and women, waited, all having immigrated to America in the thirties, all with family back in Nashok. Within ten minutes, Yankl arrived beside his Uncle Aaron Weber, a bearded man in his forties. Yankl seemed nervous, greeting people with a nod and forced smile. He was taller than Peretz remembered and his black, curly hair longer, but his face had changed most, something ancient about it as if he'd seen Masada and the burning of the Temple. He stopped in front of Peretz, and the two boys stared at each other a moment, then embraced.

"You're safe. Thank God," Yankl said in Yiddish.

Soon people began peppering him with questions, which he didn't answer, looking from one to another as if he no longer understood the language.

His uncle held up a hand. "Let him tell his story. That's why he is here."

Slow starting, Yankl fell into a steady flow of words. He had decided to try for America instead of Palestine because the world needed to know what happened, and told from here, the world might be prepared to listen. It had been a wild adventure getting out of Nazi occupied territory, stowing onto a Swedish merchant ship in the port of Klaipeda to Stockholm. From Stockholm, he made his way to Gothenburg, then serving on a merchant ship, he worked his way to Bordeaux in Vichy France, on to Casablanca, and across the Atlantic to Curacao in the Lesser Antilles. From there, he made his way up the Atlantic Coast to New York. In some stops, he spent long weeks, even months in Bordeaux, looking for another ship out. The journey had taken more than a year and a half.

Finally, Aaron Weber said softly to his nephew, "They've waited long enough, Yankl. You must tell them."

Looking at his old friend, Peretz had never seen more anguish on a human face. The room was silent.

Anguish in his voice, Yankl said softly, "They're all dead."

Everyone in the room gasped in a chorus of shock. His voice subdued and without inflection, as if he feared to stray into any emotion, he told them of the horror of German SS and Lithuanian shooters and Polish police herding the entire Jewish population of Nashok out of town to huge pits and murdering them all, the men first.

Peretz saw his uncle's face drained of color, his head shaking in disbelief.

"How did you escape?" someone asked.

Yankl sank his head into his hands for a half minute, then stared up with hopeless eyes. "I ran. Papa told me to do it. So I left them all behind," he said, his voice choked. "My father, my brothers. Everyone. My mother and sisters. All of them."

Peretz said, "You had to, Yankl. My God, you had to."

He nodded several times as if trying to convince himself, then said, "When they took us out of the square, we went by Mr. Kornberg's farmhouse. You remember where his apple orchards are, Peretz?"

Peretz nodded.

Yankl blinked as if returning to that moment in Nashok. "Avigdor Koppel, his cousin Avram, and I ducked into them and ran. The Germans shot at us. I think they hit Avigdor and Avram. I don't know. I ran into the woods. What was I to do? Stay? Pack a bag and go to the train station? I was too afraid to move from the woods. I felt safe there. Too many Germans and Lithuanians about. And Karnowski, Radek Karnowski. He was a police sergeant, the most brutal of all."

A door slammed down a hall, and he jumped. After a moment, he took a breath and went on. "The next day I heard shooting again and snuck to the edge of the woods. New pits had been dug near the Catholic church. There, they were killing the women and children. All of them. All day long. I wanted to scream. I didn't want to watch, but this needed to be witnessed. People needed to know what happened. I saw them die in gun volley after gun volley. When it was done, I sank down and wept."

Tears flowed down his cheeks now, and everyone else was crying. Uncle Morris asked, his voice cracking, "Miriam, Mila, my children?"

Yankl nodded.

Knowing the answer already, Peretz still had to ask, "Rivka?"

The air slid out of Yankl like a punctured balloon. His eyes were tortured. "Yes, I saw her go into the pit." He whispered, "I loved her. I loved her. I loved her."

Others began calling out names, and Yankl patiently answered each one. "Yes, I saw her...He was in the group that went ahead of me...He was shot by the Germans before the Apple orchard...I saw her with the first group of women." An on it went.

That evening Peretz skipped dinner and went to bed early. All he could think about before he went to sleep was Rivka, his best friend, the girl who loved him. And Mila and his sweet cousins. He thought about them till he slept, then he dreamed about them, as real as if they were in the room with him.

The next week he went to the prom with Geraldine, him in his tux and her in a beautiful blue gown with corsage, but he had not recovered from the horror and loss. She thought it was her, and halfway through the dance, she said forcefully, "If you're so displeased with my company, Pete, then take me home, please."

He looked at her in shock. "I...I...that's not it at all. Your company is fine. I mean...please. That's not it."

Throwing on her wrap, she walked out of the hall, and he hurried to catch up. "Where are you going?"

"I can walk home."

"No, I'll drive you."

When he found the Plymouth parked down the street, they got in. He didn't start it. After a moment, she said, "Let's go. Take me home." Then he heard a choke from her. "You're crying. Pete, you're crying, and I know it's not because of me. What's wrong?"

Peretz didn't know he had been and wiped the tears from his cheek, shaking his head fiercely. She put her hand on his arm, and her flesh burned through his jacket singeing his skin.

"What is it?" she asked softly.

And he told her. Told her about Yankl, about Nashok, about Rivka, about Mila, about all of them. That night he wept in her arms and swore his undying love for her. She said she loved him, too.

Three weeks later, Peretz graduated from high school, and the next day went to the army recruiting office and enlisted.

CHAPTER TWENTY

I sat in the living room armchair, four-year-old Fritz Kruger in my lap, reading to him in German. The smell of baking bread drifted through the house. Though all the windows were open, the room was stifling. A gentle breeze shifted the lace curtains but didn't cool the air. Glancing up, I saw an SS guard pass by outside, his rifle slung on his shoulder. At any one time, at least fifteen of them patrolled the grounds with three or four inside.

At that moment, across the room, the tall grandfather clock struck noon and the cuckoo raced out to coo twelve times. Fritzie and I laughed each time. We were still laughing as Generalkommissar Kruger entered, undoing his holster and setting it on the table by the door.

He grinned at us. "That bird gets you two every time."

Fritzie jumped from my lap and ran to his father, arms out, to be scooped up and hugged. In the three weeks I'd been working for him as a maid and now sometimes nanny, I'd learned he was a good father who loved his son and would do anything for him. He had an engaging and friendly personality. And he had been responsible for murdering over two hundred thousand Jews and about the same number of Poles and Lithuanians. I was there to kill him.

Earlier in July, with the Red Army threatening to encircle Kaunas, he had emptied the ghetto, sending Jews to Auschwitz, then razed it to the ground, killing anyone left. He planned to burn the rest of the city as well if a Russian breakthrough seemed likely. For now, the Wehrmacht held them back.

Fritzie in his arms, he walked over to me. "Please join us for lunch, Maria. Fritzie would like it, and I have a favor to ask of you."

"Of course, Generalkommissar. Thank you." The forged documents I used to get this position had my name as Maria Schroder, a Pole of German descent.

For lunch, we had beef goulash with spaetzle and carrots. All with thick, rye bread. Living mostly in the forest as a partisan for the last two years, I never ate this well. Usually, the cook served me much more meager fare. Each time she came in to deliver another dish, she scowled at me as if I'd usurped her place in the household.

Kruger and I chatted for a while about the warm weather and his beautiful gardens as if I were an old friend, then he asked me, "Where are you from, Maria? Kaunas? I've not heard the name Schroder among the city's Germans."

Two of the other day as the house blows. maids walked past in the hall, each shooting me a glare. I had the urge to laugh at them but focused on Kruger instead. "No, Herr Generalkommissar, I'm from Karys. It's a small village near Vilnius. My father was a farmer there."

"Was?"

"Yes. When the Russians came, they took our farm. Papa protested, so they arrested him and sent him to Siberia. We mail letters, but we get nothing back. My mother has younger children than me to feed, so I came here to look for work."

"Not Vilnius?"

"No, Herr Generalkommissar, too much turmoil in that city. Besides, Kaunas is farther from Moscow and closer to Berlin."

He chuckled. "That's a good reason. Now, you and I must make an agreement. While we sit at this table, you call me Klaus, not Generalkommissar. That's far too many syllables, don't you think?"

I smiled shyly. "Yes, Herr General...Klaus."

Fritzie was trying to spread butter on a piece of rye. Patting his arm, I took the knife from him and spread the butter, knowing Kruger was watching. My commander, Sokolov, had instructed me to sleep with him if necessary. A Red Army sergeant from Moscow, he had been dropped into the Dainava Forest two years ago to organize the partisan resistance. While training the brigade, he took particular interest in me when he realized my lust for German blood exceeded his own. He taught me to shoot, to kill with a knife, to use explosives, and to sleep with Germans if necessary.

When I balked at this last, he scoffed, "Your virtue is nothing against the death of another Nazi."

But fortunately, Kruger seemed not interested in me, at least in that way. He wiped his mouth with a napkin and set it on the table. "It's time for me to return to work. I must ask you for a favor, Maria. Mrs. Olzanski cannot stay over tonight. She has taken ill. Would you stay with Fritzie? I am so often called out, and when that happens, someone should be with him." He lowered his voice. "He has nightmares. I don't want him alone."

Of course, Sokolov had seen to Mrs. Olzanski's illness, as he had the maid whose position I took. After a few weeks, both would be fine, at least that's what he told me. It mattered not. They were sympathizers. Mrs. Kruger couldn't stay with Fritzie because she was in Berlin visiting her parents, but the guards told me she was actually in a sanitarium for drunkards. One even suggested she ran off a month ago terrified of the Russian advance. She could have waited to go with her son. With the Red Army now not more than forty miles away, Nazi families were being moved farther west, and Fritzie was scheduled on a train to Berlin tomorrow with them.

I patted the boy's hand and said to Kruger, "I understand, Klaus. I'd love to stay with him. If you're called out, Fritzie and I will have a wonderful time together."

Tonight, as Moscow had ordered, I would plant the bomb in his bedroom and finally blow Generalkommissar Kruger to hell. At three in the afternoon while Fritzie napped, I slid the straps of my large handbag on my shoulder and went out to retrieve the bomb from Sokolov. I met him downtown in a safehouse.

"It's tonight," I said. "He asked me to stay over."

The wreckage of the Russian's face always struck me. He had a crooked nose, three puckered scars along his right cheekbone as if clawed, and a stubble of red beard. His eyes were chillingly gray like the winter sky in Nashok. He had the bomb on a table, a fat block of plastic explosive with a pencil detonator already inserted. Inside the detonator was cupric chloride. When released, it would eat through the wire holding the firing pin, allowing it to strike the percussion cap.

Sokolov held up pliers. I opened my handbag, and he dropped them in. "I don't want you looking for a pair of these when the time comes." He pointed to the detonator. "When you crush the copper, the acid is released. You will then have ten minutes to get out. That should be enough time."

"I know. Relax."

He glared at me. "Oh, Madam Ninotchka. So composed. You know everything now, Rivka."

I wasn't composed, my nerves already eating at me. "You're a good teacher, Sasha."

"Pay attention. When it's done, I will meet you two blocks down on Vida Street. I'll wait till five in the morning."

I nodded. With him watching, I lifted my dress and strapped a Walther P38 to my thigh. He handed me a knife. "Take this."

I shook my head. I hated knives. Not that I was squeamish about them. Rely on a knife and you die. In training for silent kills, Sokolov instructed us to cover the enemy's mouth with our hand while cutting his carotid artery. The man would give a groan and collapse to the ground. Job done. It just never worked that way. When Anton, my boyfriend, used it for a planned attack on the Drosknik police station to free one of our people, the guard bit his hand, and though the throat was cut, the carotid only nicked. The man was able to fire his rifle and scream for help. The attack ended as police poured out of the station and soldiers out of the nearby barracks. Anton was killed, and the rest of us barely escaped. The prisoner was shot that night.

"You may need it to kill the boy if he shouts out a warning," Sokolov said.

Kill Fritzie. How to balance that against killing his father. I took the serrated blade and set it on the table. "If I have to, I can do it without the knife."

I placed the bomb in the bottom of my bag with the pliers. If the plan went wrong, I'd use my pistol on Kruger, and then either be shot down or taken into Gestapo custody. I would prefer the first. If everything went as planned though, I'd be out of the house when the bomb went off, and Sokolov and I headed back to the Dainava forest before the call went out.

A few people were out on the sidewalks when I approached Kruger's mansion with the shopping bag straps hanging from my shoulder. Thoughts of the half year I lived in Kovna with my aunt and going to school came to mind. Could I run into anyone who knew me then and remember I was a Jew? I'd made no friends, and I'd grown quite a bit since then, but people would have remembered me. The girl who walked out of class at the teacher's Jewish slur, carried her desk to the library and stayed there for the rest of the semester. No, not likely.

As I turned up the driveway, I lurched a step. A black Mercedes with swastika flags on the fenders was parked by the front door. Kruger must be back early. An SS officer I'd never seen stood beside Corporal Huttner. My heart pounding against my chest, I came up to them.

The officer held out his hand and demanded, "Papiere."

My stomach seized as I fumbled in my bag and took out the forged documents. He studied them, looking at me several times. I glanced at Huttner, who gave a faint shrug of the head as if in apology. He had told me to call him Kurt, but I doubted he'd like me to do it now.

"Search her bag," the officer ordered.

"But, Herr Obersturmführer, she works here," Huttner said.

The officer turned on him. "You, idiot, do as you're told."

Hearing the commotion, three other guards stopped to observe, two of them also new. I stiffened as the corporal reached into my bag and pulled out a fluffy, brown bear. He held it up to the lieutenant.

"Keep looking," the officer snapped.

Huttner began pulling out night clothes I'd placed on top of the bomb, setting them on the grass with the bear. When he quickly got down near the bottom, I slid my other hand into my skirt pocket and grasped the Walther on the inside of my thigh. If he found the bomb, he and the officer would be dead before they realized I'd drawn a gun, but I doubted I could get the other three. The two new men held their rifles on me while the third watched uneasily. If I ran, I would not make it down the driveway. I'd die here. Kruger would live.

"What's this?" Huttner gasped in alarm, and everyone tensed. Then, he pulled out my panties, holding them up for the officer to see. He'd exposed the bomb but hadn't spotted it yet.

That's when Kruger stepped out the front door. "What are you doing there? Let her through."

All the SS men snapped to attention, and the officer shouted, "Yes, Herr Generalkommissar."

I was already throwing my things back in the bag. Huttner handed me the bear. He had a smirk on his face, not for me though, but the officer. I rushed past them and past Kruger into the house. Fritzie stood in the alcove, looking forlorn as if I'd abandoned him.

Furious, Kruger grabbed my shoulder and spun me around. "Why did you leave Fritzie? I thought you understood that it was your job to stay with him."

"Yes, sir. I'm sorry. He was napping, and the other maids were here. I…I needed to get some clothes for tonight." I pulled out the bear. "I thought he might like this."

Fritzie reached out and took it into his arms. Kruger's face did not soften. He pointed his finger at me. "Your assignment is to watch Fritzie. Do not leave without my permission again. Even if your home is burning down."

"Yes, Herr Generalkommissar."

That evening, Kruger hosted a dinner with his top SS officers along with the kommissars of his six districts and several powerful Lithuanian collaborators. They were planning the evacuation and the burning of the city. I could hear that much from upstairs, their heated conversation carrying throughout the house. Everyone but Kruger, it seemed, were panicked about the Red Army so close. I wished I could set off the bomb in the dining room but knew the idea unworkable.

I was with Fritzie till eight o'clock, packing his bags for his trip to Berlin tomorrow with several other families. His room was on the second floor next to his father's. When it was his bedtime, I fixed him a cup of hot chocolate, slipping in a bit of Veronal to make him sleep through the night, and then went to my room across from his. There, I lay on my bed, sweating in the heat, waiting as the night wore on.

Sometime near one, the men finally left, and after a few minutes, I heard Kruger climbing the stairs and entering his room across the hall.

I lay on my bed waiting an hour, then another to make sure he was asleep and the house completely silent. By three thirty, it was time. My heart pounded. With the bomb, I crossed the hall and went in Kruger's room, pressing my back against the wall, and waited. I was breathing so loud I was sure I had awakened him. With the heat, the windows were open, but no breeze came through. From across the room, I studied him lying on his back in boxer shorts and a sleeveless t-shirt, no movement but the rising of his chest.

Trying to calm my breathing, I moved one silent step after another, knelt, and set the bomb on the floor. There it sat for a moment, blue-gray, a block of plastique that would blow the upstairs off the house. With the pliers, I crimped the detonator, releasing the acid.

Ten minutes. I slid it under the bed.

Then I heard the creak of bedsprings and flattened on the floor just as Kruger sat up. Frantically, I scooted under the bed next to the bomb, praying I'd made no noise. His feet thumped down, and he loudly cleared his throat. In the faint light, I stared at his bare, blistered heels. I willed my breathing to calm. Finally, he went to a night table and I heard him pouring a glass of water. Then he stepped to the window and stared out. I could only see his bare legs, hairy and thin. He began talking to himself in a low murmur.

There was no clock on the bomb, just acid eating away at copper wire, but I swore I heard ticking. Three or four minutes must have passed by now. I could roll out and shoot him, but then I would have no chance of escaping. At last, he finished the water, set the glass on the table, and went to the small WC. I debated if I could slip away without being seen or heard, but decided it was impossible. The WC was only a few feet away; he would surely see me, even if I made no noise. I heard him urinating an insufferably long time, then the flush.

He shuffled back and with a groan of springs and lay down above me. I waited, sweat drenching my clothes. My body trembled now. This bomb would go any second. What would it feel like? My body being blown apart? Painful? How could it not be? Moments passed, then minutes. More and more, and the damn plastique seemed to throb beside me louder and louder. Finally, I heard his wheezing snore and instantly rolled out. Without much regard for quiet, I rushed from the room, closing the door with a loud click, and made the stairs.

There, I stopped cold, cursing myself. I could not be quite the monster Kruger was. I just couldn't. I hurried to Fritzie's room, scooped him up and rushed downstairs. Drugged, he didn't wake.

No guards yet. The cook slept on the first floor near the back door, as far away from Kruger's room as I could get. Best I could do for the boy. The old woman woke as I came in.

"What is this? What do you want?" she demanded.

"Shut up." I placed Fritzie beside her on the bed.

"What are you doing?"

I drew the Walther and aimed it at her face. "I'll be right outside. If you step out of this room, you will die. Is that understood?"

She nodded.

I left and shut the door. Not waiting, I slipped through the back where my luck ran out. Two guards smoking by the garden wall looked over at me. I waved and walked up to them.

"Anyone got a cigarette?" I asked. I didn't smoke but could think of nothing else.

A soldier offered me one and the other held out a lighter. I took a breath and coughed. They laughed.

The first one said, "Not used to strong German tobacco."

I shook my head.

The other said, "Couldn't sleep?"

"Too hot."

Just then, a deafening roar erupted from the house, blowing much of the building top off in a fiery, yellow flash. The two guards hurried to the back door and rushed in just as the cook with Fritzie in her arms came out. She stared at me. I heard wild shouts about the grounds.

In the chaos, I slipped through the back gate and ran toward Vida Street and Sokolov.

CHAPTER TWENTY-ONE

BERLIN, JULY 27, 1944

I n his Charlottenburg home, Max Bauer finished his lunch alone, and the housekeeper cleared the dishes away. He missed Klara and the children. Last month, he'd finally convinced her to leave Berlin and take them down to Ostenbruck ten miles outside Nuremberg where his parents lived. Staying in Berlin was too dangerous. British and American bombers had been pounding the city for three years, attempting to take the heart out of the German people, but it did not weaken the Führer's resolve. He would call her tonight if he could get a line through.

A few minutes later, when Bauer stepped out of his house in civilian clothes, a black Mercedes swung to the curb. An SS Hauptsturmführer got out and opened the door for him.

"Good day, Herr Obersturmbannführer," he said. "I am sorry to interrupt your leave. However, Reichsführer Himmler wishes to speak with you immediately."

Bauer tried to hide a reflex swallow at hearing Himmler wanted to see him. It was a week since the assassination attempt on the Führer at the Wolf's Lair and the savage reign of terror that followed throughout the Reich. More than two thousand people already had ended up on meat hooks. Bauer had no connection with the conspirators, but you could never tell with Himmler. Bauer's old friend, Karl Schneider, who had been high up in the government, was arrested and his coffin returned to his wife two days later.

At Gestapo Headquarters on Prinz Albrecht Strasse, Bauer entered Himmler's office and thrust his arm out in salute. Sitting at his desk, Himmler peered over his pince-nez glasses, his face like cold stone. Casually, he lifted his hand in salute. "Sit down, Bauer."

He did, his back stiff and straight, the perfect officer.

"How are your wife and children? I know they are no longer in Berlin," Himmler said.

"I've sent them down to my parents in Bavaria. Thank you, sir, for asking," Bauer said. "My mother and father are getting old, and I worry about them being alone."

It was a lie, and by the smirk on the Reichsführer's face, he knew it. If for some reason Himmler was displeased with him, Bauer, too, might end up hanging from a meat hook.

"Of course. Of course," Himmler said.

Himmler opened a file and shifted through the papers in it. Bauer felt a chill in his stomach. Was he to be arrested? "You have been in the East. Your record is exemplary there."

"Thank you, Herr Reichsführer."

"We are facing uprisings throughout Ostland and the Baltics. Partisans are everywhere. Damn Jewish pigs! Those forests are dark spots on our maps. They are so large it would take a division to root them out. And that damn 'Nun.' Last night, she killed Generalkommissar Kruger. It's like Heydrich again. How did she get so close to him?"

Bauer had heard something about a woman partisan called the Nun, who over the last two years had assassinated several SS leaders, even though they were well-protected. Was this why he had been called here? To hunt down the Nun?

As if he had asked a question, Himmler waved his hand dismissively. "Of course, she is not a real nun. Do you know how she got that name, Bauer?"

He shook his head. "No, sir."

"One of the officers she shot a year ago was still alive when people got to him. In his last breath, he said, 'it was the nun.' Now what do you suppose he meant by that?"

Bauer's forehead furled in a frown. "I don't know, sir. How do they know it was her who killed the Generalkommissar?"

"The description. Always the same. Dark hair, young—the documents she gave Kruger said she was twenty-one. And she's a bit on the plain side. I suppose that's why she can get through security so easily. No one notices a plain girl."

"Is that why I am here, Herr Reichsführer? To find her?"

"No, no, of course not. It's on my mind this morning. That's all. I must send my condolences to Kruger's wife, and I never know what to say in these types of things. No, I won't use one of my best men hunting a woman who has killed only a few men, even a kommissar. We will catch the bitch." Himmler shoved a sheath of papers across to him. "These are your orders. I have a far more important assignment for you. Command of the SS battalion at Auschwitz."

He was stunned. The name *Auschwitz* hit him like a bullet fired into his chest, but he had enough sense to keep his expression blank. The duty was beneath his rank, but more importantly Auschwitz was the last place he wanted to be sent. The Russian army was just a hundred miles from the camp, if that, cutting down the once invincible Wehrmacht like Death with a scythe, and Himmler was sending him into their path. The war was lost. The Americans and British had landed in Normandy in the west. Everyone should be setting up escape plans. He'd heard rumors that the Führer had a secret weapon in the works, one that would win the war. Perhaps he would find his miracle, but in case he didn't, Bauer wished he'd be sent to the Western front instead.

Abruptly, Himmler stood, and so did Bauer. The Reichsführer walked around his desk and clapped Bauer on the back. "The Führer asked for you specifically. Much work still needs to be done with those damn Jew pigs, and you are the man for it, Bauer. We are counting on you."

I sat in the crowded car facing Sokolov as the train lumbered down the track at an excruciatingly slow pace. Outside, brown fields burned under a cloudless sky. We had been lucky to get these seats. Across the aisle, a small detachment of SS filled row after row. Men in uniform and civilian clothes with their wives and children squeezed into the other seats and the aisle. Was this the last train out of Kovna before the Russians smashed through the city?

Last night, I'd reached Sokolov on Vida Street in seconds, but instead of fleeing the city then, we made our way into downtown and the safehouse, which couldn't be safe for much longer. After the assassination of Generalkommissar Kruger, reprisals would be swift and overwhelming. Buildings would be searched. People lined up against walls and shot.

In the darkness of his room, I told Sokolov, "We need to leave. It might be too late."

"We will, but the plan has changed."

As he quickly explained, the situation was much worse than he'd let on. When we came up to Kaunas from the Dainava forest, there had been no lines to cross, no front where the Red Army and the Wehrmacht clashed. Now, there was. To the south, the front was stretched nearly to Poland. With the fury of the battle, it could not be crossed. Two civilians wandering through that landscape could not survive. Either the Germans would kill us, or the Russians would.

He began to undress. "We're going out by train. Change your clothes."

"That's madness, Sasha," I told him. "One place that will be swarming with SS and Gestapo is the train station."

"Maybe it will," he said, then shrugged. "It is the only way."

Finally, I understood. "Fritzie's train." It was scheduled at seven, three more hours.

He nodded. "Germans are trying to flee on that train. We're going to be two of them."

He put on his burgermeister clothes, a gray double breasted, pinstriped suit, somewhat worn as if second-hand, which it was, but perfect with scuffed brown shoes. A man of some importance but not too much so. For me, I put on a one-piece faded, navy blue dress, and threw on a blond wig. Before we left, he handed me my new documents. With a flick of Sokolov's cigarette lighter, I only had moments to check my name. Anna Feiler, and he was Hans Feiler, my father, burgermeister of the town of Pakai just across the Polish border.

We didn't enter the depot till just before eight. It was packed with people trying to flee, German and Lithuanian collaborators with the SS and Gestapo checking papers. A Gestapo policeman checked our documents as the train puffed steam, getting ready to depart. I wanted to yell at him to hurry but kept my smile in place. Finally, he handed them back. "You might as well leave. You won't get on the train."

We found a harried station official, who refused Sokolov's bribes till he offered rubles instead of deutschmarks, enough perhaps to survive the onslaught of the Russians. He put us on at the last moment and we found our seats, Sokolov moving a young couple out of them.

When the train finally picked up speed and travelled for nearly an hour, the landscape outside changed to hilly and wooded. This was the wrong way. I felt like I'd suddenly burst an artery. I grew up here. Panic swept over me. As a harried conductor worked his way through the crowd, I stopped him with my hand. "Why are we going to…" The word stuck in my throat. "Why are we going to Nashok?"

"Orders. The train has been diverted to pick up German families," he said.

"But there's not enough room."

"Then they will throw you off the train." He pulled his arm away and went on.

I sat back in my seat. Sokolov was watching me. I scowled at him and looked away. What if someone at the station recognized me? I never wanted to return to Nashok, not even passing through on a train. As we neared the town of my birth, the welling terror within forced my mind to go blank. I could no longer think. My body lost all feeling. Sweat beaded on my upper lip and I wiped it away. Nashok!

I'd left here three years ago to become a partisan. Out of the Dainava forest, I had been a part of derailing trains, blowing up bridges, attacking police stations, then Sokolov found I had a talent for assassinations, or at least a willingness. The only thing I felt about all of it was that I should have felt something. I didn't, except an insatiable thirst for revenge. Now I was back, and the only thing to penetrate my awareness was an urge to run.

Glancing out the window, I saw we were only a minute out of Nashok, then too soon the wheels screeched, and we rolled into the station, the station where I had kissed Peretz Frischer goodbye so long ago. Where was he now? In America some place, safe from this.

Anxious to board, a crowd clamored on the platform, several in uniform with women alongside. They would be the wives of officers. No room would be made for girlfriends. As they pushed onto the cars, I noticed a blond woman on the arm of an SS captain step up into ours. She was young and slim, a real beauty. She looked familiar, but I could not place her. It was not something to dismiss. If I might know her, she might know me.

I kept my head down. At the other end of the car, her captain forced two older civilians to give up their seats. The train pulled out, and I was glad to leave Nashok. The pain of it was slow to drain away, but as we approached the Polish border and safety from the immediate war, the long night caught up with me. I fell asleep and fell into a flood of familiar nightmares, the pit my family and friends were buried in, and me in it with them because that's where I should be. I saw myself stacked like cordwood among them. Why should I among them all be the one to live? The guilt of surviving felt like a great granite pressing down on me instead of Mama.

Someone was shaking my shoulder. Finally, I blinked awake. Four men in uniform faced me along with the blond woman, who smirked as if she'd stumbled onto the last chocolate bar and was about to devour it. The SS detachment across the aisle watched. Sokolov was glancing out the window as if it meant nothing to him.

"Papiere," the captain demanded.

I groped in my pocket and found the document and hand it to him, trying to feign unconcern. As he studied it, I looked at the woman, the smirk never leaving her face. I conjured that face as it might have looked three years ago and finally recognized her. Marta Karnowski, Radek's daughter. Her grin widened when she saw my reaction. She knew she had me.

Handing back the document, the captain asked as if I'd passed inspection, "Who are you traveling with?"

"I'm alone. I'm returning home to Warsaw."

He turned to Sokolov. "Papiere."

Looking affronted, Sokolov handed over his document. I knew they would not be the one he boarded the train with. After a moment, the officer handed it back and addressed me, "My wife says she knows you. That you are a Jew from Nashok. Rather foolish to come back."

Marta grabbed her husband's arm. "Her hair is much darker. Jew hair."

"Are you wearing a wig, or have you dyed your hair?" When I started to protest, he held up his hand to stop me. "Do you want me to pull it off?"

I removed the wig, and my dark auburn hair tumbled out.

"Hello, Rivka," Marta said with an easy smile.

"Hello, Marta."

CHAPTER TWENTY-TWO

A few minutes after eleven in the morning, Klara Bauer sat in the comfortable living room chair of her house, just south of Nuremberg, breast feeding her year old baby, August, while reading Max's latest letter. She had just posted one to him that morning. She wrote two to his one, but then that was the duty of a wife.

A fire in the grate warmed the room. Hanzi played on the floor with his toy soldiers, camouflaged tanks, and trucks decorated in swastikas, along with ridiculous miniatures of the Führer, Himmler, and a slender Goring. Klara thought her son should be outside or in school, but she'd let him stay home today because it was his birthday. Hannelore had gone to summer school today but had soon come back like she usually did. The Czech girl didn't get along with the other children and often ran off just after she arrived. Right now, she was playing outside in the chill of an overcast day. That was fine with Klara. She did not have the energy to deal with the sullen child.

She lifted the letter higher to catch the light. After endearments of love, Max wrote about his camp where they housed enemies of the Reich. Jews mostly, but many others as well. She'd had a Jewish doctor when she was growing up and had gotten along with him. At least he had a good smile and gave her a lollipop after each visit.

Sometimes she wondered exactly what those people had done that was so criminal but would never dare ask. The Führer hated them and that was enough. Max's letter described the women's camp and how they made little effort to clean themselves. They were so filthy, their hair had to be cut to the scalp to prevent lice. She shivered at the thought.

He wrote of how most of the camp commandants had their wives and children with them, which provided for a pleasant social atmosphere, especially when the Jewish orchestra played for one of their dinners. Kramer, commandant of the Birkenau camp, had been insisting that he bring his wife and the rest of his family to the camp. That caused Klara to lurch. The baby whimpered till she got his mouth around her nipple again. She did not want anything to do with that place, then sighed with relief when Max wrote he could not see uprooting them again. They were best suited where they were.

She noticed outside had grown brighter, several beams of sunlight piercing through the clouds. Hanzi stood up and went to the window, the Hitler figure in his hand. That's when she heard the sound, a distant rumble like sustained thunder. It grew louder and louder, a mounting roar.

Some miles north of them, the Americans were bombing Nuremberg again. The sound carried. But it was overcast and that was worrying. How would they know where to drop their bombs?

Moments later, an explosion rattled the windows, then another closer.

"Mama," Hanzi called, staring out.

She jumped to her feet. "Hanzi, get away from the window!"

In horror, she saw past him to the explosions racing toward them. Just as she put a hand on her son's shoulder, the next bomb blew apart the house.

Three weeks later, the three Auschwitz commandants and Bauer received a communique from Reichsführer Himmler ordering him to cease selections for exterminations on October 31 and to destroy all gas chambers, crematoriums, and evidence of their actions. As an addendum, the Reichsführer added how sorry he was to hear about the deaths of Obersturmbannführer Bauer's wife and two children in the American air raid. He added it showed how criminal the enemy was to bomb civilians.

Till that moment, Bauer hadn't known. It had been weeks since he'd received a letter from her, but he thought nothing of it, assuming it had been the erratic mail service. And his attention had been focused on the Sonderkommando revolt. Bauer had ruthlessly put that down, executing all of them and at least five hundred more. He and the camp commandants feared that all was not yet done with prisoner revolt.

Later that night, Himmler's words finally came to him, *his two children*. Who had survived? He knew which one. The Czech girl. He would not miss her. He didn't care if the girl was alive or dead. He would miss Klara. She had been a good wife. And losing the two boys tore at his heart, but he knew he must be strong. His type did not break under the worst of assaults.

The next day a letter arrived from his parents confirming their deaths. They expressed their condolences to their beloved son for Klara, Hanzi, and baby August. Also, for Hannelore, whose body had not yet been found. There had been much destruction in Ostenbruck, so Schneider was sure it would only be a matter of time.

CHAPTER TWENTY-THREE

AUSCHWITZ CAMP, AUGUST 3, 1944

After four days squeezed inside a freight car with a hundred other people, I felt myself slipping away. In the brutal heat of summer, the car was a living inferno even at night. No food, little water. Only a bucket for a latrine, but after the first day who could piss or shit? My mouth dry, I groped to hold onto reality, clasping tightly the ancient coin on my mother's necklace and prayed to God, prayed to Shelamzion Alexandra, the queen who's image I held.

No one had taken it from me. With the Russians coming, the Gestapo just shoved me onto this train. My mind found sanctuary with drifting thoughts that seemed more real than the freight car, thoughts of my years with the partisans, loving Anton then, finding a spark of life in our romance. I couldn't last long in such an escape. With my throat cracked like a dry moonscape, I soon saw myself crawling through a desert searching for water, and the moans and rattle of the freight car pushed back in.

That's when the steel of a canteen pressed against my lips. It was night, but in the glow of lights coming from somewhere, I saw the apparition of a boy who held it up for me, and I drank two large swallows, instantly feeling better.

"Henryk," I muttered after a moment.

He sat down beside me. "I had a little left. You looked thirsty, Rivka."

He was a startlingly handsome boy, maybe my age or a little older, pale, blue eyes and unruly, black hair. He'd told me sometime during the last four days he'd been on his own since 1939, always moving, ducking the Nazis. Then, one day, they caught him at a train station with false papers.

Suddenly, the wheels screeched, and the train lurched several times before it stopped hard, spilling the latrine bucket on several, who cursed loudly. When the door clanged open, it seemed a blessing. Fresh night air flooded in, cool night air. In an instant, the delusion shattered with a thunderclap of bedlam. Men in striped suits appeared at the door, shouting, "Raus! Schnell! Get out. Get out."

My heart pounded against my chest. Terror gripped my spine as I scrambled to the ground. In one glance, I took in the SS guards with dogs snapping at us and the hundreds of prisoners shouting at us. In that first glimpse, I saw barbed-wire fences, guard towers, and searchlights. Someone ordered us to leave our possessions. "You will get them back."

Immediately, the men were separated from the women and children. Prisoners rushed in to gather up the luggage while others carried the dead from our train. My eyes darted about, trying to take it all in, trying to grasp this madness. Suddenly, in the noise and chaos, a single child began screaming, overriding everything. Other children picked up the wail. Dogs barked. Women shouted they wanted to stay with their husbands and sons. The screaming grew louder, spreading up and down the line. I felt myself being dragged into the insanity. A primal scream clawed up my throat and burst out in a madhouse plea to God.

The guards fell on us with their rifle butts. Near me, Henryk was struck and went to the ground. An SS officer stepped over and fired his pistol into the back of his neck. My arms jerked up in shock. Henryk gone in an instant. Others were being shot. A blow on my head knocked me to my knees, blinding spots of light filled my eyes.

My vision cleared, and I saw the SS officer stride toward me, raising his pistol. Panicked, I struggled to get up but collapsed to one knee.

A small woman in a striped uniform lifted me up by the elbow. "I have her, Herr Hauptsturmführer."

After a moment's hesitation, the officer went on. My head clearing, I turned to thank the woman and blinked in surprise. "Sister Agneta?" I whispered. "My God, Sister Agneta."

"Keep moving, Rivka."

I knew the Nazis had raided the convent a year ago when someone had informed on them for hiding Jews. "How did you get here? Where are the other sisters? Where is Mother Johanna?"

"That's for later. Have you got any valuables on you? If you do, give them to me. They are going to take everything from you, including your clothes."

The skin of her face was stretched taut, almost translucent, her bones beneath nearly visible. Her eyes shown with fear and urgency.

"Nothing."

She shoved me forward. "Do as I tell you or you won't live the night."

She guided me into a queue that led to an SS officer who was sending people either to the right or the left. Four other officers were making the same kind of judgements. My head clearing from the blow, I noticed most were sent left where the sickest ended up in Red Cross trucks. If the Red Cross were here, I decided I needed to go that way.

Agneta squeezed my elbow. "When you get to the officer, tell him you are a nurse. That might save you. They always need nurses. Whatever happens, you must go to the right. You must."

"But the left is where the Red Cross trucks are."

Her voice was harsh. "All of them, the trucks, the people, are going to the showers and the bakery." When I frowned, confused, she hissed, "The gas chamber and the crematorium. This is a death camp, Rivka."

She left me there, hurrying off to collect luggage. The line moved forward quickly. I noticed black smoke rising out of a brick building in the distance, and knew as horrible as it was, Sister Agneta was right. We'd heard rumors. They were true.

At a nearby street, guards were tossing the weakest onto the Red Cross trucks. Separated from their wailing children, parents shouted for them as the trucks drove away. My body seemed to drain of all its blood. I thought myself hardened, but this ripped at my soul. Where was God? I heard others saying it aloud, *where was God?*

Amid this chaos and the searchlights and the night shadows, I had little view of the officer up front who was waving his hands like an orchestra conductor, sending people to life or death. In three minutes, he'd sent just one woman and no children to the right.

Then, nearing the head of the line, I finally could see the officer clearly for the first time, and the shock caused my bowels to weaken and my legs to tremble.

It was Max Bauer.

I tried to switch to another line, but a guard kept me in this one. My turn came. I lifted my head and walked up to him. "I am a nurse, Herr Obersturmbannführer." I shuddered. It was a mistake to recognize his rank.

He looked at me quizzically. "Have we ever met, fraulein?" he asked in German.

I said back in German, "No, sir. I would remember. I am a very experienced nurse. I can…"

Breaking into a smile, he turned to the SS officer judging the next line over. "Herr Doctor Mengele, this one says she is a nurse. What about that? Do you need yet another nurse?"

Maybe to alleviate his boredom, Mengele seemed drawn to the question. "So you're a nurse?"

"Yes, Herr Doctor. I have worked in many clinics and hospitals."

"And what would you do if your patient came to you with typhus?"

"In this place, I'd tell her to prepare to meet God."

Both men laughed.

"Do what you want," Mengele said to Bauer and went back to his column.

Bauer looked at me again and flicked his wrist to the right. Enormous relief flooding through me, I started off, and then abruptly he called, "Halt!"

I froze. What kind of torture was this? I turned, and he motioned me back to him. Perhaps he finally recognized me. When I stood in front of him, he snatched the chain with the ancient coin about my neck, stared at it a moment, then slid it into his pocket and motioned me to go on. I hurried away.

Marched into a large building with over a hundred other women, we were made to undress before several leering male guards, all our body hair shaved off, then paraded alone into the showers. Terrified, I stood under the nozzles, certain a killing gas was about to spew down on me. But cold water came out. Then the guards walked in and watched us wash. The last time I was forced to stand naked before Germans my family and my friends were murdered. The Jews from my town wiped from the earth. As the water fell, I shuddered with revulsion and fear, but also hate. Hate, *my dear Hate*. Still my most faithful companion.

That night, someone tattooed a number on my forearm, and I felt my humanity begin to slip away.

The next months passed slowly with constant threats of death and beatings, with bad food and no water to wash ourselves, and sharing barracks with huge rats that scurried about and sometimes feasted on those who died during the night. Like everyone, I itched from lice. Prime breeding ground for typhus. Dr. Mengele dealt with typhus outbreaks by taking everyone in the offending barracks to the gas chambers.

There was never enough food. In the mornings, we received hot, brackish water that the kapos called tea or coffee. Sometimes I attempted to wash with it. At the noon meal, they gave us watery soup made from whatever the kitchen could find, mostly rotting vegetables like turnips. The taste made us gag, yet we consumed it. For the evening meal, a few ounces of bread laced heavily with sawdust and occasionally a rancid piece of sausage.

I would have perished if not for Agneta and her friends. She and four other women had sworn to help each other survive. Already with five—too many, they said—they didn't want me to join them, but Agneta insisted, and her job as a Kanada Kommando held such importance they agreed. The Canada barracks was where the possessions of new arrivals were taken. There, she and the other kommandos sorted through them for shipping to Germany, and when they found food or a prized piece of clothing, they smuggled it to their barracks. If caught, they'd be shot on the spot.

So, through her, I became a part of the group, which eventually I dubbed the Six.

"Keep that *skata* to yourself," Eleni the Greek told me angrily. A tall, emaciated woman, she missed little with her dark eyes. "We are six now, but tomorrow we may be five or one or all of us no more."

And she was right. By mid-September, two of our people had perished. One from pneumonia and the other, a woman named Jadwiga, at Canada. One day, a guard known for his brutality named Lenke inspected the women who had just finished work, grabbing their private parts and checking every area of their bodies. Stuffed in her undergarments, Agneta had a quarter loaf of bread and a portion of cheese found in a suitcase, for us a feast. In line about to face Lenke, she frantically sought a way to escape but there was none. When she was second in line, Jadwiga suddenly ran. She carried nothing but knew Agneta did. When Lenke chased her, Agneta and the others slipped away. Incensed, he beat Jadwiga to death.

Worst of all was Helena. From Warsaw, she was a beauty, even with her loss of weight and short, chopped hair. An SS officer told the barbers to allow her hair to grow and gave her soap for a weekly shower he would provide. She took the shower but made sure her golden hair was cut like the rest of us. He raped her anyway, but then eventually tired of her. One day she came to the infirmary.

"I'm pregnant," she said.

The female doctor, also a prisoner, said, "I will deal with it."

Helena and I knew what that meant, the baby terminated.

At Helena's pained expression, the doctor said, "If the pregnancy is discovered, you will be shot. If somehow the baby comes to term, both of you will be killed outright." At our looks of horror, she added, "There are no miracles here."

She saw my nod of understanding, but Helena shook her head. "This is not the German's bastard. I was pregnant when I arrived here. It is my husband's. He is dead. This is all I have left of him. I will not kill it."

I noticed then how late she was, maybe eight months. She hid it well under the constant blanket she wore. We all knew if born alive, it could not survive long in this place.

"Babies cry. Babies take constant caring. How are you going to do that here?" the doctor asked.

"I will not kill it."

The doctor sighed heavily. "Then what do you want?"

"I have morning sickness," Helena said sheepishly.

The doctor gave a bitter laugh. "Ah, I see. Well, all I have for morning sickness, for any damn sickness, are happy words. You want some happy words?"

Helena shook her head.

Her baby was born in late September, small and weak but clinging to life. It died a week later. But it did not die from hunger. The baby was a threat to all in the barracks, but we, especially the Six, saw him as a symbol of our survival, a small light of hope and helped to keep him alive. But late one night, while Helena slept with him, someone snatched the baby up and placed him outside in the middle of the Lagerstrasse. Without his mother, he began wailing. The guards came, but they didn't know what to do.

When Helena tried to rush from the barracks, Eleni and I held her back. Others stepped outside, a violation that could get us all shot. But the guards seemed transfixed by the baby on the ground till Bauer showed up, furious at being called out, he said, for such a trivial matter.

What he ordered the guards to do snapped the thin string of humanity we had left. That image of Helena's baby carved itself into me; the sounds of gunfire and Helena's screams echoed again and again in my head. None of it would ever go away. Afterward, what were we to do? People died here. We had to step over the moment and keep going, keep surviving. The next day came and then the next, and the death of Helena's baby was left behind.

Finally, sometime in late September, Agneta told me what happened to the other nuns. When the convent was raided and the sisters and Jews in hiding hauled away, half were sent to Auschwitz. Mother Johanna and Sister Irmengard went elsewhere. Agneta didn't know what happened to them after that. Of the five nuns who came with Agneta, one died in the hell of the train and the other four were sent immediately to the gas chambers.

God, was there any surviving the Nazis?

At first, I'd been afraid Bauer would recognize me, but apparently his duties as the SS commander kept him from entering the camp very often, except when he joined his friend Dr. Mengele in one of the random selections. They both seemed to enjoy their games in choosing people to send to the gas chambers.

But in early October, that changed. The sonderkommandos revolted. These were the prisoners who led their fellow Jews to the gas chambers and carried their bodies to the crematoriums. Before loading them into the furnaces, they shaved hair for someone in Berlin to make wigs and pulled gold teeth to put cash in SS pockets. They had no choice. If they refused, the response, as it was for all infractions, was instant death. Finally, knowing they were destined for the gas chambers, they fought back. While we other prisoners huddled in our barracks, Bauer led his battalion into camp and slaughtered all four hundred and fifty of them. In the battle, only three SS guards were killed, but one of them was Lenke. He was thrown into the furnace alive.

At the end of October, the trains stopped coming. There were no more selections, and the Germans began dismantling the gas chambers and crematoriums.

In January, with winter growing colder and colder, the Russians were finally closing in on the camp. At night, seeing flashes of artillery far to the east, the SS were desperate not to be caught by the Red Army. Every morning and evening, we stumbled out of our barracks onto the Lagerstrasse for roll call, expecting to be marched out somewhere to the west.

This evening, five thousand women stood outside in the brutal, icy wind, bundled in whatever we could stuff into our clothes for warmth. Numbing cold clawed at my bones, and hunger at my stomach. I made my mind go adrift like a blackbird floating over the formations. It had been six months here. I'd lost weight, twenty to thirty pounds. My thick jacket and skirt hung loosely on me, despite the stuffing.

Black smoke drifted in over the women's camp from the crematorium while the smell of burning flesh laced the air. I gave my head a shake. No, that couldn't be. My mind playing tricks again. The Nazis destroyed the crematoriums and gas chambers, removing the evidence of their crimes. We were evidence. Soon they must remove us, too.

The SS guards were becoming agitated. A captain named Lindorf strutted in front of us, slapping his thighs with his gloved hands in agitation. Our numbers should be the same as on the list for formation. That was the German fixation. Even the sick and the dead had to make roll call. The tally had to match, and it didn't. Lindorf ordered the kapos to count us for a third time, and they moved among us.

Beside me, Agneta said in a voice weak as thread, "Something is happening. It is different this time."

"I don't see any difference," Eleni the Greek said in a harsh whisper. "The same foul *skata*. That's all I see."

"They are panicky. Can't you see it?" Agneta insisted. "They must do something with us now. The Russians are too close. It's now for us. I think we're going to leave now."

Eleni shook her head. "So what? We won't be free. They'll just march us to another hell."

I remained silent. Everyone in the clinic where I worked, no matter how sick, had returned to the barracks. No one wanted to be left behind, certain the Germans would shoot them all. I didn't know what to think or feel. Both dread and hope attached themselves to the possibility of leaving. Out of this place yet still under the boot of the Nazis.

In that endless roll call, the third count ended and a fourth began. We stood in the frozen air. Day had turned to night. Snow began to fall. At a blast of wind, I attempted to tie my scarf tighter about my head and pull my coat in more snugly. Nothing helped. I was freezing. Beside me, Agneta moaned, and her knees buckled. On the other side of her, Eleni slipped a hand inside Agneta's elbow to hold her up. On my side, I did the same. Agneta had been one of those sick in the hospital, but we wanted her with us if we left.

Finally, a woman was found hiding in one of the other barracks and dragged out. What she was doing I couldn't guess. Maybe she wanted to wait for the Russians, but it did her no good. The guards shot her and left her lying in the falling snow.

The count now matching, Captain Lindorf faced us. His voice filled the Lagerstrasse. "We are evacuating the camp."

And with that, they marched all of us out through the gate into the snowstorm.

CHAPTER TWENTY-FOUR

For much of the night, we trudged westward through the storm, a column of several thousand women prisoners, ghosts among the snow flurries. My legs burned with exhaustion, not sure how much farther I could go. Hundreds of guards frightened by the onrushing Red Army flanked us, their voices cracking again and again, "Schnell. Schnell."

They pushed us into a hurried shuffle, all anyone could manage. Those who stopped were shot. Those who fell back were shot. We passed bodies stacked on the side of the road. When Agneta fell back, Eleni and I, despairing losing our precious friend, linked arms with her and dragged her with us.

Toward morning, the column was halted, and we were allowed to rest. The three of us collapsed in the snow by the road, huddling together with four other women from our barracks. The savage cold ate at our bones. We could not see the Russian front for the storm, but we could hear it, a distant rumbling of artillery, which made the guards nervous. They stood nearby, warming themselves at a fire while trying to watch us.

"My feet are numb," Agneta said, shivering.

As she leaned back against Helena, I snatched up her boots, removed them, and buried her feet inside my coat. She was already asleep. We would all do anything for Agneta. While many of the thousands had no shoes, wrapping their feet in strips of blanket or cloth, all seven of us wore men's boots stuffed with cloth thanks to Agneta. She'd smuggled them out of Canada barracks by wearing regular shoes to work and boots out when found. Lenke never seemed to notice. She got us food, coats, pants which were warmer in winter, and gloves. Without her, most of us wouldn't have made it this far.

Drowsy, I escaped this frozen hell remembering my family, drifting back to winters in Nashok, skiing the forests and skating the Neman River with Hanna and Ben Zion and the Young Guardians. Papa sometimes would join us while Mama came only once, and that a ski outing. I was so surprised to find she was a better skier than all of us. I asked her why she didn't come out more. She had looked at me with a frown. "What? You think a house and family run by themselves?"

I wondered if their souls drifted in a Jewish afterlife. The rabbis seemed vague about that. No one would come right out and say, yes, there's a Heaven and a Hell. Everything was a metaphor. So, I did not think they lived except in my heart. If I died here on this road, they too would die.

It was out on a Young Guardian ski trip that I kissed Peretz, oh, my Peretz, for the only time before the day on the train platform when he left for America. I was twelve; he was fourteen and saw himself as a man already. I had fallen back so I could be alone with him, and as I'd hoped, he stayed with me, afraid something was wrong. We stopped to rest by a tall pine. I had been planning to kiss him all day, and now was the time.

"Are you sure you're all right, Rivka?" he asked, taking off a glove and putting a barehand on my forehead, as if that would do any good in such cold weather.

I nodded. "I want to tell you something. Lean down so I can whisper it in your ear."

He frowned, as if annoyed at playing kids' games, but leaned his ear toward me. I turned his face and kissed him on the lips. He jerked upright. "What are you doing?" He put his glove back on. "Come on, let's go."

As he skied off, I felt mortified but also furious that he saw me only as a little girl. I followed him at a distance and never caught up that day.

As I lay in the snow by the Auschwitz road, I knew in my heart he had made it to America. That he had survived all this. I don't think I could exist otherwise. I must reach him. I must find a way...

"Aufstehn! Schnell!" The guards' voices woke us up, and we scrambled to our feet. Within a few seconds, the entire column was on the road again, marching all day and long into the night before we rested again. Day after day, we slogged through the snow, skirting towns, cutting through forests and country roads past isolated homes. I was desperate just to lie down for a minute but knew when that happened, I'd be shot immediately. My muscles screaming, I pushed on.

A few people threw food to us, but most did not, hiding in their farmhouses, drawing their curtains shut. The food we'd brought was gone, and we lived on the bits of stale bread the guards tossed to us. With little to eat, hunger drained our strength, and I began to fear I would die here. They wanted us to die here. Fear was how they moved us, pushing us forward with it.

Finally, after five days, we came to a village train station where guards hustled us onto freight cars. As I climbed in, the panic I felt clasped itself around me. This was just like the cars we rode into Auschwitz. We couldn't possibly be going back. When the train soon pulled out, it lumbered slowly, stopping and waiting for hours, then moving on. Water was provided and some bread, but not even a bucket to do our business. The times the train stopped, we were allowed to climb down and relieve ourselves in the snow.

After several days, we reached a camp named Dachau where they unloaded all the cars but ours, which went on for another hour. The rumor spread that they were going to take us into the forest to shoot us, but when we got out, it was another camp that a guard called Kaufering. The names meant nothing to me. It was all the same. Skata, as Eleni would say.

We were housed in damp, cold earthen bunkers and made to work, digging out an underground factory to build Messerschmitt planes for a war that was lost. With the allies so near, we inmates, desperate to survive just one more day, went under the earth and dug out the ground as if people would actually build planes that no one would ever fly.

But the war did not end, not right away. We spent another two months with the winter hanging on and snow clinging to the ground. The bread was better here, not so much sawdust, though there was hardly enough to sustain us for too much longer, especially with the labor. Daily, I thought Agneta would die. After her bout with pneumonia at Auschwitz, she never regained her strength. I swore I would not let it happen, but all I could do was give her some of my rations as did Eleni. In the two months, my flesh melted away, my ribs stood out against my skin, my knees seemed huge against my thin legs.

In late April, typhus broke out in camp. There was no water with which to wash. Like everyone else, lice crawled on my body and in stubbled hair, which had been cut weekly to prevent just that. Agneta and Helena had typhus for a certainty with rashes and dizziness. I had a headache and had been coughing all day but no rash yet. Maybe I had something else, a cold or something. Instead of work, Helena had gone to the hospital that morning, and I thought never to see her again. A former schoolteacher from Warsaw, she had survived the ghetto and Auschwitz. Now, too weak to work, she'd likely be shot. That was the Nazi cure for typhus.

When we returned to our bunker that day and collapsed on our straw mats, Eleni said, "This damn war better end soon, or none of us are going to make it."

I looked over at Agneta with concern. She had finished work, but she could not make another day. I went over and sat beside her on her mat, feeling her forehead. It was burning.

"I'll be all right," she said in a hoarse voice. "You don't need to worry about me."

"Yes, you will."

"Do you ever think about Mother Johanna, Sister Irmengard and the others from the convent?" she asked, a glaze in her eyes. "Do you think they're still alive?"

"I'm sure they are. We are, aren't we? And we're going to stay that way." Silly talk. They were surely dead, and we were all edging closer to it. "Besides, the Germans wouldn't dare harm Mother Johanna."

While I lay beside her to keep her warm, brushing her cheek, Agneta smiled and drifted into a half-sleep. I tried to tell myself to keep this daily trudge going, don't let fear take over. That we would all make it through, and that was the big lie. Seeing Agneta's placid, angelic face, rage suddenly erupted through my body. If I could, I'd kill every damn German I saw for destroying her, for destroying so many good people. I couldn't tell Agneta this for she would then pray for my soul, which I was sure I did not have.

Just then, Helena stumbled into the bunker, breathless and pale. "Dr. Mikkelsen said the Germans have orders to execute us. All of us. The entire camp. They're transporting us back to Dachau tonight to be gassed."

It was terrifying to hear, but we were too exhausted and too sick to do anything about it. What could we do? Run for the barbed wire fences and be shot down? That night, Kaufering was evacuated, some prisoners marched toward Dachau while others loaded onto trucks. About a thousand of us were forced onto open boxcars with only the night sky overhead. This way, we'd be the first to arrive, the first to go to the gas chambers. Frightened, knowing this was the last journey, we huddled in silence as the train lurched forward and out of the camp.

Not more than ten minutes out, it stopped. Standing up, I looked out over the side of the car at the mud and patches of snow to the forests beyond, wondering if we could climb out without the SS guards seeing us, but they were soon outside patrolling. Another train packed with soldiers and weapons crept by on an adjacent track. And that's when luck turned our way.

Three planes swooped down out of the night sky, strafing the troop train with bombs. Several explosions blew apart railcars. The guards threw themselves on the ground or took shelter under the train. I could see the dim outlines of the planes looping around for another pass.

Just then, our door banged open, and someone yelled, "Run! Run!"

Eleni and I snatched Agneta, and fear pounding through us, we rushed out and struggled into the mud and snow of the field. Up and down the track, someone had thrown open all the doors. A few shots burst from the guards' rifles, but with the planes coming in again, they stayed hidden as we stumbled for the woods in the mad, slow gait of the sick and dying.

The planes dropped more bombs, tearing both trains apart, then when they flew off, the guards rose out of the fields and chased us, opening fire. Some of the women around me went down, but Eleni and I still dragged Agneta between us. Despite her illness, Helena kept up with us. With a quick glance back, I saw several guards gaining on the prisoners. They began rounding up or shooting people. When we four reached the woods, we kept running through the trees, pushed on by our desperation. Dizziness set in. Helena stopped first, then Agneta. Eleni and I went back for them.

"Where are we going?" Helena gasped. She was struggling with the last bit of her strength. I could just make out the look of despair on her face.

"Away from the damn Germans," I said.

"Keep moving, Helena," Eleni said in a harsh whisper.

We took off again and distanced ourselves from the others, though we could still hear occasional gunshots and orders of *halt*.

After another minute, Helena choked out, "Please, please, I can't move. You go on."

Eleni lifted her arm over her shoulders to keep her going.

But in only a few yards more, we slowed down. I didn't know how far or how long we'd been running, not fast, barely more than lurching jog, but we must have distanced ourselves from the Germans. We kept walking now, Eleni helping Helena, and me Agneta. After another minute, I caught the sound of thrashing behind us and felt a stab of fear. It was guards. It had to be.

When we came to a small glade, I slid Agneta's arm off me, whispered to them to keep going, and ducked into the trees. I fumbled around and found what I was looking for, a stone the size of my fist. Within seconds, two guards crashed through the brush and came upon the clearing.

"Halt," an officer cried, aiming his pistol.

A second later, even as my friends stopped and raised their hands, he fired. One of them went down.

I leapt from the trees and smashed the rock into his head with all the strength I could muster, knocking off his helmet and buckling his knees. As he was collapsing, I hit him again and again.

I turned to the other German soldier. Panic in his eyes, he was fumbling with his rifle as if he had no idea what it was for. Frantically, he worked the rifle bolt, but it wouldn't slide into place. With the moonlight, I could see he was a boy, no more than fifteen, if that. I picked up the sidearm the officer had dropped.

He threw down the rifle and raised his hands. "Please, I want none of this. Let me go. I will not tell anyone I saw you. Please."

I had no pity left. I shot him twice.

Helena was dead. The officer's bullet had caught her in the chest. We stared down at her, not wanting to believe she had come this far and would go no farther.

"Her baby," Eleni said. We all knew what she meant.

Agneta crossed herself. "Through this holy blessing and by His most tender mercy, may the Lord pardon you your sins."

Eleni cocked her head at Agneta. "She was a Jew."

"All the same to God. She is in His House now."

"We have to go," Eleni said. "We can do nothing for her now."

I pointed in what I thought was the right direction. "West, that's where the Americans are. That's the way we must go."

Beyond exhaustion, we traveled through the night and into the next day. We slept a couple hours, then struggled up by midday and pushed on. Our goal, our Jerusalem, was to reach the American troops. What drove me was Peretz. I had to reach him. He was in America. I had to get to America. It was all that mattered now.

Agneta passed out twice, and at midday, she stopped in the middle of a green field and sat down, her face white as porcelain. Between gasps, she said, "I'll just lay here. You go on without me." Then, her eyes rolled back in her head, and she toppled over.

I checked her pulse, which was rapid. "Let's move her out of the dampness."

Weak ourselves, we struggled to carry her over to a standing oak thirty yards away and set her on the dry moss surrounding its trunk. Eleni and I lay on each side of her. I knew I would not be able to get up again to go on. My body was folding in on me. Above, the sky was a perfect blue. A good way to die, I thought as I fell into a bottomless, empty sleep.

"This one is carrying a pistol. She's still alive," the voice stirred me into half wakening.

Another voice said, "So's this one. I'm afraid the other one is not going to make it."

A third voice, "We saw these people at Dachau. They're all the same."

A weary voice said, "Poor bastards."

I was not sure whether it was part of a dream. At first, I couldn't understand the language then realized it was English and opened my eyes. A man in uniform was kneeling over me. I blinked several times. It didn't make sense. He was Asian. Maybe we stumbled onto the Red Army. I'd seen them before around Nashok, not sure where any of them came from. Then I saw the uniform, not Russian. And he spoke English. Somehow American. I had not spoken English in

188

years. I needed to tell them something. What? I couldn't remember what I needed to say. Something came to me.

The words choked out of me. "Peretz Frischer."

Then darkness took me again.

CHAPTER TWENTY-FIVE

Max Bauer sat on the bank of a stream a quarter mile from the train, which he could no longer see because of the trees. At dawn, to escape aircraft bombing, the engineer had stopped in a forest and would not be moving again till nightfall. Bauer had been travelling in route to Munich with hundreds of soldiers to shore up the Wehrmacht for the last battle against the Americans, in reality, the last dying gasps of the Third Reich.

Beside him, Generalmajor Kurt Muller squatted on his haunches, tossing stones casually into the water. They had struck up a conversation on the train, two young high ranking officers, one Wehrmacht and the other SS.

Light brown hair and square jawed, Muller was short, stocky, and pathetic, whining against Hitler and the thousand year Reich chuckling, "It fell just a little short of that."

Bauer was tired of hearing it.

"Are you married, Max?" Muller asked abruptly, changing the subject.

"I was. They're dead. The bombing by your friends, the Americans."

Muller ignored the jibe. "I have not had the pleasure of marriage. Maybe someday if Germany ever recovers."

Across the stream about two hundred yards out, a man in uniform was crossing the farmer's field, hurriedly, a deserter not wanting to be in the open long. Bauer couldn't blame him. No one wanted to be the last casualty, civilian or soldier, of the war at its death knell.

Reaching in his tunic pocket, Muller pulled a bar of candy out. "Chocolate. Good German chocolate. Can you believe I found a bar in Berlin? I've been saving it for a special occasion. I'd say this is it. You and I heading into Gotterdammerung. Here, take half." He laughed and held out the bar.

Shaking his head, Bauer said heatedly, "What are you laughing at?"

"You, Max, that red face of yours, so angry when I said the damn war was over, the High Command deluding themselves, acting like it was 1941 again." Muller snorted derisively. "You know it's true. Hitler won't be satisfied till we're all dead."

"You are speaking treason, Herr General."

"So I am, Max. Our great commander is sending me to Munich with a division of men, Aryan Warriors all of them, to stop the American assault on his favorite city." He threw up his arms and boomed with laughter again. "Division! Aryan Warriors! They are all in his daft mind. There is no division, my friend. I have three hundred men. And those warriors, they are not men, but untrained boys barely in their teens and fat old men, the Volkssturm, set for the slaughter if they don't shit themselves first."

Bauer became more annoyed, partly because he knew Muller was right. The Volkssturm was Hitler's people's army, and they were worthless. "He is the Führer. You swore an oath."

Muller flipped his hand dismissively. "I swore to a madman. That doesn't matter."

"You should be arrested for such talk."

"By you, Max?"

Bauer paused as if considering it, then said, "No, I have no time for you now, but I will report you."

Muller laughed. "Who will you report me to? Everyone in High Command is fleeing or surrendering except for us poor, dumb soldiers. Well, not me anymore. I'm not getting back on the train." He pointed to the west with the hand holding the chocolate bar. "I'm going that way. I'm going up to the first American soldier I can find and surrender. That's the special occasion I am celebrating. Not your foolish war?"

"You have no honor, Muller."

"None. But a small matter at this moment. Honor is dead like so many soldiers." More exhausted now than anything, he glanced at Bauer. "Look at you, Max, with your SS uniform. I can surrender. You can't. You will be shot on sight, even by the Americans, and my guess is deservedly so. When they find you, you will face a firing squad." He looked quizzically. "What did you do, Max? What evil did you do in the name of the Führer and the Aryan race?"

"Nothing more than my duty."

"I'm sure. There is a reckoning coming to all of Germany and for you doing your duty. When the peace is signed, your death is signed. It will only be a matter of time." He grinned. "And I hope I will be there to see it."

Bauer had to admit Muller had at least one thing right. He had known the war lost since he left Auschwitz in the company of Dr. Mengele and the rest of them back in January. He didn't want to surrender. He still believed in the cause and the superiority of his race. But the armies were gone. No German air force in the skies and no navy on the seas. Nothing left but pockets of resistance at bridges and crossroads. All of it hopeless.

When the peace was signed, the allies would come after him and the others who did the dirty but necessary job of ridding Europe of the Jews. At some point, someone would recognize him and denounce him. He needed to get out of Europe, and like Muller, he had to do that by surrendering only to the Americans.

But he could not surrender as SS officer Max Bauer.

"I've lost my soul in this war," Muller was saying. He began to unwrap the chocolate bar when Bauer drew his Walther and shot him in the back of the head. The general slumped to the ground. Afraid someone might have heard the sound and come to investigate, Bauer quickly switched tunics and caps with the dead man, then swapped ID tags and Wehrpass documents.

Muller's picture didn't look much like him, but he thought it should pass as just a bad photo. He slid the Wehrpass back into his new tunic pocket. Now, he was Kurt Muller from Berlin—no, he would claim he was from Vienna—and Max Bauer, SS officer, lay dead on the banks of the small stream near Augsburg. He picked up the chocolate bar, brushed off the smattering of dirt, then waded across the stream to the west.

Two days later, around midmorning, the sky gray with drizzle, Bauer walked down the center of the autobahn with four hundred other prisoners heading for the rear. On each side of them, long lines of American tanks, troop trucks, and jeeps drove toward the front, sending up a constant spray from the slick pavement. To him, it looked like the Wehrmacht in the first years of the war. The power seemed endless. His army was thoroughly beaten. So self-confident were the Americans that only a few guards accompanied them.

An hour more took them off the autobahn and down a muddy road to an old German army camp with barracks, barbed wire, and Americans busy with vehicle and foot traffic. They passed through the gate with a sign mounted above that said *3rd Infantry Division*. Underneath that, the quotation, "We Shall Remain There." He wondered what that meant. They were led into a secondary barbed wire enclosure and allowed to stand or sit in the drizzle and mud.

Several hours later, close to sundown, he was taken by two MPs to a small room in a barracks. The room had a single wood table with two chairs facing across to a third, and a covered light above. He was told to sit in the single chair, then the two guards flanked the door in a relaxed stance. After a few minutes, when two officers entered, the MPs straightened.

Bauer knew the ranks of the American, British, and Russian armies. He felt a little disgruntled that he, a general, would only merit two lieutenants. One of them seemed formidable, as if a German specimen, athletic, tall, about two hundred pounds. The nametag on his uniform read *Lomax*. The other was a thin, little man named Greenbaum. Clearly a Jew. This second man laid a yellow notepad on the table and jotted a few things with a pencil.

Lomax smiled easily as if they were good friends. Bauer knew it was his task to smile back. Lomax spoke German, "Sorry you had to wait so long outside, General Muller."

"I speak English," Bauer said.

The American switched to English. "If you prefer. As you might suspect, we've been overwhelmed with prisoners. All we know about you is what the MPs told us, that your name is Kurt Muller. So, we'd like to learn a little bit about you if we could."

He asked questions about Muller's unit, their strength, and their disposition. Bauer answered them all, talking about the insanity of sending three hundred Volkssturm boys to fight a lost war against a trained army.

"I told them to go home," Bauer said. "The army no longer needs you, I said. Then, I surrendered to an American unit."

Lomax nodded sympathetically, then after a moment when he squinted at Greenbaum's notes, he asked about Muller's war record. Bauer thought it best to stay as close to the truth as possible, obviously without mentioning the Einsatzgruppen or his work in camps like Auschwitz. Instead, he told of his long years with the regular army on the Eastern Front fighting Russians. Throughout, he let drop hints of anti-Nazi sentiment and even tossed in that he had been aware of the July 20 plot to assassinate the Führer.

At that, Lomax glanced at Greenbaum, but the Jew didn't look up from his writing. In fact, he hadn't raised his head once, as if afraid to look Bauer in the eye. Here, Bauer thought it was time to make the important chess move. "Among my university studies, I focused on International Affairs, particularly Russia, and the army high command trained me even further in the communist menace."

Lomax didn't even pause but went on with other questions. The interview lasted another thirty minutes till a knock came at the door and a sergeant entered and whispered in the ear of each officer. Both men seemed surprised. Lomax sputtered a bit. Greenbaum sat motionless.

From somewhere outside, he heard a soldier shout, "Hitler is dead! The bastard is dead."

Bauer flinched as a cheer rose and swelled, then chants of "Hitler is dead! Hitler is dead!" The two MPs were grinning.

"Is that true?" he asked the officers.

Faces smug with satisfaction, both smiled and nodded. Bauer wanted to leap across the table and choke them. He was too overwhelmed to act anyway. Hitler dead. It could not be. Even as he sat here in this American camp, somewhere deep inside him a part of his mind still believed Hitler would find a way. He would somehow turn it all around. Now, the Reich was truly gone.

For the first time in the entire interview, Greenbaum looked up at him and met his gaze with a cold stare, as if he could read Bauer's thoughts. "You seem shaken. War is hell, general," Greenbaum said.

The interview ended then, and the MPs led Bauer to a room at the rear of the barracks. With an affable smile, he nodded to them as they shut the door, heard the click of a lock, and retreated to the bed. Outside the window, night had come, the room cast in darkness. The Führer dead. He was the Reich. And for the first time in years, he placed his head in his hands and wept.

The next morning, the two MPs took him out for exercise, then brought him a breakfast better than he'd had in a year, eggs, toast, bacon, and coffee. Just before noon they returned with a pin striped suit and shoes, all of which fit him. He had no idea what was going on but was relatively sure he wasn't about to be shot. Down the hall in the small barracks lobby, two men in civilian suits met him, introducing themselves as Mr. Flynn and Mr. Power.

They got in a Mercedes sedan, Flynn riding in the back with Bauer as Power drove out onto the autobahn. After about ten miles, Bauer asked, "Where are we going?"

Flynn was silent for a long time, at least a minute, then frowned and said, "There's a man who wants to meet you, General Muller. He will answer all your questions."

CHAPTER TWENTY-SIX

ZURICH, SWITZERLAND, MAY 1, 1945

Before seeing this important man he'd been brought to meet, Bauer was interrogated for two days in his hotel room by Flynn. Showing not a moment's hesitation, he kept to his story, having had time to add more detail to it. When asked about his time in Russia, he told about how, after decades of terrible Soviet oppression, the peasants welcomed German soldiers like himself as liberators. He had been shaken by the terror these people had lived under and provided army rations when he could.

Flynn turned to the concentration camps and rumors of Nazi atrocities, and Bauer remained calm, flicking lint off the seam of his trousers. "Of course, I'd heard the rumors, but I personally knew nothing about them. The Wehrmacht had nothing to do with that. I was raised in the Lutheran church, Mr. Flynn, and we were taught to treat all people the same."

The next day, the interview picked up again and went on till noon. Flynn pushed hard on details over and over, especially any knowledge of atrocities. Later, alone in his hotel room that afternoon, Bauer thought he had held up well. At least he was pleased with how he performed and hoped it was enough to get him to

America and to a new life, free from any crusaders who felt sorry
for the necessary unfinished business with the Jews.

After leaving General Muller, Flynn drove to an apartment near
the lake to meet with the old man. His boss, Alan Forster, looked
like a librarian, gray-haired, open-buttoned sweater, a pair of glasses
down to the tip of his nose, but all that belied the tough, ruthless
way he operated.

They met in the old man's living room, cluttered with folders
and papers as usual. "Well, Tom, what do you think?" Forster asked.

"He's lying," Flynn said. "Especially when talking about the concentration camps and other outrages. His answers are always too
pat. He's a bull-shitter, sir, but a damn good one."

"So, you think he was involved in war crimes?" the old man asked.

Flynn shrugged. "Perhaps, trivial ones. I don't know, but I'm
sure he knows about the worst ones. How could he not?"

"Do you think we can use him, Tom?"

"Absolutely. He's got the background and knowledge to be of
great service," Flynn said, then shook his head regretfully. "Too bad
I couldn't pin him down on his involvement in some real war crime.
That knowledge would be the hammer we need to control him."

The next day, Flynn drove Bauer to the old man's apartment
and left him in the hall. When Bauer knocked, a man in his fifties
opened the door and broke into a wide grin as if greeting an old
friend.

"General Muller, I've been looking forward to meeting you. I've
heard so much about you," he said. "Come in."

The man led him into the living room like a character from a
bad spy novel. Bauer could see through the man's thin veneer. This
was the leader, the man he needed to impress. With blue curtains
on the windows and orange pillows on the couch and chairs, it
looked like a child's room. Watercolors on the wall, desks and tables
and office clutter tables, and the smell of stale cigars. Through the
large window, Bauer caught a glimpse of the lake glimmering in
the morning sun.

"Lovely view, isn't it?" the man said. "Too bad I spend so little time here. I suppose you're wondering what all this is about. We will get to that, I assure you. My name is Alan Forster. Please have a seat."

He left and returned a minute later with a tray bearing a silver pot and two cups, setting it on the coffee table, sitting just across from him. Without asking if Bauer wanted coffee, Forster poured for both.

Unable to hide his eagerness, Bauer placed four teaspoons of sugar into his cup and sipped with almost a sexual satisfaction. "This is excellent. I've had nothing like it for years."

"I know. I know quite a bit about what's been happening in Germany the last few years," Forster said, opening an office folder on the coffee table. He took out the sheaf of papers and studied them a moment. "You speak English well. A bit of an accent but you could smooth that out."

"Thank you, sir."

To Bauer, it was clear the man didn't know who he really was and had no real way to find out unless someone recognized him, and that unlikely. Forster reminded him of Admiral Canaris, the traitorous Abwehr chief, and that's who he suspected he was, someone high up in American intelligence. The military, their diplomatic department, or that spy agency, what was it called, OSS. Or some other part of the government. Perfect. The next war. It would be East versus West, and he needed to display his expertise on the Soviets.

"I see from the screening interview by Mr. Flynn that you have substantial education." Forster leaned back in the chair. "Tell me about that."

Bauer shrugged with forced humility and told him about a doctorate from Heidelberg University in the Biological Sciences and threw in some studies on the Soviets and Communism.

"Why study Communism?"

"I thought they were the true enemy, and someday we would be fighting them."

Bauer thought he caught a hint of skepticism in Forster's eyes and realized he needed to tread more carefully. The man was no fool.

Forster read something on a sheet of paper, then set the entire folder aside, picked up his coffee cup, sipped, and leaned back in his chair. "Tell me about your time on the eastern front."

Bauer did, as usual leaving out his association with the Einsatzgruppen, instead placing himself in Army Group North with a regular Wehrmacht unit. He related stories of combat with the Russians he had been told by others, how ruthless the Russians were and his own passionate hatred for them, and then talked about the winter, the brutal winters. That came across to Forster.

"It is fortunate you survived. Most of your fellow soldiers did not," he said.

"It was more than fortunate. I had a friend in the OKW, the Wehrmacht High Command," Bauer said. "In '43, he reassigned me to Berlin as a staff officer. I was out of that debacle. We should have won it, but the generals failed us."

"Who was the friend who helped you?"

"Obergruppenführer Karl Schneider, commander of the Economic and Administrative Office for OKW. From that day in 1943, I tried with many others to keep the soldiers in the field fed and equipped. I knew from experience how much they depended on their supplies. But because of your bombing, it became an increasingly difficult task. I was there till a month ago when I was reassigned to command a Volkssturm division of boys and old men. That was—how do you say it—the last straw."

"Yes, I should think it was long past time." Forster set his cup down and leaned forward, his elbows on his knees, his sharp blue eyes fixed on Bauer. "Let's get to the chase. Hitler is dead, all your armies are defeated. There is no resistance. The surrender will be signed this Tuesday. I assure you that is a fact. The war is over. Now, the next war begins."

That was cryptic, but Bauer understood him. He was speaking about the real war, the big war. The war against Communism.

"You are right about something," Forster went on. "The Russian bear is our true enemy. You and I should have been fighting Stalin all along. Since the thirties and before, they have been infiltrating American life, every aspect of it, and have not waited till the Nazi surrender to wage this secret war against us once again. All parts of our government are threatened, the State Department particularly, but other agencies as well. They have targeted our financial institutions and the labor unions. They are being well-placed within newspapers and on the airwaves. Worst of all, they have penetrated our education system, especially universities, operating in subtle ways. Under the guise of academic freedom, they peddle their Marxist manifesto."

Bauer kept his face impassive. He no longer cared about wars, not his or theirs, but he did care about keeping the Führer's ideas alive and fighting communism would be part of that.

As his anger grew, Forster's face flushed, and he wagged a finger like a teacher scolding a recalcitrant student. "I have seen the intelligence myself, General Muller. Intercepted communiques, asset reports. We monitor the Soviet embassy day and night. We are now in a race against them to recruit Germans like yourself for this new war."

"I understand, sir. No sane person would want to rid themselves of Hitler just to end up with Stalin."

Forster slapped his knees with conviction. "Exactly. We need fellow warriors in so many fields fighting this battle. In government, journalism, and so many of our institutions, but the true battleground might just be education. If they can control education, they will control our youth, and if they control our youth, they will control the future. We must root them out wherever they are, or the United States will become a satellite of Moscow. You have a PHD in Biological Sciences. With that background, you'd be well-suited to it. If you're interested."

"Sir, this is the war we should have been fighting from the beginning."

CHAPTER TWENTY-SEVEN

At mail call in the lobby of Gasthaus zum Schloss, which the 82nd Airborne had commandeered six days ago, G2 Master Sergeant Bailey called out, "Sergeant Frischer." Turning about as if looking for him, he said, "Does anyone know a Sergeant Pete Frischer?"

"Funny, Sarge," Pete said, snatching the letter from his hand and hurrying down the hall to his room. Skipping morning chow, he could read alone without distractions.

Over the last year and a half since he'd last seen Geraldine, he'd yearned for these letters like a hungry babe for its mother's milk. Sometimes, he went two or three weeks without any, which nearly killed him. He was always sure she had found someone else, and the next one he received would be a Dear John letter. He dreaded that more than a German bullet, but always it was because the mail hadn't caught up with them. Then large packets of them arrived, and he was in his own dreamland for days. Long letters about home he could lose himself in. He unfolded this one and caught a hint of her soft, rose-scented perfume.

My Dearest Pete,

I walked this evening to the Botanic Gardens and sat on the bench by the pond where you proposed. The same silvery moon gazed down, and I felt you were with me. It made me happy and sad at the same time, my dearest. I am very sentimental about it. As I sat there, I dreamed we were already married and had seven children, and though that's a lot of kids, it's the life I want. What a minute!!! That's too many, don't you think? You would have all the fun, and me, I would have all the work bearing our children. It's scandalous to say, but I think I will have fun too.

He laughed and felt a little giddy, mixed in with his desperate longing. He read on and on, five pages of daily life, love for him, plans for the marriage as soon as he returned, and each word dug into his heart. Without Geraldine, he was lonesome in a crowd of soldiers.

On the final page, the tone of the letter shifted. She tried to hide it in some whimsical language, but it was distinctly fearful.

All the radio stations and newspapers are saying the war in Europe is nearly done. It's about time. They say it's only a matter of a few weeks if that. This is not the time to do anything foolish. I want a healthy Pete Frischer coming home to me, not a letter and a medal. Be careful. Be very, very careful.

I miss you so much. I dream of the day you will return, and we can get married.

All my love and kisses,
Your Geraldine

She was always forthright and said what she thought. Of course, she was right more than she could know. Everyone was careful now. No one wanted to be the last K. I. A. When he wrote back after he reread the letter, he'd tell her how careful he was and how he worked at headquarters far from the front, which was true but misleading. Often with his job in G2, he had to venture up to the front to deal with prisoners, and several times even go beyond into enemy territory to capture German soldiers for interrogation. That was anything but safe.

Nor would Pete tell her about the concentration camp.

Four days ago, as part of his job, he had visited the Wobbelin Concentration camp that the 82nd Airborne had liberated the day before. American, British, and Soviet troops have been discovering these death camps all over Europe. He dreaded going, dreaded seeing firsthand the horror done to people like himself, like those he grew up with, but he couldn't stay away.

When he got there, he found the place worse than he'd imagined. There were no gas chambers or crematoriums as in so many other camps, but the dead were here, bodies stacked like kindling around the camp, skeletal people more dead than alive drifting about, lost in some nightmarish world. The Red Cross was there trying to save as many as they could. As Pete interviewed the living in Yiddish about the camp officers and guards, more food and medicine arrived. It was not enough; it would never be enough.

Nor would Pete tell Geraldine he likely would be court martialed.

The same day the camp had been liberated, May 2nd, a German general surrendered the entire Army Group Vistula to the 82nd Airborne. It was not till May 4th that he was sent in with several G2 teams to interrogate the new prisoners. The Germans had given up their weapons, and they looked like what they were, a beaten army, squatting in the vast, green field, guarded by American soldiers. The officers, a couple hundred of them, had been gathered into a separate part of the field for preliminary screenings, and the teams began finding out who they were and what they knew. Like all the team, Pete carried his M1 slung over his shoulder.

While he listened, Major Landry, his team leader, was asking questions in German of a Wehrmacht colonel, a man with graying blond hair, an aquiline nose, and still an air of superiority, the Aryan race. The colonel seemed to be indulging the lowly American major.

"What do you know about Wobbelin," Major Landry asked.

The colonel waved his hand dismissively. "This business with the Jews was none of our affair. We knew nothing of it." He snickered. "You Americans are such sentimentalists. The Jews caused this war. They brought what happened to them on themselves."

Black rage exploded in Pete, and he swung the rifle butt into the man's jaw. A sound of things cracking. Teeth, blood, and spittle flew from the colonel's mouth, and he collapsed to the ground unconscious.

Hours later, Pete learned even Eisenhower had heard about the incident and wanted the offender to pay. The war was not over yet. The General of the Army would not tolerate the surrender be throttled by the uncontrolled actions of one soldier.

No, Pete could not tell Geraldine any of that, but she would know when he returned home with a dishonorable discharge after a substantial vacation in the guardhouse. He would have no future, and the marriage would be called off. If he had it to do over, though, he would have shot the bastard instead.

About to read her letter again, he jumped when someone knocked at the door. Master Sergeant Bailey stuck his head in. "The Old Man wants to see you. Now, Frischer."

Pete folded the letter into the envelope and grabbed his M1. "Gavin?"

"You know any other Old Man?"

He grinned. "Hell, lots of them, Sarge. Every damn officer is my old man."

Bailey gave him a jaundiced look. "Being a smart ass, Frischer, won't help you in a court martial."

Outside, Pete and the master sergeant made their way through the town of Ludwigslust, past the flood of tanks, trucks, jeeps, and foot soldiers, out to the castle where General Gavin had his head-quarters and where both Pete and Bailey worked. The castle loomed several stories above, a giant ornate building that looked to Pete more like a fancy office building, surrounded by sprawling, green lawns and gardens.

Fancifully, Pete hoped Gavin might send him out on some mean-ingless, suicide mission. At least Geraldine and his family could live with that. It was not like Gavin to do meaningless things, but you could never tell in this man's army.

They found the general out back amid the gardens in his combat fatigues with his ever-present M1 slung from his shoulder. Pacing back and forth, he seemed more a sentry than the commanding general of the 82nd Airborne. A newspaper was tucked under his arm.

"Sir, Sergeant Frischer," Master Sergeant Bailey said, saluting him as did Pete.

Gavin returned the salutes. "Thank you, Master Sergeant."

Bailey left, and Pete stood at attention with Gavin eyeing him.

"Relax, Frischer," the commanding officer said and handed him the newspaper.

It was the Stars and Stripes, the army weekly. On the front page were stories of American military pushing into Germany from the west and the south with the 82nd spearheading in the north. The banner story, though, was about the liberation of a concentration camp called Dachau. He looked up questioningly at the general.

"What is not there, Sergeant?"

"I don't know how to answer that, sir."

"I'll tell you what's not there. Anything about some crazy, American army sergeant who nearly killed a Wehrmacht colonel with a rifle butt, and how that colonel now has loose marbles for a jaw. That's not there."

Pete glanced at the paper again. "No, sir, it's not."

"You're Jewish, aren't you, Frischer?"

Pete stiffened. "Yes, sir."

Gavin held his hands up to calm him. "Easy. General Eisenhower wanted your scalp but then after a couple days decided to let me handle it. So, this is an official reprimand, Sergeant. Understand?"

"Yes, sir." Pete didn't know what to think. It was like the weight of a giant boulder slid off his shoulders. He wasn't going to be court-martialed. Not even an Article 15 hearing it seemed.

A hint of a smile appeared on Gavin's face. "Of course, if it were truly up to me, I'd have given you a medal instead. Not shooting the bastard showed remarkable control."

"Yes, sir."

Gavin glanced over toward the field where the German army now squatted more than half a mile away. His face took on a merciless intensity, and he pointed to them. "Today, we are going to bury the dead of Wobbelin in that damn field. We will put crosses on the Christian graves and Stars of David on the Jewish graves. And those bastards are going to dig them and then watch the ceremony along with all the good people of Ludwigslust."

"I know, sir. I plan to be there. The colonel has given us permission."

"Sorry, Sergeant. I have to countermand that order. You should be there, but something has come up I need you to handle." The general took off his helmet liner with the two stars and wiped his beaded forehead with a kerchief, then replaced his liner. "Walk with me, Sergeant."

They ambled easily down a path amid the flowers and hedges, always followed by a security detail a little way back.

"These camps are everywhere," Gavin said. "This Dachau is far worse than Wobbelin. A friend of mine, the correspondent Martha Gellhorn, called me last night, and she couldn't stop talking about what she saw there. She's writing about it, and when she writes about something, people read it."

"Yes, sir. I've heard of her."

"She told me about this other camp the Russians found in the east, a place called Auschwitz, worse than all of them. When the American public reads about what all these Nazi bastards have done, there's going to be hell to pay. Trials. Executions. The works. People are already enraged, and the news is just now getting out. That's why we are interviewing the camp inmates and every damn German soldier we can to build the case against them."

Pete wondered what this was about, why a two-star general was telling him this as if he were a staff officer. But then Gavin did nothing haphazardly.

The general stopped and faced him, hands on hips. "I received a call early this morning from a colonel at a field hospital outside Munich. Members of an all-Nisei unit found three women who had escaped a Dachau camp. One is near death and the two others not much better off. They survived not only Dachau but Auschwitz. How they could have done that I don't know." Gavin stared at Pete several seconds, long enough to make him uncomfortable. "Sergeant, one of them mentioned your name."

"Me?"

"Yes, you. A clerk at Third Army headquarters remembered you from basic training and knew you were in the 82nd. A corporal Smith."

"Smitty, sure, I remember him, sir, but I don't understand. How would she know me?"

"Major Landry tells me you're engaged to be married."

"Yes, sir. When I get home."

"Well, that's a problem. This woman says she's married to Peretz Frischer. That's you unless there's a lot of other Peretz Frischers in this man's army."

Stunned, Pete stepped back, exhaling a long breath.

Gavin said, "If she's married to you, Sergeant, she's an American, even if she's never set foot in the country. Martha Gellhorn is already writing about her, and that will get big play in newspapers across the country. We can't let an American citizen who survived these camps get lost in the millions of refugees already wandering through Europe, especially with Gellhorn watching."

Pete couldn't grasp how this woman could know his name and use it to claim they were married of all things. It seemed bizarre. He was about to tell the general he was not married to anyone…as yet, and he damned well was going to marry Geraldine.

The next words the general said buckled his knees. "Her name is Rivka Resnik. Do you know anyone by that name?"

Pete's vision blurred for a moment, and he stumbled, quickly regaining his balance.

Putting a hand on his shoulder, Gavin steadied him. "Then you do know her?"

"That can't be, sir. Rivka is dead. I was told she was dead. A man I trust saw her shot by the Germans and thrown into a mass grave. Sir, she's dead."

"Maybe so. Still, we must be sure. We must find out what the hell is going on. This could explode in our faces. Go down and find out who she is. Major Landry and Master Sergeant Bailey will go with you to grease the way."

In a fog, Pete nodded.

Gavin pointed a finger at him. "Sergeant Frischer, we are still at war, so don't be careless. Get your ass in gear, son. It's a long way to Munich. Major Landry is waiting for you."

CHAPTER TWENTY-EIGHT

B locked sporadically by American troop movements and check points, it took Pete, Major Landry, and Master Sergeant Bailey two and a half days to go the five hundred miles south to Munich. They had a fourth man with them, 1st Lieutenant Bascom, a JAG officer fresh from the states, sent to help investigate Nazi war crimes. Since all the other 82nd Airborne JAG officers were wrapped up in investigating Wobbelin, this newcomer was sent on the journey south, and he didn't like it.

Rumors had been swirling around the division that as soon as the war ended, the 82nd would be sent to Berlin. To Bascom, that would be the center of the judicial world where the prosecution of Nazi war criminals would take place. As ambitious as he was, he wanted to be a part of it. Now, he was being sent south on a minor case just because one of the women might be an American by marriage while thousands of other bigger cases lay elsewhere.

Bascom had a square face with a pencil thin, black mustache and arrogant pale eyes. His uniform fit perfectly, always looking as if it just came from the dry cleaners. And Master Sergeant Bailey hated him. Since his first day with the 82nd Airborne JAG unit, Bascom had acted as if he were still on a college parade ground, addressing senior NCOs, even G2 NCOs like Bailey, as if they were undergraduates.

"There is nothing so certain or in need of smacking," Bailey said to Pete, "as a fresh faced lieutenant who already knows everything."

On the drive, Bascom in the back seat attempted a couple times to interrogate Pete about this so-called marriage, which Pete avoided answering. He wasn't sure why. Perhaps because the reason the women were receiving treatment at the American field hospital instead of being shipped off to an overcrowded Red Cross camp was the possibility of one of them being his wife. If she, indeed, was American, it would be the JAG officer who needed to interview her.

In that two and a half days on the trip down, the war in Europe ended. On the 8th of May, the German army high command unconditionally surrendered. Around 2100 hours on that day, the three soldiers from the 82nd Airborne stopped for the night with a unit near Augsburg and celebrated the victory. While Bailey was somewhere reveling, Landry and Pete sat in folding chairs outside their tent, drinking German beer. Bascom was in the tent trying to sleep.

From somewhere in the camp, the sound of cheering drifted to them, Master Sergeant Bailey, no doubt in the middle of it. Pete and Landry clinked bottles. The night was hot. Relaxed, both men wore their uniform shirts out and unbuttoned, their long legs stretched out.

"With the war over now, I'm ready to go home, sir," Pete said.

"Forget it, soldier boy." Landry chuckled. "You ain't going home anytime soon, and neither am I. Our mission is just going to change."

Pete sighed. "The Russians."

"Damn right, the Russians. We still have work to do with the Germans and war crimes yet, but the Russians will be our main focus from now on." Landry rubbed his red hair and fixed his glance on Pete. "While we're in Munich, Gavin wants us to continue the work for JAG, gathering evidence of war crimes. Kind of obvious with Bascom along."

"I figured as much."

With the horrors found in so many liberated concentration camps, G2 had been tasked by the Judge Advocate General Europe to help investigate violations of the Geneva Convention, especially those camps that held American servicemen and women, and to build files on the Nazis who ran them.

"Thing is," Landry said, "Bascom being the JAG lawyer has lead in the investigation. Once we get your situation straightened out, Pete, we will be interviewing all three women. Whoever they are, they were in the camps. The commanding officer at the field hospital says they even have numbers tattooed on their arms. Can you believe that shit? The bastards even numbered them, as if they're not people but furniture."

Inside him, Pete felt anger stir and grow like an expanding embryo. He took a swallow of his beer. "Seeing Wobbelin, I can believe anything."

The next morning, after filling up the jeep's gas tank, the four soldiers started out on the last short leg of the trip to Munich with Pete driving and Master Sergeant Bailey holding his head in agony beside him. Bailey nursed a massive hangover. From the back, with an edge of amusement, Landry warned the Master Sergeant not to fall out of the jeep.

At the wheel, Pete glanced at Bailey, afraid he would actually fall out, then grabbed his shoulder to steady him as he veered the jeep to avoid a bomb crater. There were several along this stretch of road, and he slowed down to navigate past them. Just off in the field were at least fifteen destroyed Wehrmacht half-tracks, trucks, and command cars. A few ragged kids wandered among them, no doubt searching for food or anything to barter. With the devastation he'd seen all over Europe, it was going to be that kind of post war for a long time. The children stared at the passing jeep.

As they neared Munich, the thought of meeting the woman who maintained she was his Rivka began knotting at his insides. Incensed about it, he still wondered who she was. She had somehow survived those hellish camps, so he could not go after her for lying the way he would like to. Still, he was certain she wasn't who she claimed to be, but he didn't have any idea who she was or how she had latched onto his name.

He remembered the real Rivka, how she could be so shy one moment and so bold the next, ready to take on any challenge, almost obsessively. Not almost, he grinned. The girl had been obsessive about what she wanted and loved in life. She cherished her friends yet loved being alone in the forests. She always tried to get him to walk with her on its shadowed paths. Every winter, they skied through the woods together or with the Young Guardians, talking about the world, and their little part of it, laughing and thinking life could not be this good to them.

Pete remembered the summer when Rivka was ten, and she pleaded with him to help repair his roof, which had been leaking. His father had gone to America a couple years before, so Pete had taken on his role around the house. The roof's height didn't bother Rivka, and she worked so hard and intently he didn't have the heart to tell her she had made a mess of it, and the roof still leaked where she had put down shingles. He had thanked her profusely, and she beamed. That night, he'd climbed up and redid her work.

And he remembered how Rivka loved music, always singing or humming something. One late summer night, unable to sleep, he gazed out his window and saw her at the other end of the block, up in that little turret on their house, swaying gently to the rhythmic sounds of the klezmer band from somewhere in town.

Tears welling in his eyes, he wiped them away, hoping no one saw. Pete remembered those days, and also remembered Rivka was no more.

A little after 0930 hours, they reached the field hospital on the outskirts of Munich, a small city of tents with big red crosses against white backgrounds on the top. Doctors and nurses and a few patients could be seen moving along the grassy streets. A soldier on crutches directed Pete to headquarters where the commanding officer Lieutenant Colonel Granger greeted them.

"I've been expecting you gentleman," he said, coming out from behind his desk and shaking hands with all of them. He was a balding man wearing a white medical coat with steel-rimmed glasses on a black ribbon hanging from his neck. He gestured to cloth folding chairs. "Please, sit down."

"We'd like to see the woman as soon as possible, Colonel," Bascom said, "so we can clear this up and get started with the interviews."

Granger leaned back against his desk and congenially smiled at Bascom. "Patience, Lieutenant. You'll get there soon enough. Before you talk with these women and the other survivors, you'll need to know what you're facing with them. Oh, yes, we have nearly forty other survivors here. Our soldiers find them in more and more numbers wandering the meadows and forests, dying, no place to go, all of them graduates of the Dachau camps. We do our best with them, but we've lost a couple. I suppose you'll want to interview them as well."

"Yes, sir," Landry said.

"We will set that up for you. Of the women you came here to see, the fact that one was possibly an American allowed us to keep all three long term to treat. Otherwise, we'd stabilize them and then move them on to Dachau for further care like with the others."

"Dachau?" Landry said, shocked.

"Yes, where else are they going to go? Right now, they are the places where survivors receive food and medical care. Same at all the other camps."

Bailey whistled, shaking his head. "I always knew this war was fucked up."

"More than you know, Sergeant," Granger said. "We were completely unprepared for what we found at the camps. You know of Bergen-Belsen? The British had to deal with a full-blown typhus epidemic and a camp population of more than 60,000 suffering from starvation. They took what seemed like the most appropriate action, eventually handled the typhus, but for the starvation, what they did was disastrous."

Pete knew what the British did wrong, and it was tragic. And the woman he came to see had been through things like that. Though he knew she was not Rivka, he felt a deep sadness for what she must have gone through.

Lt. Col. Granger's hands closed and opened; the face took on an infinitely sad expression. "The British brought in food and let them eat, the worst thing they could have done, but they didn't know. After long term hunger, the prisoners' bodies could not handle such rich and abundant food. Thousands died. The American military learned that lesson and applied it to Dachau as we did to our patients here and your three women."

"Will they be able to talk with us, sir?" Bailey asked.

"They can talk to you. Question is will they? Physically, they are improving, but like all survivors of Nazi madness they have deep psychological problems. They show signs of paranoia and bursts of sudden anger. Like so many survivors, these women carry a deep thirst for revenge, and as far as I'm concerned, they are entitled to it. We have been treating several German prisoners here. Your Rivka and the Greek woman Eleni tried to talk the cook into poisoning their food."

Bascom gave a snicker. "I guess it's an understandable joke."

"Oh, they weren't joking."

They all fell silent for several seconds, then Granger grabbed his garrison cap off his desk. "Follow me, gentleman. Sergeant Frischer, let's go greet your wife."

Wincing at the word *wife*, Pete joined the others hurrying after the colonel who led them out and down a grassy street to a smaller tent just as an attractive woman in a uniform with lieutenant bars stepped out. She didn't salute, and the colonel didn't seem to expect one. "These men have come to see our patients."

"They the ones?" she said.

"They are." The colonel indicated Pete. "This man is Peretz Frischer."

The nurse eyed him as if he'd constructed the concentration camps himself. "They're not here," she said. "The nun is with Chaplain Henning, and the other two women are taking their morning walk. They need exercise, but at least those two are coming along. Still, you won't be able to send Rivka back to America for a few weeks. They no longer have typhus, but that and the malnutrition took its toll on their bodies. Rivka's not up to it yet."

Back to America, Pete thought. She'd never been to America. How could she be going back? These doctors and nurses were assuming the woman was telling the truth. They didn't know that Rivka had been murdered four years ago by the Nazis.

The lieutenant rubbed her forehead. "They'll be back shortly. They can't walk that far yet, but each day they're adding a little distance."

"I think this is them now." Lt. Col. Granger nodded down a side street.

Pete's head snapped around. Two women were approaching wearing US army fatigues that draped off their emaciated bodies like from a coat rack, their hair short as his own. He felt a quickness in his chest as he studied them for several seconds, finally exhaling almost in relief. This ordeal was settled and over. Neither of them was Rivka.

Landry glanced at him, and he shook his head.

But then, not ten yards away, one of them stopped, frozen in place, and stared at him. The other woman looked back at her and said something. Moments later, the first woman strode forward, halting abruptly a couple steps away as if slapped.

For a few seconds, no one spoke, then she said in Yiddish with a voice that broke at the end, "You don't remember me, Peretz?"

He blinked and shook his head. She knew his name. It could not be. He said more forcefully than he intended, "Yankl saw Rivka killed. He saw her buried."

Her eyes widened with shock. "Yankl? He's alive? He escaped?"

Looking at her quizzically, Pete nodded.

She held her fist up at him. With a twisted grin that was somehow familiar, she proclaimed, "Wheat! It must be wheat!" Her chuckle was more a cough.

What the hell was she saying? *Wheat?* Then that night four years ago roared back, striking him like a mine exploding under his jeep. That night when he walked her home after the Young Guardian's meeting, and they talked of Yankl. *Oh, God.*

His hands trembling, he whispered, "Rivka."

Tears in her eyes, she stepped into his arms. "Peretz."

CHAPTER TWENTY-NINE

Pete couldn't talk with Rivka alone till after the women agreed to be interviewed, which they would not do without Sister Agneta. But the nun arrived moments later, being pushed in a wheelchair by a chaplain introduced as Father Henning. She wore a habit and a cross dangling from a rope chain about her neck. Pete noticed she couldn't be more than thirty. When she rose to greet them, everyone quickly insisted she shouldn't stand, but she shooed them aside.

Meeting Pete's eyes, she said, "You've come for our Rivka. I'm so glad. You must do what you can for her."

He nodded. "I will."

"Then since you are here to interview us, we have much to tell."

That was all there was to it—she had agreed for all three, but to Pete, it seemed she had just struck a bargain with him. Agree to allow the marriage falsehood, and they will talk of the camps. Father Henning helped her back into the wheelchair and rolled her into the women's tent.

Walking silently with Rivka into the grassy meadow next to the hospital, Pete was overwhelmed with the miracle of her survival. He couldn't believe she was walking beside him. His mind fell into a quagmire of emotions; she was here, safe for now, and telling people they were married. He loved Geraldine, and maybe he loved Rivka, too. What would happen to her if he told the truth? Would she be sent to Dachau, and then from there to where? How could he do that to her? But how could he break Geraldine's heart? He didn't know what to tell Rivka about her, but he would have to. He sighed. How could something so good feel so bad?

"You look like you lost your best friend instead of finding her," she said as they meandered along a creek.

He watched the water rolling over rocks painted orange and yellow with lichens. "Just a little overwhelmed by it all. By what happened to you."

Even after two weeks in the field hospital, she still looked little more than a skeleton, her bones standing out stark on her face and shoulders.

"Dr. Granger said you had typhus," he said.

"We all did," she said.

She told him matter-of-factly of being bathed like a child since she was so weak, given injections, pills, her dry skin rubbed with oil daily, and fed milk several times a day. Liquid ran through her bowels, but eventually she got better.

"They even gave us black coffee, strong coffee, real coffee," she said with a tremor in her voice. "It has been years since I had any good coffee like that." She fell silent for several seconds, bent over and snatched up a flower, then said, "I cried when they brought me the first cup. Something inside me snapped loose, I think. I cried so much they thought I was having a seizure, till Dr. Granger just told the nurses to let me cry it out."

"That must have been a great cup of coffee," he said, trying to ease the hurt in her.

After a second, she smiled, then chuckled. "It was."

She picked at the flower petals. Pete had so much he wanted to ask her about what she endured, but this wasn't the time. It would have to be done coldly at the interviews. Instead, after so many years apart, they walked on in silence for about five minutes like awkward school kids. He could not help but be aware of the irony of it, so much to talk about but no one saying a word.

Finally, she asked, "How is your family? I haven't seen them in so long."

He told her about how successful his father and uncle were with the clothing business, how his mother had taken to life in Brooklyn, playing Mahjong with her friends and organizing community charities. He told Rivka that his brothers and sisters had grown so much she wouldn't recognize them.

"I probably wouldn't."

"Here, I'm boring you with this. We can look at…"

"No, I like hearing about normal things." She hesitated. "Peretz, I wonder if…"

"Please, call me Pete. That's what I go by now."

"Pete. All right. I'll call you Pete then." She shook her head as if trying to get used to a pervasive bad smell. "Pete, tell me about your family, about your life now."

So he went on talking about letters from home and the warm spring they were having in Brooklyn. He told her how Yankl had made his way to America working as a seaman.

She threw back her head and laughed. "Yankl a seaman. Oh God."

He laughed with her, noticing the warmth did not make it to her eyes. Something in her held back, yet clearly, she was starved for love. He sensed it as much as if she'd said it plain. He placed an arm around her shoulders, and she leaned into him as they walked. He did not think of himself as a coward. He'd gone behind enemy lines enough to prove that, yet here he hesitated telling her about Geraldine. How would she take that? She'd been through so much, he didn't want to lay more on her. But that was just excuses.

"I'm engaged," Pete said abruptly, finally getting it out. "Her name's Geraldine."

Her reaction surprised him. Nothing. She kept walking, staring impassively ahead. "Congratulations."

He didn't know what to make of that and felt uneasy about it. This was Rivka, but he didn't know her at all. He wondered if there was anything of the girl he once knew left of her. There followed another long silence till, to make conversation, he said, "I've been talking so much about myself. What about you, Rivka?"

She gave a harsh bark. "My last four years have not been quite so normal as yours."

Instantly, he felt guilty, not just for asking the question but escaping Nashok, escaping the horror that became Europe.

Stopping by the water, she glanced over at him with a penetrating and not very friendly gaze. He'd never seen such hostility coming from her before. Why was she so angry at him all of a sudden? But before he could step in and take her in his arms, the fire slid out of her eyes, and she dropped the flower in the creek, her hostility gone as quickly as it had come. He'd never seen anything like it. A slight breeze shifted her dark hair, which was so short he could see her scalp in the flutterings. His heart broke for her.

Still, Pete needed to ask her one question and now was the best time. "Rivka, I have to ask why you said we were married."

Shaking, she turned on him with intensity. "I had to, don't you see? There was no other way. I had to get to you. Everyone I loved was dead, except you. I was alone in the world and about to die like a cow to the slaughter. All those years in hell, and they were hell, you were all I had. Getting to you, my dearest friend. The boy I had always wanted to marry. I thought you were in America. I thought if I told them you and I were married they'd send me to you." Turning to him with a rueful grimace, she lifted her hands in an exaggerated shrug. "But they sent you to me."

He took her in his arms and felt her trembling.

In the afternoon, Lt. Col. Granger provided a small tent in which to interview the women and set out plenty of coffee and what was left of a small loaf of German black bread he'd bought in Munich yesterday. He cut a slice off it as Landry placed canvas chairs around the table so, he said, it would not seem like an inquisition. The G2 men and the JAG officer took their seats, while Granger surprised them by also sitting down.

"Don't worry," he said, holding up his hand. "I won't ask any questions. I want to observe. They're still my patients, and they're not healthy."

Bascom said to the corpsman at the tent entrance. "Bring in the first one, Corporal."

He left and returned in moments with Eleni. She took the chair beside Granger. While Bascom began telling her the purpose of this interview, she poured coffee into a metal cup, throwing in several teaspoons of sugar and snatching up a slice of the black bread. She stared at the rest of the bread, picked all of it up, and stuffed it into her shirt pockets as the men watched.

She held up the slice in her hand. "They gave us this bread. Small piece. It's made of..." She glanced at them. "Wood dust?"

"Sawdust," Bascom corrected.

"Yes, wheat and sawdust."

As she ate the bread, the tall Greek began speaking in her halting English. When Bascom interrupted and tried to ask a question, she ignored him, talking on. She told of the summer of 1943 in Thessalonica, Greece when the Germans began transporting the large Jewish community in boxcars to Auschwitz. Many died on the way. Most of the rest were gassed to death the day they arrived.

With tight-jawed intensity, she told of a hell that lasted nearly two years, of horrendous incident after the other, of little food, of constant selections of prisoners for the gas chamber. Right from the beginning though, Pete saw Bascom didn't believe her story. By the minute, the skepticism grew on his face. She'd clearly been through hell. Her appearance showed that much, but the stories she told were so monstrous, so barbaric that he could understand Bascom's disbelief. Everyone felt that way hearing such things secondhand. He had before he saw Wobbelin and the stacked bodies.

She told of four or five days she spent in a standing cell without food or water, unable to sit or lay down. She jumped to her feet and gestured to describe the size. No more than a foot square, they held prisoners not shot outright for minor infractions. Bascom shook his head. That was too much for him to believe.

Then, she told them the story of Helena's baby. With a snort, Bascom scoffed at that but said nothing. It was too inhuman even for the SS. It had to be made up.

After an hour, she began to tire, and Lt. Col. Granger stopped the interview. "Eleni needs to rest. If you have more questions, you can speak with her tomorrow if she's willing."

He rose and escorted her to the corpsman at the open tent entrance. She stopped and turned back. Her eyes burned. "Will you find bastards? Kill them?"

Landry nodded. "I promise you, Eleni. We will hunt them down."

Pete looked at his notes where he'd jotted down the names of the worst of the Nazis she'd mentioned. They included two women named Mandel and Volkenrath, a doctor named Mengele, and an SS officer named Bauer.

Bascom drummed his notepad with his pencil. "I'm sure she's been through quite a bit. I haven't been to that Wobbelin camp, but I've heard the stories. Quite a bit of starvation there obviously. But I can't build any kind of case with such obviously outlandish and exaggerated claims. I can't. The JAG will laugh me out of his office and toss my notes in the circular file."

Granger turned to him. "You and I will drive up to Dachau tomorrow."

"Sir, I'm not sure…"

Granger tapped his finger on the tabletop. "I'm trying to keep you from making a complete ass of yourself, Lieutenant, and ruining your career before it begins. I go there two or three times a week. I've seen the standing cells. All the camps have them. You will go tomorrow, Lieutenant."

"Yes, sir," Bascom said.

At that moment, the corpsman pushed Sister Agneta and her wheelchair in. Though she spoke rudimentary English, she communicated with them in Polish through Pete interpreting. When they asked her prompting questions, she relayed pretty much the same thing as Eleni. Bascom shook his head again but this time with a frown. She could only manage a half hour then Granger insisted she be taken back to her ward.

When she left, Bascom said, "An exaggeration is not a lie if it is believed."

Pete had to admit that was a reasonable point, but he knew the tales to be true even if they were unbelievable. What surprised him most was that Sister Agneta knew Rivka before Auschwitz. She said after hiding at the convent, Rivka had left to join the partisans. She had taken up arms. She had fought.

"Sir, the last one is here," the corpsman said.

He stepped aside, and Rivka walked in, her short, dark hair framing the intensity on her face.

CHAPTER THIRTY

An hour later, Rivka left the interview tent. Lightheaded, Pete felt as if his blood were rushing at great speed. His eyes glistened and he closed them, trying to keep the horrific images from flashing through his head. That such things happened to her, his closest friend, and to Mila, the cousin he loved so much, and to his aunts and uncles, overwhelmed him.

Lt. Col. Granger rose. "I have other patients to see."

Pete opened his eyes and exhaled a long breath. Soldiers were rolling up the tent walls, allowing a breeze to cut at the afternoon heat. At the other end of the table, Master Sergeant Bailey and the two officers huddled together, going over the list of Nazis involved in the atrocities they'd compiled from the three women. Rivka had identified Max Bauer as not only being at Auschwitz, but also responsible for something called the Einsatzgruppen, Murder Squads who had slaughtered the Jews of Nashok.

Bauer had buried Rivka alive with the thousands of dead, including her mother and sister. And Rivka had crawled out of the grave. Tears filled Pete's eyes, and he turned away from the officers, suppressing his own urge to run out and kill every German POW himself. Bascom still found it all unbelievable, which it was, even though Pete knew it to be true, but the lieutenant had enough sense to keep his mouth shut for the time being.

Amazingly, Pete thought, Rivka had been a partisan, his wouldn't-hurt-a-spider Rivka, and not even the youngest among them. She was blowing up bridges, attacking German patrols, and disrupting supplies while he was sitting in high school classes ogling Geraldine. Two years of it. About her time working just with this Sergeant Sokolov, she would say little.

"Blow up things. Keep the Germans busy. That's all," she said, clearly being evasive.

Pete would not be the one to press her on more detail though, and no one else did. Then, she talked of Auschwitz and Kaufering. The same as Eleni and Sister Agneta, even to the unspeakable horror of Helena's baby.

This Rivka, who sat through the hour interview by the JAG and G2 officers, was far different than the one he had known. Not intimidated by them at all, even angry at times, perhaps paranoid as well like the doctor said, not trusting them. After what she'd been through, how could she not be changed?

Once, when Landry had mentioned how the bombing of Germany had stopped on May 8th, the day of surrender, her temper exploded, and she shouted at them that the allies must bomb every German city to rubble.

Another time, Bascom explained how the JAG Corps would bring the offenders to justice, and she laughed at him. Her eyes flashed hatred so pure it made Pete sit back as if punched. "They will escape. And those you do catch will be given a pat on the back for killing Jews. Bomb them. Shoot them on sight. That's justice."

Pete and the other Americans had fallen silent for seconds following her tirade.

After Rivka left, the question remained for Pete, as it had been since General Gavin first brought all this up. What should he do about this marriage business? He wanted to marry Geraldine, yet the only way to get Rivka to the states was to say they were married. He knew the answer. He had known it the moment he realized the woman was actually Rivka.

"Major Landry," he said.

Landry looked up from the notepad he and Bascom were studying. "Yes, Sergeant."

"Sir, Rivka is my wife. How do I get her to America?"

Landry set the notepad down. "I've already spoken to Colonel Granger about it. We'll take care of the paperwork, and when she's healthy, he can send her to America with a hospital ship transporting patients."

"Wait a minute," Bascom said, eyeing Pete with suspicion. "Do you have documents showing you're married to this woman?"

"Of course, sir. They're in Nashok."

"Which with the Reds in Lithuania, we will have no access to in our lifetimes."

Pete shrugged.

In the next few days, paperwork was established for all three women, letters from General Gavin claiming Greek citizenship for Eleni, Polish for Agneta, and US for Rivka through marriage to one of his soldiers. According to Granger, it would not be for another month before any of the three would be healthy enough to travel.

Pete, Bailey, and the two officers spent several days at Dachau with Granger and volunteers from the field hospital, joining in with other medical teams and JAG investigators thankful for the help. Amid the overwhelming evidence on Nazi atrocities, Bascom quickly came around and became a passionate advocate for prosecuting even the lowliest guards. Finally, after a week in southern Germany, Pete and the others received orders to return to the 82nd.

The next morning, he and Rivka walked very slowly from the mess hall toward headquarters and the jeep, letting the other three men get far ahead. He held her hand. They were silent. Her face appeared drawn, but she smiled as hints of calm softened her expression, perhaps because she was safe, she was going to America.

"Should I count your steps till you speak?" she said with a playful smile.

He chuckled. "I don't think I'll be able to see you again till I get home to the states, and that may be a long time."

"Then it will be a long time," she said. "And when you return, you will have your marriage."

He wasn't sure whether he detected a hint of bitterness or not. Nor who she meant as the one he would be married to. He didn't know either how Geraldine would take this situation and if he could indeed marry her with Rivka supposedly his wife. "When Lt. Col. Granger assigns you to a hospital ship going to New York, he'll call me and give me the details. I'll write Papa, and he will pick you up at the docks. I've already written them about you, so they'll be looking for the letter."

"I know what you're risking for me, Peretz. I mean Pete. I know, and I'm grateful."

"When you dock, you will not go through any big immigration process. The hospital ship will have only American citizens on it, and you'll be one of them." He handed her a piece of paper and twenty American dollars. "Here. This is my address in Brooklyn, in Crown Heights. My letter home may not get there in time so nobody will be there to meet you. You'll have to take a taxi."

"What did you write them about me?"

"Only that you had been in the camps, and that you had a rough time of it. Nothing else. What you tell people is up to you, but they do know what Yankl told us."

They had reached the jeep, and the other men were waiting. She placed her arms around his neck and slid into his embrace. "Thank you, Pete," she whispered. They stood holding each other for nearly thirty seconds, then she released him.

He kissed her cheek. "I'll see you in the states." Then ran to the jeep and climbed into the driver's seat.

"My God, Frischer," Master Sergeant Bailey said. "Is that the way you kiss your wife goodbye? You need to work on your technique, son. It's terrible. The 82nd has its standards to maintain."

They drove off, and as they left the tent city, Pete glanced in his rearview mirror to see Rivka still standing by headquarters watching them.

A month later, Lt. Col. Granger told me he'd put me on a hospital ship to America set to depart Cherbourg, France on June 20th. I would accompany a small contingent of soldiers from the field hospital on their way home to continue their recovery. Eleni, Sister Agneta, and I had regained enough of our strength that it was time for us to leave. The parting was difficult.

Eleni was the first to go. She was walking to Greece. "I am Greek," she told us. "But I am a Jew. I need to find if there is anything left for me at home."

The doctors, nurses, and medics came up with a combat pack for her, stuffed with food and clothes. Nearly forty of them accompanied us to the edge of camp to say goodbye. Sister Agneta and I hugged her with tears in our eyes.

"We three are survivors," Eleni said. "You come to Greece, find me in Athens, not Thessalonica. We drink ouzo."

She stuffed her documents into one of the ruck's pockets and hefted it onto her back. As she strode from camp, she waved to the medical staff, and they applauded her, shouting, "Good luck."

Two days later, it was Sister Agneta's turn to leave. Again, I wept as we hugged. Even more of the camp people turned out for her. They thought her something of a saint. When Eleni and I had gotten her finally on her feet and walking with us, many of the wounded and staff would approach her for her blessing. She would place a hand on them and tell them, "God is always with you."

"I will write to you in New York when I am settled," she said. "I don't know how the mail will be."

Chaplain Henning waited for her in a jeep. He would drive her into Munich to the Archdiocese, where she would be moved along an underground Catholic network into Poland and eventually to Warsaw.

"If you see any of the others, let me know," I said.

She nodded, understanding what I meant. "I will always pray for you, Rivka."

We embraced again, then she was gone.

The two women I had survived hell with were gone. For a moment, when dust settled from the jeep and it had disappeared beyond the trees, it felt like Sister Agneta had died. Like she and Eleni had died. We had survived together, supported each other through all that horror, and now they were gone. I felt dead inside.

The next day, several army ambulances drove sixteen recovering soldiers, two white uniformed nurses, an army doctor, and me to an aerodrome in Munich. From there, we were airlifted to Paris, stayed in the 1st General hospital for a day, and then flown to the embarkation hospital at Cherbourg.

On June 22nd, we boarded the white ship, and that afternoon set off for America.

PART THREE: BROOKLYN

CHAPTER THIRTY-ONE

On a hot summer day, the white hospital ship slipped up the channel into New York. I stood with the others on deck, the walking wounded as they called themselves, all of them New Yorkers who would be released from their military service once healed. Everywhere ahead, I saw the massive city with great towers of stone and glass glittering in the afternoon sun, inhabited by countless millions. Against the gusty wind, I wore but a simple black skirt and white, short-sleeved blouse provided by a German hausfrau that Lt. Col. Granger had persuaded to donate.

As we slid past the Statue of Liberty, a wild cheer rose from the uniformed men and nurses on deck. Two months ago, my head was bald, but now my hair had grown a couple inches, enough to fluff into a boyish look that was popular among some of the nurses. One had told me, after working twelve hours trying to keep soldiers alive that they didn't have time to take care of long hair. In my hand, I held tight to a small suitcase containing two more dresses from this same hausfrau, along with toiletries given to me at the field hospital.

As some of the men passed by, they glanced at me, nodding a greeting. They knew I had been in the camps, and by now everyone knew what they were. Places where people starved and died. They were men of war, and I supposed they felt a kinship with someone who had known a different kind of terror. To avoid their eyes, I moved in against the rail.

The ship drew near a massive building on the wharf. My nerves jittery, I asked myself if anyone would be waiting for me. Then, when we cozied up to the dock, I saw a row of green lorries with red crosses lined up waiting and felt a rush of dread. My knees buckled and I lurched against the rail as a memory flooded back of that night a year ago when I arrived at Auschwitz and the Red Cross lorries there hauled people to the gas chambers.

Someone placed a hand on my forearm, steadying me. "Easy, young lady. Are you okay?" A handsome captain in a wheelchair smiled up at me. Under the blanket on his lap, he had no legs. A corpsman stood behind the chair.

"I'm fine. Thank you, Captain."

These trucks couldn't be doing the same thing as at Auschwitz. I saw no buildings with smoke lifting from chimneys night and day. They couldn't possibly. Still, I would not be getting in one.

Looking up at me, the captain grinned. "It's great to be back in the good old U. S. of A."

I placed a hand on his shoulder. "Yes, it's great, Captain."

It was time to disembark, to step onto the soil of America, as people soon made their way down the many gangways. MPs stood at the entrance to a hangar-like structure on the wharf. I wondered if they would allow me in their country. If the documents I had, simple letters from General Gavin and Lt. Col. Granger, didn't hold up, would they send me back to Europe? In the end, it didn't matter. The term being used these days was "displaced person." That was me. Someone had misplaced me. I had no home, only one perhaps someday to find. On the edge of the pit, Mama had said *to live*. That had been branded into my heart much deeper than the tattoo numbers on my arm. Because of that, I would live.

Inside the great hall on the wharf where the ship was docking, Mina Frischer stood with her husband Isaac and her brother-in-law Morris waiting for Rivka among several hundred other people anticipating their own loved ones to come home. She, like Isaac and Morris, had sat by the radio listening in anguish to Edward R. Morrow talk of what he found at a place called Buchenwald. From the tremor in his voice, the unbelievable horror of it had shaken the CBS man to his core. And she had read the recent article in *Collier's* by Martha Gellhorn about another of those camps called Dachau. What they had done to the Jews in them. Not even the Christian Hell could match it. It was remarkable that anyone survived. Somehow, Rivka had survived.

It had all been too much for Mina. She walked out of the living room whenever one of those ghastly stories out of Europe came on the radio and hustled the twins out as well, making sure they never listened to such real life horror.

At the harbor, she finished her coffee that Morris had gotten them from the nearby USO counter and tossed the cup in a trash receptacle. Fidgeting, she now had nothing to do with her hands and stuck them in her dress pockets, balling her fists. The men were sweating in their suits. With so many people, it was like a sauna in the building. Through the big windows at the far end, she saw the white ship docking.

Isaac wiped the sweat from his forehead with a handkerchief. "What if we don't recognize her?" he asked for the third time since they arrived an hour ago. "We haven't seen her in years. What if she doesn't recognize us?"

"I will recognize her," Mina said with conviction.

I waited till toward the end to disembark, till after the Red Cross lorries had loaded up with stretchered patients and departed, till after the walking wounded had stepped down the gangway and into the building, then I followed them. I desperately wanted someone to be there. Someone to be waiting for me. Inside, the pleasant smell of salt water changed to one of sweaty bodies while a loud clatter of talk and shouts of names filled the cavernous structure. At the end of the hall, hundreds of soldiers were meshing with the hundreds waiting for them. Everywhere, people embraced and screamed with joy. No one was checking papers. We were all Americans just coming home.

Slowly, I moved through them, searching for anyone who might be waiting for me. When Lt. Col. Granger received the details of the ship's arrival in New York, he had notified Pete, who presumably wrote home to his parents. I remembered Mina, his mother, better than his father, Isaac. At least, I thought I would recognize her if she were here. There were hundreds of people, and I saw no one I knew or anyone who looked familiar. Holding my little suitcase, I stood alone at a Red Cross station where young women were passing out small containers of milk. I imagined myself floating above everyone, gravity suspended, looking for ghosts. A displaced person again.

I am lost, I am lost.

I went on searching.

Toward the back, near where smiling girls were serving coffee at a USO counter, I saw them, and my heart burst. At least I thought it was them, two men and a woman. The woman had to be Mina, standing elegantly and erect as if she were an ancient Hebrew queen. She'd always had that bearing. At first, people thought her aloof, but her demeanor hid a truly gentle and kind person. The two men were smartly dressed in tailored gray suits with black ties and fedoras on their heads. One of them had to be Isaac and the other Moishe, Mila's father, but I couldn't tell which was which.

From fifteen feet off to the side, I stood watching them for a minute or two, then Mina glanced over, stared for a moment and broke into a smile. She strode to me and took me in her arms, whispering, "Bargrisung heym, Rivka. Welcome home."

When she released me, Isaac placed his hands on my shoulders and in a strained voice said, "It is so good to see you again, Rivka."

Beside him, Moishe stood transfixed, staring at me, at first fiercely. Then his eyes watered, and I knew what was in his mind. I had climbed out of the grave that still held his wife and all his children. Abruptly, I embraced him, and for a moment, he placed his head on my shoulder. The sound coming softly from him was an animal groan of pain.

Even though the windows were rolled down inside the car, it felt like an oven as we alternately sped and crept along the crowded streets. Smoking a cigarette, Isaac drove with Moishe, smoking also, in the front seat, Mina in the back beside me, her arm through mine, holding me close.

"Nothing is hot like July New York," Mina said, speaking English now. "Except August New York." She had a distinct accent like Moishe and Isaac, but her English was good. "We speak English in our house as much as we can," she explained as if I'd just asked her about it. "The twins Ellie and Daniel hardly speak Yiddish at all."

Remembering the twins only as dark haired seven-year-olds, I wondered if not teaching them Yiddish was a good thing, but then it was not my place. We were passing through an alien landscape of tall buildings, fancy cars herding through the streets, hordes of people rushing along the sidewalks, all of it accompanied by terrible sounds like a thousand trains screeching on iron rails. Nothing like the quaint, old buildings of Vilna and the unhurried pace of life, that was till the Nazis marched in, and it became a corner of hell.

Mina held me tighter. "You probably want to rest after your long journey. I should warn you though, we have someone waiting at home for you."

"Yankl."

"Yes, of course," she said with a humorous glint in her eyes. "Shpilkes. That's our Yankl. Since he learned you were coming, he's been so excited he couldn't keep still. He was always at our place talking about it. We couldn't take him along, though he pleaded with us. He would have driven us crazy." She squeezed my elbow. "And the children. They remember you and look forward to seeing you. I hope you don't mind, Rivka."

I sighed inwardly, but said, "No, of course not, Aunt Mina."

I did feel a surge of anticipation at seeing Yankl again. He understood. He was the only one who could know me, and I him. He had been there in Nashok through it all. I remembered that last glance he gave me when the men were marched away to their deaths. I didn't understand then what that glance meant, but he had held it for such a long time before he was pushed on with the other men by Bauer's Nazi henchmen and Karnowski's Polish police.

Aunt Mina was telling me something about the children, but I wasn't listening. I nodded, then stared out the window again, hoping she would stop talking like she had to fill every silent moment, or I would fall apart. The streets went by, each the same, block after block.

When we crossed over a long suspension bridge, Moishe glanced back at me. "This is Brooklyn. It's a good place. A safe place. You'll thrive here."

"I'm sure I will, Uncle Moishe," I said. I wasn't sure at all.

"Moishe is from another time. Please, call me Morris," he said, his eyes almost begging me. I would have to tell him about Mila, and what a wonderful girl she was. It might be painful for him, but he had to know.

Eventually, we turned onto a street flanked by rows of three-story attached houses Aunt Mina called Brownstones, whatever that was. Several boys and a couple girls were playing a game in the street with a stick and ball. They scattered for the car to pass as a couple of the boys chased after us. We pulled to the curb in front of a set of steps up to one brownstone with bay windows. Partway up the block, several women stood at a vegetable seller's cart. They all stopped to watch as if the market day fire eater had just arrived.

As the others got out of the car, the three children surrounded them. One of the women at the vegetable stand, who turned out to be a young teenager, hurried to join us. She was pretty with curly, brown hair flanking a face slightly on the chubby side. I slid across the back seat, climbed out, and stood facing them. For several seconds, everyone stared at me, and I thought I should sing and dance like a gypsy.

The teenage girl took my hand. "Hi, Rivka, remember me?"

I didn't at first, and her face fell, but then it came to me. "Tikva, of course, I do."

"It's Teresa now."

"I promise to tell you how I once was a Catholic nun called Sister Teresa."

She beamed. "We're going to be sharing a room. I hope you don't mind."

"No. I look forward to learning about America from you."

Aunt Mina indicated a sweating boy a little younger, maybe fourteen, wearing a blue t-shirt with horizontal yellow stripes. "You remember Samuel."

"Sammy," he corrected.

"And this one is Jimmy," Aunt Mina added, shoving forward a boy who was digging something out of his mouth with his finger. Mina slapped his hand. "He and Ellie are eleven now."

"Hello, Jimmy," I said, remembering his Hebrew name had been Haim. "It's very, very good to see old friends again." I placed a hand on the little girl's shoulder, Jimmy's twin. She was looking down and scuffing her shoes on the sidewalk. "And this must be Ellie." She had been Eliya in Nashok.

"You'll be sharing the room with me, too," she said in a barely audible voice.

"Then you'll have to tell me about America, also."

Up the steps, the door crashed open, and Yankl stood just outside it, staring down at me. I easily recognized him, thin, intense, dark, his curly hair a little shorter, but still the same.

The others parted as I moved to the steps and he rushed down them, tears flowing from his eyes.

"Yankl," I said softly.

He engulfed me in a big hug. "Rivka, it is you. God is merciful."

I didn't see any of God's mercy in it but kept that to myself. He released me and held my hands, tears flowing down his cheeks.

"You look good, Yankl," I said.

"You're really here." He was about to say more when the children jostled passed us, rushing up the steps.

Mina said, "Come on, you two. Let's get Rivka situated."

Taking Yankl's hand, I followed her up into the house.

CHAPTER THIRTY-TWO

Later, after supper, Yankl and I walked the neighborhood. The heat was still oppressive, but the sun had pushed down toward the horizon of rooftops forming a lane of shade over much of the block. Like Nashok in summer, people came outside to escape the heat in their homes. Here, they assembled on the stoops, seeking a cool breeze, and even sat in beach chairs along the block, some furiously working fans. Most were women, children, and older men since the younger men like Pete were still in the military. As we walked, I felt I was being inspected, people gawking at my short hair. Even though Yankl didn't live here, he knew everyone and greeted them with, *evening, aunt*, and, *good to see you, uncle*.

I spotted Sammy and Jimmy playing that stickball game in the street with several other boys while Ellie, with several other girls, jumped rope on the sidewalks. The neighborhood throbbed with life, something I thought I would never see again.

In greeting the neighbors, Yankl rambled on with them about something called the Brooklyn Dodgers. All talking with such fervor, I determined these Dodgers must be something religious. Then, as we went to the next block and the next, he fell silent, which didn't bother me. I was comfortable with silence, even though the racket of kids playing and people talking and cars honking was hardly silence.

After nearly five minutes, I said, "Keep talking about America."

He laughed. "All right. I guess you know I like talking."

"I know."

So, he did. He told me about Prospect Park, the Botanic Gardens, Coney Island, and places in Manhattan. As he went on, warming to his topic, I noticed I was slightly taller than him, which I hadn't been four years ago. His dark hair was wavy, a bit unruly. His eyes were blue but a little darker shade than I remembered, still intense like everything he thought or said deserved his utmost enthusiasm. Talking about a Yiddish theater on the Lower East Side, he spoke as if he were a young revolutionary generating rebellion. Everything excited him.

I thought of Shoshana, the Seven's great actress destined for the Yiddish theater in Vilna or Warsaw. She would have flourished here.

Toward the end of a block, a family was gathered on the stoop around a middle-aged woman who was wailing. Others around her were crying as well, the women hugging, comforting each other. The raw emotion came off them with a physical force, and I stepped back. I could not take on anyone else's sorrow.

But Yankl went in among them and said, "I heard about Bobby yesterday, Mrs. Goldberg. I'm so sorry. He was a great guy. I thought of him as a good friend."

The woman in the center got up, wiping her eyes with her hands, and embraced him, then patted his cheek. "You're a good boy, Yankl Glazman."

"Thank you, ma'am." He took my hand, and we went on.

"What was that about?" I asked him.

"She got one of those telegrams from Western Union on Wednesday."

"What telegrams?"

"Bobby was a Marine. He was killed at a place called Okinawa two weeks ago. The government notifies families by sending a telegram. You get a knock on the door and there stands this Western Union messenger. She got the message yesterday. Not the best way to learn a loved one has been killed."

I doubted if there was any good way, but I let it go. "What are you doing with yourself these days, Yankl? Knowing you, it's something where you can talk your way into or out of things."

"I'm a bicycle messenger." Dabbing the sweat from his forehead with a white handkerchief, he smiled and told me he'd finished high school last year and would enter Brooklyn College in the fall. "Right now, I'm working the summer at Uncle Aaron's law firm as a messenger boy. I'm the best messenger in the city."

"I'm sure you are."

Though he'd been joking, he seemed pleased by the comment. "I'm going to law school, and then work for my uncle. I should have a decent enough salary, Rivka."

That last was an odd thing to say. His joke aside about being the city's best messenger, Yankl was not a braggart, so why say that? With a sharp blink of my eyes, I realized he was telling me his future prospects, as if he were courting me. Yankl and me? I shook my head. No, that couldn't be it.

Abruptly, his demeanor changed, becoming both somber and nervous. His voice trembled when he spoke, "I'm sorry, Rivka. I have to know. There's so much I have to know. What happened to you in Nashok? I saw you..." He blinked several times to hold back tears. "I...how did you escape?"

I shook my head. "Not now, Yankl. I don't want to think about those times now. This is so pleasant. For a long time, I didn't know places like this still existed in the world. We'll talk about what happened to you and me some time, I promise. Just not now."

"All right, but I have another question I very much have to ask."

Upset he would go on, I said curtly, "All right, ask. What is it?"

"Are you really married to Pete? I mean, did you have a ceremony or anything like that before you came here?"

I gave a small laugh. "No, we didn't. We're not really married."

"I didn't think so but had to ask."

"Don't say anything, please. I'm worried about who knows. I'd rather not be sent back to Europe. Pete—I'm not used to that name yet—Pete asked me to explain it all to Geraldine though, so I guess I need to tell her. He's worried she won't understand."

He stopped and faced me. "That may be hard to do. Geraldine's gone. She was so upset she went to stay with relatives in Boston. I tried to tell her the reasons for what Pete did, but she won't have anything to do with him anymore. She still thinks you two are married."

I exhaled. "I suppose I'll have to talk with her."

Yankl gave a skeptical grimace. "I'm not sure she's coming back."

When the light began failing, we returned to the brownstone.

Hours later, after Yankl had gone back to his uncle's apartment, I excused myself and went up to the bedroom I now shared with the girls, and, exhausted, fell into a fitful sleep. Sometime in that night, as with each night in the last four years, I awoke, bolting upright, sucking in breath. It had been the same gallery of nightmares that played one after the other through my head, this time Helena's baby, me lying in the pit at Nashok with Mama and Hanna. Other nights Auschwitz crowded in with the figure of Max Bauer in his gray uniform, his shiny black boots, his swastikas. Now that survival had been won, these nightmares had free dominion to gouge deeper into me. They would never end.

I looked over at Teresa and Ellie in their beds still sleeping. The room was stiflingly hot, my body damp with sweat. Rising, I slipped silently out of the bedroom and padded barefoot downstairs, wearing only the borrowed pajama tops from Mina and the male underwear from the field hospital.

It was warm downstairs as well but not as bad as the bedroom. A bit of moonlight shone through the windows, and the streetlamps illuminated the living room. I went to the kitchen at the back of the house and opened the small box refrigerator. From habit, I glanced over my shoulder to see if anyone was watching, all the while realizing I could take what I wanted and not be shot for it. Mina had said I was welcome to anything, anytime. Still, anxiety crawled through me like an army of ants.

The refrigerator held vegetables, a half bottle of milk, leftovers from dinner, meat slices, and cheese. So much food. Shutting the door, I went to the counter and lifted the breadbox lid. Half of the pumpernickel Mina baked today remained. I picked it up and went into the living room where I sat by the front window, staring out at the empty street, holding onto the bread in my lap. I wasn't hungry. It just felt reassuring in my hands. And this half loaf had no sawdust, a meal for Agneta, Eleni, and me. Bread had meant life for us.

Outside, nothing moved amid the streetlamps and cars at the curbs, not even a stray cat. Then, down at the end of the block, a man appeared on the other side of the street, walking casually along the sidewalk, his hands in his pockets. I watched him steadily, thinking maybe he was a thief. Who would be skulking about this late at night but a thief? When he paused under a streetlamp, I noticed he was young and handsome. His modest size and the way he moved reminded me of Anton, my boyfriend in the partisans. I had loved him as best I could, though I seldom let my emotions out of their prison cells. Thinking of him made my heart lurch. How he had moved with such confidence like this man on the street, how he loved me with a fullness I could not match, how he died so pointlessly.

In the astral light, the man outside was Anton. I imagined a romantic interlude between us, my Anton coming across the street and bounding up the steps. I would let him in and whisper his name. We would have playful banter like in those Hollywood movies that showed in the Nashok firehouse, and he would tell me how beautiful I was and embrace me.

With that, the dream fell apart. I was a scarecrow, my legs thin as candlesticks, my body still far too underweight, maybe twenty pounds yet. Like years ago, I was the Stork again. I knew when any man saw this, he would be disgusted.

At the other end of the block, the man outside turned the corner and disappeared from sight. My feelings sank back into oblivion.

For the rest of the night, I sat by the window, holding the bread, till the morning light came.

CHAPTER THIRTY-THREE

L ong after evening chow with the light fading, Pete Frischer sat in the back of the open jeep as it passed through the wreckage of the city, heading toward the American sector's border with the Soviets where a Russian officer awaited them. The report had come in a few moments before that he wanted to defect. Since the war ended, G2's focus had shifted immediately to their former ally, the Soviet Union, and a defector right now should provide much needed intelligence.

After years of allied bombing, the Berlin they passed through was a wasteland, with some blocks completely flattened, and others with hollowed out buildings standing like skeletons. Few were intact. In many streets, huge piles of debris and bomb craters blocked the way. Women, old men, and children walked among this lost world with haunted, glazed looks in their eyes. Young German men were few. The shock of such destruction had not worn off in the week Pete had been there with the 82nd Airborne. When he first arrived and saw the devastation, he had felt a sense of satisfaction as had many others, but now that had worn off, and he just hated that war left so much sorrow behind.

"Damn, we sure blew the hell out of them," the driver Corporal Billings said, gawking at the devastation. He was hardly more than nineteen, a replacement to the 82nd in the last two months. He'd missed the entire war.

Lucky for him, he hadn't been sent to the Pacific, Pete thought. The Japs still needed killing.

Major Landry turned around in the front seat and gave Pete a sly grin. "You hear from that wife of yours lately?"

"I got a letter from her last week, sir," Pete said. "She's doing okay, fitting in. She's got a routine going, working at my father's store a couple times a week and spending time at the library the other days."

"It's a routine. That's important." Landry's smile grew. "Have you heard from your girlfriend yet?"

Billings stared at Pete in the rearview mirror with wide eyes. "You got a wife and a girlfriend, Sarge?"

"Keep your eyes on the damn road, Corporal," Pete snapped. He turned to Landry. "No, not for a while. Maybe her letters haven't caught up to us yet."

"Yeah, that's probably it," the major said. "If I could get you home, Pete, I would. I know how all that goes. My wife is a looker. Guys flock around her like moths to a flame. I worry all the time I'm going to get one of those letters. Boys, don't make a pretty woman your wife."

You couldn't always tell with Landry, Pete thought, whether he was kidding or sincere. Pete just wanted to go home. After nearly two years without seeing his family or Geraldine, he missed them desperately. He needed to be back there. He needed to explain the situation to her, but he was not getting back any time in the near future unless it was in a coffin, and not even then. They'd bury him in an American cemetery somewhere in Europe.

Ahead, fifty or so Rubble Women, many young and attractive, passed buckets of debris from one to another, the line snaking for some thirty yards, and the buckets then dumped into the back of a truck. The job paid pennies, but with thousands dying of starvation daily, Pete could understand why they worked twelve hours a day or longer. Billings slowed the jeep to a crawl and whistled. A few glanced at him and smiled as if trying to gain his attention. These women lived in such despair they would pretend that a nineteen-year-old kid's wolf whistle was somehow wildly romantic. Get an American boyfriend and your family eats for another day. After two years of war, Pete saw himself as anything but a kid. He felt only sadness for them.

"Eyes on the damn road, Corporal," Major Landry said. He propped his boot on the side panel, has hand resting on the un-snapped holster of his .45. "Step on it."

"Yes, sir."

The jeep shot forward.

Like Landry, Pete felt a wariness about the assignment. You could never trust the Russians and now one was supposedly defect-ing. The savage behavior of Russian soldiers had turned Berlin into Rape City. All the intel said they were untrained, without discipline, and given to barbaric acts. Many had been conscripted off isolated farms, thrown into uniform, given a rifle, and sent to occupy Berlin. No surprise that drunken gangs of them roamed throughout the city, raping women no matter how young or how old, murdering anyone who showed the slightest resistance, and looting anything not nailed down. Tensions between the Soviets and the other allies hung heavy, a flammable gas waiting for a match.

What riled Pete most was the order from somewhere far up the chain of command not to confront the Russians no matter how despicable the crimes they were committing. Women were raped in daylight in the street while US soldier dare not lift a hand to help under threat of court-martial.

Down the block where the entire wall of a skeletal apartment house had fallen, exposing its innards, a woman sat alone at a table on the fourth floor, sipping something from a cup. When she no-ticed the jeep below inching passed a large mountain of rubble, she stood up and slowly walked to the edge, looking down to the ground. Pete thought she was about to jump, and grasping the back of Billing's seat, rose up to shout *no!* But, instead, she lifted her hand and gave a little wave to them. He waved back.

The last of the sun filtered through the husks of several row apartment buildings, and shadows were deepening when they approached the Soviet sector on the cobbled avenue of Sonnenallee. Not a checkpoint. It had no barrier nor MPs checking documents since passage between the zones was legal.

All that indicated the border between allied powers was a large, white sign in three languages, English, Russian and French, that said, *You are Leaving the American Sector.* Three soldiers from the 82nd Airborne, one of them a staff sergeant, stood beside a couple jeeps parked near the sign. Pete couldn't see anyone that looked like a Russian defector. Billings pulled their jeep to a stop near them as the soldiers straightened and saluted Major Landry.

Getting out, Landry returned the salutes. "You have someone for us to pick up, Sergeant."

"He's hiding in the rubble, sir," the soldier said, putting his fingers to his lips and whistling.

Two more 82nd Airborne soldiers came out of a destroyed building, flanking a man in a Russian uniform, and slid down a pile of rubble toward them. When the Russian strode out ahead and out of the shadow, Pete recognized the rank as something equal to a colonel. The man had a crooked nose jutting out from a narrow, patrician face, and he walked with an air of bitter arrogance,

Following protocol, Landry saluted the colonel who returned it, but that was the extent of Landry's military courtesy. "Do you speak English, Colonel?"

"Of course."

Landry gestured to the jeep. "Get in the back, please." He turned to the staff sergeant. "Sergeant, you and your men follow us back to headquarters."

The night had come full on, and with no streetlamps or building lights, the darkness was so thick it felt liquid to Pete. Headlights pushing ahead, the convoy of three jeeps weaved its way back through the streets, skirting the debris and moving from shadow to shadow. In the forward jeep, Pete felt the same jittery nervousness before an operation behind enemy lines. Sitting in the front seat now with Landry in back with the Russian, he clasped his hand over the .45 at his hip.

Landry was talking with the colonel, who said his name was Volkov. He talked of purges before the war, of losing his family, of his hatred for Stalin.

"Then why defect now, Colonel?"

Laced with anger, Volkov's voice shot up an octave, overriding the jeep engines. "The frontline Soviet soldier has discipline, but they are no longer here. Many are dead. Now, the men occupying this city are barbarians." He spit out the back. "I will not work with such pigs. Not a second longer."

Pete wondered if there was any more to it as the convoy turned a corner and stopped abruptly. Just ahead, as if to prove the colonel's point, some twenty Russians soldiers had two women on the cobblestones in the middle of the street, ripping off their clothes. One of the women looked no more than a teenager. They were screaming, and the soldiers were laughing, cheering, and clapping. Pete could see the glint of several bottles of vodka. He drew his .45 but held it in his lap and thought about the order not to interfere with Russian soldiers or face a court-martial and time in prison. He hated this. He seethed. Finally, unable to sit by and watch, he jumped out of the jeep and started for the Russians.

"Stop, Frischer," Landry snapped.

The major drew his own .45 and strode past Pete and fired his weapon into the air. The Russians froze into a momentary tableau and stared at him. Then, they lifted their rifles and handguns. The other Americans leapt from their jeeps and aimed their rifles at the group. It was a standoff, but Pete didn't like their chances. Too many of them, and they were drunk. Anyone could fire and ignite a bloodbath. In the silence, he heard himself breathing. Felt his chest pounding. He saw a tall Russian with drool mixed with vodka draining down his thick beard. He shot Pete a look of rage. Pete decided if someone tossed the match, this guy would die first.

"Stoy!" Volkov shouted. Pete recognized the Russian word for *halt*. The Soviet officer strode forward, gesturing for the men to leave while berating them so quickly Pete couldn't follow any of it. No one moved for several seconds, then the Russians reluctantly drifted off in twos and threes till the last man, the one with the beard, disappeared into the broken buildings nearby. Relieved, Pete sighed but did not holster his sidearm. The women ran off in the opposite direction from the Russians and disappeared among the debris.

"Thanks, Colonel," Landry said as everyone climbed back into the jeeps. "Let's get out of here, Billings,"

His hands shaking on the steering wheel, Billings squeaked, "Yes, sir." He drove off, the others following.

Still alert, Pete felt the tension in his body ease. He'd thought his war done, but this damn place was just as dangerous. Billings was driving quickly through the shadows when down the block something clattered onto the cobblestones in front of the jeep.

Pete knew immediately what it was and shouted, "Grenade!"

Billings swerved, and an explosion rented the air. The jeep lifted off the street and landed on its side, tumbling out its occupants. Lying on the cobblestones, uncertain where he was, Pete saw headlight beams askew, illuminating ruined buildings. Blood streamed down his cheek. He blinked several times trying to get his bearings. What? Where was he? Then the funnel of lights faded, and everything went black.

CHAPTER THIRTY-FOUR

In those first weeks with the Frischers, it seemed I was drifting. Without the sheer pressure of daily survival weighing me down, I had no idea what to do, so I did nothing. Mina and Isaac seemed content to let me. I seldom ventured outside except to walk the block or occasionally catch a movie with Yankl. Without that purpose of survival, the light had gone out of me. My mind was crisscrossed with scars. Hellish dreams inhabited my nights, woke me up to wander the house, or sometimes sit outside on the stoop under the city lamps as hours passed.

I found comfort in the evenings when we'd gather around the large, wood paneled radio listening to *Gang Busters, The Lone Ranger, The Lux Radio Theater,* different shows each night, which allowed me to sink into imaginary worlds. On Sundays, I found myself caught in the grips of *The Shadow.* At the show's beginning, Jimmy would deepen his voice and say along with the show's announcer, "Who knows what evil lurks in the hearts of men? The Shadow knows."

I'd laugh each time.

Daytimes I spent helping Mina and Teresa clean the house and cook in the kitchen, at which I was not very good, and then in my free time I would slumber on the couch, listening to the radio while reading one of the many magazines lying on the coffee table. *Glamour, Seventeen, Life, Colliers, Modern Screen.* The words seldom stuck. Moving slowly through this living somnambulance, I told myself I was distancing myself from the terror that had inhabited my life.

But one day that old life rose out of the shadows. Alone in the house while Mina and Teresa went grocery shopping and the kids were out playing, I sat on the couch, my legs tucked under me, flipping through the latest issue of *Collier's* magazine. Halfway through, my body jerked as if shocked by an electrical current. On the page was an article by Martha Gellhorn, the journalist who spoke with me at the field hospital outside Munich. At the top was an illustration of the Gellhorn woman standing outside a red cross tent, hands on hips, listening to a tall, skeletal woman standing by the tent flap with intensity distorting her face. Though unrecognizable, it was me. That day, I'd told her everything that happened to me in detail. Suddenly coming upon the article brought to the surface the terror that lived inside me.

Not using my real name, she called me Rebecca. Scanning the article quickly, I flew passed Nashok, the partisans, and Auschwitz and Kaufering. Only one phrase stood out: *With the partisans, Rebecca built a blood count in revenge against the Nazis.* About to close the magazine, I saw the next heading for the piece: "War Criminals on the Run." I began to read.

> *Rebecca and her fellow survivors, a Greek Jew and a Catholic Nun, described several men and a few women who committed such atrocities that the deepest depth of Hell is the only place for this gallery of monsters. Rebecca and the two other women held particular hatred for two men. One was Joseph Mengele, a doctor at Auschwitz who conducted hideous experiments on his 'patients,' and the other was Auschwitz SS Commander Max Bauer, who sent hundreds of thousands*

to the pits and gas chambers. Both men are still at large, likely hiding in Europe, and the allies are pursuing them.

As for Max Bauer, there was the case of Helena's baby. It brought tears to the eyes of Rebecca in the telling. It would seem impossible in the camps...

My hand convulsing, I crumpled the page in its grip, then another, then the entire article.

On the surface, I presented a front of normalcy, engaging with the family, doing my work in the home, even laughing at the appropriate times. I was trying to live. In fact, I went to the movies with Yankl several times, being reminded through movie tone news that there was actually another war going on in the Pacific, the one with Japan, but it was sure to end soon, everyone said. It was not my war. The newsreels showed a devastated city, flattened by something called the Atomic bomb. I wished the allies had used that on Germany and flattened every damn one of their cities.

I knew my life to be aimless, but then no one was trying to kill me. One day washing dishes with Mina after breakfast, that all changed.

"You know Isaac and I love you like our own daughters, Rivka," she said, cleaning a dish and setting it in the rack. I picked it up, dried it, and placed it in the cabinet.

"I do."

"God knows, no one more than you deserves to spend her time the way she wants." She placed the dish towel in the sink and turned to face me. "But I'm worried about you. This can't be what your mother intended for you, this doing nothing. I think she wanted more for you."

I flinched, furious with her. "You could not understand, Mina."

"I know I couldn't, Ziskeit," she said, using a term of endearment in Yiddish.

Even with these people I loved and who loved me, I was alone. An alien in a strange land. She couldn't see that. No one who had not been through those years could know me.

"Whatever you do, you are our daughter and we will love you. I know this, Rivka. Your mother was the strongest woman I have ever known. And she would want you to live."

My mind returned to that moment before Mama shoved me into the pit of dead bodies and told me exactly that: *Live!* I had not told the Frischers anything about what happened to me. A profound guilt sank into my bones. For becoming a nothing girl like the Nazis said I was, for not doing what Mama wanted. For surviving. I dropped my own dish towel on the counter.

My eyes watered. I didn't want to feel but couldn't fight back the tears. "She did."

Mina took me in her arms.

And so, I started back. In the following days, I established a routine for myself, one with at least a vague goal. Mama and Papa had instilled the value of education in their children, even their girls. To find my way in America, I decided I needed to continue my learning. Pete and Yankl had no long interruption in their schooling and so slid smoothly into the American system, but for me, that would be nearly impossible. Isaac said I could surely enter the nearby high school, and he and Mina accompanied me there to register for the new school year. In the interview with the principal, I admitted I'd only fully completed the eighth grade.

"Then you must begin in the ninth," he said. "You'll be a bit old, but I'm sure you'll fit in."

I shook my head. "I'm eighteen. I'm too old to start in the ninth grade."

The principal shrugged, seemingly saying there was nothing he could do Without a word, I got up and left, and the Frischers hurriedly followed me out.

Turning his hat brim in his hands, Isaac asked me, "Now, what will you do?"

I didn't know for sure but still gave a firm nod, saying, "I will educate myself."

He nodded as if that were the wisest thing anyone ever said. "Then so be it."

Now, most mornings, I walked to Brooklyn's main library several blocks away, reaching it by nine when it opened. The librarian who always unlocked the door began greeting me, and once she learned why I was there helped me select books. With more books than I'd ever seen in one place, I read and read and read, mostly literature but also science and math. With a twist of my heart, I wished my Sarah, Sarah Shlanski, the Seven's math wizard, was there to explain it all to me.

Three days a week before noon, I took the subway that crossed the bridge into the Lower East Side and worked at Isaac's and Morris's store, doing anything they needed from a little accounting to moving great bolts of cloth. Each time, I stopped first at Goldfarb's Kosher Delicatessen to pick up lunch for everyone, usually pastrami and corned beef sandwiches, potato latkes, and a metal container of soup.

Emil Goldfarb, the owner, was a balding, rotund man who always wore a loose vest and white apron. After the first few times at his deli, he personally had my order ready for me when I arrived because the Frischer brothers had been valued customers for years, but his friendly treatment also stemmed from a moment early on. One day, as I slid the signed receipt back to him—I never paid till the end of the month—he touched my wrist.

I shot him a glare.

Barely above a whisper, he said, "May I look?"

I knew what he meant and nodded. He turned my arm and gazed at the tattooed numbers. He looked up at me, and his eyes watered. "Oh, my," he muttered, then forced a smile and handed me the paper bag of food.

I was getting along, adjusting to American life, though once in a while, a frightening sudden dread rushed over me much like it did during the war. Back then, Sokolov had called it *shestoye chuvstvo*. Best I could guess he meant a sixth sense. He said your senses pick up things that have not fully registered in your mind. "Don't dismiss the feeling," he said, "for it has served me well too many times."

It turned out that would be true for me as well. Here in America though, that sixth sense led me into a terrible situation. It happened on a Sunday when Yankl, the girls, and I went to the movies. Like a good American boy, he had two passions, the Brooklyn Dodgers, a baseball team, and the movies. I was sure he was in love with someone named Veronica Lake because he talked about her so much.

With school not beginning till Tuesday, Teresa and Ellie went with us to see *State Fair,* a musical at one of those movie palaces Yankl loved so much. And it was a palace, massive with star-filled ceilings and walls decked with ornaments. It held two thousand people this night, nothing like the old firehouse in Nashok, which was lucky to hold a hundred. Ellie squirmed throughout the film, but Teresa and Yankl loved it. I sided with Ellie. I never liked musicals, even when we put on one in Nashok.

I whispered to the little girl, "Not once in my life have I seen people on the street suddenly burst into song and dance."

She giggled.

When the movie ended about 7:30 and we started walking home, a night chill had come, and rain threatened, so we took a shortcut that Teresa knew through a rundown neighborhood. Most of the streetlamps were out, either not working or busted. Old rowhouses were squeezed together and appeared deserted. Both girls were bobbysoxers like most of the other young woman I'd seen. They wore blouses, tonight with sweaters, knee length skirts, and saddle shoes with white sox, and they loved pop music, most especially the songs of Frank Sinatra. I felt no part of this, most days wearing slacks or, like tonight, a simple black skirt and a long sleeved, white blouse.

When we were well along the neighborhood's dark sidewalks, Ellie suddenly ran ahead and started jumping into the air, throwing her arms out, and singing.

"You've gone mad," Teresa shouted at her. "What are you doing?"

"I'm dancing and singing like in the movies. Everyone does it." She twirled around, singing, "You've got to accentuate the positive, eliminate the negative, and latch onto the affirmative. Don't mess with Mister In-Between."

I joined her, and we danced down the block, and she laughed even more, though the best I could muster was a smile for her.

When I returned to Yankl and Teresa, Ellie kept dancing. Finally, Teresa shouted at her, "Stop that. Act your age."

"I am. I'm a kid." But she stopped and came back to us. After a moment, she said, "If Papa learns we came this way, he's going to be mad at you, not me because I'm a kid."

"Shut up."

"Why would he be mad?" Yankl asked.

"He told us never to come this way," Ellie said. "Too many bad people live here."

"He won't know if you don't tell him," Teresa said. "I don't want to be caught in the rain. I just had my hair done."

"Okay, Princess," Ellie said. "If you must..."

Suddenly, that sixth sense hit; fear shivered through me, and her voice drifted away. Something was wrong. Up ahead beneath one of the still intact streetlamps, a man sat on the steps drinking from a large whiskey bottle. That was not it, but he concerned me. With the threat of rain, it was cold, and yet he wore just a t-shirt. As we approached, he glanced at us with dead eyes. Days of stubble covered his face.

Yankl saw my tenseness and said, "Are you all right?"

"Quiet," I said in a hushed voice, listening.

Then I heard it. Hurrying footsteps behind us. I glanced back and saw the outline of two men in the darkness, coming fast. I would not let anything happen to the girls. I strode over to the man drinking from the bottle and snatched it by the neck, ignoring his cries of protests. I smashed it over the concrete stoop, and brandishing the jagged edge toward the approaching men, I ran at them, screaming in rage.

They were just coming into the light, two boys no more than fifteen or sixteen, Hasidic Jews with side curls, each carrying a stack of books. When they saw me, they shrieked in fright, turned, and ran. Neither dropped his books.

I froze, mortified.

When Yankl and the girls rushed up to me, Teresa said, "Wow, why did you do that?"

"I thought it was something else," I snapped, more furious at myself than anything, and dropped the bottle to the pavement. "Let's go."

As we passed the man still sitting on the step, he raised his hands as if to say he wanted no trouble. When we got back to the brownstone, neither of the girls said anything about what happened.

Later, an hour or so after we all had gone to bed, I was awakened by shouts and screams outside. My first thought was those boys had reported me to the police, but that was ridiculous. Our window faced the street, and Teresa, Ellie, and I looked out. Crowds filled the block. celebrating. Throwing on clothes, we raced downstairs and outside. It seemed everyone had gone mad, dancing and hugging, church bells and car horns blaring close by and far away.

"It's like in the movies," Ellie laughed.

"What's going on?" I asked Mrs. Lipinski, a neighbor.

"Japan surrendered. It's finally over," she said.

Shouts echoed up and down the block. "The war is over. The war is over."

Teresa and Ellie were screaming, "It's over. It's over."

I should have felt the same jubilation but all I had was a grand emptiness. I'd not even known when the war in Europe had ended, and when I learned it, I could only feel a release of pressure, as if my death sentence had been commuted. Now was different. I could celebrate with everyone else, but I saw nothing in it. I was glad it was over. That was enough.

Everyone was embracing, and I hugged people I didn't know. Mina, Isaac, and Morris came down the steps and joined us.

"Is the war really over?" Isaac asked.

"Yes," Teresa said and leapt into his arms.

We all hugged.

"Is Pete coming home now, Mama?" Ellie asked.

"Soon. He must be coming home soon," Mina answered, twisting the end of a shawl she had thrown over her shoulders. "Yes, not long now."

On Thursday of that week, the war, which was supposed to be over, crashed in on us again. I had come home from the library. School had begun that week, and the children were not at home, only Mina. We heard a knock at the door, and she answered it. She gasped when a Western Union messenger handed her an envelope and hurried down the steps. I was shaken, my heart crumbling. I knew what it had to be. But that war was over months ago. It was over.

Her hands trembling, Mina opened it and read the message. Tears came to her eyes, and a soft moan escaped her lips. Closing her eyes, she slumped against the wall and held it out for me.

Quickly, I read.

Dearest Mr. and Mrs. Frischer,

I am sorry to inform you that your son, Sergeant Pete Frischer, has been severely injured and will be returning to America for further treatment. His hospital ship is due to arrive in New York harbor on September 23. He will need some months of outpatient treatment. He has been an exemplary soldier and deserves the best we as a country can provide. It has been my privilege to call myself his commander.

Yours Truly,
James M. Gavin
Commanding General
82nd Airborne Division

CHAPTER THIRTY-FIVE

N ear the East River at Hawthorn University, Max Bauer stood in his cubbyhole of an office, organizing his desk before his first class. He hated disorder, even one paper, one pen out of place. Angrily, he stubbed his cigarette out in the ashtray. Though he'd told the Negroid janitor not to touch his desk, the man just had to put his ape-like hands on it. The typewriter had been moved off center, several notepads sloppily stacked, and the text for his first class, *General Biology*, lay open.

Incensed at the janitor's carelessness, Bauer straightened the items, then realized something was missing. The only truly personal item he had was a magnifying glass, which he had set to the front of the desk's blotter, but it was nowhere to be seen. He found it on the floor and snatched it up, relieved it hadn't been broken. It had been given to him by Heinrich Himmler, who swore it had belonged originally to Hitler. A. H. had been carved into the handle.

Finally, his desk in order, he opened the textbook to the chapter on eugenics he would assign today and marked it so he could read from it in class. Inaccurate in so many places, one passage told the truth: *To prevent the continued breeding of inferior human stock and to stimulate the reproduction of the superior type would seem unquestionably desirable in the light of man's experience in the improvement of domestic plants and animals.*

It would be a good start. With Germany and Nazism defeated, eugenics was no longer the prevailing academic doctrine, at least in most of America. He would begin to reverse that today. Shutting the book, he sighed and thought of his dead wife, Klara. How proud she would be of him. He had not only survived the fall of the Reich but found himself in such a promising situation here at the university.

Now, he led not one but three lives. First as a professor of biology at a prestigious American school. Second as an agent of one of America's intelligent services hunting communists and communist sympathizers. And the third as a fugitive from the Allies who sought his capture and execution.

All the allied governments, and even his own, were gathering forces to pursue the top Nazi criminals, as they saw it, for so-called war crimes. He could not use his own name like so many others whom the American intelligence services were recruiting could, as if they had been innocent bystanders to *Endlösung*, the Final Solution. The name of Max Bauer stood at the top of the list of those still at large with Adolf Eichmann, Martin Bormann, and Josef Mengele. Bauer's Einsatzgruppen had done halcyon work in Eastern Europe and his efforts at Auschwitz had produced needed results. Yet, that made him one of the most wanted men in the world. He could trust no one with his true identity.

When he'd arrived in America a couple months ago, his handlers had put him and seven other men through a small training program. All of them were former German Wehrmacht, SS, or party officials, and all of them so-called Russian experts, soon to ferret out communists in American life. It had been a bit of a spy school, Bauer remembered. They also took several lie-detector tests, as if they could not be trusted. He wasn't sure he passed any of his, but then no one challenged his story.

It was there he recognized two people he knew from the war. He had considered right then to leave and try to survive on his own somewhere in this vast new land. But he stayed through the day to see if they recognized him.

The first man, Otto Shaub, was just as Bauer remembered him, pale as death and slender with thinning hair. He had been a supply officer in Warsaw several years ago, confiscating jewels, paintings, gold, homes, cars from Jews and Polish intelligentsia. With some idea of where all the stolen loot might be, he'd be a wanted man by the Allies. The two had only met once, and though Bauer recalled him, the man thankfully gave no indication of knowing Bauer, but then he was apparently quite drunk.

Shaub didn't return for the second day. No one knew why, and the American intel officers wouldn't say. A rumor spread that he'd been deported back to Europe and turned over to the Soviets for war crime trials in Poland. Bauer felt relieved by his absence.

The other man was Willi Meisner, a former Nazi party official, and they had never met, but he'd seen Meisner in films. Once a top aide to Joseph Goebbels, he had appeared in many of them either as a speaker or most often in the background. Now, he claimed to have only been a low-level radio producer within the propaganda ministry, occasionally reading out lines provided him, and who was there to say differently? His crimes, whatever they were, could not compare to what the allies claimed were Bauer's. It was unlikely that Meisner knew him. Bauer had done only that one film when Heydrich presented him with a medal for his Russian campaign. As a high-ranking member of the Propaganda Ministry, Meisner might have seen it, but gave no indication when they were introduced.

Meisner ended up in New York as well, another "Austrian" working for a national radio network as an assistant producer on several programs. When both rode up to New York on the same train, they struck up a friendship. Since then they had met a couple times over coffee and schnapps to reminisce about the good old days.

Nearly ten o'clock, Bauer placed the text and class roster into his brief case, smoothed the lapels of his pinstripe suit, and cleared his throat as if about to sing an aria.

"Muller?" someone called from behind him.

He turned and saw a smallish man, his arms folded and leaning his shoulder against the door jamb. He wore one of those gray sports coats with the fake elbow patches. His white shirt was unbuttoned at the top, and the collar pulled out over the lapels. With his swarthy face, Bauer knew immediately who he was, Ira Berman, the famous Jew author who the university president had hired for the new year to teach writing classes.

At seeing the man, Bauer suddenly seethed with fury. The collapse of his world, and now this Jew standing with such cocky self-assurance at his door made the room swim by him in blind fury. Then, he regained his equilibrium. He imagined himself once again in his gray SS uniform, his pistol out, and Berman, in front of him, standing on the edge of a pit filled with bodies. Bauer pictured himself aiming the pistol and firing, the Jew collapsing into the ditch with the others.

He answered the man curtly, "I am *Doctor* Muller. Who are you?"

Catching the tone, the man lifted himself off the door jamb. "Ira Berman, the writer. It looks like you and I are going with President Walton to this damn soiree tonight. Are you ready for this crap? I hate it. I still haven't rented a tux."

Bauer clipped shut his briefcase and walked past him, shutting the office door, making Berman jump back. "I haven't time to chat. I have a class."

He left the man standing in the hall and hurried down to the first floor classroom. When he entered, the students fell silent. He stood behind his desk, checking the roll, which showed thirty-one males and six females, then rubbed his hands together, his mind flashing on how a little luck and his own cleverness had landed him here instead of on a hangman's rope.

The bell rang.

He walked to where a large pull-down chart of the human respiratory system covered the blackboard and sent it like a window blind rolling back up. On the board, he'd written earlier: *I am Dr.*

Kurt Muller, PHD in Biological Science from the University of Vienna. He strode back to the students, standing in front of them. "As you can see, my name is Kurt Muller. You will address me either as Professor Muller or Dr. Muller. This class is General Biology. If you were looking for 19ᵗʰ Century French Poetry, you're in the wrong building."

The students laughed.

A hand went up in the first row, but Bauer held his hand up to stop any questions, his eyes filling with intensity. "Before we start on the course of study, we should talk about what your ears are telling you, and then we will talk about it no more. You hear a German accent, and we just fought a long war against Germany. Has the university gone mad and hired someone who was an enemy just a few short months ago? In other words, am I a German?"

A few students squirmed in their seats.

Bauer balled his hands into fists and thrust them up in front of his face, a technique he'd seen Hitler do so powerfully in his speeches. His voice rose with intensity. "No, I am not. I am Austrian. I opposed the Nazis with everything in my power and lost everything beloved by me as a result, my dear wife and three children. If I had it to do again, my actions would be the same."

Utter silence followed his outburst. That pleased him. He knew they were his. No one said the obvious. Hitler was Austrian. He looked down at the massive textbook on the desk and flipped it open to the chapter on Eugenics. It would take a more subtle approach for them to see the light. He held the book up. "You should have purchased the class text by now," he said. "Open it to Chapter Seven."

Bauer's last class of the day, Comparative Anatomy, was on the fourth floor, and when it ended at five o'clock, he was kept from leaving by several, overeager male students who hung about asking questions as if this would somehow gain them favor. Regrettably, this was not like a German university where students would not dare such familiarity, and he had so little time to waste tonight. He needed to catch a series of trolleys back to his apartment, wash up, and put on his tux before President Walton picked him up at seven for the charity event at the Waldorf Astoria.

Walton would be attending with his hand out, looking for grant money, displaying his two new prize recruits, Muller and Berman, as if that would assure success. Unlike Berman though, Bauer looked forward to rubbing elbows, as Walton called it, with the richest people in New York. It was far away from the hell that was Europe these days.

He was aware of his new role, no longer an SS office who could give life and death orders that were instantly obeyed. Here he needed to be firm but friendly, the beloved teacher, the wise counselor. Holding his hand up, he cut a student off in midsentence. "I'm sorry, gentleman. I have an important engagement tonight."

"The Waldorf," one of them said. They understood. Apparently, this charity gala was a well-known annual event.

"Yes," Bauer said with a sigh.

"Good luck, sir. Careful you're not blinded by all those bright lights and jewelry."

When they left, Bauer placed his things into the briefcase and followed them out. The hall was empty except for the janitor at the far end, his back to him, mopping the floor. As Bauer approached the stairs, a man appeared at the top, just ten feet away. He wore a shabby suit with lint on the shoulders. He looked to the janitor, then to Bauer.

His face broke into a grin and called out. "Bauer. It's me, Otto Shaub. Thankfully, I found you."

Good god, the man was speaking German, and so loudly, he might as well have been announcing they were Nazi fugitives.

Bauer hurried to him. "Keep your voice down, Otto." He looked at the janitor who was still mopping the floor, some twenty yards away. "We can't talk here."

Shaub spoke hurriedly, not as loudly, but still in German, "The Americans were going to send me back to Europe, Bauer, so I ran. I need to hide from them. I have no money and no place to stay. You must help me."

Instantly, Bauer made a calculation. He barely had enough time to make it back to his apartment and get ready, and he sure couldn't keep Shaub there, a man who knew he was Max Bauer, but he had to deal with this. He stepped forward and placed his hand on the other man's shoulder, whispering, "Of course, I will help you, my friend. But we can't talk here. There's a park not far from here, Tompkins Square. Do you know it?"

"I think so. I saw it on a…"

"Go there now. I'll meet you at the Temperance Fountain. You'll find it. Go. Hurry."

After an instant's hesitation, Shaub nodded and rushed down the steps. Bauer didn't follow immediately, instead hurrying to his office to empty out his briefcase, then taking it downstairs into the basement. He found the janitor's private little nook and a work bench where he saw what he was looking for.

Near six o'clock, with the sun fallen beyond the tall buildings, Bauer strode into Tompkins Square, unsnapping his briefcase as he went. The park was a large, tree-filled area with thick foliage, a popular place on a warm evening like this one. He saw Shaub waiting for him at the Temperance Fountain, a stone kiosk with a woman's statue on the top. Instead of going up to him, Bauer walked past and gave a subtle nod for him to follow.

He found a tiny footpath into the thick trees and brush, not a walking path, but more like a critter trail. Shaub followed him, closing quickly. The shadows were deep, and to Bauer, they might have been the only two people in the park.

Shaub came up to him. "I was looking for a big fountain with spray and everything. It was just a damn drinking fountain. You should have told me."

"You found it," Bauer snapped.

Shaub held up his hand. "Relax, Bauer. I am your friend, not your enemy. I don't want to ruin what you have here. You want to be Kurt Muller, then you are Kurt Muller. The Americans care more about Stalin and the Soviets than we Germans. Once you were a Jew hunter, now you are a commie hunter, eh. All I need is a bit of help. The damn Americans are after me."

When a burst of laughter came from a walkway some thirty yards off, Shaub flinched and glanced that way. A young couple was passing by, visible through the trees in snatches. Bauer pulled the heavy pipe wrench from his briefcase.

Shaub wiped his forehead with his hand and turned back. "I badly need a schnapps."

That's when Bauer violently struck him on the side of the head with the wrench. The man's eyes popped, and he collapsed. Lost in rage, Bauer struck him again and again, crushing the skull, then stepped back, breathing heavily and looked around. No one had seen him. The young couple was gone, and no one else was about. Placing the wrench back into the briefcase, he waited for his breathing to calm, then slipped out of the trees onto the walkway. Reaching the square, he fell in with other evening strollers and made his way out of the park.

CHAPTER THIRTY-SIX

Just before eight that evening, Mark Walton, President of Hawthorne University, led two of his new teaching hires, Dr. Kurt Muller from the University of Vienna and renowned Jewish writer Ira Berman, up the steps into the main lobby of the Waldorf Astoria. They mixed in with men and women also wearing formal attire and squeezed into the elevators for the short ride up to the Grand Ballroom, where the Annual Arthur C. Shepherd Charity Gala was taking place.

Walton was nervous. Getting money out of these Brahmans meant the difference between a successful year for the university or a slide backward into mediocrity. It didn't help any that there was a distinct freeze between the two men he'd brought, but then Ira Berman was about as anti-social a person as he'd ever met. Now, he wished the Board of Trustees had not forced him on the school. And Muller, distracted, sweating despite the air conditioning, seemed as if he'd rather be anyplace else than here.

Moments later, stepping out of the elevator, Walton said to both men, "Remember, a signature from Arthur Shepherd or one of his friends could add a new wing to the library or an entire building to the Biology or English departments, so be ambassadors for your university."

Bauer nodded absently. He felt his armpits uncomfortably damp with chilled sweat. After disposing of the bloody pipe wrench in the East River, he'd caught the trolley and reached his apartment at seven, just before Walton arrived to pick him up. He'd only had time to jump into his tux and rush out the door.

It wasn't the shock of killing a man that had him so jittery—he'd done that often enough—but the realization that he came so close to being exposed had staggered him. Then, he'd have been the one on the run, possibly someday hauled before a war crimes tribunal. With that idiot Shaub a bomb ready to explode, the situation could have been disastrous, but Bauer told himself it was handled. No one had seen him, and he doubted Shaub had spoken to anyone about his good friend Max Bauer. To be safe, though, he would prepare an escape plan should the FBI or anyone come after him.

As they moved toward the ballroom, Bauer felt himself relax. *It was handled.* Berman leaned toward him and said with a sardonic snort, "Gee, I always wanted to be an ambassador."

To Bauer, the Jew was a comical figure, the tux too big for his slight build, his elfin dark eyes glaring at the world. But looking at the man gave him an idea, and he managed a smile.

As they entered, he was struck by the dazzling array of wealth, the throng of men in formal attire and women in evening gowns baring arms and shoulders with alluring glimpses of breasts. Their jewels glittered under the chandelier lights. A haze of cigarette and cigar smoke hung in the air. Milling about with cocktails in their hands, their conversation sounded as urgent and loud as an SS operational meeting. Moving in among them, Bauer caught the heavy scent of perfume and thought this was where he belonged.

Walton began introducing him and Berman to the New York aristocrats, and he played his part with a winning smile and a telling compliment, especially to the wives and daughters. When he held their hands a little longer than necessary, he often garnered blushes, even from the grotesquely fat old biddies.

A couple people were taken with Berman the author, recognizing his name, but soon flinched at his acerbic comments. He asked one woman if she had purchased her gown at the Lower East Side flea market. Clearly, he didn't like being among them. The wealthier they were, the more he went out of his way to be impolite. Walton was apoplectic and ordered him to venture no more opinions and to keep his mouth shut or find another job.

And Berman did. Typical Jew, Bauer thought. No courage. As he had learned days ago, the great author needed the paycheck. In confidence, Walton had told him, "His highly praised work doesn't sell worth a damn."

Across the ballroom, two young women caught Bauer's attention, one a tall blonde in a silvery gown appearing like a Valkyrie come to Earth, the other a mousy brunette clearly of no consequence. They were studying him, and when the blonde cocked her head at him and smiled confidently, he gave a nod in return, then Walton said something, and he turned back.

"That's Arthur Shepherd," Walton said, nodding toward a man speaking to a group of adoring toadies.

Bauer thought he looked like Joachim Ribbentrop, Hitler's Foreign Minister, a distinguished appearance with gray streaked hair and polished manners. But, he suspected, unlike the buffoon Ribbentrop, Shepherd was no fool. To Bauer, the height of Ribbentrop's stupidity was his action or non-action at the end of the war. The man had no escape plan, thinking he didn't need one since he was just a diplomat. Now, he resided in a Nuremburg prison, held by the Allies in preparation for the so-called war crimes trial.

Standing next to Shepherd was a short, flabby man who piped in with loud comments that added nothing except the sound of a voice that carried over the entire hall.

"Who's the other man?" Bauer asked Walton.

"Senator Henry Morton. He's very influential in Albany." Walton glanced at Berman warily. "He's a bit of an anti-Semite, so control yourself, please. We will need his backing."

Berman bridled. "How is one a bit of an anti-Semite? Is he a bit of an anti-Semite like, say, Hitler or more like Himmler? Maybe Adolph Eichmann or his henchman Max Bauer."

At hearing his name, Bauer blanched. The fear he'd just dispelled came roaring back. How had he gained such prominence, or that Eichmann had either? If true, where could you hide?

And why had he been connected to Eichmann? He'd only met the man once, and that was in a 1943 meeting with several others in Himmler's office. They took no particular notice of each other, and now, somehow, he was Eichmann's henchman.

"Keep your voice down, Berman," Walton was saying, half pleading. "For Christ's sake, you know what I mean. Keep your trap shut. Is that clear enough for you?"

Shaken, the Hawthorne president led them into the group and shakily introduced his new faculty members to Shepherd and Morton. "We have great plans to greatly expand our already great learning to its maximum, er, potential, Mr. Shepherd. It's no accident we are called the East Side Ivy League school."

"He's a real charmer," Berman said under his breath to Bauer.

"But you are not Ivy League, are you?" Shepherd said. "Save your pitch for later. This is not the time."

Gulping as if trying to swallow a lump of coal, Walton backed away.

Morton's head tipped back in surprise. "Berman you say? That's a Jewish name, isn't it?"

Berman stiffened. "I'm Jewish if that's what you mean."

Morton shrugged dismissively and leaned down to whisper in the ear of a dowdy woman at his side. In full retreat, Walton quickly guided Berman and Bauer away, but they could still hear Morton in the background. "Arthur, Berman is a Jew. Ghastly business what the Germans did to his people, but really, must we invite him to dinner? I don't think the women will stand for it. Next thing you know, he'll want to join the Knickerbocker Club."

Berman started back for them, but Bauer got there ahead of him and addressed Shepherd, "We are just humble university professors, Mr. Shepherd, so whether we stay or go tonight means little. But if Ira doesn't stay, neither do I."

Shepherd gave him a hard look before responding, "I think you misunderstand the senator, Dr. Muller. He is just expressing his concern for all the terrible news coming out of Europe these days. Of course, you are welcome. Both of you."

Moments later, furious, Berman pulled Bauer aside. "Why did you do that? Look, pal, I don't need anyone to fight my battles for me, least of all a damn German."

"Austrian," Bauer corrected patiently. "You have nothing to do with it, *pal*. I've seen enough of that anti-Semite shite to last a lifetime. It makes me sick, and I'll not stand for it. I don't care who the hell says it, that fat bastard or Harry Truman himself."

Berman hesitated, then relaxed. "All right, Muller. Just so you got the lay of the land. And sorry about the German comment."

"Sure. Forget it."

Bauer lit a cigarette, cupping it as he took a drag. He smiled inwardly. Camouflage. If the name Max Bauer was so well known, that's what was needed, camouflage, and what could be better concealment than Jewish friends?

Across the hall, the two women had watched the exchange. The blonde said, "Cynthia dearest, who is that gorgeous Alan Ladd type who was talking to your father? See the way he smokes his cigarette, as if hiding it? So continental."

"That's Kurt Muller." Drawing back her shoulders exaggeratedly, Cynthia imitated a German accent. "Excuse me. It is *Doctor* Kurt Muller, thank you. Herr Professor at Hawthorne."

"You like him, don't you?"

"Look at him, Edna. Who wouldn't?" Then Cynthia frowned. "But our Dr. Muller didn't even notice me a few minutes ago when Walton was introducing his two protégés around. His eyes went right past me."

"The other one's kind of cute. I like that tough Mediterranean look. He can break my back any day." Grinning, Edna added, "I know. Let's rearrange the seating placements."

Cynthia laughed. "I swear, Edna, you're impossible. That's just what we'll do."

A few minutes later when everyone moved to their assigned dining tables, Bauer found himself sitting between the two women who'd been watching him earlier and felt this night might prove far more interesting than expected, especially after dealing with Shaub. They were a long way from Shepherd's table where all the big donors were, but that was Walton's problem.

The blonde leaned into Bauer, her leg pressing against him. "I'm Edna Schuster, and you're Doctor Kurt Muller, and you came here tonight to pick Arthur Shepherd's pocket. Did you get anything?"

"No. We tried and failed," he replied. "He was about as interested in Hawthorne University as a dental appointment. We are poor pickpockets. I'm afraid it's hopeless."

She sat back, releasing the pressure on his leg. "Perhaps not. The Shepherd Foundation passes out all of Arthur's charitable contributions, several million a year. Arthur doesn't handle any of it. His daughter does. She's the person whose pocket you must pick."

Bauer glanced about the room. "Perhaps you could point her out to me."

"Certainly," Edna said, nodding to the other woman. "She's sitting on your left."

Shocked, he turned to the mousy woman. "Miss Shepherd?"

Edna said, "Doctor Muller, may I introduce Cynthia Shepherd. Careful, Cynthia. He's out to pick your pocket."

He gave the wealthy brunette a dazzling smile. "A pleasure to meet you, Miss Shepherd. It is Miss Shepherd, isn't it? I see no ring."

"It is. But you, sir, you do have a ring."

He gave the saddest expression he could muster. "Yes, my beautiful Klara. She and my young ones were killed in the allied bombing. Vienna was bombed you know." He did love Klara and the children still and felt horrible pain whenever he thought of them, but if they could help him now, why not?

Suddenly, with sadness on her face, she placed her hand on his forearm. "Oh, I'm so sorry, Dr. Muller. What hideous carnage wars are."

"So true, so true." He patted her hand. "That's kind of you about Klara, Miss Shepherd."

After a moment, his smile was back, but it wasn't for her or even Edna. It was for himself. In Germany, Ribbentrop languished in his jail cell heading for inevitable execution while here in America, Bauer had deepened his cover by befriending a famous Jew and sat at a fancy gala between two women, one stunningly beautiful, one stunningly rich. If he wasn't careful, he'd burst out laughing.

"Oh, dear, Dr. Muller," Cynthia said, looking at his throat. "It looks like you cut your neck. It looks like blood. You have a spot just at your shirt collar."

He blanched, then said, "I was in such a hurry tonight. It's nothing." He cocked his head at her. "You know, you have such beautiful hair." It was a genuine compliment for she did.

Her cheeks flushed. "You are such a liar, Dr. Muller." But her voice was lilting as a schoolgirl.

CHAPTER THIRTY-SEVEN

The day Pete's hospital ship docked in New York harbor I waited at the brownstone with the Frischer children and Yankl, who had come over, all sitting around in the living room. Knots twisted in my stomach at the prospect of seeing Pete again, at what his wounds might be, at what the future, our future, might hold. No one from the army had sent word of his injuries, which seemed odd to me unless Pete himself asked them not to. Why would he do that unless they were catastrophic? I remembered the legless captain I'd met on the ship when I came to America.

Pete's sisters and I had moved upstairs into a hastily constructed bedroom in the attic and our room fixed up for him. This morning Mina, Isaac, and Morris drove to the harbor to be there when Pete arrived, leaving the rest of us at home.

Isaac had waved his hand, dismissing our pleas to go. "Too many people. He'll get back on the ship and go back to Europe."

The clock above the mantel showed 11:15. The ship was due at 10:00. He might already be in the car heading home. Yankl gave me a sheepish shrug. "Rivka, I called Geraldine. I told her the situation and asked her to be here."

"Well, she's not here," I said curtly. I did not like being reminded who Pete really loved.

Yankl sat back in his chair and folded his hands across his lean stomach, closing his eyes. I noticed his dark curly hair had become shaggy. He'd never be handsome, but in repose, his face seemed pleasant. That was me as well. At times, I could be pleasant looking, I thought, but never beautiful, especially still as thin as a stork and with monthly visits to the dentist to fix my teeth almost destroyed by the poor nutrition in the camps. I was no beauty, but according to Yankl, Geraldine was. No doubt why Pete was in love with her.

The doorbell rang. Still shocked by sudden loud noises, I jumped, and Yankl sat up.

Teresa called from the kitchen to Jimmy and Sammy, "Can one of you boys get that?"

I reached the door first. A young woman stood there, a curvy, vivid, dark-eyed girl, holding an umbrella and wearing a cute beige jacket, her honey brown hair done in a bob. When she saw me, she flinched, taking a step back as if she were afraid I'd attack her. What did she see in me that made her do that? When Yankl had spoken about her, he praised her lovely hair, but I thought it too short. I hated short hair on women. Her curves he no doubt drooled over, but I thought them too ostentatious, showed off as they were in a tight, green skirt. No, not particularly attractive at all, I thought. This couldn't be the beauty Geraldine Rosen, but who else could it be?

"Hello, Geraldine," I said. "So, the fiancée finally meets the wife."

She straightened. "I think both those titles are on shaky ground."

With a slight shrug of the shoulders, I stepped back. "Come in."

Yankl gave her a quick hug. "Geraldine, thank God. It will mean so much to Pete that you're here."

"I'm not sure about that, but my mother said if I didn't come, I'd never forgive myself."

The Frischer children all greeted her with hugs, even the boys. We waited in the living room, Yankl and Geraldine talking about some place called Roxbury in Boston where she now lived with her aunt and uncle. After two years at Brooklyn College, she planned to transfer to Boston University. He tried several times to involve me in their conversation, but I just shrugged at his attempts and didn't say a word.

Finally, she looked at me. "There's a question I must ask you, Rivka. May I do that?"

"No."

"You won't answer my question?"

"No, I am not married to Pete. That was what you wanted to know, isn't it? Didn't Yankl tell you?"

"He did but what I don't understand is why he felt he needed to pretend marriage to you?"

"You could not understand."

"If you tell me, perhaps I…"

I repeated brusquely, "You could not understand."

Tension settled on the room. It felt as if any noise would trigger an explosion. But I was not bothered by it.

Eleven-year-old Jimmy broke the spell. "That, Rivka, was like taking a crap in the pool. It gets everyone out of the water."

Everyone laughed, even me.

"Nobody knows what that means, Knucklehead?" Sammy said.

It was not till two o'clock that Pete made it home. We heard the car doors shut, and Ellie ran to the window. "He's using crutches. He's got…oh, God."

Geraldine beat me to the door, running down the steps and flinging herself into his arms. It would have knocked him over but for Isaac and Morris steadying him.

Dropping his crutches, he embraced her. He wore his uniform and struggled to keep his cap on his head. Yankl rushed to retrieve the crutches. Standing at the top watching them, I did not know what to say or do. In this moment of warmth as Pete and Geraldine embraced, I felt out of place. A good person would share in their happiness, but I'd learned four years ago that at heart I wasn't a good person. And that realization then and now didn't disturb me.

Something seemed off about Pete, and I couldn't quite get it. His apparent happiness seemed restrained as if he were afraid to truly let himself enjoy the moment. It should have been euphoric for him. It wasn't.

When Geraldine finally released him, he took his crutches from Yankl and looked up at me, a lock of his hair falling across his forehead underneath the military cap. My heart lurched for that's when I saw his right leg from the knee down was missing. His face was thinner, yet still matinee idol handsome, at least to me.

"Rivka," he said.

"Welcome home, Peretz."

Later, in the living room, Pete answered a few questions with curt answers. I remained quiet, knowing he did not want to talk. In some ways, I knew him better than anyone, even his mother, and he didn't want to talk. He was about to explode, but I didn't know how to stop it.

His father asked how the injury happened.

"Injury, Papa," he answered curtly. "No, it was a wound." Before anyone could speak, he held up a hand. "Please, what's with these questions. Let me enjoy being home. Please."

Then he sat silent as we talked on. Everyone exchanged embarrassed glances, then for a while pretended as if this were just another social gathering. When I carried Pete's and my coffee cups out to the kitchen to refill, Geraldine followed me and said in a quiet voice, "I didn't know he would be like this. You and I are going to have to bring him back."

Glancing at her, I didn't answer, certain she would desert Pete at the first opportunity.

Suddenly, wincing in pain, she looked down at her shiny, black shoes. "I'm having trouble with these damn pumps," she said, lowering her voice even further so no one in the living room could hear the princess curse. "I'm sure I'm going to get a blister."

"Poor you."

She stared up at me, her lips twisting in anger. "At least, I'm not wearing clodhoppers like you. At least I'm trying to look like a woman for him and not a refugee."

She returned to the living room without refilling her cup. We were not going to be friends.

CHAPTER THIRTY-EIGHT

Max Bauer sat in his office grading papers from his Comparative Anatomy class, hating the drudgery of it and eagerly waiting for Cynthia and Edna to take him away for lunch. Aggravated with the tripe he was reading, he dropped his red pencil on the papers and snatched the *New York Herald Tribune* off his desk. He exhaled with both relief and anger as he read the banner headline. *Nazi Officials Indicted for War Crimes in Nuremburg*. Below that, twenty-four grainy pictures filled the entire page: Hermann Goring, Hans Frank, Ernst Kaltenbrunner, Ribbentrop, and the rest, all headed for the hangman. They were fools, Bauer thought. If he was careful and smart, he would evade capture.

Of course, pursuing Cynthia Shepherd was not smart. She herself was in the newspapers often, but he'd avoided having his picture taken. The promise of her wealth and the life it provided were worth the risk. It was that damn Edna, who was the bigger threat. Such a beauty, reminding him of his dear Klara, she'd dragged him into a delightful affair that could be ruinous.

All in all, he had to conclude, he was doing well for himself. His work for Alan Forster and American intelligence had already unmasked two communist sympathizers among Hawthorne's professors, both of whom who talked too much in the faculty lounge. One had been dismissed after J. Edgar Hoover himself, head of the FBI, complained to Walton about the professor's anti-American speeches. With a friendly arm about his shoulder, Bauer offered sympathy to the departing professor, commiserating about the unfairness of it all.

He was not the only one working for Forster. Willi Meisner was now entrenched in network radio and had already ferreted out three writers with communist leanings. Occasionally on Wednesday evenings, Bauer would tune into Meisner's show, *FBI Crime Fighters*. Though most often it broadcast stories about organized crime, bank robbers, or kidnappers, the show sometimes dealt with communist spies attempting to infiltrate American life.

Tonight, the new radio producer would take him to a gathering of former Nazis like himself and members of the German American Bund, a second meeting for him. The group met each month in an isolated home outside White Plains to drink schnapps and German beer, remember the good old days, and watch news reels of Hitler speeches and movies like *Triumph of the Will*.

Though association with them was also risky, Bauer had to admit he looked forward to the meetings. He missed his own kind. He would take this risk as well. He needed the connection to the old ways, to his true feelings, so he would not have to always be the milksop Kurt Muller every second of every day. These were acceptable risks, but still, he would continue setting money aside and making plans for a quick escape should it become necessary.

Suddenly, he was aware of someone watching him and recoiled slightly, then forced a smile. Ira Berman leaned against the door jam. It infuriated him that he was dating Edna, no doubt sleeping with her. He hated sharing the woman with him.

"You were so deep in thought," the writer said, "I didn't want to disturb you."

Bauer waved his hand dismissively. "Oh, I welcome it. These papers are filled with never ending stupidity, but what is one to do?"

"Drop them all in the trash can and come to lunch."

"I wish I could, the trash can that is." He caught himself, almost saying *Was ist los*, and instead fell onto an American expression, "What's up?"

"I want to show you a great new place. Come on. It's sunny out. Indian summer. We can catch a trolley. Forget the papers for a while. Let's get something to eat."

"Cynthia and Edna will be here soon. Can you wait a couple minutes?"

"Sure."

Just then, he heard Edna's voice call out, and she and Cynthia strode up. "Hey, you two."

Coming out from behind his desk, Bauer kissed Cynthia's cheek, then Edna's. "Ira's going to take us to a new place for lunch. He swears by it."

Cynthia patted Berman's arm. "Oh, sounds exciting, Ira. What's the place?"

"Goldfarb's Deli. You'll love it."

The eatery was in Lower Manhattan on the eastside with steps leading up to the entrance. Inside, people packed the booths and tables and made a racket with the thick sound of cutlery and dishes. Broadway playbills covered the brick walls. They found a booth in the back corner, and all four ordered Matzah ball soup and pastrami sandwiches from a harried waitress.

When the food came, Bauer asked, "Am I eating kosher?"

"Yeah, you're eating kosher," Berman said.

"I'm not going to turn into a Jew, am I?"

Everyone laughed, but Berman without much humor. "I doubt it," he said. "If you do, don't ask me to circumcise you."

As they were finishing lunch, Bauer saw a young woman who he thought looked familiar enter the deli and go to the counter where the old fat owner slid a bag across to her. She was tall, a bit skinny as if she'd been sick for a while, making her face, which he thought would otherwise be pretty, a bit hawkish, almost like a bird of prey. She had dark, almond shaped eyes, sharp and alert. Brown hair was tucked in a red scarf worn like a cloth crown.

He attempted to remember where he'd seen her before, perhaps one of his students, but they certainly had made no lasting impression on him. The answer seemed to be coming to him when she turned to leave. At the door, she froze as if abruptly reaching the end of a chain and looked back over her shoulder, those dark eyes scanning the lunchroom. Just then, Cynthia asked him a question, and he turned away from the girl to her.

"Can you come to dinner tonight, Kurt?" she said, squeezing his arm. "Seeing all these playbills I have a mad desire to see a play. We can go afterward."

"I'd love to. Perhaps tomorrow night," he said, appearing devastated not to see her tonight. "I have a previous commitment I can't get out of, and besides, I am swamped with papers to grade. Please, tomorrow night."

"It's a date."

He turned back to the front door, but the girl was gone. The answer of who she was had slipped from him.

By six that evening, Berman's Indian summer had become a wintry fall day with the bite of a cold wind as Bauer waited on the curb for Meisner in his overcoat and fedora. Willi pulled up in his new, shiny Buick, and Bauer climbed into a furnace. Willi had his heater blasting at full, his shirt sleeves rolled up and his tie loosened. As Bauer struggled out of his overcoat, he thought Meisner looked like a Berlin shopkeeper, paunchy, wearing suspenders, and a gray frothy mustache.

"Did you hear my latest show last night?" he asked eagerly as he pulled into traffic.

"Of course. I never miss it, Willi. I loved how you gave the FBI character the German name Kruger and then the part at the end when he shot the communist spy. Great work."

Meisner laughed. "Hoover liked that, too. You know he approves all our scripts."

"I know. You tell me often enough."

Twilight was darkening when just outside White Plains, Meisner turned up a dead-end road passing four new brick homes, heading toward a large, white framed farmhouse at the end of the cul-de-sac bounded by a pond and trees in the distance. He parked behind a row of cars, and they went in.

Inside, Bauer took in the large living room quickly, nine people standing about drinking beer or schnapps, all wearing swastika armbands. He and Meisner slipped on the armbands from a table and studied the people in the living room, most of whom were Bund. Of the three that were Germans from Europe, he was sure none knew him during the war, which was all that mattered.

One of them, Martin Mohnke, a gawky man with thin moustache on a lean horse face, stood by the unlit fireplace, holding a beer and talking to two other men. He claimed to be just a common soldier during the war. Unlikely but Bauer didn't plan to pry into his past or anyone else's. Mohnke caught his eye and lifted his beer in greeting. Bauer nodded to him.

The second German in the room called himself Carl Huttner and sat alone on the couch, his fleshy face terrifying in some deep, furrowed countenance. Heavily muscled, a clean-shaven head, he wore a brown shirt with a tie and the Nazi armband looking like someone from the old days with Ernst Rohm and his SA brown shirts.

The third was a woman, Trudi Huber, who gave him a flashing smile from across the room when he came in. At first glance, he had thought her a great beauty with wavy, blonde hair and a perfect oval face, but the edges were hard and the blue eyes vacant and pig stupid. And the body too broad-shouldered with arms as muscular as a wrestler. Again, she dressed all in white like a nurse, and she did that all the time. She recently married an American truck driver who knew nothing of her Nazi past, whatever it was, portraying herself to him and those here as a simple secretary during the war. Bauer felt certain that wasn't true.

Sporting a wide grin, Joe Hauser, the home's owner, approached him and Meisner. "Glad you came again, General Muller," he said, handing them each a shot glass of the strong German schnapps they all preferred. He had a soft, pudgy face with a bird's beak for a nose. "Welcome back to the Brotherhood."

Bauer's previous time here, he'd learned that before the war Hauser had been a leader of the German American Bund and on two different occasions spent time in an internment camp at Crystal City, Texas for Americans of German and Japanese ancestry.

"Good to see you again, Herr Hauser," Bauer said.

After a few more minutes, they all trooped down a set of stairs into a large, refurbished basement that Hauser called *the Bunker*. At the back, blood red Nazi flags flanked a movie screen, and pictures of Hitler, Himmler, Goering, Heydrich, and other prominent Nazi heroes covered the walls. Displayed under glass along one wall were several pieces of Nazi memorabilia, including a metal device to measure skull size, something Bauer knew eminently. Above Hitler's photograph was a red and black banner that read: *Endlösung. Final Solution.*

Bauer's mind returned for a moment to the work he did in Eastern Europe and Russia, cleansing the Earth of the Jewish menace, and he thought of his new friend Ira Berman again, that in some ways he enjoyed the man's company, and if the situation ever presented itself for their own personal Final Solution to play out, he would have no reluctance in ridding the population of another Jew.

They all lifted their glasses of beer and schnapps to the banner. Seeing it, Bauer couldn't help realizing the irony of his eating today with a Jew in a Jewish delicatessen. It was stupid and his own failing, but he was beginning to like Berman, the anti-social, acerbic *arsch*. The food at Goldfarb's was actually quite good, but that brat Edna kept rubbing her foot on his leg under the table. Remembering it, a smile reached his face and then grew into a grin.

Trudi Huber pressed her body up against him. "That must be a pleasant thought."

"It was, Trudi," he said, curtly, damned if he'd share his thoughts of Edna with her.

Before the night's movie, they saluted the flags and spoke in unison, "I swear to be faithful and obedient to the leader of the German Reich, Adolf Hitler, to observe Reich's law, and conscientiously fulfill the Führer's goals. So help me God." Then the room echoed with a loud, "Heil Hitler."

Afterward, they refilled their glasses and sat down in the two rows of chairs to watch a German newsreel of Hitler's January 30, 1941 speech at the Berlin Sportplatz. Back then, Bauer was preparing for Operation Barbarossa and read newspaper accounts of the speech. It had been an anniversary celebration of his coming to power. When the lights went out and the projector began to flicker and the image of the Führer appeared, Bauer felt a jolt of the man's old power coming off the screen. He sank into his chair and let himself drift back to those days when the thousand-year Reich was very much alive. In his heart, it would never die.

Later that night, as everyone was leaving, Hauser asked him to wait so they could talk. Meisner stayed behind also as did the three other native Germans all gathering in chairs near the fireplace where a blaze heated the room. Standing at his liquor cabinet, Hauser held up a bottle, speaking in his heavily accented German. "Jägermeister. A little brandy to finish off the evening."

He filled each glass with a couple drams and brought them on a tray for each one of them. Then, unbuttoning his vest, he settled into the leather armchair and sipped his drink.

"Well, sir, what did you think of our little rally?" Hauser asked Bauer. "Not like before the war, I can assure you, when the Bund filled Madison Square Garden, but we still have the same passion."

He raised his eyebrows and took in all of them with his glance, then answered honestly, "What I think? It's good to be part of a group that knows and reveres the old ways." He lit a cigarette and waited, but no one spoke, so he asked, "But why are we still here?"

Setting his brandy snifter on a table, Hauser sat forward, hands on knees. "The Brotherhood, Obersturmbannführer Bauer, the Brotherhood."

Bauer flinched at hearing his real name, seeing the world he was building collapsing before him. About to deny it, he saw the other Germans including Meisner grinning at him as if Hauser had just announced the coming of the Fourth Reich.

Mohnke, the lanky, horse-faced one, said, "I recognized you from the Russian Front. I knew who you were the moment I saw you last month and told the others."

Hauser held up his hand. "Relax, Max. We are not here to threaten you. We are here to support you. You know Willi. Let the others introduce themselves, and you'll understand."

Mohnke cleared his throat, sat forward, and explained that as a former general, he had commanded a division of the Waffen SS. As part of his operating procedures, he'd had killed every Russian prisoner his units captured. "I could not fight effectively if my division hauled around hundreds of prisoners. And they were only Russians, after all. Still, I am on the list."

By that, Bauer knew he meant he was a wanted man by the allies, especially the Russians. Having led his Einsatzgruppen in the general's field of operation outside Leningrad, Bauer knew of him, so they must have crossed paths, though he didn't remember it.

Then the woman Huber spoke, "I am Trudi Heidegger. I was a guard at Treblinka." With pride in her voice, she told him how she dealt with female prisoners, carrying a hardwood baton and beating them with it when they were slow to follow directions, often to death. "I followed orders. So, me, a simple camp guard, is put on the list."

When the third German, the one with the clean-shaven head, gave his real name, even Bauer had heard it before. Anton Bruck. Once, a Gestapo interrogator at Prinz Albrecht Strasse, few people lasted a day with him before they wet themselves and gave up all they knew. Now, he used the name Carl Huttner and worked as a chef. An odd transformation, Bauer thought. When his name had come up while Bauer was in Berlin in 1943, someone joked he was *wahnsinnig*, insane, circling his finger around his temple and rolling his eyes.

Bruck definitely was on the Allied list of top war criminals.

Hauser looked as if a knockout punch had been delivered. "You see, they are all in the same boat as you. That's an American expression. You are the same. The Allies want to hang all of you, perhaps no one more than you, Herr Bauer, but all of you just the same."

He explained though his Bund organization was prudently secret, no one pursued them, not even the vaunted FBI. He laughed. "They don't care anymore, focused as they are on the Red Menace. Listen to Willi's shows. You'll see. But if someone recognizes General Mohnke and tells the FBI he has found a Nazi war criminal, they must do something, and they will. It can happen to any of us, even me for my support of Germany before the war."

Bauer listened intently. That they knew who he really was had shaken him, and yet he saw the possibilities.

"The Bund is all over the country still," Hauser went on. "If any of us must run, we have people who will help us. We have escape routes, safe houses." He handed a small piece of paper to Bauer. "This is the combination to a safe in the basement below the Führer's picture. There are passports and money inside. Get me a photo, and I'll have a new passport under a different name for you in two weeks. If one of us needs to run, what's in that safe will lead to a new life."

"We must support each other," Bruck said. "That's why you are here, Herr Bauer. That's why we are all here. We support you. You support us."

Hauser, the American, laughed. "United we stand; divided we fall."

They all fell silent for several seconds till Bruck lifted his glass of Jägermeister to everyone and with a tinge of nostalgia in his voice said, "To the good old days."

"To the good old days," the rest said in unison and drank.

Then, they stared at him, and Hauser asked, "Are you with us, Obersturmbannführer?"

At first alarmed by this situation, he now felt it an opportunity, an insulated layer of protection should it ever be needed. And besides, he told himself, the promise of being a part of people who still treasured the Führer intrigued him. "The Brotherhood?" he muttered reverently.

"Yes," they answered together.

"Then I am your brother." He stood, extended his arm, and burst out, "Heil Hitler."

They all jumped up, saluting, and shouted, "Heil Hitler."

CHAPTER THIRTY-NINE

In the weeks that followed Pete's homecoming, he struggled to adjust to life with a missing leg, losing his temper occasionally at inanimate objects like the radio when he couldn't tune it and the coffee pot when it wouldn't boil coffee fast enough. Once, he screamed at no one in particular, "What the hell could a one legged man do for a living?"

Most of the family ignored his outbursts, but I told him to quit feeling sorry for himself. Jimmy, always the comic, saw Pete holding his crutches to hop up or down the stairs and dubbed him Hopalong Cassidy, someone I didn't know, but everyone else seemed to.

Some days when Geraldine visited—she had moved back from Boston—he did not even come downstairs. I had to give her credit. She didn't desert him, sticking it out, at least so far.

Though we maintained politeness toward each other, I knew immediately that first day she didn't like me, and I certainly didn't like her. Always so pleased with her looks, she dressed sensually, flirting with any male in sight, including Yankl and the older Frischers Isaac and Morris, who seemed smitten with her.

She or I or both of us went with Pete on trips to the hospital till the Veterans Administration finally provided him with an artificial leg. They left it up to him to learn how to use it. Unfortunately, it was a cheap piece of goods. We learned from other military amputees that the lowest bidder supplied the prosthesis, and it showed. The contraption had metal rods encased in wood with thin, leather padding. A spring permitted the knee to bend and the ankle to flex, but it broke down more than it worked.

One day with just the two of us there, he practiced with it, walking gingerly around the living room. "Does it hurt?" I asked.

"Like a son of a bitch," he snapped.

Despite the pain, Pete tried day after day to walk with it. He wouldn't allow anyone to help him, and when they tried, he told them to leave him alone. Finally, when the metal spring broke again, he tossed the thing into the closet and went back to his crutches.

In November, he joined thousands of other amputees to flood the U.S. capitol, hundreds including Pete getting inside the halls of congress. Each man held his prosthesis in the air, waving it at the congressmen as if they were grenades about to be tossed. The veterans were heard, and a new law was passed. After a few more months, new arms and legs arrived at the New York VA, and these worked. On his own, Pete learned how to use his and wore it all the time. It wasn't painless, but it was workable. You couldn't tell he had a missing leg, except going up steps, which he did with precise, slow strides. Jimmy now called him Peg Leg Pete.

Then, came the New Year and 1946. The war receded another couple of months into the past, but its damage clung to me like a cat with its claws in my throat. I knew I was just one of millions in that regard. Every day, I brought back good memories of my family to offset the ones of horror, but the images of those last days in Nashok and at Auschwitz flooded back at any time, catching me off guard and wracking my body with pain. They would never leave me.

One evening while walking home with Yankl from his uncle's apartment, he and I finally shared our stories. I owed him mine. In the telling, we didn't say much about Nashok, both having been there. He told me about his adventures escaping Lithuania to Sweden, then going from port to port for a year and a half till he reached America.

When he prompted me, I held nothing back. I told him about the partisans, about my love for Anton, his death, Sokolov's arrival, and my work killing high ranking Nazis. He seemed saddened by this, which I couldn't understand. I felt a sense of pride. I thought, let him see the real me. Angrily, I said, "They were hardly the only ones, Yankl. These men were guarded. I shot them down, too."

This was like a punch and saddened him more, like he was judging me.

In January, using something called the GI Bill, Pete joined Geraldine for the term at Brooklyn College. Though they didn't have the same classes—he was a freshman and she a junior—she came over to study with him. It turned out she was reasonably smart, taking business courses, while I had completed only the eighth grade. Watching her at the dining room table with Pete studying, I began to see how actually pretty she was, how physically good looking, that beautiful, honey brown hair falling loosely across her chest, a face dazzling, especially when she smiled, the full breasts that gleamed white above her blouse with two buttons undone. In this, I realized I could never compete with her.

One evening in the attic bedroom I shared with the girls, Teresa caught me staring at myself in the long mirror, pulling at my hair, longer now, down to my shoulders. It gave my narrow face a haunted appearance. I combed it straight but that did nothing special for me. Suddenly, looking at it, I felt ugly. My hair was awful.

Teresa stood beside me, both of us looking into the mirror. "I've been thinking we should do something with your hair," she said. "You'd look really beautiful with the right perm."

"To make me beautiful, that perm must be a real pip."

Wetting my hair, Teresa put it in pin curls, then when I looked in the mirror, I shrieked, and watching us, Ellie laughed.

"It will be better in the morning when we comb it out," Teresa said.

And it was. Just after we got up, she combed my hair for half an hour, giving me a deep side part and long, loose waves down the sides.

"Veronica Lake," Ellie said.

"Veronica Lake," Teresa agreed, admiring her work.

When Pete saw me at breakfast, he gave a double take, as did everyone else. I started to feel good about it. I hoped it would attract more of his attention. Yankl had talked of Veronica Lake. I would have to learn who she was.

During those early months of 1946, Pete, Geraldine, Yankl, and I spent time together going to movies, Coney Island, and jazz clubs, New York razzmatazz as Geraldine referred to it. Yankl called us the Four Musketeers. My new effort to appear more attractive was a waste of time. By then, Pete had clearly made his choice between Geraldine and me, and it was not the skinny, broken one with the sad attempts with makeup. There was never really a choice for him. He loved us both, but he loved Geraldine romantically, me only as a friend. Inside, that ripped my heart apart, while on the surface I pretended it didn't matter. Geraldine knew differently, but she never gloated, instead treating me like a leper by avoiding speaking to me directly.

Sometimes Pete, Yankl, and I would talk about our childhood days in Nashok, which left her out, which was all right with me. At other times, I shifted to Yiddish, which she actually couldn't understand. Surprisingly, many second and third generation Jews in America no longer spoke the language. She sure didn't. That was not my fault. Pete always apologized when we left her out, but the damage was done, and she blamed me because I was the one who always steered the conversation there.

What had to drive her to madness, though, was the fact I was the one who lived in the same house with him, no doubt thinking of me like a spider spinning a web to entrap him. Mostly, though, I believed she hated the Nashok bond Pete and I shared because in many ways it was deeper than her relationship to him.

It bothered me, though, how much I hurt Yankl, playing my part in our "soap opera." He loved me, I knew, but I didn't love him, not in that way. That sore broke open like a festering wound one night the four of us went to the Pair of Kings, a jazz club not ten blocks from the Frischer house. Trying to look my best, I wore Teresa's navy blue skirt with a burgundy blouse, nylon hose with seams up the back that I had to keep straight or face dire fashion consequences and, dear God, black pumps like Geraldine's. I was taller than Teresa, so the skirt didn't fall even to the knees, garnering constant glances from Yankl and other men. I didn't mind at all.

The four of us sat in a booth, drinking dry martinis and listening to Negro musicians play what Geraldine called Bop. It had a pounding, throbbing beat that found its way inside your body. Except for the stage, which was brightly illuminated, the place was lit by gas lamps, and had sawdust scattered on the floor. She ached to dance. Pete couldn't because of his leg, and Yankl didn't know how. She dragged him up onto the floor anyway. Poor Yankl looked so out of place. For her, it must have been like dancing the jitterbug with a telephone pole.

When they came back, we talked and listened to another set from the band. Glancing over at Yankl who was talking about someone named Thelonious Monk, I began considering Yankl, really considering him as a lover. He sat next to me, his foot tapping to the throbbing beat of the music. I didn't want to admit to anyone, but I desperately longed for physical contact; I wanted to feel human, and I wasn't going to get it with Pete, whose arm was draped around Geraldine.

I slid closer to Yankl. "Anyone ready to go?" I wanted to get him alone. I hoped he'd pick up on my hint.

Geraldine said, "Go where? Great music. Great booze."

"Go home. I'm tired. I've had enough jazz for one night. Anybody else ready to go?"

Sipping his drink, Yankl said nothing. His black hair, smoothly combed at the beginning of the night, now fell down close to his eyes from his dancing. Geraldine spoke again. "Why in the world do you want to go home now? We just got here. The band's got two more sets."

"Why all the damn talk? It's a simple yes or no." I finished the drink and stood. "I'm going home."

Not sure what to do, Yankl looked to Pete and back at me, before jumping up to follow me out. Now, I hoped Yankl would take advantage of his opportunity. Kiss me in the shadows of trees away from the streetlamps, touch my breasts inside the coat, hold me in his arms. He did none of these. I even bumped him a couple times and was about to grab his hand and lift his arm over my shoulders when his face tightened in thought. "Rivka, remember the movie we saw last week, *Gone with the Wind*?"

Not another damn movie. That film was so popular that the second re-release still packed theaters. "Sure, why?" I said, annoyed.

"I was just wondering if you saw any similarities between the movie's four main characters and the four of us."

At first, I didn't know what he was saying, then I understood, and it infuriated me. "No," I snapped. "That's ridiculous. Who am I supposed to be? Conniving Scarlett O'Hara? And sweet Geraldine is dear, dear Melanie? You're crazy, you know that. Pete, I suppose, is Ashley, and you, you must think you're Rhett Butler. I can tell you now, Yankl. You're not Rhett Butler."

My words cut him like a knife. He stepped back, his mouth hanging open, his face pitiful and pale. "I think I'm a perfect Rhett Butler."

I knew I was being mean and apologized. He shrugged. "So what else is new?"

And that hurt *me*. Was that how he saw me? How everyone saw me? As an unfeeling, scheming Scarlett O'Hara?

We made it back to the brownstone, and I dashed up the steps, going in without saying goodnight. Poor Yankl. I went to the window and saw him walking slump-shouldered away, back toward his uncle's apartment. He was as inept in these social situations as me.

Around this time, a miracle happened. The Ford Foundation donated money to Brooklyn College to evaluate people who were 'self-taught.' Though America still would not open its doors to Jews and other refugees in Europe, many, like me, had made their way here anyway. The donation was to open a path for us to a university education. We were the 'self-taught.' It was not guaranteed. I was to be tested and interviewed. But I had hope now.

As it turned out, when the interview took place on a cold day in early March, I got through it without too many nerves, though it was impossible to tell how well I did because the dean never changed his stern-faced expression. He asked me question after question about my educational background, stopped cold at eighth grade, the state of my current knowledge, I could blow up a bridge, fire a soviet army rifle, and hit your eye from twenty yards with a Walther P38—I didn't tell him that. When asked, I only told him my family were all dead, and that I did what I had to do to survive. A couple times he came back to those years, but I only repeated what I'd said before. This was not the man I wanted to discuss those times with.

So I left the interview sure I'd failed and pushed this disappointment from my mind—I could do nothing more about it—and went on with the routine of my days, worst of which was that irritant Geraldine. But then not long after the interview at Brooklyn College, something happened that changed my relationship with her. The four of us attended a movie titled *the Blue Dahlia* at the Paramount Theater. One of the stars was Veronica Lake, the actress Teresa patterned my hairstyle after, and Yankl's favorite. He had come to think I'd done that just to please him. I thought it would be just another of our movie excursions. It wasn't.

In the darkened theater, we sat as a Popeye cartoon played, watching him downing a can of spinach to miraculously build muscles in seconds. We had Mickey Mouse in Nashok but not Popeye. Sitting beside Yankl, I hoped he'd put his arm around me, wondering if I'd have to throw myself at a man to get some attention. Pete's was certainly around Geraldine. Yankl's gaze was fixed on the screen, and he abruptly laughed at something Popeye did. His chances with me were rapidly passing.

Then, the newsreel came on, and I went rigid.

I never expected to see again what came on the screen. A concentration camp, not Auschwitz, not Dachau, but another one, and mountains of bodies were being bulldozed into pits, then the doors of ovens stood open to reveal human bones, then skeletal people in familiar striped clothes wandered vacant-eyed behind barbed wire. The deep voiced announcer used words like *horror* and *evil*. "Men toughened by combat were sickened by the sights and smells of what the Nazis had done."

My body trembled.

Rising, I slid along the seats, then ran from the theater.

They followed me out, my friends, but some fifty yards back. Child's play for me to lose them among the alleys of downtown Brooklyn, then I began to walk, fighting to keep the images at bay, what I'd lived through, but finally they overwhelmed me, bending me double. Flashes of all the pits, all the dead, all the monsters marched through me.

I sat down on a stoop somewhere and wept, the tears flowing. I didn't know where I was and didn't care. It must have been at least an hour till my sobbing stopped. Other images came, of Mama and Papa, of Hanna and Ben Zion, and Baba all telling me to get up, to live, to not let the Nazis destroy the last Resnik. *Do not waste this life we gave you.*

I did. I got up.

When I arrived home late, maybe three AM, Pete, Yankl, and even Geraldine waited in the living room for me along with Mina and Isaac. I did not want to talk; I did not want their pity. Giving a casual wave to them, I went straight to the stairs and up to my room.

As I lay down in bed, Teresa said, "Ah, you're back."

"Yes."

"Good."

Within seconds, I heard her gentle wheeze of a snore. She had waited up for me too.

The next day when Geraldine came over after school, she cornered me in the kitchen. "What we saw in the theater last night, you were in those camps? That's what you survived?"

I stared at her to gauge her intent and saw concern. "Yes."

"You were right, Rivka. I couldn't possibly understand that." Her voice came out tinged with sadness, which I hated. Wanting no one's pity, I pushed past her and returned to the living room.

Our bristling, little war didn't end after that, but we did settle into a truce, keeping our distance from each other so we didn't snap at each other like jealous hens anymore. I couldn't tell whether Pete was relieved or disappointed. I still wanted the engagement to breakup.

The next week, I received a letter from the Dean of Admissions at Brooklyn College. When I got home from work with Isaac and Morris, Mina handed it to me. "This came for you this afternoon."

The entire family was there, including Geraldine, who was staying for dinner as usual. They all looked on expectantly when I ripped the envelope open and read the letter, then bowed my head, tears filling my eyes, and handed it back to Mina.

She read aloud, "It is with great pleasure I write to inform you that you have been accepted to Brooklyn College..."

There was more, but she stopped when everyone cheered. One by one, this new family of mine hugged me, even the boys, even Geraldine. They could never replace my own family, but they loved me. And I loved them.

"We have an announcement, too," Pete said smiling, his arm around Geraldine. "It's a night for good news. We might as well share it now. Geraldine and I have set a date for our wedding. June 11th."

My knees weakened as another cheer went up. What was I to expect? Despite hoping otherwise, I knew this was coming. Still, my childhood dream of marrying Pete had just shattered. I feared I'd crash to the floor with my dreams, but I stood, offering a blank expression. Best I could do. And hugged them both like everyone else.

Uncle Morris clapped Pete on the back. "Tuesdays, these are the best days for a Jewish wedding."

Pete nodded. "Yes."

Jimmy was disappointed. "June! June! Everyone gets married in June. October would be better. We can have the wedding on Halloween and wear scary masks and costumes."

Fortunately, everyone laughed and didn't see my face frozen in a grimace of sorrow.

CHAPTER FORTY

On a Sunday afternoon in early May, Max Bauer drove his green, 1940 Chevrolet convertible up the long driveway of Shepherd's Castle on Long Island's Gold Coast, thinking about how his life had landed among these hated Americans who had destroyed his fatherland. When he bought the vehicle last year, he'd been extremely proud about the great deal he'd gotten. Because of the war, it seemed, new model cars had not been made in this country, and he felt pleased that he could best the Americans around him by purchasing and flaunting this sporty-looking Chevy in front of them.

That was till he turned up this same driveway three months ago and saw the mansion looming near the sand cliffs in the distance. More gaudy in its ostentatious wealth than *Göring's great Carinhall lodge*, it appeared like a medieval castle, containing turrets and battlements as if they expected Vikings to invade. His poor Chevy fit here like an SS officer at a bar mitzvah.

He was in a foul mood again, still upset at September wedding was planned. In March, he'd proposed, and Cynthia had accepted. He'd wanted a quick, small wedding, but she only laughed, saying her parents would cut her off at the knees if she tried something like that. It'd be a big wedding with her high society friends and political cronies of her father like the governor. All that had to be worked out, and it took time, she'd said.

At his apparently sour expression, she'd laughed again. "In New York, engagements can last two years or more. Six months is a short engagement, dearest. I want my wedding to be perfect. Father had to practically get a papal decree to have the ceremony outdoors at the Castle. The bishop only agreed after a generous donation to the church, so us waiting till September will just have to be a hardship we both endure."

She could be tough when she chose, Bauer admitted. When he parked the car in front, Hastings, the butler, stepped out the great oak door, his nose cocked high as if the Chevy gave off a terrible stench.

"Good afternoon, Mr. Muller," he said, refusing to use the term *doctor*. "Miss Shepherd is waiting for you on the tennis court."

Without a glance, Bauer tossed Hastings the car keys and went in.

After changing into his whites, he found Cynthia practicing her serve, whacking the ball with some accuracy into the opposing court. He called out to her, "That's not fair. Practicing. You're already too good."

Grinning at him, she rushed around the net with her racket in hand and hugged him. He kissed both her cheeks.

"I'm glad you could make it today," she said.

"I come almost every Sunday. What's special about today?" he asked.

"Mother and Father are in New York this weekend," she answered with a coy smile.

He laughed. "I see. This *is* a special day."

He called his Sunday afternoons with her their Festival of Sex, and she always feigned shock as she did now, playfully slapping his shoulder. "You're such a satyr."

"Only around you."

Whenever her parents were in residence on the weekends, they had to use subterfuge for their lovemaking such as riding or long walks over the massive estate to be alone. But today, after tennis, they would spend a couple hours in her bedroom before he had to return to the city. It surprised him how much he found sex with her more enjoyable than with Edna. So beautiful, Edna seemed to think all that she had to do was just lie on the bed and be admired while Cynthia loved their romps together, always ready to do whatever he wanted.

They played two sets of tennis in which he barely won the first and she edged the second.

"I think you let me win the second," she said as they walked off the court, toweling the sweat from their bodies.

"No, of course not," he said, keeping the smile on his face. In fact, she was a much better player than he and could have easily won both sets. But then he'd had little opportunity to practice his game on the Russian front or at Auschwitz.

It didn't matter. He and Cynthia rushed to her bedroom and attacked each other the second the door was closed. Bauer thought every servant in the house, including Hastings, must be listening to them rutting wildly, the bed creaking, the loud groans of pleasure, and he was pleased at that.

Afterward, they showered together, washing each other's bodies and drying each other off. Back in the bedroom, still naked, he lit a cigarette, cupping it in his hand.

"What's that tattoo under your arm?" she asked.

"What tattoo?" he said.

She pointed. "It's under your arm by your hairy armpit," she said with a chuckle. "Looks like some gothic letters."

He cursed to himself but did not let her see any unease. He should have gotten rid of the tattoo long before this, but he was proud of it. The blood type of every SS soldier was tattooed under his arm, and it became a badge of honor for him, so he'd not had it removed.

"That? It's just a birthmark," he said casually. It was a lie, and he could see she knew it.

She shrugged and began to dress. "I'm coming into New York tomorrow on business, Kurt. Can you get away for lunch?"

"What business does my beautiful, soon-to-be wife have in New York?"

"I have to write all those checks to Hawthorne University so you can keep construction going on your new Biology building. I also have other charities that need their money."

"In that case, of course I can get away," he said, slipping on his trousers. He pulled on his shirt, buttoning it. "I usually take lunch with Berman these days. I can cancel."

"No, don't. Bring him along. We can go to that place we went last year, what was it? Goldman's, no, Goldfarb's Deli. I'll bring Edna. She's dating Berman, you know."

"I know," he said a little too acerbically. To cover his tone, he slapped her playfully on the bottom as she passed him. "Goldfarb's it is."

On Mondays, Pete had classes at the same time as Geraldine, and he waited outside the brownstone for her to pick him up, holding onto an old, leather briefcase, which he kept his books in. I kept him company before walking on to the library. I parted a strand of hair and listened to him talk about his Freshman Composition class, which he found boring because all they did, besides a couple essay assignments, was study grammar and diagram sentences.

That day, trying to look my best around him, I brushed out my Veronica Lake hair and dressed in a dark skirt and long sleeved green sweater, which I wore to avoid people asking about the tattooed numbers on my forearm. Instead of heels, I had on flats, since by American measurements, I stood 5'9" and that was tall. I didn't like looking down on all the men I knew, including Pete and Yankl, both an inch or two shorter than me. My height made me feel as gawky as it did when I was younger when kids called me the Stork. Odd how those little pains stay with you, despite all that's happened.

"That's not composition?" he groaned. "I have a lot to write about, and he wants me to find prepositional phrases. Wow."

He checked his watch and glanced up the street for Geraldine. As if remembering something, he unsnapped his briefcase, took a square envelope out and handed it to me. "We sent out the wedding invitations a couple of weeks ago, but I wanted to give you yours personally."

I bit my lip, restraining the urge to toss it to the curb. "Oh, good."

Pete shot a look at me. "You know I love you, Rivka. You're still my best friend."

I said it straight out. "I know, and I love you, too, Pete, but in a different way."

"No, you don't. I think you'll eventually see that. Someday, they'll be someone else you'll really love in that way."

"Yeah, as soon as Clark Gable comes along."

He chuckled. I didn't think he minded being loved by two women.

Just then Geraldine drove up. Waving goodbye to me, he hurried in a jagged hobble for the car, and they drove off. I turned up the sidewalk and headed for the library.

A little after eleven, I left the library and caught the trolley for Manhattan. As we passed over the Williamsburg Bridge, I considered Yankl, realizing I was becoming more and more fond of him. If I couldn't have Pete, I liked Yankl well enough. I wanted somebody. I would not be a secluded old maid. I knew he wanted to kiss me, but he just wouldn't get off the damn start block. It seemed I'd have to be the instigator. Tomorrow night, the Frischers were throwing a birthday party for his Uncle Aaron. Perhaps, then I'd ask him to come outside and kiss him.

I got off the trolley at the underground terminal and hurried up the steps onto Delancey Street. Buttoning my sweater against a chill, I made my way through the crowded streets over to Goldfarb's. As usual, when I entered, the deli was crowded, the aroma of pastrami, sharp cheeses, and chicken soup pleasantly sharp in the nostrils. I saw Emil Goldfarb, the owner, the same time he saw me, and he waved me over to an empty spot at the counter.

"There's my college girl," he said.

"Hello, Emil. My God, it smells so great in here. What's the soup today?"

"Matzah ball, what else? Isaac loves his matzah ball." He packed five sandwiches wrapped in wax paper into the bag on top of a cannister of the soup. "You can have my pastrami either lean or good. Isaac and Morris want it good." He handed me the bag. "Rivka, when are you going to marry my son? His heart is pining for you."

"Frankie is engaged, Emil. Marrying two women is illegal I think." I signed the receipt and slid it back to him.

"I have another son. It's him I'm talking about."

"He's sixteen."

"You can have a long engagement."

Laughing, I picked up the bag. "What am I going to do with you, Emil? You're hopeless."

As I started for the door, he called out, "See you next time, college girl."

Outside, I was walking south the four-blocks to the Frischer Brothers store when out of nothing panic struck as if it were 1943 and a wave of Panzer tanks roared over the ridge above our camp, bearing down on us. I stopped dead on the sidewalk. Dread pumped through my veins. I could hardly breathe. Was I crazy? This was New York. This was 1946. Yet, something was not right.

I studied the street, searching for what had triggered my alarm. Like any other day on the Lower East Side, the place teemed with endless people, flowing in an endless stream, a woman pushing a baby carriage, several women standing in front of a vegetable cart, an older man handing out balloons to children, people going in and out of countless shops. Nothing seemed wrong. Nothing seemed out of place. Yet, something my conscious mind couldn't recognize gripped in a shock of fear.

Across the street, two young men slouched in the doorway of a bakery watching me, but they didn't look worrying, just loungers. On this side of the street, an Orthodox Jew in a black suit and broad-brimmed black hat walked past. Beyond him, two couples were entering Goldfarb's, the men in sport coats with those fake patches on the elbows and wearing fedoras. I could only see them from the back.

It was the women who stood out, dressed so elegantly they didn't seem to belong in this part of town. Clearly, they were not from the Lower East Side. One was a tall blonde with a striking figure. The other a brunette, shorter, plumper. She glanced over at me. She smiled warmly then entered the deli with the others. I could find nothing that had set off the sirens crying in my head.

I hurried on, trying to distance myself from the feeling as if it would remain back at Goldfarb's and reached the Frischer Brothers' in minutes. When I entered, I set the bag on one of the front counters. Isaac, Morris, and Jacob, a young tailor in training, were waiting on customers, fitting them out in new suits.

Morris looked over his shoulder at me. "You will have to take the trolley back home for a while, Rivka. The car is in the garage. No need for you to stay late."

With pins in his mouth, Isaac called, "Tell Mina we will be along. We won't be late for dinner." He took a pin out and slid it into the cuff of the jacket. "Rivka, while you're here, I need you to look at the ledger. We need to order new fabrics and you have to clear the money for us."

"Bring it home tonight, Isaac. I'll look at it there." Then I must have shocked them because I turned and walked out, quickly hurrying back to Goldfarb's.

I didn't know what to look for, but the moment of such sudden ferocious anxiety was too real. I knew not to dismiss it. I had to discover the cause, or I would not feel safe.

Across from the deli, two women sat wearily on a bench in front of a haberdashery, talking about how much it cost to feed growing children. I leaned back against the brick wall next to them, just another lounger as the throngs of pedestrians flowed by. After a few more minutes, the two couples I'd seen from the back earlier entering Goldfarb's were now leaving, stepping onto the sidewalk. The blond-haired man put on his fedora, sliding his fingers along the brim, and turned in my direction.

It was Max Bauer.

CHAPTER FORTY-ONE

I slunk back into a nook by the haberdashery door, the granite walls of hell crashing down around me. On the other side of the street, the murderer coolly smoothed the brim of his hat. My temples pounded; my shoulders trembled, and my breathing flared. The image of Bauer on the Lagerstrasse in Auschwitz plunged into my brain, him tossing Helena's baby into the air, me turning my head as the guards fired their rifles, the baby's cries instantly silenced, Helena's bloodcurdling scream.

Trembling, I stared across the street at him in front of Goldfarb's. My first instinct was to run, but I didn't. The most important lesson Sokolov taught me was how to survive when your body, seized by panic, betrayed you.

"Don't listen to it," he said. "Force your mind to take control." Then, he slapped me so hard I stumbled back. He drew a knife and thrust it at me. Shocked, I froze, and he cut me.

He stepped up to my face and shouted. "Control your body!" He tapped my forehead with his finger as my forearm dibbled blood from the small cut. "It's the mind. The attitude. The fearlessness. Always ready to fight, to kill."

For the next several days, he'd hit me again and again, attempting to stab me. Each time, I froze. Stunned, I flailed at him, and each time he cut me. Not seriously, hardly more than a scratch—he was so good with the blade—but enough to cause sharp pain and blood.

"Are you going to cry now like a girl?" he would say mockingly.

"No," I'd shout back at him, desperately fighting tears.

But finally, I learned. One day, after he spent hours training the partisans in the use of the Russian rifles just airlifted in, he told me to wait as the others dispersed back to camp. I knew what was coming and was ready. Even so, he almost cut me again. Suddenly, punching me in the chest, knocking the air from my lungs, he drew his blade and came at me, but after that first acid rush of panic, I gained control and turned the knife aside. I easily parried the next thrust and punched him in the face, causing his nose to bleed.

Blood running into his mouth, Sokolov beamed like a proud father whose daughter had just come home from school with a red star for spelling.

It was identical here on the Lower East Side. Ignoring the rush of fear, I focused on what I needed to do. Kill Bauer. That screamed at me. Kill Bauer.

On my side of the street, I fell in with the thick flow of people and followed the two couples as they headed north. The day was overcast, grayness beckoning like a lid on a coffin. Fear gone, rage pounding my chest, I watched while Bauer talked animatedly to the others, the center of attention. Such good friends, such fun and laughter, such a good life he had, appearing anything but what he was, an evil, merciless slaughterer of the innocent.

The other man, small and dark, hung back like a wobbly loose wheel, ignored, much in Bauer's shadow.

Then, suddenly, dodging the traffic, they hurriedly crossed the street, coming straight for me. I held back and let them get ahead by some twenty feet. At the end of the street, they climbed on a trolley as it began to pull away. Fearful I would lose him, I sprinted after it, caught up, and at the last, leapt on at the back. A hand grabbed my arm and pulled me aboard. I looked into the blue eyes of Max Bauer, vacant as a dead sea, his expression blending mockery, scorn, and amusement.

"Careful, young lady," he said.

Rage and fear welled up in me. I wrenched my arm free and managed to say, "Thank you," before pushing through the crowded trolley toward the front.

After the next ten blocks, the nature of the buildings changed to stone and brick four or five stories high. When the trolley stopped across from a complex of old, ivy-covered buildings, Bauer and his friends got off. About to fight my way through the throng after them, I found that half the trolley emptied onto the sidewalk. Most of them seemed my age, young people carrying books. When the stoplight hit red, Bauer, his friends, and the entire crowd crossed the street, and I followed them. They all headed for the ivy buildings.

I lost Bauer for a moment and when I saw him again, the two women were climbing into the back of a black sedan that reminded me of the Mercedes important Nazis used. While the car pulled into traffic, Bauer and the other man headed into the complex of buildings. I kept thirty paces back. The grassy areas were filled with young people. I knew this had to be a school of sorts and saw on a brick pillar a bronze plaque that read: Hawthorne University. At a crossroad of cobblestone pathways, the two men separated, and I stuck behind Bauer. It was not unlike tracking a Nazi official destined for assassination. That was Bauer to me now.

After a moment, I stopped a male student and pointed to Bauer. "Do you know him?"

He broke into a slight smile. "Sure. That's Dr. Muller, but forget about it, honey. He's engaged to some rich hoity toity broad." He must have thought I was love-struck.

"What is he, some kind of professor?"

He squinted curiously at me. "Yeah, some kind of professor. Biology." Then, he hurried on his way.

Bauer entered a four-story building with scores of students. I stood for a few moments staring in a state of disbelief. I'd found Max Bauer. I'd found the man who had murdered my family, murdered my dearest friends, murdered every Jewish life in my village. Walking to a nearby oak tree, I sat on a bench and absently watched students go by. A deep calm settled over me. A light illuminated the dark places of my mind, revealing the path ahead. Since that day of slaughter in Nashok five years ago, Bauer had been my purpose in life, sending him to meet God. That was as precise and clear to me now as the slash of a knife across his throat. My soul felt unshackled.

That night at the Frischers, I said nothing about my encounter. With my silence through dinner and afterward in the living room listening to our usual radio dramas, Mina gave me the occasional worried look.

Later, when I went upstairs to bed, I drifted into a fitful sleep, dreams and nightmares converging, my mind floating through a netherworld between waking and dreaming, and always the presence of Bauer with his swastika eyes. I split apart. I was two people. I saw the old Rivka lying beside me, a dead husk. Rising out of it was a creature with twelve wings and wearing chains of fire, the Angel of Death, unbreakable, invincible.

Where I appear, there is no escape.

In the morning when I awoke, I had no moral unease, no guilt for what I planned to do. I saw only the cold equation that Sokolov taught me: gather intelligence, plan, prepare, execute. Downstairs, I helped Mina get the children off to school and the men off to work. Around then, Geraldine swung by in her car to pick up Pete for their classes.

"You're feeling better now," Mina said after everyone was gone and we sat at the dining room table, sipping a final cup of coffee together. "Last night, it seemed something was bothering you. Is it your period?"

"No, I'm fine, Mina."

"Tonight should be enjoyable. I'm looking forward to it."

I didn't know what she meant. "Tonight?"

"Aaron's birthday party."

Yankl's uncle. "Oh, yeah."

"Are you sure you're okay, Rivka?"

I gave her a reassuring smile. "I'm fine, Mina."

And I was. This morning, I walked the several blocks to the library, considering what I knew about Bauer. The most obvious, he thought himself safe. That gave me a sense of power. He didn't know it, but he wasn't safe. He would never be safe again.

It would be easy enough to buy a gun, walk up to him, and shoot him, but I might be caught. More than that, the idea of such a quick execution left me feeling cheated. It wasn't enough. My entire family lay in a mass grave along with the people I most loved, while the ashes of millions he helped murder at Auschwitz drifted in the endless clouds. Bauer would not get off that easy. No death in a blink for him. He must know the terror my family felt. His past must be exposed. The perfect, safe life he had built for himself must be destroyed.

That night, the Frischers held the dinner and birthday party for Aaron Weber, Yankl's uncle, a small, thin man in a coat and tie who sported a trim, brown beard. At something Jimmy said, he gave a deep-throated laugh, his eyes sparkling with delight. He slapped his knees. "You are such a funny one, Jimmy Frischer. You're going to be another Jack Benny."

Liking praise and being the center of attention, the boy's chest swelled. What boy didn't?

Yankl and his uncle, Pete and Geraldine, me and all the Frischers sat in the living room after dinner exchanging memories of Nashok. Tonight, there was much laughter. The stories everyone told were joyous ones raising up images of shtetl life when I was a happy child and when my family lived each day with a love and contentment that seemed then the natural order of things. I wanted to carry these with me always. Perhaps, someday they would remain while the nightmares faded.

But this night I had told no stories of my family and had not laughed. For me, tonight was about Max Bauer. It was as if he stood in the middle of the living room in his SS uniform, pointing at loved ones to die but unaware the Angel of Death was coming for him.

Earlier, Yankl noticed my distraction and gave me a questioning look. I shook my head and went back to listening to Morris talk about his wife Miriam, Aunt Miriam, how they'd first met. It was about as far as he could go with the storytelling. He could not talk about his children, none of whom survived, and I doubted he ever would.

I decided Yankl, who'd been at Nashok and lost his own parents, brothers, and sisters, had a right to know about Bauer. Telling the others would be a cruelty to them. What could they do now? After Bauer was dead, I would tell them. When Morris finished, I told everyone I was going outside for some air and asked Yankl to join me.

Though the sky was overcast and starless, the streetlamps illuminated the block of jammed brownstones and parked cars. The pavement glistened after an earlier shower. Still it was a pleasant night with just a little chill. From down the street, we heard Mr. Greenbaum playing his clarinet. He would stop at nine so as not to keep the school children up late.

Folding my arms across my chest, I leaned against Geraldine's car. None of us had a car, not even Isaac and Morris with theirs in the garage. Uncle Aaron had one, but that was not like Geraldine, our age, having one, a gift from her father on her birthday. A brand new Packard Clipper. She talked about it like it was her first child.

"What is it?" Yankl asked.

"I saw someone today."

He raised an eyebrow, waiting for me to go on.

"Max Bauer."

Confused, he gazed at me, clearly not remembering the name right away. Then, he blinked as if punched in the face and took on an expression of shock. "Bauer? That Max Bauer?"

"Yes."

He ran his hand through his hair. "Here in New York? How can that be? Are you sure?"

"I'm sure. I've spoken to him before more than once."

"We need to tell someone. We can't let him get away."

"He won't get away. Tell no one."

"But…"

"Yankl, no one."

He exhaled and took a step back. "All right, but you should let me tell Aaron. He has…"

"No."

He held up his hand. "Wait. Let me finish. He's a lawyer. He has this code called attorney client privilege where he can't tell anyone what you tell him. He knows an attorney who just came back from Nuremburg. His cousin is one of our lawyers. This attorney worked on the trial team prosecuting Nazis. He might be worth talking to."

That actually intrigued me. As one possibility, the idea of Bauer on the end of a noose after a trial in which he was exposed to the world as a mass murderer had its attractions. It was not the revenge I wanted. I would deal out my own. But I would see this person and hear what he had to say. I nodded. "All right."

Yankl bounded up the steps and went inside. A few seconds later, he came out with Uncle Aaron.

"What's this all about, Rivka?" the older man asked. "Yankl said it was important."

I told him what happened today but used the name of Klaus Kruger as the man I saw, and though Yankl frowned at me, he didn't correct me. He said to his uncle, "I thought you could put us in touch with Richard Shapiro. He might be able to tell us the best way to proceed."

A frown creased Aaron's face. "We should take this to the US Attorney's office."

"No," I snapped. "Tell no one. Yankl said you wouldn't. I don't trust anyone to deal with this but me. I don't trust this Shapiro, and I sure as hell don't trust some government official."

My vehemence surprised him. He'd never seen that side of me, and his frown deepened. He glanced at Yankl and back at me, seemingly about to argue, but then said, "Look, this Shapiro fellow, I don't recommend him. I doubt if there's much he can tell you, Rivka. He was only a low-level paper pusher over there. He didn't have much to do with the actual prosecution."

"He knows what's happening over there, doesn't he?" I asked.

"Yes, but listen." He hesitated as if searching for the right words. "The best way I can describe Richard Shapiro is this. He's an ass. He's someone who proclaims he doesn't suffer fools gladly and then thinks everyone else but him is a fool. No one can work with him. He accused Dodd of mollycoddling the Germans."

I didn't know what *mollycoddling* meant, but I got the gist from Aaron's tone. Too soft on the German prisoners. "Who is Dodd?"

"Thomas Dodd, one of the lead prosecutors and a damn good attorney. He tossed Shapiro out on his ear. So, that's…"

"I'll see him," I said.

"We'll see him," Yankl corrected.

Shaking his head, Aaron sighed, then shrugged. "All right. I'll call him tonight and see if he'll meet with you tomorrow. If he agrees, you can use my car. I have a deposition in Manhattan at three, so don't wreck it." He fixed his eyes on me. "Beware of crusading Jews, Rivka. Don't say I didn't warn you about Shapiro."

"Thank you, Uncle Aaron," I said, giving him a quick hug.

"Please, don't tell anyone I'm such a pushover. It will ruin my business."

CHAPTER FORTY-TWO

R ichard Shapiro agreed to meet with us the next day at 11:00 AM. A half hour before the appointed time, Yankl picked me up in his uncle's Ford and drove us to Williamsburg's Grand Street where Shapiro lived in an apartment on the second floor. Five minutes early, I knocked on the door, waited a minute, then knocked again.

Someone within called, "Hold your horses."

Another minute passed before I knocked a third time. Within seconds, the door flew open, and a disheveled, dark-haired man eyed us with a mixture of confusion, anger, and disdain. Maybe thirty years of age, he was barefoot and wore creased, brown pants with a sleeveless t-shirt. He took a toothbrush from his mouth and pointed it at us. "You're the people Aaron Weber called about."

Yankl said, "Yeah, this is Rivka Resnik and I'm Yankl Glassman. We came about..."

He held up his hand. "Stop. Not yet. Give me a minute." Reluctantly, he waved us in.

The apartment was a mess, not dirty but cluttered by open boxes and two open steamer trunks overflowing with folders and loose paper.

He brandished the toothbrush at us again. "You're so eager. Sit down. I'll be with you in a minute. I need to finish my morning ablutions."

As he vanished down the hall, Yankl said, "Oh, wow, ablutions. He knows a big word."

He and I sat on the couch to wait for the Nuremberg lawyer. A few minutes later when he returned, he'd put on shoes and a white dress shirt. "Anyone want coffee?"

I nodded; Yankl said, "No thanks."

A few moments later, Shapiro came in from the kitchen with two cups and a single bagel, set them on the coffee table, then dragged a chair up to face us. I sipped my coffee. Even with a stubble of beard, he struck me as someone who would be handsome but for the intensity of his expression, as if a math problem must be solved immediately or the room would explode.

Abruptly, with the bagel in his hand, he gave a dismissive wave. "So, you two kids think you saw a Nazi."

Yankl started to speak, but I clasped his shoulder, silencing him. Then, I rolled up the sleeve of my left forearm, revealing the tattooed numbers.

His mouth opened in surprise. He leaned back in his chair and stared at me. "You were at Auschwitz?"

At least he knew that Auschwitz was the only camp that tattooed its prisoners. "Yes, and I saw Nazis there. I saw one of them yesterday."

Thinking, Shapiro rubbed his temples as if that hurt for him to do, then finally asked uneasily, "Okay. What is it you want from me?"

"Information," I said.

"About what?"

Yankl leaned forward. "What should we do? Report him to the authorities?"

Shapiro laughed. "What authorities? Who the hell do you think you would report him to? The goddamn police?"

Nonplussed, Yankl shook his head. "No, but I thought…"

"How about the Justice Department?" he said, his voice mocking. "Maybe the State Department. Those two shitass agencies have allowed hundreds of Nazis into this country based on their supposed anti-communism, Nazis that should be hanging from the damn gallows." He looked up in a caricature of thought. "Let's see. Who else can we report your Nazi to?"

Yankl suggested, "The FBI?"

"Ah, yes, the FBI. Mr. Hoover. No, I don't think so. Hoover would hire concentration camp guards as agents if he could."

Squirming uneasily now, Yankl fell silent as the attorney studied us for a full minute. Though annoyed by his behavior, I returned his smug gaze and waited.

Finally, he sat forward, elbows on knees. "Listen to me. Even if there was some agency to report him to, it wouldn't matter. It's all about the math. We are trying twenty-four men in Nuremberg for murdering twelve million people, six million of them Jews. Do you think just those men alone killed all those people?"

"No, obviously not," Yankl said.

"Now, you're getting it. But they sure as hell had a big hand in it. Still, not all of the twenty-four will be hanged. They all should be, but some will be freed. Others given prison sentences, which they will dutifully serve and then be released after a few years. There will be other trials of other war criminals with the same results. Here and there, men will hang, but most will receive slaps on the wrist."

He stared down at his coffee as if seeing it for the first time, lifting the cup, then set it down without drinking. Yankl and I exchanged glances.

"Consider this," he said, his voice growing impassioned. "In time, a few hundred war criminals will be hanged or sent to prison, especially if the newspapers get involved in a case. But most won't. What about the engineers that drove the trains with Jews crammed inside, what about all the camp guards, what about the men who provided the Zyklon B and those who dropped the tablets into the showers, what about the SS and the Waffen SS, what about the men from other countries who herded Jews to mass graves and shot them for the Germans."

My body shuddered as images of my family standing with me at a mass grave flickered through my brain. Beside me, Yankl's hands clenched. He had seen his own family shot and dropped into the pit.

But Shapiro was right, and I hated it. Most of the guilty would get away.

The Nuremberg lawyer went on, "Everyone in Germany was either involved or knew about it. They're all guilty. We don't have enough people to pursue them even if we wanted to, and believe me, we don't want to. There are no governments with the will to pursue the guilty. Nuremberg is for our conscience. Not for justice."

Yankl's voice wavered, "Then what do we do?"

Shapiro thought a moment then said, "A few Jewish survivors and some Jews in Palestine have the right idea. On their own, they hunt down Nazis and kill them. They are called the Nakam, the Revenge. But it's no more than a Jew's tear in the ocean."

My tear in the ocean was Bauer. That was my path to nakam. Shapiro fell silent, drifting off into his own thoughts, then finally took a bite of his bagel.

"So you won't help us?" Yankl asked.

Shapiro said in a tired voice, "Well, since you're here, who did you see?"

I leaned forward on the couch. "Max Bauer."

The bagel dropped part way from his mouth. He caught his breath. "Are you sure it was Bauer?"

"Yes, he led the einsatzgruppen in Nashok. That's where we're from. I first met him there. I saw him again at Auschwitz. I know him. I've spoken to him. And I saw him yesterday on the streets of New York."

Shaking his head, Shapiro said, "Damn, that's a big fish if it's true."

"It's true, Mr. Shapiro," I said.

He looked for a place to set the bagel down, then tossed it onto the coffee table. "Okay, we'll operate under the assumption you're right. He's one of the top Nazis still at large. We caught all the main einsatzgruppen commanders last year, except Bauer. Every government will want him to prove what dedicated Nazi hunters they are." Excitedly, he wiped his hands on his pants. "If we get Bauer's name to the right people, they'd take him into custody. I think…"

I interrupted him. "Will he hang?"

He stared at me but said nothing.

"Will he hang?" I repeated.

He gave a shrug of his head. "Probably."

Probably wasn't good enough.

"That's the question, isn't it?" Shapiro added. "The other einsatzgruppen commanders won't be tried for at least another year, if that. Look how long the current trial is taking, and we have at least eleven more to go. Eventually, these men will be tried and likely sentenced to hang, including Bauer. Will they actually hang? It's hard to say. They all should, but I can't predict who will and who won't. Before any execution, some sentences could be commuted, and then all bets are off."

Yankl blinked, uncertain. "But you said if we get this information to the right people, he would be arrested. My uncle's a lawyer, and he knows people at the US Attorney's office in Brooklyn. They will arrest him."

"Maybe," Shapiro said. "I don't know those people. Not everyone will pursue Bauer with all due speed and zeal. They could just sit on it and he could melt into the population elsewhere."

Yankl argued with him, and I let them talk though my mind had long been made up. Only I knew how to find Bauer, and though I trusted Aaron's good intentions, I did not trust this US Attorney's office or Shapiro. As he said, too much could go wrong. Escape too easy. I needed to follow Sokolov's rules: gather intelligence, plan, execute.

After a couple of minutes between the two men, I stopped them. "We are not going to report him to anyone. No one else will control Bauer's fate but me."

Frustrated, Yankl said, "Rivka, you don't plan to let him go?"

It was Shapiro who answered him. "No, she doesn't, do you, Miss Resnik? You have something else in mind."

"Yes. I plan to introduce him to God."

For the first time, a smile spread on his face. "That's not an easy thing to do."

I didn't answer him directly. "Do you have a man named Klaus Kruger in your files? What if I saw him yesterday? What if he was also at Auschwitz?"

Shapiro's eyes flashed recognition. "Kruger? I know him. My god, two of them."

He rushed to one of the steamer trunks and began rifling through the folders. Eventually, he yanked one out and opened it. "Yes, this is it." He brought it back to the coffee table and read the papers inside. "He was the Generalkommissar of the Kaunas Region. A war criminal of the first order. So, you knew Klaus Kruger at Auschwitz. Wait." His eyes darted up at me, and he scowled. "You couldn't have seen him there. He was never at Auschwitz. He died in 1944 in Kaunas. It says here he was killed in a…"

"Bomb blast," I said, completing the sentence.

In surprise, he stared at me for several seconds. "How did you know that? It's only rumor. The Soviets tell us nothing."

"Because I placed the bomb under his bed." I stood up. "Yankl, I'm leaving. Are you coming with me or staying to chat with Mr. Shapiro?"

I stepped around the coffee table and started for the door. Frowning, Yankl followed me. I turned back. "Mr. Shapiro, you've been helpful, and I'm grateful. You told me what I had to know."

Dropping the folder on the table, he watched us go, a quizzical look on his face.

A few minutes later, as Yankl drove in the heavy traffic of Grand Street, we remained silent. The constantly blaring horns grated on me. When I first made it to America, a car backfiring had me scrambling to the ground, and the loud sounds of the city kept me continually on edge. I doubted I'd ever get used to it.

Finally, Yankl glanced at me. "So, let me understand this. You plan to kill Bauer yourself?"

"You figured that out finally. I do."

With a pronounced grimace, he shook his head. "That's such a bad idea, Rivka. It's crazy, in fact. Can't you see that? There is such a thing as the law."

Furious, I turned on him. "The law! Where was your law when our families were slaughtered in Nashok? Where was the law when Max Bauer pulled out his pistol and shot Hanna in the head? Don't talk to me about your law."

"Rivka, please." He swallowed then said, "I was there, remember. I saw it. But it's different here. The law means something here. Uncle Aaron has…"

I wanted his support, and he was betraying me. My anger swelled like magma. "You don't know. How would you know? You ran. You have no say."

His face went pale. His hands gripped the wheel.

I regretted it immediately. It was inexcusable. "I'm sorry, Yankl. That was awful of me to say. I didn't mean it. We both ran. What else could we do? It's just you're such a close friend. You're the only one who can truly understand, and you have to be on my side."

"I am on your side, Rivka. Don't you see, you alone, a young girl, are going to deliver some sort of vigilante justice to this war criminal. It won't work. I don't want to see you hurt."

Easing to a stop behind a line of cars at a light, he didn't see my reaction and went on, "The best thing we can do is take this to the US Attorney's office in Brooklyn or to the Southern District. Either would get you what you want. Aaron knows people in both. He'll make sure they work every hour on this so Bauer's brought to justice."

He hadn't listened at all, speaking to me as if I were a seven-year-old, not someone who had fought with partisans while he rode his ships to America. The firestorm ignited in me. I shoved open the door and jumped out into the street.

Alarmed, he yelled, "Rivka, what are you doing?"

I leaned back in, my voice scoffing. "You didn't hear a damn thing Shapiro said, did you? Or me? Go home and hide under your bed, Yankl." White heat blew through me. "And keep your mouth shut. Tell no one about this. If you do, I'll hate you. And believe me, the Nazis taught me how to hate."

He flinched as if slapped. Before he could respond, I slammed the door and hurried onto the sidewalk, quickly losing myself in the crowd. I had been brutal to him. Right then, I didn't care. I didn't need his pathetic good intentions getting between Bauer and me. I walked blocks with my temper incandescent, burning through me. I'd put so much trust in Yankl. He was my friend, a brother. He suffered the same loss I'd suffered. That he would not support me was like a blood betrayal.

After half an hour and blocks of walking, the fire inside began to burn off, and I regretted the way I'd acted toward him. I didn't want to lose him. Who was I to behave that way? Who was the real Rivka Resnik? Was I now wholly the Angel of Death? Nothing more? Would my parents be proud of me? Mama had told me to live, live for them all. I had been closing toward a good life when I saw Bauer and became the Angel. Those doubts settled into me.

Still, I would not apologize to Yankl or pretend I'd been wrong. At that moment, I realized I stood in front of Shapiro's apartment again, heading here all the time. I went up to the second floor and knocked on his door.

When it opened and he gazed at me in surprise, I said, "I need a gun."

CHAPTER FORTY-THREE

S hapiro took me to his uncle's shop five blocks away. A sign above the door read, *Pawn Shop. Loans. We Buy Gold.* Before we went in, he said, "Uncle Leo's connected."

"To what?"

"The mob."

"I just want a gun."

Inside was a cramped and dark room with a shipwreck of junk displayed as if a king's treasure. Beneath glass were watches laid out in rows, and rings and bracelets. Elsewhere, pots and pans, guitars, trumpets, a saxophone, drums, radios, clothes, furs, boots, all the flotsam of people's lives. In one corner stood an Egyptian mummy.

And a gun section with pistols, rifles, and ammunition on the shelves.

In a back room, I met Uncle Leo, a burly man in his mid-fifties with a hard face under thick, gray hair. He smiled with effort. "So, who's this young beauty, Ritchie?"

"This is Rivka Resnik. Rivka, my uncle, Leo Shapiro."

Uncle Leo stared at me a long moment. "Ritchie called and told me what you needed, Rivka. What's a young lady like you want with a gun?"

"I have a rat problem."

He laughed, then nodded toward a man who had been standing in the shadows near a back door, a duffel bag slung on his shoulder.

When he stepped into the light, I saw his face had been scarred by burns. He began pulling handguns from the duffel bag, displaying them on the desk, about twenty pistols in all.

Leo said, "Charlie got back a few months ago from fighting the Japs. He's a real hero. Got a Silver Star and a Purple Heart. Seen every damn island in the Pacific. He's an independent contractor now and doing me a big favor bringing his wares here."

I stepped to the desk to look them over as Leo went on, "He brought back a few guns as souvenirs, bought some other ones from his Marine and army buddies, and built himself a damn nice business. Everything top of the line. You pay cash, you walk out of here with the piece, no questions, no paperwork like the ones out in the main shop. No damn New York record of you with the gun to muck things up." He shrugged. "But this way will cost a little extra."

I studied the weapons, several I recognized. The same army 45s Pete and Major Landry had carried, a couple German P08 Lugers, several revolvers, and even a Red Army TT33 semi-automatic, Sokolov's favorite weapon. The rest I assumed were from the Japanese, but I didn't recognize them. Of the pistols spread out on the desk, there was only one for me, the Walther P38, and I reached for it, sliding back the bolt to see the chamber empty. "This will do."

Surprised, Leo said, "You are familiar with this one?"

"Yes. How much?"

He began rubbing his chin, a practiced pose. "Since you're a friend of Ritchie," he said, "Charlie will sell it to you for fifty dollars. That sound fair to you, Charlie?"

Charlie shrugged.

I didn't have that much money, not close to it, and it seemed like a lot. In the main store the pistols cost between ten and twenty.

Leo seemed to read my thoughts. "Those guns in the shop come with state paperwork. Let's say your boyfriend gets clipped, and the cops find a nine millimeter slug in him. They look at state records and see you just purchased a piece that fires nine millimeter slugs.

I'm not saying you plan to knock off your boyfriend, especially if that's Ritchie, but you see what I'm telling you here? Up to you."

"I'll take this one," I said. "I don't have enough with me, but I can …"

Shapiro interrupted, "Put it on my account, Uncle Leo."

Leo grinned. "Then we got a sale."

Before we left, I bought a large, black purse with a shoulder strap, more like one of Yankl's messenger bags, and dropped the Walther inside along with an extra clip and a couple boxes of 9mm ammunition, accessories every girl should have.

"Let's grab some lunch," Shapiro said. "I have a couple things to talk over with you."

I was about to refuse but realized I was hungry. We walked several blocks to a diner and found a booth. He ordered chili, and I had a grilled cheese sandwich with French fries and coffee. For some reason, my leg pumped under the table, and I fidgeted with the napkin, far more nervous than when I went to meet Shapiro's gangster uncle. I couldn't figure out what was wrong with me, then realized I was attracted to Shapiro. Like a schoolgirl.

Shapiro held up his cup. "The food's not good here, but the coffee's great. I suppose if you can do one thing great, you're ahead of the game."

"Then why are we eating here, Ritchie?" I asked.

He looked as if I'd slapped him. "God, don't call me that. My friends call me Rick. You know, like in Casablanca?"

"No, I don't know."

"Well, it's Rick. The food's filling, and you looked hungry. So, you probably won't notice that this isn't Delmonico's."

Then he leaned against the booth and stared with such leering eyes and for such a long time at my chest, I looked down to make sure one of my breasts hadn't poked through the blouse. I thought he would ask me to undress right here in the diner. As a girl, I had dreams like that, being naked in a public place like a street or a café, people gawking at me in horror at the skinny, flat-chested girl. Now, with Rick's stare, it both terrified me and titillated me.

But then what he asked blew that up. "Why did they call you the 'Nun?'"

I was startled by the question and at first thought to deny it. How did he know that, and how much did he know?

He must have seen my expression because he answered the question. "When you and Yankl left I went back to the documents. The Nun came up more than a couple times, with Kruger and others. It was you. I found ten references, and I only went through about a quarter of the documents. That's quite a tally, lady."

"Six. I was only assigned six of the bastards to assassinate." I shrugged. "I wish it had been more, but, you know, the war ended."

"How did that name come about? Being Jewish, you were hardly a nun."

"Actually, I was. I hid in a convent with other Jews. The mother superior made the women and some of the men wear habits in case the Germans came. One day they did."

The memories of that time flooded back, of Mother Johanna, Sister Agneta, Sister Irmengard, Sister Humilitas, the other sisters, and the Jewish fugitives. I hoped they were all still alive, but I doubted they were. I told Rick about working in the convent infirmary the day Major Dietrich and Lieutenant Schwarz arrived, how I had treated Schwarz for days and gotten to know him, a decent boy who murdered Jews and who I would have gladly poisoned if it wouldn't have brought instant retaliation on the convent.

I explained that when I began working with Sokolov, the first person I was ordered to assassinate was Major Dietrich. He was a butcher but then they all were. The partisans hated him, and Moscow okayed it. I got a job working in German headquarters as a cleaning woman but could only enter his office after he was gone. We considered placing a bomb near his desk with a timer, but Dietrich went in and out too often. A side door led to back stairs down to an alley, but the exit was guarded. Still, Sokolov thought I might be able to go in the side door when I knew he was there, ex-ecute him, and escape out the front in all the confusion. I refused. I sought no suicide missions. But after another week, Dietrich solved the problem for us. He called me to his office to clean up a broken porcelain tea pot.

When the waitress came and refilled our coffee cups, I fell silent. After she left, I resumed the story. "I have to say I was nervous. I was afraid Dietrich would see my hands shaking, but he worked at his desk, not noticing me sweep up the broken pot. The Walther—I used a Walther then, too—was hidden in my woolen dress. Just as I reached for it, Schwarz came in, the man I'd treated at the convent infirmary months before. He saw me, looked stunned for a second, then said. 'You!'" Remembering it, I went quiet.

Rick leaned forward. "Well, what did you do?"

The question seemed odd. "I shot him, of course, twice in the chest, then turned the gun on Dietrich and shot him two times in the head, then ran out the side door. I made it down the stairs to the back where the two sentries and a desk sergeant guarded the exit. One of the guards told me to halt so I shot all three." I leaned back in the booth. "That was a bloody day. It didn't bother me, Rick. I felt nothing then and nothing now except maybe satisfac-tion at a small portion of revenge. How awful does that make me? But I still burn with hatred for them. You have attached yourself to a very bad woman."

He raised his eyebrows in mock horror. "That's what I like about you. Your immoral ways. What about the nun part?"

I chuckled. "That. I heard later. It seems Schwarz's last words were, 'It was the nun.'" I shrugged, then, after a moment, said, "Now you. Nuremberg. Tell me why they sacked you."

He frowned heavily, clearly not wanting to answer.

"Talk, Shapiro," I said.

"All right. I called my boss, Tom Dodd, a horse's ass. It wasn't the first time, but it was the first time I did it publicly. He actually liked me, thought I did good work, but couldn't let it pass this time. So here I am."

"Why'd you do it?"

"I told you before. They didn't plan to hang all those bastards, only some of them. They were mitigating the murder of millions. It still drives me nuts. I knew it was coming, this leniency. I could see the writing on the wall." After a moment, he added, "It means …"

"I know what it means. I studied the Old Testament."

We sat for another two or three minutes without speaking while I pushed the French fries about on my plate. Then Rick smiled, stirring his coffee. "How old are you, Rivka?"

"Nineteen. Why?"

He smiled. I liked his smile. It was warm but something else. Seductive? Was that it? I didn't know, not about such things. "Damn, you're nineteen," he said. "You're a teenager."

"I skipped my teenage years." That wiped the smirk off his face. "Yes, you did."

"How old are you, Rick? Forty-two?"

He laughed. "Hardly. I'm twenty-eight."

I raised my eyes and looked across the table at him. Our gazes caught. His ruffled, black hair looked as if I'd just run my fingers through it. Suddenly, he placed his hand over mine, jolting me, a shiver racing through me down to my toes.

"I think you deserve some living," he said.

I snatched my hand back. "Are you thinking I owe you something for you paying for the Walther?"

He shrugged. "You owe me nothing. I just think you are a damn attractive woman, and I like looking at you."

I frowned. "You need your eyes checked."

"Don't do that. Don't sell yourself short. Come out with me to-night. A little razzmatazz. I know a great jazz club in Manhattan."

"No," I said, then added quickly, "I would actually like to. Very Much. But evenings are going to be busy for a while."

He nodded. "Max Bauer."

"Yes, Max Bauer." I met his eyes.

A cocksure grin on his face, he said, "Well, then, come back to my apartment with me."

His eyes burned with something I couldn't recognize till it hit me. It was desire. The thrill of it roared through me. "I can't." Then added, "Not yet."

He sighed theatrically, then after a moment, grew more serious. "Anything I can help with on Bauer, let me know."

"There's one thing. Do you have a car?"

CHAPTER FORTY-FOUR

Sokolov's principles of surveillance: nobody spots you. If the target catches you following him, the mission is ruined, and you should be shot. Always appear to belong exactly where you are. Look the part. A woman with a baby carriage. A woman shopping the store windows. Walking arm in arm with a male partner as lovers. If you come suddenly upon the enemy, don't lose your mind like a squawking chicken. He may not realize yet you are the tracker. If you must talk, do it calmly. Remember no matter where you are, you are always in enemy territory.

It had been a short recitation. I glanced over at Rick Shapiro for his reaction. In the quiet neighborhood, we sat in his Plymouth Coupe down the block from Max Bauer's apartment on our second night of surveillance. It was after nine, and once again, the murderer had come home from the university and not gone out.

"Quite the manual," he said with a skeptical raise of his eyebrows. "I can understand now why we won the war. Any more rules?"

His lack of seriousness annoyed me. "A bit more. Sokolov had an endless supply of tactics. Do it his way or he would punish you. Painfully."

He grinned. "Then I'm glad you're here and not him."

Suddenly angry, I turned on him. "This isn't a date. Approach every moment as if our lives depend upon you. Because with Bauer, it does. If you won't do that, I'll get out now."

I heard the vehemence in my voice. I could almost touch the fearful anger inside me but also stand outside of it and see it like a spectator, something always pushing to bust free.

He nodded several times, then after half a minute of dead silence, turned to me, his dark eyes serious. "I get it, Rivka. I'm sorry. I'm a lawyer, and I'm not used to this, but I'll learn. He sounds like a bit of a monster himself. Your Sokolov. Why did you put up with all that?"

"He was helping me."

"To do what?"

I leaned my head back on the seat and recited, "Sokolov's rule number one: when it becomes necessary to fight, kill. He taught me how."

We fell silent for a while, watching the empty street and Bauer's apartment on the third floor. To follow him without being seen, I had to change costumes to take on another character. That night, I wore gray slacks that Yankl called Katherine Hepburn trousers and a long sleeve, black blouse, clothes I could move quickly in if necessary.

Earlier, I'd changed in the car out of a bobbysoxer getup while Rick pretended not to look. Most of the day, I'd been at Hawthorne where men vastly outnumbered women on campus, so just by the numbers a woman stood out. Some were bobbysoxers, but most dressed as if they worked in an office. For me to fit in, it was not so much clothes as attitude. That makes the spy. Fall out of character and you'll be spotted.

Putting his hands behind his head, Rick leaned back in the driver's seat and sighed. "Is this guy just going to stay in his house every night? Spy work is a lot harder than I thought."

He looked to me, expecting a response, but I said nothing.

In two days, Rick and I had learned little about Bauer. His class schedule: five separate classes per week. That he drove an old, green Chevrolet convertible. And that he lunched today with Ira Berman, a Jewish writer on the Hawthorne staff that Rick recognized, at a small café down the street from the campus. Rick and I went in and, though crowded, found a small table only a few feet from them. I made sure my back was to Bauer and instructed Rick never to look his way. Their conversation and occasional laughter seemed to indicate they were good friends.

After they left, Rick dropped a couple dollars on the table, and we followed them out. They went back to the university, and we followed Bauer home when he left again.

The night was growing chilly, so I put on a sweater as we sat in the car watching his apartment. Abruptly, out of a fifteen-minute silence, Rick turned to me and said, "You know, you have nice legs."

After a moment, I replied, "Thanks."

"When is your friend getting married? Soon, isn't it?" he asked.

"Another month. I don't want to talk about that." I had pushed all thoughts of Pete's wedding to the back of my mind. I didn't have enough room to think about it and Bauer, too. Each burned far too much energy. "Don't talk of it, Rick."

He held up his hands in surrender. "Sure. No more questions."

The light went out in Bauer's apartment. Almost in unison we leaned forward in the seat. He was either going to bed or going out. We set in to wait. But nothing more happened. A half hour later, Rick checked his watch. "It's ten o'clock, Rivka. What do you want to do? I'll sit here all night if that's what you want."

I sighed. "No, no point. Lights are out. He's in bed. Let's go, and, oh, if you see Mina, we were visiting friends of yours for Shabbat."

"Okay." He started the car but before he pulled out, turned to me. "It's late. You can stay at my apartment. Nothing expected, Rivka. I'll take the couch. You can have the bedroom."

I debated with myself whether I wanted to actually sleep with him and couldn't come up with an answer. If I did go to bed with him, that would complicate things too much. "No, you might get confused about where you're supposed to be sleeping."

Shocked, he placed his hand to his chest. "Me? Confused? Never."

"My home, Rick."

On the next night, watching again down the street from Bauer's apartment, we got our first bit of luck. In the darkening twilight, a new model automobile stopped in front, and he hurried down the steps in a formal coat and tie. A chauffeur jumped out and opened the back door for him, and he slid in. As it drove by us, I saw him kissing a woman on the cheek.

Rick started his car and swung out to follow. Darkness had fallen and the streets were crowded with taxis, busses, trolleys, and other automobiles honking horns and lurching forward. Block after block, we struggled to stay two or three cars behind into Midtown.

"Who's the woman?" I murmured. "We need to know the woman."

He shrugged.

After almost forty blocks, the car turned onto 55th Street and stopped in front of a restaurant that a large awning identified as Le Pavillon.

Rick whistled. "That ain't cheap."

Bauer and the short brunette I'd seen him with at Goldfarb's got out and headed for the entrance. Elegantly dressed in a burgundy gown, she sparkled with jewels on her wrists, fingers, and neck. A man uniformed in red livery opened the door for them.

"Look at those jewels," Rick said. "How can she move under so much weight?"

"I need to find out who she is," I said again and started to get out.

Rick clutched my arm. "Wait. I'll go with you."

He parked in front of a hydrant, and we jumped out. On a Friday night, the sidewalks were crowded, and we hurried in among them, the sound of soft jazz drifting from across the street at the St. Regis Hotel. As we approached, the doorman at Le Pavillon looked at us with disdain and shook his head, refusing us entrance. Rick wore his sports coat with no tie, and I had on a long sleeve blouse and the same gray slacks as the night before. No jewels.

"We weren't planning to eat here. I gave my valet the night off," Rick said.

"Sure." The doorman smirked.

I said, "I thought I saw an old professor of mine just go in. Kurt Muller."

"The tall blond man," Rick added. "Just now."

The doorman shrugged. "Might have been."

Rick slipped him a ten dollar bill, and he looked at it. "Gee, thanks, pal. I can now make a down payment on that Rolls Royce the misses wanted." But he stuck it in his pocket. "I believe that's the man's name."

"Who was the woman with him?" I asked

"Are you kidding, lady? That was Cynthia Shepherd."

At my look of complete ignorance, he flicked his wrist at us as if shooing mosquitoes away. "Move along now."

We walked back to the car. "Who's Cynthia Shepherd?" I asked.

"She's the daughter of Arthur Shepherd, the richest man in New York, richer than Rockefeller. The newspapers say she may soon be engaged. If so, that must be to Bauer. He has not only escaped the noose but landed here in New York with a wealthy fiancée."

We got in the car. Before starting it, Rick turned to me. "If they're engaged, will you kill him before the wedding?"

I considered it. "No. I want him married. I want him happy, a happy Nazi, with everything to live for and thinking himself safe." Folding my arms across my chest, I leaned back against the seat and sighed. This was what I had been looking for in his life. Something he wanted that I could destroy. It seemed odd talking so casually about a murder, but then it was Bauer. To me, that made all the difference. It wasn't murder; it was retribution. "In fact," I told Rick. "I plan to attend the wedding."

As we drove back to his apartment, a plan began to form in my mind. I asked him, "Do you still have contacts in Nuremberg, or have you made everyone angry at you?"

He laughed. "Funny. Not everyone hates me there. Some even agree with me. Why?"

"I need a picture of Bauer. Germans kept records about everything. There should be something somewhere. In his uniform preferably."

"Damn, Rivka, you're not asking for much. It will be like looking for a needle in a million haystacks. I'll call in the morning. It's too early over there now."

For the first time, I decided to stay at Rick's. As promised, he took the couch, giving me the bedroom and a pajama top to wear. The place was hot, and the windows open to feebly gather a breeze. When I lay down, I wondered if he had fallen asleep yet. Though exhausted, I imagined him beside me, his bare chest glistening with sweat. I thought about how he looked at me. No one had looked at me like that since Anton three years ago, not even Yankl, whose gaze had been more about worship than desire.

Thinking of the man out in the living room, I tried to force myself to sleep but couldn't. While in the partisans, it always struck me as odd that after a battle in which some of our people died, we survivors returned to camp and that night, instead of sleep, made love. The sounds echoed through the camp like night birds squawking and groaning. I lost my virginity to Anton that way, though the preciousness of virginity had long faded with the world it was so prized in. I never understood why after such a close dance with death, people so often turned to sex. Was that what was happening to me now? Bauer, a dangerous man, would have no hesitation about killing anyone who threatened him.

Getting out of bed, I went into the living room and flicked on the lights. He was sitting up on the couch in his underwear. The pajama top I wore barely reached below my hips. My long, bare legs drew his gaze immediately. I didn't think I'd ever been so nervous in my life.

"This is ridiculous," I managed to say. "Come to bed, Rick."

Two days later at the Hawthorne University library, I searched through New York society pages while Bauer was in class. It took no more than twenty minutes to find a wedding announcement dated March seventeenth for socialite Cynthia Shepherd and Hawthorne University professor Dr. Kurt Muller, her picture alone above the article. The date for the wedding was Monday, September second to be held at Shepherd Castle on Long Island. The text said some of New York's most prominent citizens would be in attendance, including hizzoner the mayor and the governor. At the reception, toasts were expected to be led by best man Ira Berman, the noted author, and a film of the young couple made and shown by Hollywood's own Herbert Gold, academy award winning producer.

"Ach So," I muttered aloud in German, seeing the first inkling of true vengeance.

For the next two weeks, we kept up our surveillance, learning a little more each day about Bauer's activities, but didn't see Cynthia Shepherd again. Then, on a brutally hot night, a man we'd never seen before picked him up from his apartment on Thursday evening. We followed the car an hour from Manhattan to a farmhouse outside White Plains.

And there, everything changed.

CHAPTER FORTY-FIVE

Twilight had lapsed into darkness by the time the car with Bauer turned off the country road outside White Plains and drove up a lane. Stars had blossomed out, filling a moonless sky.

"Go past the road," I told Rick. "Go a hundred yards, turn off the lights, then come back."

He did. When we drove up the lane, our lights off, I saw the outline of a handful of what seemed like prosperous country houses, each sitting on at least an acre of ground. A couple hundred yards ahead, the car with Bauer parked behind other vehicles at the last residence, an old farmhouse with lights from inside illuminating the front lawn. The rest of the houses seemed vacant or had no one at home.

Bauer and his friend hurried to the door. It quickly opened, and they went inside.

"What the hell. A party?" Rick asked.

"I don't think so. Something else is going on."

We coasted slowly up the pavement to the first house and backed into the driveway. Just as Rick turned off the engine, another car sped past us going to the house at the end. Two more men went inside, then one car after another, rolled by.

Rick muttered, "I don't think this is a meeting of the Catholic Benevolent Society."

After ten more minutes in which no cars arrived, I suddenly reached for the door. "I need to see what this is."

"I'll go with you."

"No, I've done this kind of thing before. You haven't."

"But…"

I said bluntly, "Rick, I can't have you out there stumbling over your feet. Stay here."

Anger and humiliation flared in his eyes, but I didn't have time to worry about that. I took the Walther from my bag, shoved it into my trouser pocket, and slipped out into the night, surprised at how frightened but also how excited I was.

I darted across the street and into a sprawling backyard. The grass had grown tall. Sixty yards farther on stood the farmhouse, lights glaring in the front windows. Hurrying the distance, I stopped a few yards short in a clump of trees and studied the structure again. Etched against the black sky, it was imposing, two stories with a gabled roof, and a Frankensteinesque air to it. Most of the windows were open against the heat and shouldn't prove difficult to enter. Behind the brightly lit front windows, several men stood about as if chatting, as if it were some sort of party. That couldn't be it. I was about to move toward one of the open windows when I saw the flare of a cigarette near the back porch. I slid behind a tree and waited.

There was no porch light. To best see an object in the dark, I was taught not to look directly at it but slightly off to the side. Then it becomes distinguishable, which this figure did, his outline distinct, twenty yards away. Whoever it was, he appeared to be alone. I waited. Tried to keep my breathing calm and silent.

After another minute, someone stepped out onto the porch and called to the smoker, "We're going down."

He stubbed out the cigarette with his shoe and went back in. I waited another five minutes to be sure no one was outside, then sprinted for the side of the house, squatting down, catching my breath.

Slowly, I moved to the front window with lights on and hunched under it. I heard nothing. No shadows moved through the light. At an angle, I peered ever so slightly inside and was surprised to see no one there. Where had they gone? This could be something innocent, but I doubted it. An icy chill prickled the back of my neck. I caught a strong sense of malevolence.

I was afraid to go inside. There were too many of them. Yet, more than that, more than overbearing fear, I wanted to know. Everything told me this was the crux of it all.

Liquid fear pumping through my heart, I hurried to the open window in back and climbed into the dark room. It was not very big, a small bed close by as if for a child. After waiting a moment to make sure I was alone, I went silently to the door and stepped into the hall.

No one was about, not in the living room, nor the kitchen. Everyone had disappeared. In the hall, I noticed a painting hung at a distorted angle as if a hook had failed. It was of a young, naked man, his mouth wide, screaming in agony, pain draining down his body. Other of the paintings were the same, men and women in contorted poses of horror and distress.

Focusing back on the four rooms in the hallway, I checked the next toward the rear, an empty office, then moved to the end of the hall. Opening the door there, I saw a set of stairs leading below into utter blackness, and in my mind, I saw something deadly lurking below waiting for me. Despite staying on the sides of the steps, each creaked too loudly.

Finally, reaching the bottom, I sighed. No monsters yet. Once my eyes adjusted, I could make out dusty bottles of wine on shelves. To the left was the shadow of a door almost hidden in the corner. I checked it and saw it led to a set of stairs going up to another door that no doubt opened onto the backyard.

Turning back into the wine cellar, I noticed a faint light coming from down a narrow passage to the right. I listened and at first heard nothing, then the muffled sound of voices, and moved cautiously toward the source of light. A closed door was framed by a ribbon of brightness. Here, the voices were louder, then they abruptly stopped. I froze. Had I made a noise? A second later, they roared again, this time in unison, reciting something as if calling forth the spirits of the dead.

I had to find out what was going on. I had to open the door.

Turning the handle, I heard a click and winced, then slowly opened the door a sliver and peered in. My heart lurched and pounded. From slightly behind, I glimpsed a formation of men wearing swastika armbands, their arms outstretched in the Nazi salute toward a portrait of Adolf Hitler. Bauer tall and prominent stood among them, his voice powerful and distinct.

A pudgy man stood next to the main basement stairs, alternately studying the men and making notations in a book as if taking a roll. Hurrying, he finished, shoved the book into a drawer of a cabinet, then rushed over to stand with the other men just in time to pledge everlasting loyalty to the Führer.

"I swear to be faithful and obedient to the leader of the German Reich, Adolf Hitler, to observe Reich's law, and to conscientiously fulfill the Führer's goals, so help me God."

Rage swelled in me. These men were among those who murdered my family, murdered millions of people, and in a convulsion of madness destroyed worlds. Inside me, I felt the wings of the Angel of Death unfurl, coming out to take her vengeance. I wanted her to fly. I wanted her loose on them. I wanted her to slaughter them all.

I drew the Walther from my pocket and cocked it. With a full eight-round magazine, I picked out the eight men I would bring down, starting with Bauer. The urge to fire was overwhelming, but I knew, too, that it was a terrible plan and would not accomplish the cold justice those who'd died deserved. I had to control the angel. There were too many of them. Nothing here for me to do but die. I forced the angel, seething all the way, back into her burrow.

Slowly shutting the door, I backed into the wine cellar, slipping the Walther into my pocket, and made my way in the darkness toward the stairs. Bauer, all those Nazi monsters here, living well and reliving their past murderous glories. It sickened me. They had not paid for their crimes. They had not met any justice. Bastards. Monsters. Butchers. The sound of their voices tore at me, but I said to them, vengeance was coming. It's coming hard. The voices ceased. I hesitated a moment, then by twos, rushed up the stairs. Time to get the hell out of here.

On the first floor, I headed for the child's room when a door at the far end of the hall opened and a man stepped out. Exposed, desperate, I took two quick steps and entered the kitchen. In front of the refrigerator, a man and a woman stood holding glasses of beer. Like two characters from a madhouse, the man had a massive shaved head with bumpy knobs at the top, coal black eyes under thick, knitted brows. The woman, a pretty blonde with broad shoulders, was grinning, revealing yellow, crooked teeth. At my appearance, they glowered at me with surprise that turned quickly to alarm.

"Guten abend," I said with a smile and went to the sink where several dirty glasses had been stacked.

I rolled up my sleeves, making sure not to reveal my tattoo, ran the water, and one by one began rinsing the glasses and loading them in the rack. I could feel their eyes on me. Sweat drained down my spine. I started humming *Lili Marlene*, and finally they went back to talking, something about the Nuremberg trials. I imagined turning on them and saying, "You know, there's a lawyer from the trials right outside. How about that?"

I'd give this another minute and if they hadn't left, shoot both and get out through the back door. That's when the man from the hall entered the kitchen. "Ein bier, bitte, Bruck," he said, and the first man reached in the refrigerator and handed him a beer. The new man didn't seem to take any notice of me at all.

"Hauser is showing *The Campaign in Poland*," the man said in German and laughed. "A very short film."

From the corner of my eye, I saw he was stocky, with thick shoulders and legs and wore odd looking shoes I thought were named spats. His slicked back, black hair glistened as if wet from a shower. His voice crackled like a frog.

The other two laughed, and the woman said, "Almost as short as the Campaign in France."

Finishing the glasses and acting as if I knew precisely what I should be doing, I dried my hands on a dish towel and walked out of the kitchen into the hall. Quickly, I stepped into the bedroom and climbed through the window. Outside, I ran along the back lawns, retracing my route in, and reached the car in less than half a minute.

Rick wasn't there.

I cursed. I yearned for the days with the partisans when people did as they were ordered, then remembered before Sokolov came it was always chaos. No one did what they were ordered. Plans were poorly conceived, poorly executed, and everyone followed their own impulses.

I drew the Walther again and hurried down the sidewalk. This would have been the way Rick went if he'd left the car. Straight toward the house. A crescent moon could be seen rising above the horizon beyond the farmhouse. Sokolov had called it a stalking moon, enough light to see the enemy but not enough for him to see a practiced killer. The Dainava Forest and my days with the partisans came back to me in a flood as I neared the end of the lane and heard the scuffle just ahead.

Rick was complaining, "What do you think you're doing? I live here. I'm just out for a walk. Can't a man go for a walk?"

"Move or I shoot you," came the hoarse reply.

The voice was familiar. I'd just heard it. The man in the kitchen, the stocky one with slicked back hair, had a pistol pressed against Rick's back, shoving him forward. As I rushed toward them, he glanced back over his shoulder.

I waved, smiling. "Herr, einen moment, bitte."

He stopped. Rick looked at me, fear in his eyes, but he had enough sense to keep his mouth shut.

"Was ist los?" the stocky man said suspiciously and turned slightly toward me, the pistol coming around in my direction.

Quicker than him, I brought the Walther up and shot him in the head, the report in the silent night like a thunderclap. He collapsed, and Rick jumped back with a strangled scream.

Quickly kneeling down, I searched the man's pockets. "Take his watch," I told Rick.

He stared at me incredulously. "What? Steal his watch?"

"Take his goddamned watch."

He slid it off the man's wrist. I found the wallet, and we ran back to the car. "Can you drive?" I asked, thinking of how shaken he seemed.

"Yeah, I can drive."

"Keep the lights out."

We jumped in, and he started the engine. Instantly, we were out on the road, speeding away. It took Rick the full hour back to his apartment before he calmed down. He nearly wrecked the car before I got him to slow down outside White Plains and turn on the lights. His jumbled thoughts colliding, he talked without pause like a man hopped up on stimulants. He insisted he'd never been involved in anything like what'd just happened. Yes, he'd been part of the Nuremberg trials and seen the awful films about the camps, but he'd never actually gone to them. Did not have the courage to go among the walking dead and see the bodies personally.

On the Bronx River Parkway, he was able to keep with the flow of traffic moving south, though now driving slower, though he was still agitated.

"I'm a big coward." Suddenly, his mind went off in a different direction. "Why did we steal from him? That makes us thieves."

"So Bauer will think this was a robbery and not run. He might suspect something else now, and he's got too much to stay for. I want all of them coming back again and again, so I'll know where to find them when the time comes."

To emphasize the point, I tossed the wallet and watch out the window. I didn't tell Rick I'd already pocketed the money in it. No reason to waste that.

"That man somehow got behind me," he said abruptly, "and I couldn't run without being shot. Then you came." In disbelief, he shook his head and repeated, "I've never been a part of anything like that."

Later, we lay in his bed, both on our backs, separated by at least a yard, no cover, no sheet, the window open. The room was warm but not oppressively hot as it would likely be in the summer. Wearing just my panties, my arm tucked behind my head, I lolled in a stateless world between sleep and awareness. Beside me in his boxer underwear, Rick stared up at the slow moving ceiling fan, creaking gently. It had only one speed, and slow was it. We were silent, not holding one another. He had seen me kill, and that had sunk him, even to save his life. I felt abandoned, but I wouldn't apologize for who I was.

I told him what I'd seen inside the house, but I was unsure he heard me. As we lay there, I wished he would say something. I liked Rick, much more than I thought possible. I didn't want someone else I cared for to fail me, either by dying or by not backing me. He must now see me as a monster, too.

Then he asked, "Do you see the faces of the people you killed? Do they haunt your dreams?"

The question bore a hole into my chest. I sat up. "No, I do not. You sound like Yankl. When I sleep at night, I see the fields of slaughter. I see my mother. I see my father. I see my family and friends lying dead. They haunt my dreams, Rick. I see Bauer shoot my sister. Not a single Nazi I killed bothers me. Not one. They deserved it. And killing Bauer will not bother me."

When he didn't respond, I said, "Do you want me to leave?" When he still said nothing, I put my feet on the floor. "I'll leave."

He lifted his head to look at me. "God, no. Why would you do that?"

"You don't seem to want me here. You knew what this was, what we were doing. Now, it seems you've changed your mind."

Desperation on his face, he scooted across the bed. "God, no, Rivka. You saved my life. I failed you. That's hard for me to come to grips with. I couldn't help you. I did something stupid that almost got us both killed. Not exactly the heroic, manly type we see ourselves as."

Though I'd been furious about what he'd done at the house, I had kept that to myself. I knew what I said next would not only be important to our relationship, but to him personally. But I could not lie. He would see through that. He had failed us.

"When I was a partisan, I didn't know how to use a gun," I began. "I was scared all the time. I dreaded when we went out on an operation to tear up railroad tracks or bring down telephone wires because the Germans might show up. I wanted to kill them, but I also wanted to survive."

He squeezed my hand. "That's how I felt when I got out of the car."

"But eventually it changed. Sokolov taught us how to use the weapons properly. How to handle our fears, even use them to focus on the details of a mission so it would be more likely we'd come back alive. Rick, we learned to follow orders, to do what we were told, to trust those with more experience. You need to understand this. You endangered both our lives tonight. You didn't trust my decision. That must never happen again."

His pallor drained, and he turned away from me. I knew Rick was someone who could make a tough decision and stick with it under great pressure. I knew this would be hard for him to hear, and I knew this would threaten our relationship. I did not want to lose him, but this mission, and our lives were more important. I waited for his response, hoping he would understand and not kick me out of his life.

He moistened dry lips and said in a steady voice, "I won't make the same mistake twice."

I picked up his hand and kissed it. "I know people, at least as far as courage and bravery goes, and I know you have it, you have courage, or you wouldn't have gotten out of the car. Not the brightest move though."

His shoulders eased. He exhaled, then suddenly pulled me down to him and kissed my mouth. Sparks erupted along my skin as his hands caressed my breasts, my belly, my hips. I drew down his shorts and wrapped my leg over him.

The next morning, I called the White Plain's police. When a male voice answered, I said, "Sir, last night, my husband and I were driving outside White Plains, just west of town, when we heard what we thought was a loud car backfiring and didn't think anything of it. Now, I'm not sure. It could have been a gunshot. Has there been anything reported about it? Anyone hurt?"

The sound of paper shuffling came over the phone, then the officer said, "I don't show anything, ma'am. No reports of gunfire. No incidents reported. Pretty slow night actually. Give me your name in case something comes up. We can get in touch with you."

"I don't want to become involved," I said and hung up.

Rick was leaning against the wall next to me. "What did he say?"

"Nothing. They didn't report it. They must have disposed of the body themselves."

"Why would they do that?" he said, then answered his own question. "They didn't want any attention from the police. Maybe they really think it was a robbery."

"Maybe so." I wasn't so sure, dreading Bauer might be escaping now.

CHAPTER FORTY-SIX

A bove the buildings, slate-gray clouds rolled in with a chill and a rumble of thunder as we approached the synagogue. We'd arrived in two cars, the Frischer family, me, Yankl, and his Uncle Aaron, we women with dresses and jackets that covered the shoulders and the men in their black suits and black fedoras. The wedding I had been dreading and trying to keep from my thoughts had finally come.

How many days growing up had I dreamed of Pete and me in such a synagogue as this, performing the marriage ritual and then living our lives out in Nashok? Numbed, I felt like a sleepwalker, carried along in a stream of people. I had loved Pete all my life and now he was marrying someone else, youthful dreams grown fierce over the years soon to be shattered with the breaking of glass.

Inside the synagogue, Mina and Isaac went off with Pete. Yankl, the best man, disappeared down a hallway. The rest of us filed down the aisle to the front pews where the bride's and groom's families sat, women to the right, men to the left. I scooted in next to Teresa, Ellie, and two of the bride's aunts and several cousins. Excited, almost giddy, Teresa was chattering at me constantly till she realized I wasn't responding, and she turned to her sister.

Thank God Geraldine didn't ask me to be one of her brides-maids. She wasn't a hypocrite. She didn't like me and wasn't going to act like she did. She should have asked Teresa though. Up in front, a wide band of gauze covered the chuppah along with a garland of red, purple, and yellow flowers. Soon she and Pete would be stand-ing under it, a symbol of their new home, welcoming to everyone like the tent of Abraham and Sarah.

Later—I didn't know how long—Rabbi Salzman led the bride's grandparents to the front pews and took his place under the chup-pah. Pete's grandparents were lying under the ground in Nashok and wouldn't be coming. A procession of people followed, grooms-men including Yankl, and bridesmaids, then Pete, escorted by Isaac and Mina. I noticed Pete grinning. He smiled a lot these days but never grinned. Now he was. He was happy. This was the happiest day of his life.

The bride came in white.

The rabbi conducted the ceremony, each part administering small cuts into my heart, and soon Pete stomped on the glass, break-ing it to pieces, and it was done.

"Mazal tov!" everyone cried out.

A revelation struck me so hard I blinked. I was still alive. This marriage hadn't left me in a puddle on the synagogue floor. It came to me that the girl Rivka had died in that pit, not here with the breaking of the glass. She was the one who loved Peretz with such burning, romantic, youthful passion. Pete was a man now, just married, and it didn't bother me like it should have, as it would her. If she had been here, she would have broken apart. I had been holding onto her by loving Pete. With the ceremony's end, the last vestiges of that youthful love crumbled, and I was not devastated. No, not devastated. And I was still alive. Yes, alive.

Looking up at the wedding guests swarming the couple, I saw Geraldine in tears of bliss, and Pete grinning still, flushed with joy like I'd never seen, and suddenly I couldn't help but feel happiness for him, my best friend. Always my best friend. I rushed to him, telling him how I truly wished him well with his new bride and new life.

"Thank you, Rivka. It means so much to me that…" Then he was overwhelmed by several of his buddies from the 82nd Airborne, some still in uniform.

Geraldine would be harder. I pushed through the crowd to her and took her hands. "He is happy. You may not believe me, but that's important to me. I wish you both the best."

Her eyes misting, she swept in, hugging me.

When we went to the festivities afterward, I watched while Geraldine was carried about on the shoulders of the women. I could not help but envy her. We sang and danced well into the night, and when I crawled into bed, I was exhausted physically and emotionally, but convinced I'd finally breached a wall into my true future, whatever it may be.

As was tradition for Jewish couples to begin their married life as part of the community, Pete and Geraldine didn't rush out on a honeymoon. They remained for the Seven Days of Feasting ordained by Moses, inviting family, friends, and neighbors. Mina was put to the test to keep everyone fed. Teresa, Geraldine, her mother, and even me, worked in the kitchen as every night a dinner was held for guests.

Teresa, Ellie, and I had moved back to our old bedroom, and the attic had been fitted into a studio apartment for newlyweds. Her parents offered rooms in their house, which was bigger, but Pete and Geraldine decided on the attic till they graduated from college and he found work. That first week, we heard the bedsprings above us cranking steadily through the night. At first, I felt an old pang of jealousy, but the girls couldn't stop giggling. It was so infectious I found myself laughing with them.

During that week, I met with Rick three times to keep track of Bauer. By then, it might have been more prudent to call off the surveillance, since it was unlikely he would run now with Cynthia Shepherd waiting at the altar, but I couldn't. Every part of me cried out against it for fear something would scare him and set him running.

Rick agreed. "We have to watch him, Rivka. He might contact other Nazis hiding in this country. I don't want to let any of those bastards get away, and neither do you."

Rick was right. I wanted Bauer to feel safe, and he did. I wanted him to have the world opening before him, and that was about to happen. When it did and I took it away from him, it still would not be justice for his crimes, it never could be justice, but it would be vengeance.

In Nuremberg, Germany, Ralph Graves, Senior lawyer on Thomas J. Dodd's staff at the war crimes trial, sat at his cluttered desk long into the evening. For supper, he'd eaten only a ham sandwich and washed it down with coffee, lots of coffee. Graves was a thin man by nature but had lost almost fifteen pounds since working the trial for the last year. So much so, that on occasion people mistook him for a concentration camp survivor brought in to testify.

His small cubicle was crowded with steel files and open folders. An American flag stood in the corner. He was organizing witness statements from allied POW camps and OSS intelligence sources that would be used to support the films of Nazi atrocities Dodd planned to show again to the court. Some of these films were made by the Germans before war's end, but others by Hollywood filmmakers working for the army who took their cameras into the camps.

He also had to prepare a slide show charting all. His own aides he'd already sent back to their quarters for the day. They worked hard, and he knew better than to wear them out. He needed to get things ready for them to finish when they came back in the morning.

About to take another sip of coffee, the phone rang, making him spill some on his fingers.

"Son of a bitch," he spat, set the cup down and wiped off his hand with a tissue, then snatched up the phone. "Hello!"

"Ralph, did I wake you?" the voice joked. "You're working a bit late, aren't you?"

He recognized Colonel Payne of the JAG corps in Berlin. "Hey, Bill, how you doing? Yeah, I'm working late, but you're calling me, and I doubt it's social. What's up?"

The colonel got right to it. "We've been going through Propaganda Ministry documents—my God, the Germans documented everything, even the amount of toilet paper they ordered. Anyway, you asked me to see if I could find a photo of Max Bauer, one in his uniform if possible, for your boy Shapiro. Apparently, Bauer could be in America, right? Well, we found one and he was in uniform. But get this. We found something else. And it's major league."

"Terrific, Bill. I appreciate it. Can you get it to me ASAP? I'll send it on to Shapiro."

"It'll be in the courier packet tonight. Wait till you see it, Ralph. You won't believe it."

Summer heat had come in a blaze and lasted for weeks. Steam lifted off the pavement outside the brownstone, but the boys played their stickball, and the girls jumped their ropes. Daily, a few clouds drifted across the skies, sometimes threatening rain, but it never came. It was then, with the arrival of the package from Nuremberg, a plan finally began to take shape. For the first time, I felt there was a chance it might actually work, though massive problems remained. The biggest was simply needing more men to carry it out. Rick and I alone could not do it. The only thing certain was when it would take place, September 2nd, the day Bauer would marry Cynthia Shepherd and his wonderful new life lay before him.

At Rick's apartment, after a couple hours trying to patch the holes in the plan, we'd given up for the time being and spent the rest of the evening in his bed. As much as I enjoyed the lovemaking, my mind was not fully on it.

Finally, I got out of bed. "I'm hungry."

A few minutes later, we sat on his couch, eating grilled cheese sandwiches he had just fried, me in a pajama top and him comically wearing just an apron to keep grease splatter off his privates.

He set down his half eaten sandwich on his plate and looked at me. "Rivka, can we talk about you and me?"

"You and me?"

"Our relationship. I think I'm falling in love with you."

I placed a hand on his bare chest. "No. Rick, I can't think about anything like that. Not till all this is over, maybe then." I saw the disappointment in his eyes and added, "But it feels good to be loved by you."

He muttered a *hmm*, his expression not revealing what that meant, but I doubted it was good. "When will you kill him?"

I frowned. He really had a knack for abruptly changing the subject of a conversation. "After the wedding. He won't get away." I held his gaze. "I'm going to bring Pete into it."

Rick's eyes raised. "Is that wise?"

"He said he would help if I ever needed him. He was a soldier, and he can get around on his leg well enough. He has friends who served with him, and I need some work done watching the farmhouse." Then, I added sarcastically, "It's either him or some of your uncle's friends. I don't want to have to work with Lucky Luciano."

Rick smiled. "He's in Italy."

"Good. Then I'll take the 82nd Airborne."

CHAPTER FORTY-SEVEN

In the fading twilight, Pete Frischer stood while two of his former army buddies lay in the shrub at the edge of the tree line a quarter mile from the farmhouse, all three watching through binoculars. They wore dark shirts and baggy, dark green pants. To help Rivka, Pete had enlisted the two former members of the 82nd who led dull lives after the war and were eager to help. This was the third week they'd been observing this farmhouse for activity, Nazi activity of all things, here in America.

Former battalion Intel Sergeant Jack McCarthy lay nearby. In his thirties, he was a tough Irishman, having grown up on the streets in Brooklyn's Bay Ridge. Stocky with red hair and a pale complexion, he had another feature that gave him and Pete a special bond. McCarthy had an artificial limb, a metal glint coming off his hook of a hand. The sergeant had been one of those who had joined Pete in storming congress for workable VA prosthetics. Pete knew the man ached for a cigarette but that would expose their location if anyone in the house was alert.

The other man, Corporal Raymond Stiles, was no more than twenty with a cherubic face and pale gray eyes. When he joined the 82nd in February last year, he was a shy kid who became a hell of a soldier, awarded a Silver Star. But in his heart of hearts, he was still a teenager.

"Are we really taking orders from a girl, Sarge?" he asked, glancing up. "I don't mind sitting out here. I got nothing better to do. But really, does she know what she's doing?"

"Believe me, Stiles, she's fought in more battles and killed more Germans than all of us put together, even you."

"If you say so."

"And use the G. I. Bill if jobs are scarce. Go to college. Get yourself an education."

"I don't know, Sarge. I was never much of a student."

"College," McCarthy said. "That's where the girls are. They love soldier boys."

Stiles dropped his binoculars and looked over at him. "Now maybe I actually should become a college man."

At mention of Rivka, Pete thought about her with sadness. He'd wept for the girl she had been. In the last six years, the world had gone mad, and few people had suffered more or had a harder struggle to survive than her. Having passed through her valley of slaughter, she was different, vastly so, intense, acerbic and cynical, and focused with a marksman's crosshairs on Bauer. He wondered if there was anything of his old Rivka left. When she'd come to him at the end of June and asked for help, he could hardly refuse, but after she told him about Bauer and the Nazi enclave right here in New York, he very much wanted to be part.

Suddenly, in the binoculars, Pete saw movement at the farmhouse. "Here we go," he said.

A car was rolling in and two men got out. The door of the house opened, and a man stood framed in the light holding a rifle. Lowering it, he greeted the men as they entered. Soon a second car approached, followed by a third. In another ten minutes, several more arrived, and Pete counted fifteen men in all go in, maybe one of them was a woman; he couldn't tell from this distance. Some carried rifles as well, and Pete assumed all were likely armed in some fashion.

Stiles glanced up at Pete. "Sarge, it looks like we may be going to war again."

I was up that night when Pete came home, and we talked out in the backyard under the moonlight. Leaning over the wire fence, we looked into Mr. Mendelbaum's yard of junk, old mattresses, furniture, a broken bicycle, a toilet seat, and much more lay about, like the debris after an army had swept through. In that wasteland, a strange thing happened. I caught the scent of Pete's aftershave, a green, almost pine scent that pierced the unpleasant odor of old Mendelbaum's junk. Not exactly romantic. He had come home, washed up, and shaved again before coming downstairs, and for a brief moment in the backyard I let myself return to that overwhelming passion for him. It ran through my bones like an electric shock.

Then he coldly gave his report, and the feeling washed away.

From his days in the army, the report was concise, telling me the Nazi group still met at the farmhouse, how many people showed up, and how long they stayed.

When I asked him for help three weeks ago, I'd told him without hesitation about shooting the man outside the farmhouse. "They believe the killing was a robbery, then," I said.

"Whether they do or not, they clearly don't fear the police or FBI showing up. They're armed to the teeth for anyone else. Should we contact the FBI?"

"No."

"I hate the thought of a bunch of Nazis, even if some of them are American, living right here under our noses."

"So do I."

"Is this a private conversation?" Geraldine asked. I'd heard her come quietly out the back door.

"No, hun, we're finished." He looked at me. "We can talk more tomorrow if you want, but there's not much else."

Stepping over to Geraldine, he wrapped an arm around her waist and led her into the house. The aftershave was for her.

That week, I began using his buddies for surveillance on Bauer, varying the days. Afraid he would spot one of them, I went over the basics of following a target, leaving out Sokolov's more drastic penalties for failure.

"Getting spotted by Bauer could finish us," I told them. "If you think he's seen you, just walk away. You're done for the entire operation. He can't spot you a second time."

"Yes, ma'am," Stiles said from a chair, eager to get started. He was enjoying himself too much.

"Steady, lad," McCarthy said. "You ain't Sam Spade."

I went out once with them to ensure they could do the work without sending Bauer fleeing across the country. They both seemed capable. I thought the older man might keep the younger man's freewheeling impulses in check. I told McCarthy I wanted him driving all the time, leave the street to Stiles.

He frowned, holding up his prosthetic. "You think I can't handle it?"

Stiles laughed. "Sarge, look at you. Your red hair practically glows in the dark, and you got a pirate hook for a hand. You'd stick out like Joe DiMaggio in uniform."

I figured DiMaggio must be an airborne buddy of theirs. Still frowning, McCarthy nodded, scratching his head with the hook.

"Besides," I said. "You're the best driver we have."

As I had hoped, they turned out to be a good team. Even with his steel hook, McCarthy handled a car with expertise, using the wheel's knob like a race driver, and Stiles was a natural out on the streets. Sometimes, I couldn't even spot him, and I was looking for him.

In early August, disaster struck, and all my plans crumbled. What I'd feared most happened. Bauer disappeared. Over the span of four days, he wasn't spotted once by the men. I became suspicious on the first day, going out myself three more straight days. By the fourth, it was clear he was gone, and I was frantic.

Pete told me to relax. "It's the summer. People go on vacations in the summer. He'll be back. He has too much to lose."

"There's nothing in the papers," Rick added, tapping one opened on his lap. "Nothing in the society pages about a break up between the lovebirds. Nothing about the Shepherds at all."

We sat in Rick's living room going over almost every New York newspaper. Stiles and McCarthy stood in the kitchen, leaning against the sink, drinking from cans of beer, and listening.

"I need to know for a certainty," I insisted. I was trying to read through the New York Daily Mirror on the coffee table, my hair falling in front of my eyes and brushing it back with an angry flip.

"Ma'am," Stiles said from the kitchen. "I don't know whether this helps, but I went up and knocked on the door of the mansion."

"You did what?" Rick said, alarmed.

I held my hand up to silence him. It's what I would have done. "What did they say?"

"Nothing, really," Stiles said with a shrug. "I told this snooty butler I was a newspaper guy and wrote wedding announcements. I think he bought that. Anyway, I told him I was supposed to meet Dr. Muller to get a couple comments about things and was he here. The butler said he was not. I asked if he knew where he was, and he said he did not. Real snooty like. Then he shut the door in my face. I felt insulted for every newspaper reporter everywhere."

Pete chuckled, then asked everyone, "Well, where does that leave us?"

"I still have to find out," I said.

"Here's something in the classifieds." Rick lifted his newspaper. "It says that Miss Cynthia Shepherd will be interviewing for house-maids at the Shepherd mansion this Friday. Call this number to set up an interview. References must be impeccable." He set the paper down and looked at me. "If you could get in, you might find your answer."

"I'll need some references," I said.

"You've got mine," Stiles said with a grin.

I smiled back at him. "Thanks, Ray, but I might need a few more."

"I can handle that," Rick said. "Uncle Leo has some connections."

Pete said sarcastically, "It won't do any good to have a reference from Lucky Luciano."

"I keep telling you people Lucky's in Italy." Rick looked at me again. "Don't worry. The references will be copacetic."

I leaned back on the couch with my first smile in four days. "Well, boys, it looks like I'm going for an interview with the expectant bride."

Two days later, during a rainstorm that cooled off the burning streets, I arrived, umbrella in hand, at the Shepherd mansion for my job interview. To appear the part, I dressed in a worn, gray suit, dark rimmed glasses, and hair tucked in a bun.

The snooty butler Stiles had mentioned stared disdainfully at me as I dripped water on his floor. "Put that umbrella in the stand," he said. "This way."

With my purse held in front of me with both hands, I followed him down a hallway to a bench beside a polished, wood door. A blonde woman sat at a small desk, going over sheets of paper.

The butler pointed to the bench. "Sit here."

"Yes, sir. Thank you, sir."

Without acknowledging me, he turned and walked away.

"Miss Gladys Ingle?" the blonde said.

I nodded. "Yes, ma'am."

"I'm Edna Schuster, Miss Shepherd's assistant. She's presently with another applicant and will be with you in a moment."

"Yes, ma'am."

I sat with my purse positioned firmly in my lap. I was not nervous but pretended to be, fidgeting occasionally and patting my hair. It occurred to me that actually getting the job might be difficult to resist. Like with Generalkommissar Kruger, I would be inside the bastard's house. That had a delicious taste to it. But I'd already decided not to take the temptation. I could have killed him weeks ago. I didn't need to work my way into his household to do it now. Vengeance must be more than a simple bullet to the head. I wanted him to lose everything first and then see who it was that did it to him.

Suddenly realizing my teeth were clenched, I forced myself to relax. Outside, thunder rumbled, and I resisted the urge to look at my watch. That's when a voice came through a small device on the blonde's desk. "Is Miss Ingle there, Edna?"

"She's here."

"Send her in, please."

As I was walking to the door, another woman was coming out, buttoning her raincoat. I gave her a friendly smile and went in. Cynthia Shepherd sat behind a desk in a room so large a typical house in Nashok could fit in it. It had high windows, paintings of seascapes on the wall, a grand piano in the corner, a long curving couch, and antique chairs covered with soft fabric.

The woman rose and walked out from behind the desk, extending her hand. "Good morning, Miss Ingle. I'm Cynthia Shepherd."

I took her hand and curtsied as if she were royalty. "Pleased to meet you, ma'am."

"Do have a seat." She indicated a leather chair facing the desk.

Sitting down, she slid on a pair of horn-rimmed glasses that had been dangling from her neck and studied a sheet of paper. After a moment, she looked up at me. "I'm conducting interviews for two housemaids, and they must be ready to start work immediately." She glanced again at the sheet of paper and set it down. "I must say your references are stellar, Miss Ingle, very much so. The Trebelhorns and the Grahams heap praise on you."

"Thank you, ma'am." I wondered what pressure Uncle Leo's friends put on the two families for such good references but decided not to think about it too hard.

At first glance, Cynthia Shepherd seemed a short woman but, in fact, was at least mid-height. Her stockiness gave that impression. She wore a polka dot, mid-calf skirt and a navy blue tunic, her arms bare, pale, and plump. From her neck hung a gold chain with an old, worn coin.

I stiffened. I knew that coin. My mother had given it to me. On it was the image of Shelamzion Alexandra, the old Judean queen. My Mother's necklace. Seeing it on this woman drove an ice pick into my chest. I hated it there shinning against her black sweater and fought the urge to rip it off her neck like Bauer ripped it off mine nearly two years before at Auschwitz. I couldn't allow myself so raw an emotion, and though a tremor rolled through me, I steadied it and attempted to maintain a blank expression, though not completely successful.

"Are you all right, Miss Ingle?" she asked.

"Yes, ma'am," I managed to say in a flat voice.

She saw where I was looking and fingered the coin protectively as if I'd steal it.

I asked, "What is that you're wearing?" It was a presumptuous question under the circumstances. I added, "Ma'am."

She studied it a moment. "I believe it is an ancient coin, maybe Greek or Roman. Not a fake anyway. My fiancé gave it to me as a birthday gift. God knows where he got it. Says it's a secret." She picked up my references again. "Do you enjoy the work, Miss Ingle?"

"Very much, ma'am," I managed, glancing once more at the coin. I did want to steal it. Someday, I would. "It's always a pleasure to work in one of the city's great houses."

Miss Shepherd went on with the interview, and I gave short, terse answers. She still had a fiancé, it seemed, but I needed to know where he was.

She asked me something that I didn't hear completely. "I'm sorry, ma'am. Would you repeat that please?"

She marked something on a sheet of paper. "I asked if I offered you the position, when could you start. The house will need caring before we move in."

"Whenever I was needed."

Putting her pen down, she leaned back in the chair, and I sensed the interview over. "As I said, we're hiring two maids for my husband's and my new home a block from here and..."

"Oh, how romantic," I interrupted. "Will he be interviewing me as well?"

Shaking her head, she gave the hint of a grin. "No, right now, he's sailing about the Bahamas with my father, and I shall be joining them Monday. He trusts me to make these kinds of decisions."

She stood, extending her hand again, the interview over.

As I left, another woman was about to enter, her head bowed as she pressed her hands along her brown suit to smooth out any remaining wrinkles. She looked up, and our eyes met. Both of us blinked with recognition. It was the blonde woman I'd seen in the White Plains farmhouse. Her tiny eyes sank farther into her head as she stared hard at me. That night, she'd only seen me for a couple seconds before I turned toward the sink and pretended to be hired help. She might not recognize me, but already that hope sank. I could see in her eyes she knew me.

When I pushed passed her, she went in. I turned back to the tall blonde. "Ma'am, I believe that was an old friend of mine who just went in. We only had time to exchange a greeting, and I'm afraid I've forgotten her name."

She was lighting a cigarette but looked down at her appointment book. "Oh, you mean Trudi Huber."

"Trudi. Yes, of course. But Huber must be a married name."

The blonde shrugged.

"You wouldn't happen to have her address so I can get in touch with her?" I asked.

Hesitating, the blonde studied me.

I blushed and murmured, "She was actually my older sister's friend. They were so close, Claudia will be so happy to find her again."

The blonde sighed, wrote it out on a sheet of paper, and handed it to me. I thanked her and left. If Huber tried the same tactic to get my address, she'd find a beer hall in Greenwich Village.

The next day, Rick found out she was married to a truck driver named Eric Huber and that her maiden name was Heidegger. Another day's research through his stacks of files discovered a woman by that name who had been identified by survivors as a brutal, murderous guard at the Treblinka women's camp.

Holding the folder up, shaking it at me, he said, "She's wanted, Rivka. Her name's Trudi Heidegger and she was a guard at Treblinka. A goddamned war criminal of the first stripe. Several sworn statements say she beat to death women inmates, often from whim. That's two of the bastards now. There's probably a den of them there. We have to go after them too."

Sometimes I thought his hate as deep and vicious as mine. Bauer filled my soul with the weight of oceans. Was there room for more? But these others. They too had to die.

CHAPTER FORTY-EIGHT

Bauer had been back from his voyage to the Bahamas on Arthur Shepherd's sailboat a week when he called this emergency meeting of the Brotherhood's inner circle, Martin Mohnke, the Waffen SS General, Anton Bruck, the bald Gestapo interrogator who called himself Huttner now, the woman Trudi Huber, Hauser, and Willi Meisner. On Wednesday morning, they'd all gathered in the basement of the Hauser house amid the swastika flags.

Each person carried a handgun, even Bauer, while Hauser had a hunting rifle propped against a table. Since Otto Krause was shot and killed in May, everyone had arrived at the regular meetings prepared to fight the last battle of the war. Bauer believed some of them, the American Bund men especially, longed for some grand, heroic death. Gotterdammerung. That was foolish. Living was the best way to honor the Führer and his cause

Hauser didn't think Gotterdammerung would happen. "It wasn't the government that killed Krause," he said a couple days after Krause's murder, "otherwise, they'd have been all over the farmhouse by now. No, not them, and I don't think it was a robbery either. I don't know what it was, but we should be prepared for anything."

Back in May when Krause had been murdered, Bauer became hesitant to continue attending. In fact, he considered briefly whether to take Hauser's escape route out of New York into another life somewhere. He quickly dismissed that. The former Bund leader was right. No police came. No FBI. Not that night, not since. And soon, after the wedding, he'd be rich, untouchable. In America, like everywhere else, the wealthy and powerful never went to jail. That was worth the risk. Now, there was a new peril. He was being followed.

Two days ago, he'd met Berman for lunch at a popular, smoke-filled diner on 1st Avenue and squeezed into chairs at a small table at the back wall. Berman and he lunched so often together that Bauer asked him when he ever had the time to write.

The author waved that away. "I've got writer's block. I've had it for months. I stare at the blank page and nothing comes. It's like someone crawled into my head and shot my muse."

Bauer chuckled. "Sounds bad. I thought you were working on something about a Jewish doctor."

Berman snorted. "What do I know about medicine? I stuck the damn thing in a drawer."

Bauer forced a sympathetic smile and looked for the waitress who was taking an order three tables down. Instead of coming their way, she hurried along the counter to the kitchen window where she picked up three plates of food on one arm, then rushed back to other tables.

He turned to Berman, then suddenly shot a glance back at the counter. At the far end, a man was watching him. When their eyes met, the man quickly turned back to his coffee. He had a boy's face with pale gray eyes, and Bauer had seen him before. Two days ago, he'd been window shopping with Cynthia along 5th Avenue and noticed him down the block only because he was staring into a store window that they had just been at for some minutes. They almost went in. The store window was full of wedding gowns. For a young man, that struck Bauer as odd, but he thought no more about it till now. Seeing him a second time at this lunch counter was too much of a coincidence, and it unnerved him.

Now, in the farmhouse with his friends, he spoke German, telling them every detail.

"Could he be from the FBI?" Mohnke asked.

Using a match to light his cigarette, Bauer shook his head. "No. When Berman and I left, I glanced back and saw him hurrying into a truck with another man. They stayed behind our trolley till I got off. This man had an artificial hand, a hook. I don't think the FBI hires cripples. They were following me."

Meisner looked at everyone. "Does it have anything to do with what happened to Krause?"

"Yes. It's her," Huber said emphatically. "The one I told you about. She's behind this."

Hauser said, "You might be right."

"Who?" Bauer asked, confused.

"Remember that woman who penetrated the meeting in May?" Hauser said. "We thought then she might have something to do with Krause. Now I'm sure of it. Trudi saw her again."

Gripping the folds of her dress, Huber leaned forward, excited. "Yes, I saw her a couple weeks ago at your fiancée's house applying for the same maid's position. You were sailing so there was no way to tell you."

"Are you sure it was her?" Bauer asked.

"Yes. She looked different. I knew I'd seen her before. I'm sure it's the same woman."

They all exchanged glances.

"We need to do something," Mohnke said.

Bauer wondered if he somehow knew her. "What does she look like?"

"Young, maybe twenty. Tall, thin, dark hair. Nothing stands out except her height."

Everyone fell silent a moment, then Hauser said, "This is a threat to all of us. I'll bring some of the others in." He rubbed his hands together. "It's time we follow the followers."

Bruck's entire forehead creased as he smiled. "When we find her, I will interrogate her."

We needed more men for the plan we'd developed, and Pete brought in three more of his 82nd Airborne buddies. With not much time to get them briefed, I met them for the first time that Wednesday evening before Labor Day at Rick's apartment. Pete had told me about them. I said nothing to him, but they didn't seem promising at all.

Former Tech Sergeant Eddie Bishop was a lean man with a florid face and a thick, brown beard and unkempt, auburn hair. His clothes, mostly army stuff, were as unkempt as his hair. He'd been a part of the 82nd when it became the army's first airborne division in August of 1942 and fought through all its European campaigns. Having survived so long, he would throw out a wide grin and call himself a fugitive from the law of averages.

Since his mustering out of the army, Pete said, the world drastically changed for Bishop, and he changed with it. He'd let himself go, finding little interest in anything. In that time, he'd had a few odd jobs, but mostly he was a panhandler and vagrant up and down Broadway, who occasionally made his way across the East River to Brooklyn to stay at his mother's house in Flatbush for a week or two. That's where Pete contacted him. He was desperate to help. I felt less than enthusiastic.

Mark Shaw was a heavy, somewhat overweight man, not much taller than Bishop. He sported a Jerry Colonna moustache that reached his bulging cheeks. I didn't know who Jerry Colonna was, but Pete assured me this was true. Shaw had been a G4 supply sergeant and, Pete insisted, still had a knack of getting anything we might need. I'd believe it when I saw it. He smoked so incessantly his fingers were painted yellow with nicotine stains. An overflow of nervous energy made him seem more like a bull pawing the ground in front of a china shop.

The third man was former sergeant Thomas Jackson, who hated the nickname "Stonewall." A short, thoughtful man, he had a calming voice, and everyone respected him. Pete had said he never got excited, even in combat under fire. He was the only one I had confidence in. But we had no choice. All three were in.

In his kitchen, Rick spread a large sheet of paper out on his table that showed a detailed plan of Shepherd's Castle. Pete, the five 82nd airborne men, and I leaned in to study it.

"How did you get this?" Pete asked.

"Herb Gold drew it from memory. He's been there before." He shrugged. "Hollywood bigshot."

Gold was our entry to the wedding Monday. When he brought the projector and film can into the large hall where the reception would take place, Pete, Rick, and I would be with him as his assistants. The wedding itself would occur outside on the cliffs overlooking Long Island Sound. It was a good location for us because isolated on sea cliffs, we could block any escape route Bauer would take.

I smoothed the sheet out. "Boys, let's go over Operation Nakam."

As I described it, the plan had three parts: Destroy Bauer's life before all his new high society friends. Take him prisoner. Kill him.

Stiles looked me. "I can do it. God knows he's got it coming."

Ice settled into my voice. "He is mine."

He gave me a two fingered salute. "Yes, ma'am."

Quickly, I went over everyone's task. Stiles and McCarthy would park midway down the driveway to block Bauer if he escaped us. Jackson, Bishop, and Shaw had perhaps the most important and trickiest part of the operation, snatching Bauer, but nothing could be done about that.

I said to Bishop, "You'll have to shave that beard off and clean up."

He nodded. "Yes, ma'am. My mother won't recognize me."

When I finished going over the operation, I saw it the way everyone else must have seen it, a flawed plan with little chance of success. Hundreds of people in attendance, including Governor Dewey, created too many opportunities for chaos. Enormous obstacles remained.

Rick said, "I don't see why it shouldn't work."

"Something will go wrong," McCarthy said.

Annoyed, Rick shot back, "Why do you say that? It's going to work."

Pete was the one who answered, "Something always goes wrong. We need to prepare for that. But, Rivka, it's about as good as it's going to be."

I didn't believe it, but Stiles agreed. "General Gavin couldn't have done it better."

Later that night, with everyone gone and McCarthy and Stiles out tailing Bauer, Rick cooked a meal of spaghetti and peas for me, a strange combination, I thought, and for dessert added chocolate babkas from a bakery down the block. After dinner, we sat on the couch, his arm around me, and talked details of the plan, but it had been talked about and talked about. I loved being held.

Rick gave me a quick kiss on the cheek. "I know what you're feeling. The wedding can't come fast enough. I feel that way, too. Get this thing over with."

"It's the end," I said. "One way or another, it's the end."

He leaned back and stared at me. "Almost sounds like you're sad."

"Hardly." I thought about it a long time. "It would be like putting down a sack of apples."

He gave me a quizzical look. "What?"

I smiled. "When I was young, we had land near town with rows and rows of apple trees. We were harvesting some apples for Baba and Mama to sell at market. I was eight and I told everyone if Hanna could carry a sack of apples to the car, I could too. 'No, you can't,' Hanna said. 'You're just a little tadpole.' So, I filled a sack and hefted it on my shoulder. It was only fifty or sixty yards to the car, but I knew immediately that the sack was far heavier than I thought." Lost in the remembrance, I fell silent.

After I didn't go on with the story, Rick said, "Well, what happened?"

"It took me ten minutes at least to go that sixty yards. I kept stopping and resting, and I think that made it harder."

"But you got it to the car?"

"Of course, but I was never so glad of anything when I got it off my shoulders. Now, I want this done. I want Bauer out of my every thought." I looked at Rick hopefully. "He has so much to live for now, doesn't he?"

"Oh, boy, does he."

"Good. Then it's time."

"What happens, Rivka, when all this is over?"

I knew what he meant. What would happen to the two of us? I shrugged. "I don't know."

He pulled me close and kissed me. "I do."

I thought I wasn't in the mood, but my body was like an electric light switching on. My lips moved hungrily against his, and he slid his hand up under my sweater. I groaned as he touched my breasts, the force of my desire frightening.

"Quick," he said, sitting back and sliding out of his pants.

I pulled my sweater over my head and undid my bra just as a knock came at the door.

"Shit," Rick cursed.

I gave a sardonic laugh and hurriedly dressed while he threw on his clothes and went to the door. It was McCarthy and Stiles. They came in, and red-faced Rick went to the kitchen and brought beer from the refrigerator for all of us.

"Nothing much to report," McCarthy said. "We sat outside his apartment mostly. About four, he caught a trolley to Broadway, and we followed in the car, but he just went shopping by himself."

"That seemed odd," Stiles said.

"In what way?" I asked.

"Well, he's about to marry this rich broad, and instead of being with her, what is he doing? Just browsing along Broadway with his hands in his pockets, looking in windows but with no real interest."

I looked at Rick, who raised his eyebrows in a shrug.

Stiles downed the rest of his beer. "Then, he went in Wannamaker's department store and wandered about the floors." With a puzzled expression, he shook his head. "He bought nothing. Then, get this. He suddenly turns and walks straight out of the store and gets on a bus. I scrambled for the pickup, and McCarthy caught up quick-like. We see him jump off and walk to his apartment." He shrugged. "I don't know. I just think it's odd."

"It is odd," I said, "but I don't know what to make of it. Anybody?"

No one answered.

McCarthy finished the report. "We planted ourselves down the street like always. He didn't go out again. After the lights went out, we waited a half hour and here we are."

"Good work," I said. "With the wedding close, I'm going to call off the surveillance."

They nodded. "Nazi bastard," McCarthy muttered. "All the boys are with you, too, Rivka."

I was grateful. "Thank you. Can you boys drop me off? I better get home."

With an apologetic look, I kissed Rick on the lips. "Pick me up in the morning at nine?"

With his typical, comical exaggeration, he sighed loudly. "I guess."

A couple minutes after Rivka and the two men left, Rick was stacking the dinner dishes in the sink when he heard the knock and hoped Rivka had decided to return and spend the night. Wiping his hands, he hurried to the door and opened it.

In the hall stood two men he'd never seen before, odd looking and frightening. One was tall and thin, the other heavy and completely bald, Laurel and Hardy from a carnival House of Horrors. Abruptly, the bigger man drove his fist into Rick's jaw, knocking him to the floor. Tying his hands and feet, they dragged him to a chair and threw him in it.

"Look at this place," the thin one said, speaking in German. He was staring at the boxes and steamer trunks of folders. He scanned through several, reading them quickly.

"Gottverdammt," he exclaimed, turning to the other man and holding up one of the folders. "He is a Nazi hunter." He tossed the folder back on the pile. "A damn Nazi hunter."

Rick understood every word. Both men walked back to Rick. The bald man placed his hands on the arms of the chair, his face in Rick's, grinning. In thickly accented English, he said, "Who is the woman?"

Knowing he was going to die, Rick forced a smile. "The Angel of Death."

The man's fist slammed into his face, and everything went dark.

With Max Bauer driving, Trudi Huber rode in the passenger seat as they followed the battered, old pickup truck heading out of Williamsburg. It held the woman who had left the apartment with the two men. She had not been surprised to see her. This was the woman who had come to the Shepherd mansion, attempting to get herself hired as a maid, the woman who had broken into the meeting house and no doubt killed Otto Krause back then. She was the center of the threat facing them all.

In the light traffic this time of night, Bauer kept a discreet distance, yet keeping the target vehicle always in sight. Clearly, he had done this kind of work in the past. That reassured her. She didn't want to lose the woman. Trudi had been frightened all day since

Bauer told them that he was being followed. Before the war, she'd been a German hausfrau. Now, she was an American hausfrau, married to a man who insured her a serviceable marriage, a safe life, even if lacking the passion of her first husband years ago. Right now, after barely escaping allied capture and retribution, that safe life was the most important thing of all, and she would kill to protect it.

"You're sure it's her?" Bauer asked, interrupting her thoughts.

"Yes, she's the one," she said, her voice tense.

The pickup took a straight line down Sumner Avenue through Bedford Stuyvesant and turned right on Fulton Street, then turned left on New York Avenue into Crown Heights. When it entered a maze of block after block, turning often, Bauer had to close the distance to keep from losing them.

Finally, the pickup stopped in the middle of a street, and the woman got out. She said something to the men, then shut the door. The pickup drove away.

"What are we going to do with her?" Huber asked.

"We're going to wait."

"For what?"

"Till we need her."

That confused Huber, but she didn't ask what he meant. This man was the only person she trusted to handle this situation.

He turned down the block and cruised toward the woman as she climbed the steps. When the car went by, she glanced over her shoulder at it, framing her face in the streetlamps, before using her key in the door. On the second floor, a curtain fluttered aside, and a little girl's face appeared, looking down at the woman.

Bauer looked up at the girl, then to the woman, and hissed through clamped teeth, "We got the bitch."

CHAPTER FORTY-NINE

After breakfast, I sat with Pete at the window waiting for Rick to pick us up. Mina was upstairs on her sewing machine, making a dress for Ellie, everyone else out of the house already. Except for the distant thrum of the machine, the place seemed ghostly in its silence, Pete not speaking, no laughing boys, no Ellie following me around, no Teresa trying to teach me how to look a beauty, which she was becoming.

Rick was late, and I dialed his number, but the line was busy, and I shook my head at Pete's questioning look. Returning to the window, my mind went to last night, wondering if I should have stayed over. I didn't know how I felt about Rick and maybe that was why I didn't. I loved being with him, but that wasn't love, yet, if I was still capable of that. My concentration on Bauer made it hard for romance, but a spark was there between Rick and me. Perhaps someday it would become fire.

Today, Rick was to drive Pete and me to Herb Gold's New York apartment in upper Manhattan, where the three of us would discuss last minute operational details with him. This whole scheme would not work without the Hollywood producer.

At 9:30, I called Rick once more and heard the busy signal again. I dialed the operator and asked her to try the number. She did, then the phone went silent for a few seconds. When she came back on the line, she said, "I'm sorry. That number is currently out of service."

"What's wrong with it? It should be fine."

The operator said, "I don't know, ma'am. It just says that the number is out of service."

I hung up and for the first time became worried. Then I heard him outside coming up the steps. "There he is," I said to Pete.

Rushing to the door, I threw it open. But it was Yankl. "Oh," I muttered, stepping out onto the stoop. "Sorry, Yankl, I was expecting Rick. He's late, and I can't reach him."

His face dissolved into shadows of sorrow.

"What is it, Yankl?"

Taking both my hands, he gazed at me. "I'm sorry to be blunt, Rivka, but there's no other way to do this. There was a fire at Rick's apartment."

At his words and expression, I stumbled back, and Pete caught me. "What? What are you talking about?"

"Rick's cousin phoned Aaron to explain that was the reason he wouldn't be into work today. It burned down half the block before the fire department got it under control. We don't know much yet. Everyone got out of the other buildings, but five people were killed in Rick's." He paused, then added, "It was arson. Rick is in the hospital, badly burned. He might not live."

The full impact of what he said hit me. Tears slipped down my cheeks. I wanted to feel Rick's arms around me again. I wanted to smell the sweet scent of his cologne, to hear the chiding humor of his voice. *He can't die.*

One word stood out. "Arson?" I said.

"That's what I heard. I have Aaron's car. I can drive you to the hospital."

I hesitated. "No, drive us to Herb Gold's apartment first." I pushed past him down the steps.

His voice came after me. "Rivka, don't you want to see Rick? I think you ought to."

I whirled around on him. "I need to see Gold first." My gaze must have been savage, because he stared at me as if struck.

"Rivka, please, I'm trying to keep you safe. I don't understand why..."

This time it was Pete who interrupted him with a sharp call of his name. "Yankl, this is not a Young Guardians meeting arguing about wheat. You've known Rivka all your life. Do you really think you should be telling her what to do?"

He thought a moment, looking at both of us with a pained expression, then pulled the keys out of his pocket. He sighed. "All right. I'll take you to Gold's."

Only Pete and I went up to see the Hollywood producer. He was a short man with eyes that gleamed with intelligence. Maybe in his mid-forties, he sported a thin moustache so popular these days and had thinning, gray hair. He wore loose, gray slacks and a white shirt. The balcony of his second floor apartment looked out over the Hudson River. He knew who I was and what I intended and supported it. For nearly an hour, we went over what he needed us to do as his assistants so we could get into the wedding.

Afterward, we drove across the Manhattan Bridge to Brooklyn Hospital to see Rick. Yankl had not seen him and didn't know his exact medical status, only repeating what he'd heard, so I didn't know what I would find. I feared he was on his death bed or badly burned. If he did survive, would he be months or years recovering? He was on the hospital's fourth floor. When Pete, Yankl, and I approached his room, Leo Shapiro, his uncle, was pacing outside, his face wrinkled in fierce concentration. Two men, clearly Leo's, sat flanking the door to the room, both stone-faced, one's sport coat opened enough to see a holstered gun. I remembered his mob connections. Suddenly aware of us, Leo looked up and focused intensely on me.

"What the hell happened?" he demanded.

I shook my head. "What are you talking about, Leo?"

"The police have been to see him. They told me a fireman found him on the second floor landing and dragged him out just before the apartment collapsed." Leo stared at me, his anger building. "His hands and feet were tied."

"What?" I muttered, shocked.

"It was arson. Someone was after him. So I ask you again, Rivka. What is going on with you two?"

Hesitating several seconds, I looked at him. "I need to see Rick first. Wait here."

Leo's jaw set, but I pushed past him into the room.

Rick lay in the bed, a small tent with a plastic faceplate over his head. From a machine, a tube ran to the tent while a nurse monitored its gauges. His eyes darted to me, and he gave the hint of a painful smile. His face was bruised, and one eye swollen shut. His left arm was swathed in bandages.

"Can he speak?" I asked the nurse, a woman of thirty or so, brown hair pushing out from under her white cap.

"He can, but it's best he doesn't," she said with a practiced smile. "His throat is sore from the inhalation, and it will reduce the effect of the oxygen treatment."

"I can talk to him, can't I?"

"Certainly."

I leaned down to the plastic faceplate and said with sudden vehemence, "Don't die. Don't you dare die."

Smiling again, he lifted his hand in a casual salute and seemed to mouth, *I won't.*

"How are his burns?" I asked the nurse.

"His arm will heal," she said. "His health problems are in his lungs from the smoke inhalation."

"He'll get better.'

She nodded. "Eventually. It will take a little time."

I squeezed Rick's hand while in my mind I saw him bound hand and foot, fire all around him. I knew who did it. Who else could it be? "Bauer?"

He gave a slight shrug of his right shoulder and mouthed something I didn't get. He pulled my hand toward him and drew a symbol on the palm. It was a swastika.

"His friends did this, but he was responsible."

Rick nodded. He tried to see out of the plastic window at the nurse but couldn't and turned back frustrated. Then suddenly, he lifted the tent off his face and set it aside.

Horrified, the nurse insisted, "Mr. Shapiro, what are you doing? You can't do that." She didn't seem to know what to do, then tried to fit the little tent back over his head. He shoved it away, sitting up in bed. In a ragged voice, he said, "Not now, Miss Shaw. I'm sorry, but would you leave us?"

The nurse blinked several times. "Sir, I must complete your treatment. You can't just forego it."

"Then come back in ten minutes. I'll be ready then. Now please go." His raspy voice emphatic.

"I'll have to inform the doctor about this." Miss Shaw strode from the room.

Sitting on the edge of the bed, I took Rick's hand and gave him a wry smile. "I would never have guessed you'd be such a difficult patient."

"I'm not. Usually, I'm a perfect angel. I needed to talk with you alone." He paused to catch his breath, and I became a little worried. He went on, "They were German. Two men, one completely bald, the other tall and thin with a thick moustache. They must have followed McCarthy and Stiles back to my place. There's no other explanation."

"I should have called off the surveillance before that," I said. "I was so afraid he'd disappear, but he was never going anyplace. Now, they know about us."

389

"It was no one's fault. I wanted the surveillance to continue, too. There must be hundreds of fugitive Nazis in the New York area. If he'd met with someone else like a Bormann or Mengele, I wanted to know about it."

"Well, it's done."

"What will Bauer do? What will the damn Bund do?"

I thought about it. "Nothing. Bauer's not going to run, and the Bund, they don't know who we are, but they know we're not the government. They're not going to do anything. They may even think you're dead."

He looked dubious. "You're probably right. Why would Bauer give up Cynthia Shepherd? To him, she's got to be worth just about any risk."

"So he will go through with the wedding Monday. Operation Nakam is still on."

His brow creased with worry. I noticed one eyebrow, the one over the swollen shut eye, was singed off. "They might be waiting for us Monday. They must know that we're coming."

"You're going to be here. You must…"

At that moment, the nurse came back in with the doctor, both upset. I picked up Rick's hand and kissed it. "I have a few things to take care of. I'll come back."

As I started from the room, the doctor demanded, "Who are you? Only family are allowed to visit."

Rick answered, "She's my wife."

I smiled sweetly at the doctor and left. Now I was married to two men. Outside the room, I said to Leo, "We need a quiet place to talk."

Across from the hospital, the four of us found a picnic table in Fort Greene Park. Above the treetops, the cloudless sky burned in a hot haze.

His eyes angry, Leo folded hands in front of him and stared at me. "What's going on, Miss Resnik?"

I looked at Yankl, asking him with a questioning look if I could trust him. He read my expression and nodded. I said to Leo, "Do you know the name Max Bauer?"

"No."

I told him the German's story, how I knew him, and how he was among the most wanted Nazis still at large. Also, that there was a farmhouse some distance from Manhattan where he and other Nazis in hiding met with the American German Bund. I said, "This Monday, Bauer's getting married to Cynthia Shepherd. That's when I plan to assassinate him."

His face impassive, Leo gave a slight nod.

Pete spoke for the first time. "And, Mr. Shapiro, we need more men, now more than ever. Can you help us?"

Leo sat back and folded his arms across his chest. "Hmm." He didn't speak for several seconds, then said, "You know, Rivka, Ritchie was born in Berlin?"

"No, he never told me."

"When Hitler came to power, his parents sent him to America to live with my family. He was fourteen. His father and mother stayed because they had their own parents to look after. Ritchie's two sisters stayed also. They were older and had families of their own." He shrugged sadly. "And no one thought Hitler was such a big problem."

I nodded, understanding. "Nashok was like that."

"When they tried to get out, it was too late. None of them could. After the war, Ritchie worked hard to get himself assigned to the Nuremberg prosecuting team. He wanted to see if he could find his family. All he learned was that they had been shipped off to ghettos in Poland and Lithuania sometime in '42. There, they disappeared."

With eyes unreadable and distant, Leo fell into a silence that lasted half a minute. When he focused on me again, he said, "I can't give you any of my people. This wedding is big news, and the papers say Governor Dewey will be there. He's the one who sent Luciano to prison and burned Lepke in the chair. His cops will be there with him. I can't chance one of my men being spotted."

"We'll be all right," I said.

"But I will give you Charlie, the man who sold you the Walther. He is not one of mine. Like I said, he's an independent contractor. Dewey's boys don't know him."

Pete looked up. "One man?"

"Don't dismiss him. He can help. Like you, Rivka, he's still fighting the war. But for me to provide his services, it will cost you." Suddenly, his eyes darkened, and he stabbed the tabletop with his finger. "No one fucks with my family. I want to know where that goddamn farmhouse is."

CHAPTER FIFTY

Sunday, the night before Operation Nakam, I couldn't sleep with the details of the plan swirling in my head. I threw on slacks and a sweater and went downstairs into the backyard. I sat at the lawn table and for a moment wishing I smoked like everyone else. Anything to calm my nerves. The night was cool and dark with a crescent moon over the rooftops. The air felt sweet with the promise of rain, but was mixed with the strong odor of moldy furniture drifting over from Mr. Mendelbaum's backyard.

Mina and several of the neighbors had demanded he clean up the place, but he'd refused. She'd always been someone to reckon with, even in the old days back in Nashok when Isaac and Morris had immigrated to America. I thought after I dealt with Bauer, I would set fire to Mendelbaum's junk.

When a chilling breeze worked its way down the cavern of backyards, I pulled my sweater tighter around me. With the thought of Nashok, my mind returned to my family. That immortal loss would never fade, nor did I ever want it to. The image of Papa sitting on the steps outside his clinic came to me. I remembered that exactly. I was seven years old and hurried toward him, carrying a basket with the lunch Mama had prepared. The spark of joy at seeing him, even if it had only been a few minutes since the last time, rushed through me. He was studying his hands. Grinning, I was about to shout out, "Hi, Papa," when I noticed a look of infinite sorrow on his face and stopped suddenly.

I approached slowly, muttering, "Papa?"

He looked up and smiled, but even then, I realized it was a sad smile. I heard the soft murmur of someone crying inside the clinic. He took the basket from me, stood, and chucked me on the cheek. "Tsigele, you go back now. Tell your mother I might be home late tonight."

As he was going back inside, my mind snapped back to the present. Someone was approaching me from behind and trying to do it quietly. I tensed, wondering if somehow the damn Bund had followed me home that night. It had to be a possibility. But the tread was too careless, making too much noise sliding over the flagstones, and I knew who it was.

In pajamas and a robe, Ellie stood hesitantly to the side, watching me. She was barefoot.

"Come sit down, Ellie," I said.

"It's all right?" she asked hesitantly.

"Of course."

She slid into the chair across the table. Her head bowed, she studied her hands much like Papa had done all those years ago and her face was as troubled. I worried that she'd heard Pete and me talking about what would take place tomorrow, and she was scared something would happen to us.

"Tsigele," I said, calling her by my old nickname. "Are you all right?"

Not looking at me, she nodded, but clearly she wasn't all right.

"What is it?"

She gave a hefty sigh. "School starts Tuesday." She seemed to think that was explanation enough.

"I thought you liked school."

394

"I do," she said. "But Papa has put me in high school. I'm twelve. My friends will be in middle school." Her voice became anguished. "Everyone will be bigger than me, and they'll think I'm a freak. I don't even have breasts. No one will like me."

This was the most important thing in the world to her. "You're smart," I said.

"Jimmy's smart, too, but he doesn't have to go to high school."

"His grades are not so good."

"He doesn't try." Then she perked up. "You think I shouldn't try?"

"No, don't do that. Learn everything you can. That's important. The more you learn, the more you know. It can give you control over your future."

She was frowning. It was not particularly good advice. It hadn't worked for me, but then a war had gotten in the way. At that moment, I realized how much more I wanted to be dealing with these kinds of problems than how to kill murdering Nazis. I wanted to marry and have children. The last of my family, I wanted to carry on generations. That's what Mama meant when she screamed out just before she died, *live, live, live.*

Killing Bauer was as irresistible to me as water to a woman crossing a desert. The other was the life I desired. The life I owed my family. *By the end of my days,* I asked myself, *will my mother be proud of how I lived?*

I turned to Ellie. "I'll speak to Aunt Mina about it. I don't know if it will help, but I'll suggest that maybe you can take one or two classes at the high school but return to middle school for most of the day."

Ellie looked at me hopefully. "Will you do that, Rivka?"

"Yes, Tsigele. I can't promise anything, but I'll speak to your parents."

Near midnight, Joe Hauser awoke to go to the toilet, which he was doing more and more these days. It had been years since he'd slept through the night. As he finished and came back, he heard a creak somewhere in the house and stopped to listen. This old farmhouse creaked and groaned from the slightest wind or shift in temperature. Hearing nothing more, he dismissed the sound, crawled back under the covers, and turned off the lamp on the bedstand. Within seconds, he was asleep.

Another noise startled him awake again, and he wasn't sure how much time had passed. It had been distinct, like the clap of hands. He reached for the lamp, but a voice said harshly, "Leave it off."

Startled, he focused in the darkened room. He could make out the shadowy figures of four men standing about his bed, all of them aiming handguns at him. His body stiffened in shock and terror. With an effort, he kept his bowels from erupting but was unable to stay the quiver from his voice. "What do you want? I don't keep money in the house."

"Where's the book?" a man asked.

"What book?"

"The one with the list of your Bund friends. It's in a cabinet in this house. Where is it?"

How had they learned about that? "I don't know what you're talking about." He shrugged, hoping the bluff worked.

A gunshot exploded in the silence, and his kneecap blew apart. He shrieked in pain. Quickly, he spilled out the words, telling them where to find the record of the Brotherhood. One of the men left the room and returned within a minute, holding the book up. "I got it, Leo."

Holstering his pistol, Leo took the book, went to the bedside lamp, and flicked it on. His face harsh, as if his only willing smile would be a false one, he flipped through the pages, then glanced at Hauser.

"I have given you what you want," Hauser said, grimacing from the pain. He pulled the blanket up to his chin as if that were protective armor and croaked out, "Please go. I have nothing worth stealing."

Leo nodded. "Don't worry. We're leaving." Carefully, he turned off the lamp and drew his pistol again. "Let me give you something to help you sleep."

Then, the four men shot Hauser again and again, lights flashing from the muzzles in a frenzy of fireworks, the smell of cordite drifting thick in the room.

CHAPTER FIFTY-ONE

O̲ur panel truck headed up the long drive toward Shepherd's Castle, passing a pasture with a couple horses on the left and a row of parked cars on the right that stretched a half mile from the main road to the doorstep. Warm and sunny, it was a perfect day for an outdoor wedding overlooking the water, a perfect day for Nakam. Leo's man Charlie was driving, his shotgun between him and Herb Gold, who sat in the front seat, while Pete and I rode in the back with the projector and sound equipment. The rest of the team was coming in two cars at least a half hour out. Timing was key.

The wedding should have already started by now. Gold was the only one of us dressed in a tux because he would not only be presenting his movie at the reception, but he was also a guest. Posing as technicians, Charlie and Pete wore dark slacks and white shirts with ties, their sleeves rolled up. As Gold's assistant, I'd considered wearing a dress and heels but decided against it. I wanted to be able to move if I had to. My long hair in a single pony tail, I wore the gray Hepburn trousers, my Walther tucked into a pocket, and a long-sleeved linen blouse of soft blue. Gold said not to worry. I looked the part.

399

When we reached the mansion, there were fifteen or twenty uniformed policemen standing outside their cars, smoking in groups, and watching the society people arrive. Others had to be inside with the governor and mayor.

Gesturing toward them, Charlie said, "What the hell's this?" The cigarette in his mouth flipped up and down as he spoke. "Too many damn cops."

"They're here to protect the governor," Gold said with a shaky voice. When he learned that Muller was really Max Bauer, he had been willing to help, but now that the operation had begun, he turned pale, fidgeting and squirming like a three-year-old, and I worried he wouldn't go through with his part.

"Did you know about this?" Charlie looked in the rearview mirror at me.

"I knew. I told Leo. He should have told you. It changes nothing."

Charlie rubbed the burned side of his face. "It changes everything. Nothing we can do about it now though."

A security man waved us to a parking spot next to two catering trucks where we unloaded the equipment onto a metal cart. A few feet away, several waiters were carrying trays of food out of the catering trucks into the house. They were supervised by a large, bald man in a white chef's uniform. Seeing him, my bones felt a chill. It was the man from the farmhouse called Bruck, a Gestapo interrogator according to Rick. He identified the man as one of those who had invaded his apartment and tried to kill him.

Why would Bruck be here? To protect Bauer? What was Bauer doing? Could he know of our plans? I doubted it, but even so, I was going ahead with it. The chill in my bones turned to fire. I swore, after I dealt with Bauer, he would be next. I gave a quick glance around but saw no one else I identified from the farmhouse. It would be stupid to have the American Nazi Bund wandering around at his wedding, but that didn't mean more weren't here.

I feared Bruck would recognize me and kept the large projector on the cart between us, but when he followed his waiters into the house, we rolled the cart up to the door where a new worry awaited. The butler from my job interview at the Shepherd mansion in town was greeting guests like a well-practiced toady. He now wore red livery, a servant uniform from a bygone era, with silver buttons on his coat and silver buckles on his shoes. I doubted he would remember me because my appearance was completely different. Still, I didn't look at him, keeping my attention on the sound equipment.

As it turned out, there was no need to worry. In the hierarchy of servants, I was beneath his notice. He met Gold, the Hollywood producer, with a broad grin and snapped his fingers for another liveried servant to take us to the ballroom, then turned to a couple late arriving guests.

In the massive foyer, I noticed two men dressed in suits and ties observing the late people hurrying in. Both gave us a studied glance.

"Cops," Charlie whispered. "What is this place? Fort Knox?"

"Close," Gold said in a hushed voice.

I saw two more men upstairs walking along the balcony.

The servant led us past the foyer and grand staircase to the ballroom. Gold had told us not only was this hall used for banquets and balls but movie showings, and in the winter, an indoor tennis court for Cynthia. Now, it was filled with banquet tables set up for two hundred of New York's elite. On one side, sunlight radiated through four tall windows. At the far end, a massive curtain covered the movie screen on which Gold's film would be shown.

"Should we start setting up the projector?" Pete asked him.

"No, God no. All you people have to do is plug the damn thing in. I'll do the rest." Feverishly, he ran a trembling hand through his thinning hair. "For now, just guard the equipment. Don't do anything till I get back." He glanced at his wrist watch. "I'm late already. I'm going to the wedding."

When he was gone, I said, "You two stay here."

"Where are you going?" Pete asked, surprised.

"Upstairs. The Shepherd woman has something that's mine. I want it back."

"That's not in the plan," Charlie said.

"It's in my plan. Stay here."

As I left, I heard Charlie say, "It's like in the Marines. Everyone giving us orders."

Pete replied, "Yeah, the army too."

According to Gold, Cynthia Shepherd's bedroom was on the second floor, but he had no idea which one. I didn't want to go out into the foyer where I'd be spotted by the cops, but I remembered in Gold's diagram, there were nearby stairs down a hallway, so I made my way to them. If my presence were challenged, I'd be looking for the toilet.

A long hallway crossed the foyer balcony on to the far end. Along the way, I guessed at least four bedrooms on one side and four on the other. One of them had to be Cynthia Shepherd's. I didn't have the time to wander through all of them and took a calculated chance that hers would be at the back of the house, overlooking the water of Long Island Sound.

Inside the first door was the sleeping quarters of a king and queen. A canopied bed and its bedstands took up one side. All around were couches, cushioned chairs, and coffee tables. I went to the closet, which was larger than Teresa's, Ellie's, and my room at home, and saw both men's and women's clothes and more shoes than in most stores. This was the master suite, *her* mommy's and daddy's bedroom.

When I set out to leave, I heard male voices coming toward the room. I only had time to slide behind the door, but they went on, and the voices drew more distant. I peered out and saw the two policemen turn down a corridor. I hurried to the next door and went in.

Forced to move with care from room to room, it took far too much time, fifteen or more minutes, to find Cynthia Shepherd's bedroom—as luck would have it, the last one on the far side of the balcony. I slipped in and found another room befitting royalty with a canopied bed, furniture, chest of drawers, closets, and mirrors. Everything sparkled and shined.

When I entered the room, I heard a commotion outside the house and stepped to the window. Below on the back lawn, two hundred people were rising out of white folding chairs, watching breathlessly as Bauer kissed Cynthia Shepherd. At the sight of his blond hair gleaming in the sunlight, I wished I had a sniper's rifle.

Soon, the couple turned and faced their audience as applause rang out. Then they started down the aisle. The wedding was over. I had no time left.

Quickly, I went to the dresser and sat down, staring at the ornate jewelry box. It was a black lacquered container that looked more like a small chest of drawers than something to hold jewelry. It was decorated with scenes of snowcapped mountains and forests along with diamonds and other rare stones. Mama had a small jewelry box made of worn elm that held a couple bracelets and necklaces and rings. So many of her things had been passed down over the years, even centuries, most destined for Hanna or me. Of all her things, only my old coin necklace was left.

Opening the third small drawer, I found it and held it in my palm. On my twelfth birthday, Mama had given it to me, placing it in my hand.

"This is Shelamzion Alexandra, the last queen of Judea," she said, closing my fist around the coin and leather chain. "It has been in our family for centuries, and now it's yours, Rivka. Cherish it. Every time you look at it, think of us, think of the people who have gone before. Think of the hands that have held this same coin and remember the people you love."

It was in my hand again, no longer with a leather chain but one of gold. Smoothing my thumb over the queen's likeness, I blinked back tears. I thought never to have it again. I slid it over my head and around my neck. Suddenly, noise from the hallway drew my attention, people approaching. I looked at the door as it started to open.

Instantly, I dove for the floor and rolled under the bed.

Two women entered, talking so animatedly they must not have heard or seen me. Once again, I was hiding under a bed, this time with no bomb beside me like in Kovna. I could see the bottom of their dresses. One was the bride with the white lace along the hem, Cynthia Shepherd, now Cynthia Bauer.

"You should change out of your dress, Cynthia," the other woman said. "You want to leave right away, don't you?"

"I suppose," Cynthia replied.

"Come on. I'll help," the other woman said.

They hurried to the closet but came back out immediately. "No," Cynthia said. "No. I want to stay in this dress as long as I can. Edna, this is the happiest day of my life, and I want this moment to last."

From their tangling feet, it looked like they might have hugged, then one of them said softly, "Let's go downstairs. They'll be waiting."

A second later when they left, I slid out from under the bed and sat on it, waiting, giving them time to leave the hall. I thought about what she said. Happiest day of her life. This would be hard on her, but that couldn't be helped. If she stayed married to him, her life would be on a ticking clock to misery or death

After a minute, I sprung up and hurried from the room. The play was about to begin.

When I returned to the ballroom, the reception had started, people milling about drinking champagne and talking. I slid into a chair next to the projector at the back with Pete and Charlie. Gold was fiddling with the film loop in the projector, getting ready for what was to come. Several of Governor Dewey's guards stood about the room, some in highway patrol uniforms, trying to look unobtrusive but failing miserably. It was worrisome. Their presence might blow up our plan.

Suddenly, cheers went up as, hand in hand, the bride, still in her white wedding gown, and the groom entered the room. Clapping, people made a path through the tables for them. I watched them come, saw the smug grin on his face, a molten rage swelling within me. Staring at him as he shook hands with people, I felt the Angel of Death unfurl her wings and begin to rise, her force swelling in power. Reaching into my pocket, I clutched the Walther. Get it over with. Walk up to him now and put a bullet into his brain.

I felt Pete's restraining hand on my forearm, and I looked at him, furious. Instantly, he released me. "No, Rivka," he whispered. "Stay with the plan. This would make him a murder victim and you a murderer."

Pete was right. I hated Bauer's smug, self-satisfied face, but the time for justice would soon be upon us. "Not yet," I muttered. The angel drew in her wings and sank back into her chamber, but I could feel her churning there.

With a deep breath, I stood up and said, "It's time, Mr. Gold."

For a moment, I thought he'd balk, but taking a deep breath, he made his way slowly through the crowd toward Bauer, Cynthia, and Arthur Shepherd. Rolling up the sleeves of my blouse, I followed right behind him. Another couple stood talking with the Shepherds and Bauer, a man with square jaw and a movie moustache beside an attractive, older woman in a blue cocktail dress. Gold approached the group, kissed Cynthia on the cheek, and shook both Bauer's and Shepherd's hands. "Congratulations, Arthur. Not only have you got yourself a son-in-law, but a new vice-president."

Shepherd laughed and patted Gold's shoulder, then gestured to the other couple. "You know Governor Dewey and his wife."

"We've met," Gold said, extending his hand to the mustachioed man. "Good to see you and Francis again, Governor."

They exchanged quick pleasantries, and Shepherd said to Gold, "Are you ready to show our new production?"

"Yes, we're ready. I think you're going to like it."

"I better," Shepherd snorted. "I paid enough for it." He turned to his daughter and Bauer. "This is a wedding surprise for you two."

Moving aside for me to step up, Gold introduced me as Rivka Resnik, his assistant, to the governor and his wife. This was an unusual thing, him presenting me like this. I was just hired help and hardly dressed to match the formal clothes of the day, but Dewey and his wife smiled easily.

I remembered Rick talking about him, how as a special prosecutor in New York he gained fame for bringing many famous mobsters to justice, including Luciano. That got him elected to the governorship. I couldn't decide whether or not it was a good thing he was here. I extended my hand, surprising him, and we shook.

"It's an honor to meet you," I said.

Then Gold turned to the Shepherds. "Rivka, this is Cynthia Muller, Kurt Muller, and Arthur Shepherd, our hosts."

They seemed uncertain what I was doing among them. Being this close to Bauer, my body shook with tremors of fear and rage, which they seemed to take as my nervousness at being among my betters. Instantly, I drove down my emotions and stared back at them. Abruptly, expressions changed. Both the bride and groom stared at me quizzically as if they'd seen me before, which they had, of course, but seemingly, they couldn't quite place me. All of them waited for me to speak, perhaps to curtsy and profess my undying gratitude for the high honor of meeting such fine people, but staring hard at them, I said nothing.

This unsettled Cynthia, and then she saw the necklace. "Where did you get that?" she demanded.

I fingered the coin with my left hand, revealing the numbers tattooed on my forearm. At seeing them, Bauer flinched, his eyes narrowing sharply and rising to meet mine. They bore into me. By his expression, it was clear he recognized me. From Nashok or Auschwitz? That seemed unlikely, but I was sure he knew me.

"From my mother," I answered. "This coin has been in my family for centuries. You see, it's Shelamzion Alexandra, the last queen of Judea. Unfortunately, I lost it about two years ago when someone tore it off my neck." I gave her a smile without humor. "It has recently come back into my possession."

Before she could respond, Arthur Shepherd said, "Well, nice to meet you, Miss Resnik." Then he stepped to the nearest table, snatched up a spoon, and clinked his wine glass with it. When the room fell silent, he announced, "If you'll take your seats, we'll begin the festivities."

As the guests made their way to their tables and Gold and I back to the projector, I said to myself, yes, it was time to begin the festivities.

CHAPTER FIFTY-TWO

At the head table, Shepherd stood, waiting for the room to settle. Next to him sat the bride and groom and beyond them a row of people I had been assured were the greats of New York society, Bauer's new world. All looked expectantly at Shepherd. When the room fell silent, he gestured to his daughter and her new husband, and in a booming voice announced, "Let me be the first to introduce to you Dr. and Mrs. Muller."

People stood and applauded; the couple beamed. After half a minute when they sat back down, Shepherd went on, "As you know, Kurt is a professor at Hawthorne University, but I have prevailed upon him to resign his position and join Shepherd Enterprises effective immediately. I believe there's something called a honeymoon in there somewhere, but we'll work that out."

People laughed and Cynthia blushed.

Grinning broadly, Shepherd held up his hands for silence. "So it is customary at this time to have a few speeches starting with the father of the bride. I am to talk about the bride and her new husband, but instead I thought we'd do something a little different. I asked my friend Herb Gold, the Oscar winning Hollywood producer, to make a film introducing them to you. I hope you enjoy it." He nodded toward us at the projector.

Gold told me, "Flip that switch on the sound panel,"

I did, creating a loud pop in the speakers. At the huge windows, Pete and Charlie closed the black curtains, casting the entire room into darkness. The projector light beamed down the center passage onto the far screen, my eyes adjusting quickly. It was not theater dark, but still the images on the screen came through distinct and sharp. I looked over at Bauer whose attention was firmly on the film. Then, for a second, he glanced my way and saw me watching him. He turned back to the film.

State troopers manned the two ballroom entrances. I searched among them for Jackson, Bishop, and Shaw, but they hadn't appeared. I didn't expect to see them yet, but still became a little worried. The timing had to be perfect.

On the screen against a wine-colored background were the words: *An Arthur Shepherd Production*, along with a mellow voice singing a song called *Swinging on a Star*. Fade to the words: *First, the Bride.* While the song continued, a baby picture of Cynthia Shepherd with fuzzy, auburn hair appeared. Swathed in a white blanket, she looked up at the camera with a wide grin, and the audience responded with oohs and ahs.

A strong voice out of Movie Tone News announced that Cynthia was a cute, well-behaved baby, the joy of her parents. With the song still in the background, a series of black and white photos of her growing years followed, at five riding a bicycle, at ten standing with a tennis racket, at sixteen in a prom dress.

The song ended, and we saw her in a black and white film at her Radcliff College graduation, walking across the stage to receive, as the narrator told us, her summa cum laude honors. Next came snatches of her valedictorian speech, her voice confident even in the tinny movie recording. Finally, there were a few clips in color of her as director of the Shepherd Foundation passing out checks to grateful recipients.

On screen came the words *Now, the Groom,* accompanied by a short trill of Wagnerian music that abruptly stopped when the movie began. Little was known of Kurt Muller, so the audience fell silent, and some leaned forward in their chairs. Then, they gasped as the clear black and white film rolled. A thin-shouldered, narrow-faced German in an SS uniform was pinning a medal on another officer, their blond hair distinct. The movie tone announcer identified the first man as Reinhard Heydrich, Chief of the SD.

The original sound accompanied the film, and the Nazi's high-pitched German filled the ballroom. An English translation ran along the bottom. "Hauptsturmführer Max Bauer is awarded the Knight's Cross for continuous bravery before the enemy and for his excellence in removing Jews, Polish intelligentsia, and other undesirables from occupied territory."

The clear image left no doubt as to the identity of Max Bauer. It was Kurt Muller.

I watched Bauer, who stiffened imperceptibly. An uneasy commotion crept through the room. At nearby tables, I could see people exchanging stunned looks.

Suddenly on screen, a map of Eastern Europe appeared, crowded with coffins and numbers attached of Jews killed at each location. It totaled in the hundreds of thousands.

A black and white movie began with a closeup of Max Bauer's and two other SS officers' faces, all three posing and grinning widely at the camera with such joy they appeared to have witnessed an angel's visit. There was no narration, no sound. Behind them was a large crowd of civilians, men, women, and children, watching as if at a sporting event. By the sunshine and light clothing, it was a summers day.

The audience in the ballroom had grown quiet.

As the camera slowly drew back, it revealed three bearded Jewish men kneeling in front of each officer, pistols aimed at the backs of their heads. The camera continued retreating, this time revealing a large pit filled with bodies gaping before the kneeling men, a small spotted dog dashing back and forth yipping soundlessly.

At the same moment, Bauer and the other two men shot the three Jews, their bodies tumbling into the pit. At the shots, the dog

411

darted back toward the civilians and leapt into the arms of a boy in short pants. Bauer and the two other SS officers were still grinning.

Though I knew it was coming, the scene cut deep into me. I shuddered and groaned and turned away as Pete's reassuring hand pressed against my back.

In the ballroom, several people screamed, followed by a rumble of agitated chatter. A few people called out, and Bauer shouted, "What is this monstrous trick?"

But Gold's presentation went on. The English announcer was saying, "Heinrich Himmler was so furious that pictures and even movies were being taken of the Murder Squads that he forbade any more recordings. Max Baur's Murder Squads moved on to the next village and to the next. Killing and killing. Never tiring. Never resting. Never satiated by blood."

I was watching Bauer, who rubbed his hands together and glanced back and forth from Cynthia to her father. She had buried her head in her hands, her shoulders shaking, her sobs mixing in with the sound of the film. Shepherd was transfixed on the screen.

Baur's gaze shot to me and held. It must have hit him that his world had fallen, crashed like the giant swastika blown from atop the Reichstag by the allies, and I had done it. It was too dark to read his eyes, but I imagined them burning like fireballs of rage. This gave me intense satisfaction.

A photo of Bauer and three other German officers appeared on screen, standing like tourists under the gate at Auschwitz, above them the sign *Arbeit Macht Frei*. Then to bodies stacked at the crematorium.

By now, the ballroom was in chaos, people fainting, others screaming. I couldn't have been more pleased.

The announcer said, "Auschwitz Death camp, the crematorium where Max Bauer led..."

A piercing scream came from the main table. I looked up. It was Cynthia, her hands gripping wads of the white tablecloth.

"Stop!" Shepherd cried out above the din. "For God's sake, Herb, stop this!"

In the flickering projector light, I saw Arthur Shepherd standing at the main table. "Please, we've seen enough," he said. "Turn it off. Turn it off."

Gold stopped the projector, and the lights came on, revealing a frozen tableau at the main table that included four men standing behind Bauer's chair as if guards. By their ill-fitting uniforms, three of them appeared to be state police. They were an odd trio. One sported a thick, brown mustache while another's face took on a two-toned countenance, jaw pale, upper half tanned. The third trooper's forehead dripped sweat; dampness stained his armpits. These were my men, Jackson, Bishop, and Shaw, and they looked to me about as much like state troopers as the Marx brothers. Yet, no one had seemed to notice, not even the fourth man standing with them

This was Governor Dewey, focusing a scowl intently on Bauer. Beside the German, Cynthia's face and shoulders quivered in spasms of shock, sorrow, and horror. She had scooted her chair at least a yard away from her new husband. Silence locked the rest of the room in its own tableau.

The only moving part was me, heading for the table.

Abruptly, Bauer reached his arm out to his new bride, the pained expression of a wronged man on his face. "Cynthia, you can't believe any of this. It's a terrible trick." He jabbed his finger at the movie screen. "Clearly, that film is a fake."

Her face grew stiff with fury. She ripped a garland of flowers from her wedding dress and hurled them at him, screaming, "That was you. That was you. What kind of monster are you?"

He saw everyone staring at him in distaste and horror. You could see the realization settle on him that his mask had been peeled back to reveal the beast beneath. Like a trapped animal, he searched frantically for an escape route, but none existed. His shoulders sank. His new world of wealth and power had collapsed utterly and with finality.

Was it enough? No, it would never be enough. There could never be justice that matched the crime. But this was the best I could do.

As I came to the table, he looked at me with recognition. "You're the one who did this to me," he said in German. "Who are you?"

I displayed my tattoo again.

"So you were at Auschwitz. I did not pack the showers with you Jews. Others did that. Yet now you want revenge. Too bad you didn't die with the rest of your Untermenschen. You're like vermin. There's no end to you."

My words, also in German, came out like cubes of ice. "Yes, I survived Auschwitz and before that, Nashok. Now it's time to make worms' meat of you."

He covered a flash of fear with a contemptuous flutter of his lips. "Foolish girl, I won't hang. The American government brought me here. I work for them. They'll just send me somewhere else."

This shocked me, but I didn't show it. Finally, Governor Dewey's voice cut through the room. "Max Bauer, as the chief law enforcement officer in the State of New York, I am arresting you for crimes against humanity. Get up."

Two of my state troopers yanked him to his feet, turned him, and bound his wrists in front with handcuffs. When they began escorting him out, he glanced back at me with a smug grin. "You survived Nashok and Auschwitz, but I got so many others of your kind."

I turned away, not giving him the satisfaction of a response. I saw Pete and Charlie hurrying to catch up with them as my troopers shoved Bauer out of the ballroom with Dewey following. This was the crucial part. We couldn't let other police take charge of our prisoner but had to brazen our way out through a cordon of them, and the governor's presence was not helpful.

In the ballroom, chaotic chatter rippled through the guests. No one seemed to know what to do. Wiping tears, Cynthia rose and clinked her glass, saying with venom, "Well, I guess you'll never

414

forget this wedding. I'll return your gifts, of course. God, I couldn't keep them now."

She started to say something else, gave it up, and flopped back down, falling into the arms of her blonde assistant Edna. Several people rushed to her, including Herb Gold.

Arthur Shepherd stood, calling for attention, "I'm sorry for this. May I suggest that we end the day. Thank you for coming. Exit through the two doors please."

As I started from the room to meet with the others outside, someone grabbed my arm and held it tightly. I turned to face Cynthia Shepherd. Her face was a mess with tear tracks running down through her makeup, but her eyes locked on me with fury and maybe a hint of madness. "Who are you?" she demanded. "You looked different then, but you applied for the maid's position. You never intended to take the job."

I didn't have time for this. "Let go of my arm."

She did. Around us, the departing guests had turned into a rush, some of them laughing. Flushed with anger or embarrassment, Cynthia muttered, "First person to a phone has a hell of a story to tell." Then she ripped the ring from her finger and hurled it across the floor. "This is the worst day of my life. My life is ruined."

"You'll get an annulment."

"Why did you do it? Can you even imagine what pain you've caused me? I don't deserve this humiliation."

Time was wasting, but I felt a fragile crack in the hard surface around my heart. Not much, but just enough that I could see the hurt in her. I stepped forward, backing her up, my voice intense. "Five years ago, I crawled out of a pit filled with bodies like what just saw on the film. Your husband put me in it. I was fourteen. He thought his shooters had killed me like everyone else, but my mother had shoved me in just before the guns. Her dead body lay on top of me for more than an hour."

Aghast, Cynthia's mouth dropped open.

I went on. "My family, my friends, my life, everybody I loved, is buried there. Your husband did that. There will be no annulment of his crimes. No true justice either.

A groan escaped her. "I'm...I'm sorry."

"You'll survive."

Suddenly, Jackson in his state trooper uniform was next to me, his face emptied of color, and I realized something was very wrong.

"You better come," he said.

"What is it?"

"The Bund, they have Ellie."

CHAPTER FIFTY-THREE

I t didn't make sense. Ellie kidnapped. My heart pounded so hard it threatened to burst out of my chest. Not another one I loved taken by the monsters. If something happened to her, the fault would be mine.

"You'll see, you'll see," Jackson was saying as we crossed the foyer, weaving through the guests fleeing the castle.

I tried to focus on what he was saying, something about talking to the Huber woman. "What?"

"He's talking to her now. In here," he said, pushing open the door.

What I found when we entered an office library shocked me back to awareness. It couldn't have been worse. Men were facing each other in a deadly standoff. Anton Bruck, the Gestapo interrogator, his bald head gleaming with sweat, pressed his gun against Governor Dewey's ribs. Bishop and Shaw were pointing their weapons at the German. Bauer, handcuffs in front of him, sat on a leather couch, his face tight, staring straight ahead while Charlie covered him with his pistol.

And Pete was standing at the desk talking frantically into the phone.

I looked at Bruck again and saw this impasse was about to come apart. The Gestapo man with the frightening record of torture darted his eyes frantically from one man to another as if finding himself cornered by a pack of wild dogs. I'd seen men who suddenly found themselves in desperate situations they could not handle, and he had finally grasped that fact. Holding a gun on the governor of New York while police officers surrounded the house was not a particularly good idea. The realization was in his eyes. Whether he shot Dewey or not, he would not escape this. Bauer might; he wouldn't.

Pete's dark eyes sparked with rage. "If you hurt my sister, I will…" he shouted into the phone, took it away from his ear and stared at it a moment, then slammed it down.

I looked at him questioningly.

"They have Ellie," he said, closing his eyes in anguish. "The Huber woman let me talk to her. They have Ellie."

Charlie explained what happened when they left the reception with Bauer in tow. Bruck had abruptly appeared, his gun pressed against Dewey, told them that his people had Pete's sister, and gestured them into the library. In there, Pete could talk to her.

Inside me, the angel shook, her wings flapping, trying to get out. I knew what she wanted: carnage. I drew my Walther and marched over to the German. "You bastard."

His eyes locked on mine. "Well, you knew that."

I couldn't shoot him now, and when he saw my gun drop, he relaxed and motioned his cuffed hands to encompass the standoff. "This is why we had to take the girl. We knew about you. You made yourself a threat. We couldn't wait for your Nazi hunter boyfriend to come after us, and I really couldn't trust your government. Not for someone like me. So, here we are. If that pretty, little girl is hurt, it will be your fault."

Pete cut in, "Huber wants to exchange Ellie for Bauer. She wants you and me to bring him to her, no one else, just us two, and she'll release Ellie. We have to do it. We have no choice."

I checked my watch. Five-thirty. I asked him, "Do you know where she's holding her?"

He shook his head, then indicated to Bauer and Bruck. "These two know."

Disdainfully, Bauer said, "Of course, we know. What's the point of this if we don't?"

I turned to Bruck. "We don't need you then." I lifted the Walther, intending to kill him, thinking the blasts of horns outside would mask the sound.

He must have seen it in my eyes for panic washed over his face like a splash of red dye. This man who unmercifully tortured so many couldn't drop his gun fast enough, and Bishop scooped it up. Like so many of his kind, Bruck was a coward at heart.

"Feigling," Bauer accused him. Bruck could not meet his eyes.

The angel fluttered her wings, dissatisfied, but still stirred as I lowered the weapon. Stepping away from the Gestapo man, Dewey demonstrated more composure than I had expected. He wiped his sweating forehead with a white handkerchief then said calmly, "I'll get some men in here to..."

"No," Pete interrupted him, a harsh tone in his voice. "Governor, we're taking Bauer out of here. We need him to get my sister. No offence but the police will screw it up. Stay in the room, sir. Give us five minutes."

It wasn't a request, and I wasn't confident Dewey would agree. He didn't answer.

I said, "Shaw, stay here to help him watch Bruck." I didn't add aloud, *and to keep the governor in here.*

Shaw understood and nodded.

Charlie yanked Bauer to his feet. "Come on."

As we shoved him out the door, Dewey called after me, "Miss Resnik, you call my office when that girl is safe."

Trudi Huber paced back and forth in the living room of the farm-house. Martin Mohnke sat on the bricks of the raised fireplace, his head buried in his hands, those hands periodically digging through his hair. Two of the American Bund men, brothers Walter and Karl

Berger, stood watch at the windows. Both worked at Hauser's distillery and had broken heads for the cause before. Their hands fondled the guns in their holsters. They were eager for a fight. Silent for a change, the little girl was curled into a worn chair, her hands tied behind her and her feet bound.

And upstairs, Hauser lay dead in his bedroom.

Trudi was enraged. "Es war Irre," she muttered. *This was crazy.*

At his wedding, Bauer had been exposed and captured. Just after they'd arrived at the farmhouse, Bruck had called her, explained the situation, and said they'd be making an exchange, Bauer for the girl. At first, she'd gone along with it, but now she saw the hopelessness of it. In one afternoon, her life had come apart...again. She had escaped Europe. Now, the Valkyries would be after her once more.

"This was not supposed to happen," she said to Mohnke in German, which she knew the Berger brothers didn't understand very well. "It was not supposed to happen. I survived the war. I have a husband. Now, it's all gone to hell because of Bauer. Mein Gott."

In frustration, she kept folding and unfolding her arms. Last week, they'd tried killing the Nazi hunter by burning down his apartment, but he'd survived, which meant real trouble for all of them. If they wanted to keep the lives they had built in America, they needed to do something quickly, and Bauer said he had a plan. She and Mohnke were to snatch the little girl today, hold her till evening, then release her. Show the Nazi hunters the peril their families faced if they continued pursuit.

Like the old days in the Reich, threaten, intimidate, frighten, control. That was all it was to be. It seemed a good idea. Once Bauer was married, he'd be too powerful; they'd all be too powerful. Bauer assured them the plan would work.

She spoke aloud again, "Release the girl then, he'd said. The Nazi hunters would back away when they saw the danger their families were in. Bauer assured us it would work. We'd all be safe." She threw up her hands and bellowed like a trapped animal. "Safe? No. Now, we are all gefickt."

At her shout, the Berger brothers glanced at her, then after a moment, turned back to their watch.

Mohnke looked up. "What are we going to do?"

She walked over to him and said in a low voice, "We have to kill the girl, then clean out the safe in the basement, you and me, and drive to Canada."

He frowned. "What about Bauer? We need to wait for him. We pledged to support each other. Our honor demands it, Trudi." After a second, he said, "Besides, Hauser changed the combination. I don't have the new one. Do you?"

Shaking her head, her lips pulled back over her teeth in fury. "The fool. If Bauer doesn't have it…"

That's when the girl spoke again. "I'm hungry. Can I have something to eat?"

"Shut up! You will eat when we eat," Huber snapped in English, then switched back to German, her face as pale as her starched, white clothes. "Don't you understand, Martin? We kidnapped a young girl. The FBI will be after us now. You remember the Lindbergh baby. It was in all our newspapers. It means the electric chair. She has to die." She shook her head in frustration. "This was not supposed to happen."

"We can't. Not yet. We must wait. The Nazi hunters may want to see her," Mohnke said.

Exasperated, Trudi thought for a half-minute, then settled on something. "All right. Walter, Karl," she called, and the two men looked over their shoulders at her from the windows. "You understand when Herr Muller arrives, you must kill whoever comes with him. There should be just two, and one of them is a woman. If we exchange the girl for Bauer, they will call the FBI before we get a mile down the road."

"I'll go out with you to negotiate," Mohnke said. "At the first opportunity, we'll shoot the two Nazi hunters and free Herr Muller. Can you do that?"

They nodded and said eagerly in unison, "We can."

"I have to go to the bathroom," the girl demanded in a tone that infuriated Huber. She strode over and slapped her hard. Tears came to the girl's eyes, and she shrank back.

Rising, Mohnke approached and picked her up like a sack of flour. "I'll keep her quiet till they come."

He took her upstairs to the master bedroom and dropped her on the bed next to Hauser's body.

"Stay here and shut up. The woman wants to kill you."

He turned and walked out. Ellie heard the click of the door locking. Staring at the dead man next to her, she felt vomit roil at her throat and like a shot rolled off the bed. The impact with the floor knocked the air from her lungs. Her hands bound behind her, she lay on her side, catching her breath, and tried to put the thing on the bed out of her mind.

She had been scared since they'd taken her off the sidewalk this morning while walking to Anita Broder's house. Once in the car, the woman had hit her hard, twice, stunning her, causing her to cry. That's when sheer terror engulfed her. She could not think. Her body sank into paroxysms of shaking.

That lasted till she slowly began to realize these two apparently didn't intend to kill her, at least right then, and they didn't know what they were doing. The man, who was driving, couldn't find his way out of Brooklyn. The woman yelled at him till they found one of the bridges over the East River and made it into Manhattan.

With her tied up on the floor in the back wearing a blindfold, they ignored her, arguing in a foreign language most of the time. German, Ellie thought. Though she couldn't understand it, she remembered people speaking it occasionally in Nashok. She was a young kid then. Where were they taking her and why? While they squabbled, she rubbed the scarf on her eyes against the seat enough that she could just see. From time to time, she'd pop up and peek out the window and soon saw they were leaving Manhattan, heading north.

In the bedroom of the farmhouse, she asked herself what kind of kidnappers these people were. She'd read "The Ransom of Red Chief" in school. This must be those kidnappers. What did they plan to do with her? Papa didn't have much money. It didn't make much sense, but maybe crooks never made sense.

Moments ago, before the man left, he'd said the woman wanted to kill her. Terrified again, she realized she could not lay here and do nothing. Quickly, she sat up, worked her butt under her hands, and brought them up in front of her. Then easily, she undid the rope around her ankles and next worked her hands free. The man had not tied her up very well. Jimmy had done a better job several times. With a flash of insight, she understood these were the dumbest crooks she'd ever seen. The crooks in the movies and on the radio were a lot smarter than these two.

Once free, she hurried to the door and propped a chair under the doorknob. She'd seen that in the movies too. Next, she went to the gabled window, looking onto the front lawn and street, still light out. The window wouldn't open, but she could break the glass. Then what? Jump? It was too far down to jump, and heights bothered her. She could scream, but the other houses were far away and looked empty. No one but the crooks would hear her.

She considered tying sheets together. That might work. But how many sheets would she need? Surely more than the two on the bed. One was barely enough to reach the window. A second would only get her to the roof's edge. Besides, she didn't want to touch the dead man on the bed.

Turning back, Ellie began studying the room for any way to escape but saw nothing, then thought again about the window. She could go out onto the roof, but what good would that do? She couldn't fly. After a moment, wanting to stay as far as she could from the thing on the bed, she slid down to the floor below the window and, trembling, wrapped her arms around her knees.

CHAPTER FIFTY-FOUR

Twilight was fading when Charlie stopped the panel truck on the shoulder of the road just before the turn to the farmhouse. We couldn't be seen from it, a couple houses and some trees shielding us. Pete, Jackson, and Bishop were in the back with Bauer. An hour and a half ago, we had made our way through the clogged traffic trying to rush from Shepherd's Castle with Charlie bumping cars and even driving up onto the pasture. That's when Bauer told us where the exchange was to take place. The farmhouse was no surprise. He said he'd give us directions, but I told him we all knew where it was.

We'd lost McCarthy and Stiles at the castle when their car, posted in the middle of the driveway, was hopelessly blocked. I hated losing the two, but we couldn't wait for them.

During the drive over from Long Island, Bauer had said nothing, and I was thankful for it. Sitting in the same vehicle with him, my rage was never far from the surface. If I killed him before the exchange, Ellie would die. I could not trade her life for his death. That was unthinkable. Yet, I didn't want this fact thrust in my face with a single word of his. I could see by the burning scowl on Pete's face he felt the same.

Several stars poked into the darkening sky. I told Charlie, "Now."

Without a word, he grabbed his shotgun and jumped out of the driver's seat while Jackson and Bishop scrambled out the back.

They hurried through the high grass, racing up the field toward the farmhouse. I took the driver's seat. I would give them ten minutes to go the half mile up behind it. Pete and I, with Bauer in tow, would cover the front.

"You just switch me for the girl," Bauer said, "and we can all stay alive."

With the hand holding his gun, Pete smashed him across the face. Blood spurted from his mouth. "Shut up."

After ten minutes, I drove slowly up the lane and parked in front of the house. When I stepped out, Pete came around from the back of the truck, controlling the German by clutching tightly to his collar, pistol pressed against his head. He joined me, waiting by the passenger door. The hairs on my neck rose. I could feel weapons trained on us from the house.

A minute passed. Two. The sky was darkening, daylight fleeing. Then the porch light came on.

Holding pistols down at their sides, three men emerged from the house. Two of them, who looked like brothers, same build, same square faces, flanked a lean man with a thin mustache. I recognized him by Rick's description as one of those who attacked him. Even without that, I would have known him to be a former German officer by his stiff bearing.

Light was still strong enough to see their faces. Despite the evening cooling off, the brothers were sweating, continually glancing to the German, their faces tightening with each step. I was sure these two were not trained men. Likely, they thought themselves tough, but nervous fear lifted from their very bodies like steam. I doubted they'd ever fired a gun, either in passion or cold-blood. If this were a simple exchange, why were they so scared?

"This is not an exchange for Ellie," I said to Pete in Hebrew, a language of study we both understood. "It's a trap."

He exhaled. "Looks like it. We need to find out where she is." He pressed his pistol harder against Bauer's temple and switched to English. "Bring Ellie out here," he demanded.

426

"She's safe," the lean German said. "We need assurances first that you will not call the police. That we can leave undisturbed. That this will be the end of it."

"No," I said. "Ellie first."

He stared at me for several seconds, then called out to the house, "Huber, bring the girl."

His eyes darted toward Bauer as if signaling. It couldn't have been more obvious. Beside me, Bauer's body tensed. It was coming.

Just as I started to shout a warning, he wrenched free and fell to the ground. The three men had been waiting for that and lifted their weapons, but Pete and I were already firing.

My first shot hit the German officer in the chest. Bullets plunked into the panel truck around me. My second shot missed the brother on my side, and I was hit. A searing pain flared in my left shoulder and back. My next shot hit him in the throat.

In the exchange of gunfire, I'd barely been aware of Bauer scooping up a pistol and racing for the house. My snap shot clipped the door frame as he ducked through. Inside was dark now. We had shot out the lamps. Only the porchlight was on.

The third man was clutching his stomach. On one knee, he aimed at Pete, who fired a second faster and finished him with a bullet gouging out a bloody hole in his chest, ending him.

It felt like a full minute had passed, but in reality, the gunfight probably lasted no more than twenty seconds, if that. The three lay dead on the ground. Pete was unhurt; I had been wounded but, despite the burn in my shoulder and back, was not about to give it up now.

Then, the night erupted with weapons' fire again, not at us, but the fight somewhere inside the house. I knew it was Charlie and the other two coming in the back. With a quick glance at, Pete, we dashed to the door, him hobbling up a couple seconds behind. I turned the knob and flung it open but held back, not wanting to show myself in the dead zone of the frame. No shots came.

"Oh God," Pete muttered.

427

I caught the acrid smell of things burning and the flicker of flames.

"If she's here, we'll get her, Pete," I said.

He didn't wait, diving into the room, and I stood, pumping covering fire for him toward the hallway where the lights were still on, then leapt in after him. I saw a flash of blonde tresses flinging about as the Huber woman snapped off a couple shots and ducked back into the hall. I changed magazines and fired, trying to keep her pinned down.

Like most partisans, in the heat of battle, I never felt fear, only before and sometimes after. With what I saw around me, now I did. It stabbed into me and pierced my heart with dread. Flames were rushing up the window curtains, spreading onto the walls and ceiling. This old farmhouse was not going to last long.

Huber had seen it too. "Hurry up, Bauer!" she screamed in German. "Verdammt noch mal. Hurry!"

Where Bauer was, I couldn't guess. Likely with Ellie.

Huber's head flashed out again and she got off two shots. I'd been waiting for this and returned a quick volley, but she'd already ducked back. We were pinned down as the housefire grew.

Frantic, Pete crawled out into the open toward the hallway. It was suicidal, but with his sister here somewhere, he would die in the effort to reach her. *No* screamed in my head. I couldn't let that happen. About to rush Huber, I rose just as she inched out again, pistol raised. Her head exploded, bone, blood, and brain matter spewing out. Trudi Huber flopped lifeless on the rug.

Charlie stepped over her, racking his shotgun. "Bishop's wounded. I sent him out to cover the back with Jackson. It's just the three of us."

Behind us, the fire was devouring the furniture and crawling along the ceiling. Black smoke billowed up, taking the air from the room. Heat had risen to scorching, and breathing was becoming difficult.

Without a word, Pete rushed for the stairs, hopping up two at a time.

"Go with him," I ordered Charlie. "Cover him. I'll take the basement."

As he ran after Pete, I went to the door to the wine cellar and opened it onto the black below. Knowing it was utter madness to descend into this darkness, I started down and in seconds felt immense surprise and relief when I reached the bottom without being shot.

In the corner, the door to the outside stood shut. A dimness of light shown from down the narrow hallway that led to the Nazi meeting room. If Bauer was down here, that's where he would be.

I took the dark passage.

My heart pounded, and I tried to swallow, but it felt like a lump of coal had lodged in my throat. Reaching the door, I inched it open and saw no one. My heart sank. Was Bauer upstairs about to ambush Pete? Was Ellie not here? Then I heard a rustle of motion from around the corner. The Walther ready, I stepped into the room.

Trembling in fear below the window, Ellie heard the fire growing louder, coming nearer, and caught the smell of smoke seeping in through the cracks in the door. The house was on fire, and she had no way out.

And it was getting hotter.

She buried herself deeper into her knees, her arms covering her head, her body shaking. She'd never thought about dying before. She knew her cousins in Nashok had all died. All her friends there had died. Everyone she knew back then had died except Yankl and Rivka. She could not see any of them in her mind very well anymore. What she did remember was the emotion of loving them. Now, for the first time, she understood that she too could die. Really die.

She told herself she would not burn to death. If she could, only if she could, she'd break the window glass and jump from the roof before that.

Then, she heard things bang outside in the hall and someone shouting her name. It sounded like Pete. She jumped up and raced for the door, knocking the chair under the knob away. She couldn't open it. She stood back and screamed, "Pete!"

Seconds later someone rattled the knob, then the door burst open. A man she had never seen stood there, a haze of smoke swirling about his head, the side of his face scarred. She was about to scream when another man stepped from behind him into the room. It was Pete, and she leapt into his arms, crying, saying his name over and over.

Kneeling beneath the picture of Hitler with his back to me, Bauer was yanking money out of a safe with both cuffed hands and stacking it in a briefcase. His pistol lay on the floor beside him.

"Bauer, turn around," I said.

He stiffened.

My voice was glacial. "Stay down. Don't touch the gun."

Slowly, he inched around, giving a slight glance at his pistol a foot away on the floor. I saw he thought he could reach it, but it didn't worry me. I placed a wooden chair ten feet away and sat facing him, holding the Walther loosely in my lap. The odor of burnt things filled my nostrils and reminded me of Auschwitz, of the constant smell from the smokestacks. Pain shot through my back and left arm. Blood dripped from my fingers as a monstrous fatigue settled into my bones.

The fire would soon reach us. Bauer knew it; he could hear it. His eyes darted about, searching for a way to escape, to run, anything, but I left no route for him. Except perhaps the gun.

I heard Charlie's voice from up the basement stairs. "Rivka, are you all right?"

"Yes," I called back. "I have Bauer."

I heard his footsteps on the stairs, cautiously coming part way down. "Pete has Ellie. They're already outside. This place is going to come down. We need to get out."

"You go," I said. "There's a way out through the basement. I'll be along in a minute."

An instant of silence, then he hurried up the stairs.

Bauer eyed me, saying nothing for several seconds, speaking in German now. "Surely, you're not going to shoot me, and we can't stay here. Turn me over to your FBI. I will not resist. They will reward you, I'm sure."

I didn't answer.

Even as the smell of smoke thickened and the heat in the room increased, he watched me with calm. Perhaps, he was waiting me out, thinking when death closed in, I'd panic, and he'd have his chance. He gave a slight shrug of his head. "Of course, we wouldn't have harmed the girl. We never intended to. We planned to return her. The only purpose in taking her was to encourage you to leave us alone. That's all. Nothing more."

I nodded to Bauer as if listening intently. The Angel of Death rose and hovered at my shoulder, her chains clanking. She had come for the kill, intent on forcing me to it.

There was a crash upstairs, things collapsing in the flames. His eyes darted upward, but still he showed no signs of alarm.

He spoke quickly, trying to save himself, trying to justify the evil. "I know what you want. You want vengeance. I would too in your place. Your people died, and you blame me for it. I understand. But you see, you don't fully comprehend the situation I found myself in. You have not seen the orders I was given. I was personally not of such a high rank that I could make these decisions to persecute the Jews. I never gave any order on my own to harm anyone. What I did was by order of someone higher. We were at war. How could I disobey?"

My mind returned to that day in Nashok, to the moment when Bauer and his shooters lined us up naked in front of the pit to be shot and Bauer calmly winding his watch. Then the volley of gunfire, the bodies dropping into the pit. Me falling in on top of the dead, the dead falling on me.

In the basement, I didn't speak or move to flee, just looked at him. Finally, his eyes showed a flicker of fear, and he spoke rapidly, "Let me finish, Miss Resnik, then I'm sure we can leave here. It is important that you know that I personally detested the horrors perpetrated against your people and have always detested them. I grew up with Jews. Jews were my friends. I learned Yiddish. I think those who committed the terrible deeds against the Jews should stand trial and receive justice. I do. But not me. It was not me."

I nodded at the assertion of his innocence as if it made sense. Beside me, the angel beat her wings, the chains clanking. She wanted it done.

Bauer glanced at the gun again. Upstairs, the fire popped like cannons, and black smoke funneled into the basement, hovering along the ceiling. Our breathing became labored.

His eyes had already shifted around in terror. "We must leave," he said. "Not yet."

He swallowed and began breathing rapidly through his mouth. His words raced out one on top of the other. "You must understand before you make a terrible mistake. There is a difference between the leaders who gave the orders and we the soldiers who were forced to follow them. I was not a leader. I think a fair person would see I am not responsible for any of it. Please, I am not myself guilty of anything except doing my best as a soldier."

I was back on the Lagerstrasse in Auschwitz seeing him hurl Helena's baby into the air.

"I have one question," I said. "Two years ago at Auschwitz, I saw you toss my friend's baby up for your soldiers to shoot. Why did you do that?"

With his cuffed hands, he shoved the question away dismissively. "People have asked me that before. Why we did that with babies. They always misunderstand as I'm sure you do. It was not from boyish exuberance. The little creatures are so small, bullets pass right through them, and that puts our soldiers at risk. It's safer for all, you see, to throw them into the air."

Beside me, the angel rattled the chains on her wings and let loose a cry like a thousand demons from hell.

In one quick motion, I lifted the Walther and shot Max Bauer in the forehead.

An instant later, behind me, fire crashed down into the basement as much of the first floor collapsed. I darted over the timbers into the passage. My final image of Bauer was of his lifeless body lying below Hitler's portrait, the Angel of Death hovering above, flapping her wings and screeching.

EPILOGUE

On a cloudy, cold morning, I pushed the baby carriage with my year-old son Ben Zion, toward the Frischer home to drop him off with Mina so Geraldine and I could drive to Brooklyn College for our nine o'clock classes. As usual, while I strolled along the sidewalk, I ticked off the moments of my life, good and bad, year by year, placing them in a ledger. While the appalling ones have such monstrous weight and still haunt my dreams, I'd come to realize the good ones outnumbered them, and Rick and I were building more every day. Three months pregnant, I was creating a new generation as Mama had wanted.

Rick left the hospital a week after his apartment was burned to the ground, but it took another few weeks till he could breathe as before. But he gave up smoking. The day he left the hospital he asked me to marry him. I'd not even thought about that possibility, and he told me he'd court me for years if necessary. He was wrong. His courtship lasted five minutes.

We were married in January, a small wedding with just close friends since neither of us had family left. Soon I was pregnant with Benny. And after his birth, a few months later, I was pregnant again. In private moments, I realized that I was at times happy.

Yet, in other moments, I asked myself, when my children were older, how could I tell them about the horror? I hoped the ledger would help.

The Nazi Bund in White Plains was no more. That night, we burned the house down with the four bodies inside, then learned later from the newspapers that the other members did not live out the week. Leo had delivered his vengeance swiftly and brutally. When I read it, I had sighed, both relieved they were dead and that I did not have to do it.

Of all those gunned down mob style, the only one who garnered any protracted attention was a radio producer named Willi Meisner. After a few days though, when no suspects were found in any of the killings, interest faded. Someday I hoped I could put the balance sheet away and just live with the good memories, but for now it filled a need.

In filling in this balance sheet, I considered those events two years ago and wondered where they fit. Not among the good but not the bad either. I decided to slide them into their own column, a neutral zone between the two. They had brought justice of a kind, but I didn't lie to myself about them. For me, an overwhelming need for vengeance had been the driving force for which I felt neither regret nor guilt.

When I reached the Frischer house, Geraldine was breast feeding her four-month-old twins both at once, and I thanked God I didn't have twins while at the same time feeling envious.

"I'll be ready in a minute," she said. "These boys are ferocious this morning. They're going to dry me out."

"Lucky you didn't have triplets," I said, cueing her for our old joke, as if her third baby would be named Tat.

Geraldine grinned. "No tit for Tat."

When the twin's older sister, twenty-one-month-old Mila, saw me, she trundled up on wobbly legs, arms outstretched. I took her into my arms as Mina came in from the kitchen and picked Benny up out of the carriage.

She nodded to me. "I have something for you. A letter that came last night."

"What mailman delivers at night?" I asked, puzzled.

"You'll see." Carrying Benny, she went to the dining room table and brought the envelope back. "A priest from the Brooklyn Diocese delivered it. He said it's apparently been on a long journey so his bishop thought they should hurry it over immediately."

My heart fluttered. I had an idea who it was from and set Mila on the floor. Up in the corner the name of the sender read Diocese of Hildesheim in Germany. It was addressed to the Brooklyn Diocese, and it had been opened.

Carefully, I drew out another envelope, one faded and addressed to Rivka Resnik, care of Pete Frischer, Brooklyn, from Sister Agneta at the Archdiocese of Krakow. Gently removing the letter as if it were ancient parchment, I saw it was written in Polish and the date was eight months ago. I sat on the couch beside Geraldine, and everyone left me alone, even Mila, while I read.

My dearest, dearest Rivka,

I send all the love there is to you and miss you deeply. Never forget that you are a gift from God on this Earth. I hope you have found the life you sought, and the past does not draw you down into its black depths. We must live for those we lost but also live for the future.

As you must realize by now, I've sent this letter by an underground route from parish to parish, across this new Iron Curtain, across borders. Our Soviet masters would never let such a letter as this be mailed. Already, they have confiscated church lands and closed seminaries. I sigh every hour like a hungry, little bird for freedom, but it is a long way off. We survived the Nazis. We will survive them too.

I truly want to explain how I would have never endured those days at Auschwitz without you, Eleni, Helena, and so many others. All of you were my light during the darkest times, my light at midnight. God led me to all of you.

I believe He provides a different light to each of us in the darkest hours of our lives. I don't know what that light was for you, but I do know it illuminated your way like a fire that turned night into day.

Write to me and tell me what Brooklyn is like. What America is like. Send the letter back through the same channel, and hopefully it will reach me here in Krakow.

Love, prayers, peace,
Sister Agneta

When I finished the letter, I closed my eyes and sank deeply into thoughts of my dear friend as the powerful emotions that bound us together closed over me. That she was alive touched my heart like few things could. That she was surviving in another hideous world, not much better than the Nazis, unsettled me at the same time.

I knew exactly what she meant by the light at midnight, the darkest of times. My light was Mama. She made me live, live for my family then and now, live for our future generations, and she was always with me providing that light, as were Papa, Ben Zion, Hanna, Baba, the Seven, and so many others who would live in my memories throughout my days.

I would write back and tell Sister Agneta about them and my life in America, my marriage to Rick, my children, one still inside me, and my college classes.

That night two years ago outside White Plains, the Angel of Death remained behind in the burning farmhouse. I hadn't seen her since. In my return letter to Sister Agneta, I would tell her many,

many things, but with her still caught under the heel of the Soviets, I didn't think I should burden her with any of that. I would write only about the good side of the ledger.

ACKNOWLEDGEMENTS

Creating any work of fiction, especially this one, is made possible by the assistance of so many people. First, my thanks to the members of the Sandpoint Idaho Writers League, who offered critiques throughout the writing process, especially Mame Cudd, Dr. Foster Cline, and Ken Fischman, who gave his personal insight into WW2 Brooklyn, illuminating that place and time for me.

Mostly, I give thanks to those who wrote memoirs of their lives and survival during the Holocaust, including Yaffa Eliach's remarkable *There Once was a World, a 900-Year Chronicle of the Shtetl of Eishyshok*. Without all of them, so much understanding of then and now would be lost to us.

ABOUT THE AUTHOR

Tom Reppert is a veteran who served with 5th Special Forces Group in Vietnam. After earning a BA in English and History at Western State College and master's degrees in Creative Writing from Colorado State University and Professional Writing from University of Southern California, he spent decades teaching History, Literature, and Writing all over the world, mostly in Africa and Asia to international students. He has written several well-received historical and time-travel novels including *The Far Journey, the Captured Girl,* and *Assassin 13.* Look for them on Amazon and Audible.com or ask for them at your favorite bookstore.

Printed in Great Britain
by Amazon

60654560R00261